Tales from the Bookshop

Tales from the Bookshop

by

Nimue Brown

Steven G. Davis

Jon Hartless

Feline Lang

Ash Mandrake

G. H. Randle

Laura Jane Round

Hannah Simpson

Stu Tovell

Wulfenstæg

An anthology from the
Tenebrous Texts publishing house

This anthology published in England in 2023
by Tenebrous Texts

© individual artists

Cover © Steven C. Davis
Internal art © C.D. Phillip
Internal photography © Steven C. Davis
Edited by Steven C. Davis & Laura Jane Round

1 3 5 7 9 10 8 6 4 2

This book features works of fiction. The names, characters and incidents portrayed in it are the work of the authors' imaginations. Any resemblance to actual persons, living or dead, is entirely coincidental.

A CIP catalogue of this book is available from the British Library.
ISBN 978-1-914246-28-9
Typeset and designed by Tenebrous Texts

Tales from the Bookshop

The Giants' End

by

Ash Mandrake

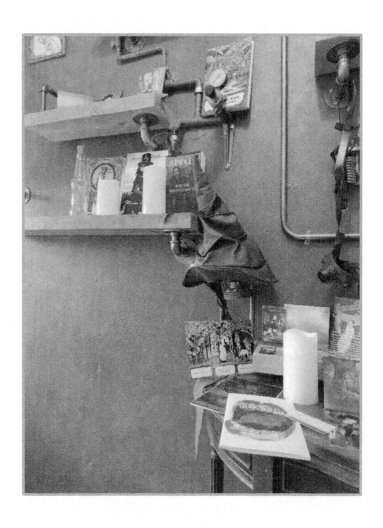

Prologue

Many have written of the ending of the giants – those magnificently ugly brutes that shook the earth with every stride, tore down castles as if made of cardboard, and brought terror to the hearts of villagers the length and breadth of Albion. Some say they were trapped and killed by men, others that their bones became brittle from the eating of metal armour; I have even heard the outlandish mention of them becoming addicted to exotic biscuits and eventually exploding. But none of these flights of fancy bear the slightest resemblance to the true tale of their extinction – a tale of guile and great mischief; I cannot speak for the ending of all giants; only those of the Isle Of Albion, a story that has been passed down through my line from parent to child, for a hundred generations. Being the bearer of such knowledge has at times been trying. The secret of the giants lay in their teeth, you see. Nothing on our earth was stronger than the teeth of giants. Very few know that giants ate rocks; that little giants ate boulders, and that bigger giants ate mountains. We have so little faith in the skills of our ancient cartographers. We all assume they misdrew their maps. But, in fact – it was the land masses that constantly changed as they were eaten and redeposited by herds of voracious giants. As a child in school, my protestations were met with derision. "Diamond is the hardest substance known to man, and giants DO NOT exist!" came the reply. The jeers and bullying would of course continue into the playground –

and so I am happily relieved, in these – my later years – to occasionally find a welcoming pair of ears.

The Giants of Albion

The giants of Albion were as follows: they were "Briggs the Bigger", named on account of his size. "Birdy Boy", so named because all manner of winged creatures followed him wherever he went; "Bodger", who didn't like the heat, and walked north whenever the sun shone brightly; "Henry", whose insatiable appetite for rock had led to his strengthening of his teeth; "Stanley the Artist", so named because of his creativity with snot. Then there were the "Lanky Twins", "Good'n" and "Bad'n". They had been named such by their mother, who being over tall and very thin at the hips had suffered terribly while birthing. The mother named the second twin Bad'n, for taking so long and not wanting to come out. It was in fact a stroke of luck that the twins were born holding hands for it was the first born, who eventually pulled her brother out by the hand and was thenceforth known as Good'n by her grateful mother.

There is little to be said about the politics of this herd. Little is known of Bodger, other than that she was thought of as a loner, because she always wandered off when the rest wanted to party in the sun. Briggs the Bigger looked down on Henry, when there were no clouds in the way, simply because he could – it was nothing personal really. Henry of course did take it personally and would shake his fists at Briggs while shouting about the strength of his teeth and how he could out-eat Briggs while devouring competition any day. Good'n was of a pleasant disposition, and had a soft spot for Birdy Boy, who was burdened with the task of carrying the ancestral necklace of the herd: a chain of teeth, the teeth of their grandfathers and grandmothers. Some 70 weighty gnashers; so heavy in fact that Birdy Boy often walked with a stoop under the load. It was at such times that Good'n would offer to help, and carry the necklace for a day or two. Birdy Boy was very pleased with this arrangement, for he disliked the name that had been given to him by the other giants and once free of the necklace, would sweep away the many winged creatures that added to his misery. Good'n was peace loving, making only one concession to the use of violence – she carried a sling shot and a meteorite, which she had occasionally needed while protecting her brother from giants that he managed to annoy – he did after all feel the need to live up to his name. It was this meteorite and the habits of an old human woman that are the key to the sorry tale of the giants' end.

The Old Woman of the Forest

The old woman of the forest lived in the woodland that bordered Cumbria. She had the habit of grinding her teeth. An affliction that started after a great sadness. So precocious was she in this act, that many of her teeth were now broken. To hide the habit from her kins folk, she created stories to explain how each had been broken. Her stories had become famous for their outlandishness and she became revered by her people, as a person who walked the line between madness and the world of reason, exploring a wisdom unseen to others.

A Puddingly Picnic

Briggs the Bigger had invited the Lanky twins to chew upon the crystal mountains of Cumbria; pudding after the hard granite of Cornwall. A tribe of humans had built their village in one of the valleys and were dismayed by the avalanche of boulders that were falling near to their homes. Mere crumbs to the giants, but sheer devastation to the villagers whose wooden huts were shattered and crushed by the shower. In desperation they went to the Old Woman of the Forest. "Can't you tell them a story?" they implored. The old woman shook her head and protested that the giants would only listen to someone of great ugliness and that although her teeth were goodly broken, and despite her rather long beard (a family trait) she still carried some of the beauty of her youth. Machismo was very important in the culture of giants. They often smashed themselves with rocks, to make themselves uglier and more impressive. The old woman only ever told stories to Stanley the Artist. If she tried it with the others, she feared that she would end her days beneath a boulder.

'Show them your teeth,' said a little girl.

The old woman was fond of the little girl who came to listen to her stories every day. Her heart was melted by her pleading. So with a deep breath, she resolved to go to the giants, and try.

Briggs did not like humans, and on catching their scent, grabbed a big boulder and prepared to hurl it at the approaching posse. It was Good'n who stayed his arm. 'Let me,' she said. And turning to the villagers she warned them that their lives would be short if they did not leave her kinsmen to their feasting. The villagers stood fast, and the old woman of the forest stepped forward. Good'n, her patience tested, gave them one more chance.

'Do you see this meteorite that I here keep upon my belt? If you do not leave this place, I shall launch it at your village, and reft a broad fiery gully through your fields and crops and forests. Your winter shall be all the colder and your bellies all the more empty if our meal is once more interrupted.'

The villagers shook in their boots, but the little girl ran forward and pulled upon the sleeve of the old woman.

'Show them your teeth!' she implored.

And in that moment, as the giant Good'n reached for her sling shot, the Old Woman of the Forest saw a way to save the villagers and rid the world of giants for all time. She flung back her head and let rip a loud cackling laugh – her mouth wide open and the battered stumps of her few remaining teeth jiggling in her jaw bone as the laugh grew louder.

None so Clever as the Crone

Briggs and Badden turned from their meal to look at the abomination that wheezed before them. This bag of rags that dared to mock them with her guffawing. But it was her mouth that locked their gaze. As if manacled in a macho staring contest they dared not blink, for they had never beheld such ugliness. They were awed by the extremity of its grotesquery. It was Good'n who once again spoke.

'How did you come by such an arrangement of teeth, old woman? They are ugly beyond compare and I wish to know how we too can improve our appearance in this way.'

'The answer lies upon your belt, good giant,' declared the old woman, pointing.

Good'n looked at the sling shot woven through her belt and then looked back at the old woman, confused.

'The meteorite upon your belt, good giant,' said the old woman, smiling. 'When I was a little girl, I used to watch the night sky, and hold my mouth open to see if I could catch a falling star. It was on one of these occasions that a tiny meteorite came hurtling from the heavens … moving faster than even a giant could throw it,' she added.

'It hit me square in my open mouth, and lay stuck there for three days, until my grandmother managed to prize it out with a pitch-fork. My teeth were so badly broken, that I was cast from my tribe on account of my ugliness, and I have lived in the forest ever since.'

The old woman ended with great satisfaction, seating herself upon the earth and folding her arms with a look of completeness.

Good'n looked at Birdy Boy, Birdy Boy looked at Bad'n, Bad'n looked at Good'n and then all three of them looked back at the old woman. The giants had managed on many occasions to make their faces more ugly, but had failed miserably when trying to rough up their teeth. Could it be the old woman had found the key to their ultimate fashion accessory?

'You caught a meteorite in your mouth?' asked Bad'n.

The old woman kept her arms folded, and nodded.

'And it breaked your teef?' asked Briggs.

'Yes,' said the old woman, 'but you need to keep moving, if you want to catch one, because they travel very, very quickly.'

The giants grunted in approval, nodded to each other and began whispering, very loudly. The old woman rose slowly and quietly, and ushered the villagers away.

The Quest for Ultimate Ugliness

Briggs the Bigger sent a message to his brother, "Briggs the Swindler" to return from his business on distant shores. And soon, all eight giants of Albion walked the earth with their heads in the air and their mouths wide open; all hoping to be the first to catch a tooth breaking bullet from the sky. So fierce was the competition between them, that they looked to the earth not once, and forgot about their eating mountains. Weakened by their hunger, they began to stagger, trip and fall; but still they continued, pulling themselves to their feet and soldiering on in their quest for ultimate ugliness. The two Briggs brothers were the tallest, and so they fell the hardest. This happened for the last time in Cumbria at a place called Ambleside. The two brothers had spotted a falling meteorite and backed into each other trying to catch it in their upturned mouths. Briggs the Bigger fell northwards, hitting the ground so hard with his open mouth, that his teeth pierced the bedrock of the Keswick plane, and remained stuck fast, while his brother, "the Swindler" fell southerly, his teeth becoming embedded close to the mouth of the river Dudden. There they lay, unable to move, till exhaustion and hunger robbed them of their final breath.

Knowing from her previous journeys, that the night sky was more dramatic beyond Scotland, Bodger walked north, eventually tripping over the tiny isle of Graemsay and burying her teeth into the sandstone of the Orkney mainland on the banks of Loch Harray.

Henry and Birdy Boy had followed Stanley into the southern reaches of Albion, Henry had always been secretly interested in the larger giant's love of the aesthetic, and thought that he might be onto something. It transpired that Stanley had been working on a brainwave. Associating the fire of meteorites with the fire of volcanoes he ventured to a place giants had once dined on volcanic rocks and it was here that Stanley stubbed his toe on a piece of partly chewed magma, plummeting headlong into a plain of rock, narrowly missing the village of Pensford. With his teeth firmly rooted in the earth, he was able to see the shimmering light of the setting sun, reflecting over a nearby lake. And with this little pleasure Stanley's eyes fell shut. Henry and Birdy Boy, mourning the loss of Stanley, headed east. It was while they were passing the village of Calne in Wiltshire that the two of them simultaneously spotted a shooting star in the sky. They began running, and as their weak legs tired, began to wrestle each other to the ground. As Henry glanced upwards with his mouth open wide, only to see the shooting star fizzle and die, Birdy Boy caught him under the chin with a knuckle sandwich and sent him flying many miles over the Vale of Pewsey. With his energy all spent, Birdy Boy breathed his last, and hit the earth, his teeth clenching into the hard rock and his ancestral necklace embedding itself around him. After a long arching flight, little Henry hit the earth by the village of Amesbury, with the force of an asteroid (and it is said that the ground shook in Mongolia).

Good'n and Bad'n were told by villagers that a giant carrying a huge necklace had headed south and so Good'n led her brother in that direction, for she wished to be close to Birdy Boy. Eventually they came to the sea without finding him, and Bad'n insisted that they should paddle. So they paddled, and kept paddling until the water raised above their waists and eventually to their chests. Their journey exhausted them so completely, that when they finally reached land, they could do nought but stumble, and when after a few days journey, they reached the sea once more their resolve faltered and they fell with their mouths still stretched open into the bedrock near Vannes, on the southern coast of Brittany.

In Memoriam

Many years later, an old bearded woman and a young maiden were seen placing a sign next to Stanley's disintegrating hulk. The headstone bore witness to Stanley's artistic tendencies and the love of the old woman for the only giant who had ever enjoyed her stories. The sign read "Stanley Drew". Over the centuries, the flesh and bones of the giants wasted away. Only their teeth and their names remained. The names became changed over time, as letters were dropped here or there. For example, "The Circle of Briggs the Bigger" became known as "Castle Rigg" and "The Circle of the Swindler" because "Swinside", as some names became favoured over others. "The Circle of Stanley Drew" became known as "Stanton Drew", "The Lanky Circles" in Brittany were named the "Circles of Er Lannic" by the French, who also named their nearby villages Larmor-Guden and Larmor-Baden. But it was the Romans who changed "The Circles of Birdy Boy" to "Avis Circulos" and later, Avebury. "The Circle of Bodger" in Orkney became "The Ring of Brodgar". Much attention has been endowed upon "The Ring of Henry". Particularly about the strength of his teeth. It seems that Henry's teeth were in fact fused under his gums. There are precedents for this phenomenon in the animal kingdom; it can be found in the fossil remains of the Megapedete rodents, and in the generic phenomenon of tooth germination where a single tooth develops into two, the root remaining fused. In any case, "The Circle of

Henry" became simply known as Stone Henge and Henry's strangely powerful molars can still be viewed to this day.

Epilogue

Of the giants of Albion, I have spoken. Needless to say, there were other herds of giants in other lands, and as news spread of the old woman's trickery, the mischief was repeated elsewhere. Giants from distant continents succumbed to a similar end, some wandering onto our shores in the name of vanity. It has been thousands of years since the last giant turned to dust – all that remains is their strange dentition. Some revere them; many have formed theories which they defend with fury and vigour. The real pity though, is that people can be so preoccupied these days with things like tellies and smart phones, that they don't even know where most of the giant circles are, let alone the reason they got there. And this, I do believe, is a great shame. It has been the burden of my ancestors and it will remain the burden of my children to pass the truth to you all. Wish us strength, for we shall need it. My tale is at an end.

Gelert's Hound

by

Steven G. Davis &

Wulfenstæg

In his dream, the forest was snow-lit. Black and snow-white, frosted flakes floating round like fragments of flower petals, discarded, fragrant and forgotten. The trees pierced the stars, icy fingers stretching out to challenge the gods themselves, to challenge Cernunnos, Wōden, Ullr. To challenge Caerne.

The ground was hard bastions of ice, crenellations of curious castles of frost and flowers. Pale, ice-lily blue flowers, stark, yellow-green stems wielding them. Flowers like a trail of tears, leading from where he stood into the dark iciness of the forest.

The forest was a castle in itself. A living castle, its borders protected by the dark tree-soldiers, taller than a score's worth of warriors. Wind-tossed at their heights, cascading crumbling snow caught by the curious wind and whipped once more.

Snow flurries. Dark breath. And deep within the forest –

'A white stag!'

Llewellyn looked around, realising he'd sat up. They were in one of his hunting lodges, far from his castle at Clun. The fire burned low in the grate, heating the room. Flickering shadows flashed across the cradle where his infant son slept. Flashed across his hound, stretched out beside the cradle, eyes half open and watching him.

He shook his head, stretching. His axe was on the floor beside him. There were knives under his pillow. Sælvatici stood guard both outside and inside the lodge. Cwn dozed beside his son and the dog had formed a deep bond with his descendent. The hound was still young; his son was still young. They would grow up together. They would grow old together.

Llewellyn stood up, crossing to the grate and warming his hands. Crossed to Cwn and knelt beside the faithful dog. The hound raised its head, licking his shoulder, as he rubbed its flanks and back.

'Good boy.' He rubbed the creature warmly. 'We go hunting today, Cwn. You cannot come. To you I entrust my son, though we are deep in Sælvatici territory. You will keep him safe. You will keep him company.'

Cwn was lean and wiry, part wolfhound, part something else. Llewellyn had seen him catch hares; had seen him bring down riders and armoured warriors. Had seen him wrap his body around his son to keep him warm.

He scratched Cwn's head. 'Good boy. The Champion's Portion shall be yours tonight! I hunt the White Stag.'

There was a knock on the door.

'My lord,' asked a voice, 'is the young Sælvatici awake?'

Llewellyn looked at his son. Stroked his cheek gently. The baby responded, shifting closer, murmuring, eyes fluttering.

'He wakes, Aneirin. Come in.'

The door opened. Aneirin walked in, broadsword in hand. She wore a single piece of cloth, a woollen sheet knotted at her right shoulder. She smiled at him, dark eyes only softening as she looked at his son.

'Warrior woman.' He smiled. 'Smith of words.'

She drove her sword into the floor. Came and sat beside him, leaned over Cwn and lifted his son gently from the cradle.

He was awake and smiling, burbling.

Cwn slipped out from in front of her and re-positioned himself, his head on her thigh.

Aneirin held his son tenderly in the crook of her arm. Guided his questing mouth to her breast.

'Purveyor of milk, steel and words.' She smiled, and there was almost warmth in it.

Llewellyn looked away. His wife was not long dead, had borne their son late in life. Some had said – he looked to the fire, noting it was dying down.

He rose awkwardly.

'Will you feed the fire with us going hunting?'

'I want the lodge warm.'

'I can carry him at my breast while we go hunting. He'll be warm and snug and not thirst for milk.'

Llewellyn shook his head regretfully. 'For three nights I've dreamed of the White Stag. I must hunt it: find my destiny. It is a good omen.'

'Your son would be safer at Clun. Or at my breast.' She stroked Cwn's head. 'Even with his faithful guardian and friend to protect him.'

'It could be –' he could not say her name. The wound was too cold, too recent. To lose his wife in childbirth –

'It could be a message,' she said, looking up at him for the first time.

Llewellyn looked away.

'We ride for the stag.'

'I could stay with him.'

'You are my warrior!' he blustered.

'Am I to be his mother as well, Llew? I love him. I would give my life for him, you know.'

He nodded mutely, warring with himself.

'My courses have stopped, Llew. I cannot bear. I can nurse,' she shook her head. 'You cannot make me your wife. You need a wife you can get with child.' She held her hand up. 'And you cannot simply come to me in the night and expect me to receive you.' She scowled. 'You need a younger, fruitful, woman.'

He glowered at her.

'We ride,' he replied, finally.

**

In his dream, the forest was dark and still and he hunted alone. Silvered moon slithered through snow-cased branches, silhouetting eerie fingers raised in silent cries. Owls on black wings whispered in the wind-tossed branches. Foxes yipped and hares danced silently, their eyes upon him.

The forest resonated. It creaked and stretched, wood stretched thin over a lake, too much weight, the ice threatening to crack. The ocean rumbled far beneath. Something slumbered, something stirred. Something rose.

An owl screamed. A fox barked. Hares howled.

The white stag walked towards him, hand outstretched –

His wife walked towards him, crowned with majestic antlers –

His wife was the stag, the stag was his wife.

His wife lay on the ground, drenched in blood.

His son screamed lustily for life.

The stag lay on the ground, drenched in blood –

'The white stag!'

Aneirin looked at him oddly.

Llewellyn looked around. The path twisted and turned, rising up and plunging down steeply. The hills were high and sharp, the path rocky and overgrown in places. The air buzzed with bees and insects. Warmth prickled: no hint of snow.

Three of his kin rode ahead of him, swords and axes drawn in readiness. It might be his territory – Sælvatici territory – but some Welsh were traitors, supporting the Normans.

Not that he supported the Anglo Saxons. And the enemies of his enemy were often still an enemy. But to betray his country, to support the Normans –

Aneirin rode close behind him. She held the reins in one hand, naked broadsword in the other.

I should have married her.

The thought was unbidden, making him flinch.

Two more Sælvatici rode behind him. They carried short bows, arrows on strings. Strict instructions not to loose at the white stag. The white stag was his.

Llewellyn tried not to scowl.

Morning was passing and the woods they hunted were not large but there had been no sign of the white stag. No sign of his wyrd. His destiny.

31

He almost flicked the reins. They moved too slowly but the path was treacherous, the hills tumbledown. The edge of the forest was all of this twisting and turning, shingle and shale, as if an ancient ocean had been here once. Plunging deep and roaring high; only once deeper into the woodlands did the land level off.

Haunting hallows and heaving hollows, full of malevolent memories and grim grievous galleries of knife-edged vales. No sun penetrated the depths of this forest: no sun but permanent shadow shrouded o'er the land. Trees grew dark and twisted. Trees grew twisted and tortured, straining for the never-present sun, straining but caught, leashed, held fast in the deep, tumbled-down forest.

The forest of the white stag.

Heat rose. Insects chittered and chattered and chittered and chattered, cheeping curiously, buzzing belligerently. This was their forest, the tumble-down forest, the forest of night, the heat-forest of forbidden fortunes.

Llewellyn mopped his brow.

'My lord!' one of his men called.

He raised his head. Deeper in, in the heart of the forbidden forest, a white stag stood.

She blinded through the green-tinged gloom. She incandesced. She gleamed and glowed.

Llewellyn cracked his reins and his horse leapt forwards, leapt upwards, ascending the steep hill. He heard Aneirin call after him, follow him, but he was off, his horse was off – and the white stag was off!

The hill rose and plunged and ever ahead of him was the white stag. At times a wisp. At times a willow-thin thought hidden behind trees to emerge again, gleaming and glowing. At times the white stag watched and waited and would only move on when he drew close.

No thought of loosing, no thought of ending –

Llewellyn chased and the hills rose and fell, and night rose and fell, and the green-gloom thickened and descended and at other times it was golden-green, struck through with risen morning-sun hues.

At last he came to a circular field and the white stag was there, cropping the grass. He slipped off his horse and the creature stumbled and fell, worn beyond existence.

Llewellyn took trembling steps towards it. Fell to his knees.

The white stag cropped the grass.

Sounds. Movement.

He managed to tilt his head. Aneirin was there, naked broadsword in hand.

'Aneirin. My wife.'

She stalked towards the white stag.

The white stag looked up at her.

Held out her hand.

His wife, wearing a crown of horns.

Glowing, radiant, resplendent.

Blood dripped from her hands.

He struggled to move, to call out, to warn her.

Aneirin raised her sword and the sword fell.

The stag fell.

There was blood gushing and blood spouting and blood washing the field.

Aneirin hacked, severing the neck, severing the stag's head from its body.

Severing his wife's head from her body.

Aneirin picked the stag's head up. Held it triumphant. Flung it to him.

Llewellyn cradled his wife's head, bloody horns and all.

He passed out.

**

In his dream, he stood in the ruined court at Londinium. The Normans were routed, the rulers deposed, beheaded, heads on spikes as a warning to would-be conquerors. Walls had crumbled and walls had fallen and snow swirled in. Snow swirled and wolves howled.

Fires raged and fury spent, bands of Sælvatici stalked the streets. Neatly ordered roads were ripped up and the Forest returned to the city: the wildness returned.

An owl screamed. Foxes barked. Hares howled.

A house cracked and crashed and a tree crescendoed into being, crisp leaves stark against the night sky. The air smelled of the damp, dank, dark, Forest.

Rivers ran where roads once walked.

Rivers of blood, of steel, of bone. Rivers of bodies.

From the dark rivers ran.

Rivers ran dark and deep.

And through it all walked –

'The white stag!'

Aneirin looked at him, condescension in her gaze.

'Was it all a dream?'

She looked away, sword in hand.

They were riding back to the lodge: it was in sight on the brow of the hill.

In her lap, Aneirin carried the head of the white stag. 'A Champion's Portion for Cwn,' she said softly, glancing at him, 'and one for me.'

Llewellyn shook his head. 'I remember chasing the stag. There was a round clearing, a field. You were there,' he accused.

Aneirin nodded. 'You were – entranced? Fallen under the spell of the stag.'

'You slew my wife.'

Aneirin raised an eyebrow.

'Pain slew your wife. Birth slew your wife. I would not hold your son responsible. I would take that pain if I could. He is like a son to me, though I am not his mother.'

She turned away.

Llewellyn sighed. The lodge was in sight. He missed his son. Missed Cwn. The hunt – he shook his head.

No more to the hunt will I ride. No more to the hunt. No more.

As they neared the lodge he dismounted, glancing back. The Sælvatici warriors were returning behind him, weary and tired.

'Cwn? Son? Are you –'

He pushed the door open and strode into the lodge. The fire was dead in the grate, the room cold. The cradle was pushed over, the clothes blood-stained and dry.

Being told by his wife that she was pregnant, his heart had somersaulted.

It somersaulted now, but in winter colours, not summer.

His son was dead, gone. Cwn was – where?

Aneirin screamed his son's name.

He pushed his way through to the inner chamber. There was a jumble of furs, of robes, a rough bed – Cwn pushed his way out of Aneirin's bed, growling lowly, teeth bared.

Llewellyn stared.

There was blood on Cwn's jaw.

'Cwn?' he stared.

The hunt had been for nothing. His wife was dead, the stag had been no messenger, he had been deluded, lost, unforgiven – he had nothing to be forgiven for – he had everything to be forgiven for –

But his son was dead.

His wife was dead. There would be no more hunts, no more feasts, no more light or laughter. The Sælvatici would live in darkness. And his faithful hound –

His murderous hound.

His malevolent, malicious, murdering monster-hound –

Sword and axe were in his hands and Cwn came to him and he cut and stabbed and slew and slaughtered and cried, wailed, and Cwn wailed, their cries piercing the skies.

The ground crackled and split. Weapons fell from his hands. He was soaked in blood. Tears stained his cheeks and he sobbed, sobbed, helpless and lost –

A child's cry troubled his ear.

Llewellyn sniffed, lifting his head.

Aneirin knelt beside him. Drew the robes and the furs aside.

His son cried.

His son wailed.

Llewellyn stared.

Aneirin fetched his son: put him into his arms.

'I thought you lost,' he whispered.

His son gurgled, looking up at him.

Aneirin threw the furs aside: gave a cry.

Llewellyn stared. An immense black wolf was stretched out, throat ripped open and life's blood spilled across her bed. The creature was twice the size of faithful Cwn. Faithful Cwn, who'd given his life – who'd protected his son's life –

He kissed his son's head. 'You live. You live. That is all that matters.'

He lifted his gaze to Cwn. 'You will not be forgotten. Never forgotten.'

'My lord,' said one of the Sælvatici.

He heard voices outside. Lifted his head.

'Someone's come, my lord. A warrior.'

Llewellyn cradled his son to his chest.

'My lord, should I take him –' Aneirin began.

He shook his head. 'Draw blade. Accompany me.'

He stalked out of the room, out of the lodge.

A red-haired warrior rocked on his heels. He wore arrogance like a cloak; he wore slaughter like a cloak; he wore vengeance like a cloak, and power flickered around him.

'I am Llewellyn. I command here.'

The man thrust his hand out. 'My name's Paol. I've heard of the Sælvatici. I'd like to join you, if you'll have me.'

Jack the Theorist

by

Jon Hartless

Prologue

For three months, the denizens of London had been held in thrall by a faceless killer operating within one of the most densely populated areas of the city. The public quivered in fear at the unknown slayer, felt indignation at the lack of progress made by the authorities, and waited eagerly for the next death, secretly hoping it would be gorier, bloodier, more horrific than the last.

Not many considered the women who had been killed, but many speculated wildly and gleefully at the identity of the killer: his face, his character, his social standing. Who was this man who could take life without being seen or caught? Everyone had a theory, and everyone knew what sort of person it had to be — someone different, someone abnormal, someone other. Not one of *us*, but one of *them*.

One man, however, did think of the murdered women – and of the developing myth that was more melodrama than reality. Looking back over the three months, he and one other had seen the creation of Jack the Ripper, for they had both been there from the beginning.

And now both men were here, at the end.

Chapter One

Rattling along in a hansom cab through the foggy streets of night-time London, Sir Arthur Smythe groaned against the swaying motion and hoped fervently he wouldn't have to use his glossy top hat as a makeshift vomit repository.

The dinner he'd attended at his old college had been, at best, indifferent; at worst, it was calculated to send the digestive system into a spasm of shock. Sir Arthur's companion in the cab, Professor John Wolf, had wisely only nibbled at his own dinner, even though a free meal was normally welcomed by the impecunious academic and ex-physician.

'It's no good,' whimpered Sir Arthur. 'I shall have to get out and walk. You carry on in the cab. I'll get out here.'

'I wouldn't dream of abandoning you in this God-forsaken district,' replied Wolf, glancing out of the window at the Whitechapel slums. Besides, he rather doubted he could afford the cab fare by himself. 'Hoy, driver! Stop here, if you would.'

'You gentlemen sure you want to stop here?' said the driver. 'This ain't the place for decent folk.'

'That's all right,' said Sir Arthur, his stomach settling the instant he got out of the swaying cab and onto firm ground. 'Here you are. Keep the change. We'll walk from here.'

The cabbie touched the brim of his battered bowler hat, palmed his fare, and took off into the night. The sound of the horse's hooves and the wheels of the cab echoed down the cobbled streets, although the cab itself was almost immediately lost to view in the thick fog and drizzle.

'That's better,' said Sir Arthur, feeling his stomach settle. He then made the mistake of breathing deeply; the stench of animal and human effluvia, coupled with the masses of rotting rubbish lining the streets, made his stomach turn a fresh summersault. 'Any idea where we are?' he asked, when the power of speech had returned.

'Buck's Row, I think,' said Wolf, squinting around. 'It's rather difficult to tell with this mist, but I'm certain that's New Cottage, so over there must be the stable block. Yes, this is Buck's Row.'

A piercing blast of a policeman's whistle sounded, and was answered by several others in the distance.

'What's going on there?' shouted Wolf into the fog.

'Murder,' came the answer.

Wolf and Sir Arthur exchanged glances and hurried down the fetid street towards the source of the voice. From out of the fog, the thick-set figure of a policeman appeared, looking pale and shocked.

'What's going on, officer?' demanded Wolf.

'Haven't I seen you before? asked the policeman, suspiciously.

'I am Professor Wolf. I often give lectures and talks in this area.'

'Why, of course it is. Sorry sir, I must have been thinking about someone else.'

'Murder, you say?'

'It's murder, sir, right enough. I was doing my rounds, saw this shape on the road, and saw it was a woman. Cut up something terrible, she is. I've never seen anything like it, and that's a fact.'

'Murder? In Whitechapel? Rather unusual, isn't it?' Wolf saw Sir Arthur's surprised look and explained. 'You certainly run the risk of being attacked, intimidated, bothered by the dregs of the street and having your pocket picked, but murder itself is unusual. Isn't that right, officer?'

'Yes, sir. Why, they're always shouting out 'murder' around here, 'specially a wife when her husband's had a drop too much and raises his hand to her, but actual murder is rare.'

'You know a lot about this sort of thing, Wolf?' asked Sir Arthur.

'Yes, I'm often around here, delivering lectures in the churches, working men's clubs, women's guilds and the like. I fancy I know most of the folks in this den at least by sight, and quite a few by name. And I'm sure I know you, officer. It's Nolan, isn't it?'

'Yes, sir. James Nolan.'

'Well, Nolan, let's take a look at her.'

'Just as you like, sir,' responded the policeman, who respected the learning and class of the professor. He stood back and let Wolf approach the body, while Sir Arthur maintained a queasy distance from the blood. For a moment, Wolf looked a sinister figure in his top hat and swirling, red-lined cloak, standing over the body of an unknown victim, but the illusion was dispelled as he lit a match over the corpse and gasped in surprise.

'Why, it's Mary Ann Nichols!' exclaimed Wolf, recognising the face of the woman through her contorted expression of fear and pain.

'Yes, sir,' agreed the constable. 'She's known in this area.'

'Hmmm,' muttered Wolf as he probed the body. 'She's on her back, arms by each side, legs extended. You haven't moved her, I suppose, Nolan? No? Good man. Now, the legs are warm, though the arms are cold...a great many cuts are visible to the throat, though not much blood...killed elsewhere, perhaps? And almost certainly within the last half hour. Hmm, there seems to have been a certain amount of mutilation in the abdomen area.'

For one ghastly moment, Sir Arthur saw a glimpse of intestine, and despite the grimness of the situation and the terrible fate that had befallen the woman, he couldn't help be reminded of what he'd eaten at the college dinner some hours beforehand. He would definitely recommend to the Master that the new caterer, *S. Todd, Gourmet Caterers and Pie Makers Extraordinary*, should not retain the culinary contract.

'Tell me, Nolan,' said Wolf with authority, 'the nearest mortuary is at Old Montague Street, isn't it?'

'Yes, sir. We'll have the body sent there.'

'Good man. Hello, what's this? Oh, just a bonnet. Wonder if it belonged to the woman? And what do you people want?' said Wolf, straightening up and glaring at the assembling crowd of locals.

45

'Just looking,' muttered one of them.

'Should I move them on, sir?' asked the constable.

'No, get some statements taken,' said Wolf, looking critically into the small gathering. 'Did anybody see anything?'

The crowd slunk back and shook their heads sullenly.

'Someone must have seen something,' hectored the professor. 'You, Mrs Anderson, what did you see?'

Mrs Anderson started at being picked out of the group by Wolf's sharp eyes. 'Didn't see nothing,' she mumbled through broken, rotten teeth.

'Nothing?' roared Wolf. 'You dreg! You sit in that pub over there every night at the window, drinking what your daughter earns, so don't tell me you didn't see anything.'

'Saw her walking along with a man,' admitted Mrs Anderson. An appreciative thrill ran round the crowd, and the old woman perked up at suddenly being the centre of attention. 'Yes, I saw her, and him. He was dressed all in dark clothing, and I felt a shiver as I looked at him, I did. It was a premonition, a premonition from the Lord!'

'More likely from the gin bottle,' growled Wolf, to the crowd's amusement. 'Aside from your imagination, what did you see? What age was the man?'

'Don't know.'

'How was he dressed?'

'Dark clothes.'

'Rich, poor?'

46

'About the same as anyone else,' muttered the crone, wiping her dirty sleeve across her mouth.

'Can anyone add anything?' snapped the professor in disgust. 'No? Well, if no one can be of any help, you'd better leave.'

The crowd muttered but moved back, revealing a nondescript individual hidden behind the masses.

'Come on, out of it,' ordered Constable Nolan, overlooking the unremarkable figure as he focussed on organising the crowd.

'What about you, sir,' said Wolf to the man. 'What did you see?'

'Nothing,' replied the man as he pulled his hat down over his eyes. His face was difficult to see and almost impossible to define, and under the arrogant gaze of Dr Wolf, he seemed to dwindle even further into obscurity.

Before Wolf could respond, the sound of an excited crowd intruded as a dozen journalists swept into the street, shouting and arguing with each other as they came to investigate the heavy police presence gathering in the area.

'Ah,' said Wolf, recognising many of the newcomers. 'The press.'

**

'What's going on, Professor?' demanded a babble of voices as the reporters surrounded Wolf, obscuring the nondescript man completely. Sir Arthur tried to keep his eye on the strangely unimpressive figure, but he simply melted away behind the media frenzy.

'A woman has been murdered,' announced Professor Wolf, pleased at being the centre of attention, even if the affair was thoroughly sordid and uninteresting.

'Great!' exclaimed one of the men. 'Would you describe it as brutal, or abominable?'

'I wouldn't describe it at all,' said Wolf with a sniff of disdain.

'"Man of learning lost for words,"' interpreted the journalist as he wrote in a notebook.

'"Shock robs Prof of power of speech,"' muttered another, scribbling furiously.

'Cor, there's plenty of blood here!' said a junior reporter, one of the few to actually look at the body.

'"Mutilated body of lone woman found,"' said a further example of Fleet Street's finest, never once looking up from his notebook before turning to interview his closest neighbour. 'What do you think?'

'I think it's horrible.'

'"It's horrible,"' wrote the first hack. 'I agree,' he said. 'Terrible crime.'

'"Terrible crime, says man at scene,"' echoed his partner, writing furiously. '"Whitechapel reaction to brutal...brutal..."'

'Murder?'

'Killing?'

'Stabbing?'

'Slaying?'

'Yes, slaying is good. 'Whitechapel reaction to brutal slaying — "It's a horrible, terrible crime," says local.' Great. Let's go and write this up at the gin shop.'

48

The tramping of heavy boots obscured the sound of scribbling pencils as Police Commissioner Sir Craig Burrow appeared with a retinue of uniformed officers.

'What is going on here, Constable?' he demanded of Nolan, who had just returned from chasing away the residents.

'Hmm, a bad business, this,' said Burrow, flaring his nostrils in disgust after listening to Nolan's report. 'All right, get the body out of here. I'll bet it was a Jew or some other foreigner who did this. It's just what you'd expect from that sort.'

'Exactly the attitude you would expect from an honest, upright citizen or police officer,' muttered Sir Arthur in repugnance to Professor Wolf. 'I wonder what they'll make of it?'

'Oh, all sorts of things,' said Wolf absently, his attention still on the reporters. "Maniac on rampage." "Killer on loose." "No woman safe." The usual irresponsible sort of stuff. Pity there's not much else happening in the news at the moment; it may have relegated this tragedy to a small paragraph or two.'

'I was thinking of the police; it seems to me the investigation has been botched already thanks to their xenophobic assumptions,' said Sir Arthur, nodding at the uniformed constables as they searched for suspicious-looking foreigners to question.

'I don't suppose we're needed here,' agreed Wolf, somewhat wistfully. 'I suggest we slip away.'

**

49

'Would you care for a bite to eat?' offered Sir Arthur once both men were settled in the scarlet study of his town house, though he was usure how anyone could think of eating after picking through someone's lower intestines.

'Perhaps some dry toast?'

'Very kind,' said Wolf, who was scribbling furiously into a small notebook. 'But I think I caught a whiff of kidney and bacon on the way in. With a fried tomato, if possible.'

Sir Arthur blanched a little, blew down the speaking tube, and placed the order. 'What are you writing?' he asked as he poured out two drinks.

'Hmm? Oh, this. Well, as we were leaving, you noticed the man in the dark check overcoat who spoke to me? You did? Oh, I thought you'd missed it. Anyway, he works on the *Morning Star,* and he wanted an exclusive. You wouldn't believe the cash he was offering, so I said I'd write a quick account.'

'Ah.'

'And then we were stopped by Mrs Miggins — the lady with the huge fur muff — who represents the neighbourhood Christian Voluntary Committee, and she asked if I could do a lecture on the murder and the living conditions of the poor in the Whitechapel area, so I agreed.'

'Isn't that a bit...off?' asked Sir Arthur, feeling that making capital from the woman's death was ghoulish at best. 'After all, I'd be surprised if either group is really interested in the truth of the matter. The press will want a Midnight Phantom to scare the public and sell papers with, and the Christian Voluntary Committee no doubt want it confirmed that the right sort of religion needs to be disseminated through the area.'

'Possibly, but it's a paying brief,' muttered Wolf in reply, firmly closing his notebook under Sir Arthur's scrutiny.

Sir Arthur was disturbed at the idea of profiting from the ghastly events of the night, but he reminded himself the professor was both poor and proud, and he no doubt welcomed the extra income. He said no more.

**

The inquest on Mary Ann Nichols, held the following week at the Whitechapel Working Lads' Institute, closed as expected with a verdict of murder by "person or persons unknown."

Sir Arthur strode from the building, observing the crowd around him. Journalists were running back to their offices to write up the story on the unknown killer; the Christian Voluntary Committee were passing out leaflets on 'The Light of the Lord and the Demon of Drink'; police officers were busily expanding on their own theories, while the general public were looking suspiciously at one another, as though they believed the murderer could be among them.

In Sir Arthur's view, the killing was the inevitable result of having several thousand people penned into one small area by crime, poverty, and social neglect. The resulting violence had happened before, and no doubt it would happen again, but this particular affair was over. He glanced up at the sky, in which the filth of London's air was mixing with the dark clouds of an oncoming storm, and shivered. It was a one-off event, he reassured himself. Done. Over and finished with.

A one-off event...

Chapter Two

Just over a week after the first death, Sir Arthur was updating his files on the paranormal when the butler, Harker, announced Professor Wolf was at the door.

'Professor?' said Sir Arthur in astonishment, noting the man's feverish appearance.

'Sorry to burst in like this,' replied Wolf, sinking into a chair, 'but there's been another.'

'Another what?' asked Sir Arthur, trying to drag his attention back from the Carpathian past to the immediate present.

'Another murder,' said Wolf, trembling in interest.

'What? Are you certain?'

'Absolutely.'

'Who was the victim?' asked Sir Arthur.

'Another night walker; Annie Chapman.'

'Wait; do we know the first victim was a nightwalker?'

'It's a fair assumption; why else would she be out so late?'

'Homelessness, illness, fleeing a domestic scene...'

'That's as may be,' huffed Wolf. 'But now there are two and I want to know more.'

'Whatever for?'

'Call it morbid interest, altruistic concern, whatever you fancy.'

'How about a nice extra income?' observed Sir Arthur with gentle sarcasm, nodding at the new notebook sticking out of the professor's pocket, the first page of which revealed the heading 'Whitechapel Killing: theories.'

Wolf patted his pocket and smiled. 'Will you join me again? I'm going to look into this myself, come what may.'

With great misgiving, Sir Arthur rang for his hat and coat.

***

The professor and Sir Arthur started by calling on Constable Nolan, as Wolf knew the policeman would have just come off duty and would probably be at his lodgings. The young detective looked tired and pale when he answered the door.

'Hello, Professor,' he said in surprise. 'I didn't expect to see you again so soon. Come on in.'

Nolan took the two men into a small, cramped room stuffed with cheap ornaments, bulky furniture covered in moth-eaten, furry cushions, and numerous pictures hung to conceal the damp patches on the walls as much as for any artistic concern.

Nolan turned to the settee and prodded two of the cushions. These turned out to be his landlady's cats, which stretched out and treated Sir Arthur and the professor to a malignant glare for depriving them of the warm seat. Then, correctly deducing Sir Arthur was a sap for animals, the two cats jumped onto his lap and settled down on his knees, where they dribbled happily.

'I just wondered if the police had any new leads when you left the station?' said Wolf.

'Not a blessed thing, sir,' said Nolan, turning to the coffee pot on the table. 'Would you like a cup?'

Sir Arthur and Wolf looked at the large ginger tom wrapped around the tarnished pot, warming its stomach, and politely declined.

'So, there are no leads at all?'

'Just a couple sir. A woman called Darrell claims she saw Annie Chapman walking with a man in the alley she was later killed in; that was about five thirty in the morning. At about the same time, a cabbie called Cadosch says he heard a voice coming from a back yard in the alley where the body was found, and the sound of something falling against the fence. Scone?'

'Er, no, thank you. Let the cat finish it as she's started,' replied Sir Arthur.

'Any description of the man?' demanded Wolf.

'Dark and foreign looking, according to Darrell.'

'Who was the doctor called out to the scene?'

'Doctor Barnard.'

'Ah, good. I know of him. Our next stop, Arthur,' said Wolf, turning to his companion, 'is to visit the doctor. Do you have a clothes brush, Nolan, before we go? I appear to be covered in tabby hair, and I do believe there's now a fur ball or three on Sir Arthur's lap...'

**

An hour later, Sir Arthur and Wolf were shown into Doctor Barnard's surgery, located at the back end of the Whitechapel district. At first, the doctor didn't seem to be keen to discuss the victim, Annie Chapman, especially upon hearing of the professor's close interest in the

55

murders, but Sir Arthur's visiting card opened the way into Barnard's confidence.

'She came to my surgery at about midnight for some pills to counter the shakes — she was a habitual alcoholic,' said Barnard disapprovingly as he busied himself at his drink's cabinet, having seated his two visitors. 'Her body was found at about six this morning, in a yard in Hasbury Street. The man who discovered her, a resident of the street who was leaving for an early shift, rushed out of the road, found two others, and they split up to find a policeman.'

'Thank you,' beamed Wolf as Barnard handed his guests their drinks.

'A policeman was found,' continued Barnard, settling into his chair behind his desk, 'but he was on fixed point duty, and consequently couldn't leave his post. Eventually, one of the men reached the Commerce Road Police Station, and Inspector Joseph took control and sent for me.'

Barnard swung around in his swivel chair and looked out of his window at the filthy street below, a strange, internal light illuminating his eyes. 'Ah, the squalor, the horror of the filthy lives of these people, these people without a God!' As suddenly as the strange mood settled, it lifted again; Barnard swung back to his visitors and continued as though he hadn't broken off his narrative.

'She'd been dead, I would guess, for about two hours, so she was killed at about four in the morning.' He swung back to the window and the inner light came back into his eyes. 'Probably she had just finished with her client, some brute of a man she dragged down to her own level of sin and degradation!' Abruptly, the doctor swivelled around and addressed his two visitors in his former smooth tones.

'Her possessions had been left by the body in two neat piles. They included a coarse handkerchief, a comb, and the pill slip I had given her earlier from my surgery store. The pills and the container were above her head, while the comb and handkerchief were below her feet.'

'Did you perform the autopsy?' asked Wolf.

'No, but during my examination, I saw that certain organs had been removed from the body, so the murderer must have taken them away with him. They included the uterus and the bladder, part of the spleen, and also some intestinal tract. This demonstrates some surgical knowledge and skill. It would have taken me about half an hour to do something similar. How the killer could have walked away unseen, I do not know.'

Barnard again turned to stare out of his window. 'It is terrible, terrible...' he mused. 'The crime, the degradation, the sordid lives of the penny whores and their clientele in the doorways and alleys of the Whitechapel slums... Terrible!' he exclaimed, banging his fist down on his mahogany desk. 'The immorality, the vice, the squalor, the starvation, the pathetic children, nought but walking skeletons covered in filth – and all with no religion!'

'Oh, the degradation of the soul!' roared Barnard, oblivious to Sir Arthur's nervous fidgeting. 'I'm making a collection to save these women by handing them free bibles to put the righteous fear of God into them. Will you gentlemen donate to the worthy cause, the saving of souls for our Lord?'

Before the two men could respond, the door opened and the maid came in, weighed down by a huge pile of newspapers. 'Here are the evening editions you wanted, sir,' she said to the doctor.

'Thank you, Pamela,' said Barnard dismissively, though his eyes lingered on the maid for a few seconds longer than necessary. Wolf seemed to find this significant, and dug his elbow into his companion's side.

Sir Arthur winced, wondering why Wolf was so excited. 'May we look over them?' he asked as Pamela left the room. 'There may be some new details available.'

'Hmm, "Whitechapel Murderer strikes again!"' quoted Wolf, glancing over the first headline as Barnard spread the papers over his desk.

'"Post-mortem result; see later edition,"' muttered Sir Arthur, picking out the meagre factual content.

'"No woman safe...street sluts slaughtered... foulness and immorality of women,"' muttered Barnard as he read over the accounts, picking at the most appealing words and phrases. '"Night walkers in fear...streets of sin."'

'I think perhaps we've intruded enough,' said Wolf, abruptly. 'Thank you for your time, Doctor Barnard, but we must press on.'

'If there is anything else I can do to help you gentlemen, you just have to ask,' responded Barnard. 'I'm often to be found in the Barber Street mission, set up in an old gin shop. As you may know, I successfully campaigned against the iniquitous drinking establishment and closed it down before converting it to the higher calling of God. I hope to see you there, one day, Sir Arthur,' continued Barnard, a slight line of foam appearing in the corner of his mouth. 'Your rank and station would go a long way in helping these poor, degraded, filthy whores.'

'I may be looking in soon,' mumbled Sir Arthur, carefully keeping his distance from the frothing medic. After all, he thought, *some of those Barnard has 'saved' might well need saving from him.*

Barnard nodded in satisfaction as he rang the buzzer on his desk. 'Pamela; show these gentlemen out.'

**

'Why do you want to leave so suddenly?' asked Sir Arthur to Wolf as Pamela ushered them out of the building. Wolf had been getting progressively more excited as he questioned Barnard, and it seemed odd he would break off for no good reason.

'Can't you see?' hissed Wolf in excitement. 'Barnard is obviously a disturbed religious fanatic! He hates prostitutes but yearns after them, and he knew of the missing organs before the autopsy, which is no easy matter in a dark street with no adequate light to see by.'

'I certainly noticed Barnard couldn't even bring himself to use Annie Chapman's name,' replied Sir Arthur in distaste.

'You need a post-mortem to get a full idea of what's happened to a body, yet Barnard knew precisely which organs had been removed,' continued Wolf, waving Sir Arthur's observation aside. 'And bear in mind doctors are called to verify life is extinct; they don't usually rummage around the corpse in a darkened alley in front of everyone.'

'I sometimes forget you started in medicine,' said Sir Arthur, discreetly stepping around Wolf's career-ending scandal.

'You never lose the taste,' muttered Wolf before brightening. 'But Barnard could well be the killer!'

'Really?' said Sir Arthur, doubtfully. 'And what of the fact that Barnard's medical testimony conflicts with the witness statements? Darrell and Cadosch both believe they saw or heard the woman at about 5:30, yet Barnard thinks she died at about 4.'

'A blind!' said Wolf in excitement. 'A blind to throw us off the scent!'

'And from these haphazard scraps you arrive at the conclusion that Barnard has to be the killer?'

'The links are all there. We merely need the proof. The first step is to research Barnard's life. Then we shall see.'

**

'Look, there he is,' said Wolf, looking significantly at his companions. He, Sir Arthur and Inspector Abler of "H" division were at Annie Chapman's inquest, squeezed onto one of the benches in the public gallery. They followed Wolf's gaze and saw the back of Doctor Barnard's head.

'And you're absolutely certain about this?' asked Abler, wearily. He firmly agreed with Sir Arthur that there was no actual proof against Doctor Barnard. Indeed, the only 'proof' offered by Wolf was the professor's own determined claims, and Abler had only agreed to attend the inquest in the hope of stopping Wolf from bothering him any further.

'Do you have a warrant?' demanded Wolf by way of reply.

'Not enough evidence,' said Abler, disingenuously. 'The chief wouldn't hear of it.' *Well, I never told him,* he thought, *so in a sense he really didn't hear of it.* 'And I still don't understand how you can be so certain Barnard is the killer.'

'It's very simple,' said Wolf with authority, looking up from his diary in which he was cataloguing his theories and upcoming lectures on the Whitechapel murders. He also had contracts from various publishers spread out over his knees, each one offering lucrative terms for his 'specialist' speculations on the two crimes. His pen paused over a dotted line as he lectured the Inspector.

'I have been researching into Doctor Barnard's past, and I've discovered he had a disturbed childhood, which of course explains the fanatical nature of the man himself, as witnessed by myself and Sir Arthur. Barnard was the fifth child, and the delivery was complicated — in fact, his mother almost died during childbirth. As a result, Barnard was placed with a wet nurse, meaning he never bonded with his mother in the way a normal child does, causing irreparable mental and emotional damage.'

61

'Cod-theorising,' interjected Sir Arthur.

'Codswallop,' said the Inspector, bluntly.

Wolf ignored the two men, his eyes shining as he continued his analysis. 'By all accounts, he was not a prepossessing child. Another son was born just under a year later, a golden-haired, cherubic child, who was doted upon by the mother and father. This child was frequently the centre of attention when visitors called, while Barnard himself would be locked in the cold, lonely nursery, unwanted and unloved, rejected by those nearest to him...

'Barnard was sent to several schools but excelled at none of them. And he was punished continually for infringing the school rules. He secured a job as a clerk, but soon after he was drawn to the church where he would come to believe he was God's instrument on Earth, thus leading him to committing these appalling acts...'

'And where exactly did you obtain these "facts"?' demanded Abler, incredulously.

'Research,' replied Wolf, his tone suggesting he wasn't going to say anything more on the subject. Instead, he signed his name with a flourish across all the publishing contracts before stuffing the papers back into his coat pocket. 'What do you think, Arthur?'

'Hmm?'

'I said, what do you — what are staring at?'

'Oh, nothing of any importance,' said Sir Arthur vaguely, who had let his attention roam as Wolf presented his theory.

'It must be something,' insisted Wolf.

Sir Arthur sighed. 'You see that man at the back of the crowd, just to the right of the pillar, richly dressed?'

'Yes,' replied Wolf and the inspector.

'And see there, another man in brown check-trousers, and over there a third man in a fawn overcoat?'

Wolf and Abler looked in bewilderment at the three separate men Sir Arthur seemed to have plucked at random from the crowd.

'What of them?' asked Abler. 'With the level of press interest in the crime, it's no surprise the place is packed.'

'Indeed; my attention was simply caught by their insignia. Their pocket watches, rings, seals on their bags and so on.'

'What's worrying you about them?' asked Abler.

'I'm not worried,' replied Sir Arthur. 'I just happened to notice they're all Masons.'

Wolf started in surprise. While he knew Sir Arthur wasn't quite the vague sort of chap he pretended to be, he had never guessed such powers of observation lurked beneath the bland surface. Intrigued, he turned to a fresh page in his notebook and began scribbling down the observations.

'The inquest is over,' observed Abler as the coroner left the court.

'Barnard is heading for the door!' exclaimed Wolf. 'And so is the Mason by the pillar – and the other two!' Ignoring Abler's acerbic observation that people were leaving because the inquiry had finished, Wolf began pushing zealously through the crowd. 'Quickly, before they escape!' he cried in excitement – just as one of the Masons happened to look directly at him before turning away.

'Follow him!' bellowed Wolf, pushing his way forward as a new, superior theory began bubbling through his mind – a theory proved beyond all doubt just moments later when Wolf saw the Mason was standing in the street *with no sign of Doctor Barnard anywhere near him*, proving to the professor's satisfaction there was some link between the Mason and the medic.

'Where is Barnard?' demanded Wolf of the Mason. 'What have you done with him? Are you in league with him, by God?!'

'What are you talking about?' asked the man, taking a nervous step back.

'Damn it, he was just here!' insisted Wolf, his eyes glowing with a strange light. 'It was you, wasn't it? It was the Masons who did it!'

'Did what?' asked the man, nervously.

Wolf looked ready to grab the man on the spot, but he was restrained by Abler and Sir Arthur.

'Good day, gentlemen,' said the man in an affronted tone. He jumped into his carriage, which had just arrived, and slammed the door shut.

Wolf swung round angrily to Sir Arthur, his pen poised over his notebook. 'Do you know who him?' he demanded.

'No idea,' replied Sir Arthur.

'Well, I want to know who he was and what's going on,' said Wolf fervently, to the groans of both Sir

Arthur and Abler. 'And I won't rest until I know why the Masons are concerning themselves with this affair of dead prostitutes. The conspiracy is afoot!'

Chapter Three

'All right, so you now think the Masons are somehow connected with the murders,' said Abler impatiently after he and Wolf had settled in Sir Arthur's study. 'But I don't see how you intend to prove it.' They had been arguing all the way to the house about Wolf's latest theory on the Whitechapel killings.

'To begin with,' replied Wolf, looking up from his notepad on which he was scribbling everything down, 'the very fact that no fewer than three Masons were at the inquest is suspicious in itself. As is the abrupt disappearance of Barnard. There must be a link. There has to be.'

'You're saying the Masons spirited Barnard away?' exclaimed Abler.

'That is exactly what I am suggesting,' responded Wolf. 'It explains why the Masons were at the inquest and how Barnard disappeared so swiftly.'

'You don't think the Masons, like everyone else, may have been there out of ghoulish curiosity, and Barnard may, for example, have just walked round the corner and got lost to view in the crowd?' asked Abler, witheringly.

'The Masons!' insisted Wolf.

'Why?' demanded Abler, unwisely playing Wolf at his own game. 'For what reason?'

'There we have no data, and therefore no answer,' said Wolf, somewhat unexpectedly. 'To find out, we need to get into the Masonic community. Which won't be easy. Arthur, what are you looking for?'

Both Wolf and Abler watched in bemusement as Sir Arthur rummaged in a large wooden chest and lifted from it a ten-inch spike, a collection of silver bullets, three shrunken heads, a stuffed black cat, and other sundry objects.

'Got it,' muttered Sir Arthur finally, lifting out a thick, black cloak complete with a tarnished silver seal. 'The Order of the Middle Knights,' he explained to the two men. 'Not actually mine. I, er, acquired it from the former owner some time ago, but it should get Wolf into the Masonic lodge. Then he can see for himself the only thing the Masons play at is silly buggers, and we can forget the whole ridiculous issue.'

**

'Brothers; are we assembled?' intoned the Supreme Master of the Middle Knights.

'We are assembled!' chanted the dozen or so black-clad figures standing in a rough shape of a pentagram.

Behind them, Wolf shrank against the far wall, hidden in the deep cowl of the robe, waiting for the true horrors to be revealed to him. So far, he had stood and watched the Ritual Locking of the Doors, (which had to be unlocked when it was realised one of the brethren was still outside), the Ritual Opening of the Book of Knowledge, (which had been disturbed by a gentle but persistent zephyr from the upper windows, and the Book of Knowledge was now being held open at the right page by the Master's strategically placed thumb), and the Ritual of the Ritual, a brief prayer offered to a God who seemed to be made up of bits and pieces of all the other Gods who had ever been worshiped in the past.

'Brothers!' intoned the Master. 'The Time Has Come! The Peril is Here! Our Way of Life is Threatened! But Fate has put in our hands the Instrument of Retribution! Step forward, Brother!'

One of the hooded figures strode forward and prostrated itself at the Master's feet, causing Wolf to shake with anticipation.

'Brother, know thou of the Dark Time upon Us?' intoned the Master, enunciating clearly so all could hear the portentous capital letters of imminent doom.

'I do, Master,' replied the slightly muffled tone of the hooded figure, for he had yet to learn how to speak clearly through a thick cowl.

'A recent addition to the ranks?' muttered Wolf, voice as sotto as possible. 'Possibly even...Barnard himself!' The more he thought of it, the more obvious it seemed that Barnard was being used by the Masons for some purpose of their own, something which coincided with Barnard's own murderous activities...

'Hear now of the Dark Time!' thundered the Master, much to Wolf's relief. He had been hoping the Master would be grandiloquent enough to declaim the plot, despite the room being full of men who presumably already knew what the aforementioned plot was. *A self-aggrandising absorption is the hallmark of many secret societies,* thought Wolf smugly, who had never before seen a secret society at work, or given them any thought. 'Our noble lineage is in decay! Our most sacred tradition is in danger of utter annihilation! We must fight the good fight!'

Wolf pondered on what he was hearing and a half-remembered news story about the raiding of a male brothel patronised by the wealthy elite, combined with the talk of lineage, made a link in his over-active imagination and the Truth Was Revealed To Him: the heir to the throne had committed the most despicable indiscretion and taken a Catholic wife! And if this were true, it therefore followed that the union had produced a child!

'This, my brothers, is only the start,' continued the Master, 'for always there are terrors to be faced and trials to overcome. But we will face these trials!'

Wolf made the next deductive jump in his reasoning. Obviously, the woman the Prince of Wales had married was a penny whore, and her low and filthy friends were now trying to betray their country by demanding hush money from the authorities!

'The danger is three-fold, and three-fold must our response be,' declaimed the Master.

So there are three women in the matter, thought Wolf. *Which means another murder is to be done!*

'Mas-tah!' intoned one of the brethren with a fine oratorical flourish. 'Are we to fulfil the ancient prophecy?'

'We are! And we begin now!'

Wolf turned and ran, knowing he only had moments to act. Behind him, the acolytes watched in bemusement as the figure rushed from the hall, lurching in a hunched posture designed to make the entire body disappear from view.

'I wonder who that was?' muttered an acolyte before shrugging the matter off and turning back to the Master, who was looking in annoyance at the brotherhood.

'Perhaps next time,' said the Master testily, 'we can all remember to go the bathroom *before* we start?' The Master sighed before turning his attention back to the supplicant in front of him. He always enjoyed initiating a new member; he liked the three-fold rite, which allowed him to read the sacred incantations which in turn fulfilled the ancient prophecy.

He also liked gathering the brethren in a circle to mumble a few mantras to protect the symbolic lineage of the land, (always a certain way to boost a chap's self-esteem), followed by the symbolic trials of the new recruit, which were always most amusing to watch. Especially the one with the oversized turnip.

After which they would retire to the common room for a plate of hot crumpets, where the Master would ensure that his fellow acolyte, Alderman "Tubby" Jenks, was going to award the contract to build the new city library to the Master's own construction firm, and no one else.

A thoroughly worthwhile way to spend the evening, thought the Master, happily.

'We must be quick!' hissed Wolf as he scampered to where Sir Arthur and Inspector Abler where waiting in the gloom outside the Masonic Hall.

'You know something?' asked Abler, incredulously.

'The victims of this plot! But we must act immediately; even now the Masons are moving. Look, there!' Wolf pointed to a dark alley, in which a few strands of early fog swirled around four dappled horses and a black carriage. A figure strode out of a side door of the Hall and entered the carriage, giving a curt order to the driver as it did so. The driver gently whipped the horses and the carriage set off down the street.

'Damn!' whispered Wolf. 'I've only got a trap waiting. He has the advantage in horsepower.'

'Who is that?' asked Sir Arthur as he and his two companions squeezed into the trap. Wolf clicked the whip, and they rattled off into the developing mist.

'The murderer,' replied Wolf, his voice hoarse.

'The murderer?' echoed Abler disbelievingly.

'Yes.'

'Perhaps you'd better explain exactly what you heard in there,' suggested Sir Arthur wearily, suddenly aware he most likely had a very long night ahead of him...
***

Half an hour later, Inspector Abler was reaching the end of a very long rant. 'And if I went to the chief with that bag of nonsense, I'd be demoted down to traffic duties! You have no evidence and no witnesses. All you've given me are a few random events strung together with your own biased conjectures.'

'It all fits,' insisted Wolf, sulkily.

'Anyone know where we are?' asked Sir Arthur as they followed the black carriage through the fog.

'Berner Street,' replied Wolf. 'The black heart of Whitechapel!'

'No it isn't,' snapped Abler. 'It's nowhere near the centre. It's more to the side – hey, where the devil are all the foot patrols? I gave instructions they were to be stepped up in the whole area.'

'Ah ha!' exclaimed Wolf. 'Perhaps they've been pulled back by a higher authority? Who knows what control the Masons wield?'

Before Abler could respond, a suspicious voice shouted out; 'Who's there? Identify yourselves!' Three figures loomed forward in the thickening fog.

'Inspector Abler,' replied the officer. 'Now you identify yourselves.'

Sir Arthur slipped his hand around the butt of his revolver but relaxed when the men who had challenged them moved willingly into the flickering light of the closest gas lamp.

'It's only us, Inspector,' said the leader of the three men.

'Mr. Lusk,' identified the Inspector. 'The Whitechapel Voluntary Watch,' he explained to Wolf and Sir Arthur. 'Have you seen anyone this evening, Mr. Lusk?'

'No, no strangers, no Jews, no aristocrats,' replied Lusk, overlooking Abler (third generation Jewish) and Sir

Arthur (aristocrat). 'I think we're safe for the evening.' A piercing scream echoed around the street. 'Good God!" exclaimed Lusk. 'That came from down there!'

The men ran down the dark road and into Dutfield's Yard, where they stopped in horror at the sight of a body on the ground. 'We're too late, gentlemen,' whispered Wolf as Lusk struck a match. 'The Masons have taken another victim!'

**

'It's Elizabeth Stride,' said Lusk, who knew many of the denizens of the district. 'Looks like her throat's been cut!'

'And we know who is responsible!' insisted Wolf.

'Then where is he?' demanded the Inspector. 'Where is the man we were following?'

'He has been hidden by the powerful hand of the Masons!'

'Actually, he's over there,' said Sir Arthur, pointing to the man as he walked out of a public house and toward his carriage.

'We can take him on the spot and confront him with his crime!' hissed Wolf in excitement as he ran over to the startled man, shouting 'Ho! Barnard! Stop, killer!'

'We'd better go after him, I think,' said Sir Arthur to the inspector.

'I'll be there in a moment,' muttered Abler as several constables crowded into the area, attracted by the shouts of alarm.

'Stop, murderer!' shouted Wolf as he ran.

'I beg your pardon?' said Wolf's suspect as he opened his carriage door.

'It was you who did it, to protect the status quo of the establishment!'

'What? Who the devil are you?'

'Don't play games with me, Barnard!' So saying, Wolf pulled down the muffler covering the man's face to reveal features which were quite definitely not those of Barnard. 'Ha!' exclaimed Wolf after a moment's shock. 'They have sent another emissary to do the deed!'

'Professor...' murmured Sir Arthur.

'Yes?'

'Where is the blood?'

'What?'

'The blood. The murderer will have blood over him. This man hasn't. How can this be?'

Wolf stared at his suspect, who was indeed utterly devoid of any signs of tell-tale gore. He lifted the man's cape in case any body parts were secreted there, but found nothing more than a grubby lining. 'But, but, but,' stammered Wolf, thinking fast. 'We saw him come out of the Masonic meeting!'

'What is all this?' demanded the man in alarm, believing Wolf to be a dangerous haberdashery fetishist.

'Did you just leave a Masonic meeting?' asked Sir Arthur, handing over his calling card to show his social credentials.

'Well, we're not supposed to reveal anything,' mumbled the man. 'Secret society and all that.'

'We're very discreet,' replied Sir Arthur.

'And this is a murder investigation,' added Abler, striding over while his men spread out behind him to search the area and question any witnesses.

The man hesitated but gave in. 'Yes, I was there tonight, but nothing was happening, so I left to check on my businesses. I like to make sure the landlords are doing their jobs properly.'

'You own that pub?' asked Abler, nodding at the building behind the man.

'Yes, and several more. I often pay them a surprise visit; keep 'em on their toes.'

'Nothing happening?' squeaked Wolf, desperately scrabbling to keep hold of his theories. 'You were talking about murder!'

'Murder?' cried the man in shock.

'Yes, the "Time has Come," and "Sacred Traditions" and all the rest!'

'Oh that,' said the man dismissively. 'Just a lot of rot when we allow someone new to join. They have to go through the initiation and the rituals. Always found it a bit embarrassing myself, but the contacts are good – social and business.' The man glanced appreciatively at the calling card in his hand. 'I'm surprised you're not a member, Sir Arthur.'

"Not really my thing," said Sir Arthur pleasantly.

'But the threat to the throne, and Barnard,' said Wolf.

'Eh?' said the Mason, utterly flummoxed.

'I think we've heard enough,' said Abler. 'Come along, Professor, let's go.'

75

Still protesting, Wolf was taken away.

**

'It's a conspiracy,' insisted Wolf a few moments later.

'It's a cock up,' replied the Inspector.

'The Royals,' protested Wolf.

'You decided on that theory with no proof at all,' snapped Abler.

'Besides, the Prince can't take any wife without his mother's consent,' pointed out Sir Arthur.

'Er, er; they could have been married in secret!' blurted out Wolf.

'Then the match would be illegal,' replied Sir Arthur. 'Her Majesty's offspring need her permission to wed, and they can hardly obtain official blessings if they plan to marry someone without a title in the family, wealth in the family, or an inbred imbecile in the family.'

'But the scandal...' mumbled Wolf.

'Would hardly cause the Royals to fall,' countered Sir Arthur. 'An illicit marriage would certainly cause indignation, but the English are, at heart, deferential and traditional. It's been many a year since this country saw any hint of a genuine revolution. Nowadays, people prefer performative outrage.'

'See how a veil has been drawn to deceive us,' responded Wolf, feebly. Further debate was curtailed as a young constable came running up.

'Sir, sir, there's been another one, sir!' he gasped.

'Where?' demanded Abler. This time a clue might be found... *And Wolf's ridiculous theories be damned,* he thought.

'Down there, sir,' said the constable. 'In Mitre Square.' The four men hurried toward Mitre Square, where they found another constable standing guard with a rather unsettled expression on his face. 'Why, it's Constable Nolan again,' said Wolf as they drew nearer.

'Hello sir,' gulped the constable, saluting with one hand while clutching his stomach with the other. 'Mind yourself, Inspector,' he said to Abler, his voice cracking with the strain. 'This one is the worst yet.'

Abler and Wolf passed the constable to examine the body, while Sir Arthur offered the young man a nip of brandy from his flask before joining his two comrades. 'Do you know her?' he asked as he drew near.

'Yes, it's Catherine Eddowes, sometimes known as Mary Kelly,' said the professor, holding a handkerchief to his mouth as he stared at the mutilated corpse. 'The ferocity of this attack is appalling. Could that man have moved quickly and committed both crimes? Or was it another Mason? Or, no, wait; just a moment, perhaps...Oh, what have you got there, Nolan?'

'Where, sir?' asked the constable.

'That newspaper.'

'I haven't got a newspaper, sir.'

'Yes, you have; it's sticking out of the bottom of your tunic. Let's see it, please.' Under the glower of his inspector, Nolan pulled out the penny paper.

'It's only the early edition; the one with the Ripper letter in,' he mumbled.

'The what?' asked Sir Arthur.

'The Ripper letter. You know, Jack the Ripper?' Nolan's eyes shone as he said the name, rolling it around his tongue. 'The name the murderer's been given?' he added under the glare from Inspector Abler.

Abler held out his hand until Nolan shamefully passed the newspaper over, after which the inspector smoothed the large sheet out so the three men could see the relevant article.

'Hello, it seems the supposed killer has sent a letter to the papers,' observed Wolf. '"Jack the Ripper Speaks! Chilling letter dripping in blood sent to press offices!' Oh really, whatever will they make up next? 'Breaking news…Sensational crimes…Vicious murders…' Ah, here we are, the letter.

"Dear Boss, I keep on hearing the police have caught me but they wont fix me just yet. I am down on whores and I shant quit ripping them till I do get buckled. Grand work the last job was. I love my work and want to start again. I saved some of the proper red stuff in a ginger beer bottle to write with but it went thick like glue and I can't use it. Red ink is fit enough I hope ha ha. Keep this letter back till I do a bit more work, then give it out straight. My knife's so nice and sharp I want to get to work right away if I get a chance. Yours truly, Jack the Ripper."'

'What do you make of that?' demanded the professor.

'It will cause every idiotic wretch in the country to send in a similar letter," groaned Abler. 'And now they've named him, too. It's turning into a damn *game* for them.'

'They?' asked Wolf.

78

'The press. You don't think this is genuine, do you?'

'Well, it could be, and allied with the Masonic plot...'

'Give it up, Professor!' snapped Abler. 'Your theory is a washout, and we're no closer to finding who the murderer really is, so stop going on about Royals and mad doctors and Masonic conspiracies because I don't want to hear anymore. Understand? Just keep out of it, and let me try and catch the real murderer. Before he kills again.'

Chapter Four

Despite the sensation caused by the double murder, interest in the crimes declined over the following four weeks. With no new leads – and more importantly, with no new atrocities – it seemed Jack the Ripper's time was over, and life was returning to normal.

This was certainly the case for Professor Wolf, who found his diary was getting progressively emptier as after-dinner speeches, public addresses, and requests for articles on the Ripper began to lessen, and he was left facing a return to his old work: teaching the idiot offspring of the parsimonious wealthy the rudiments of passing exams so they could attend the University once inhabited by their fathers, and their fathers before them.

Sir Arthur also believed the affair to be over, and he began to settle back into his normal routine of pushing back the boundaries of known wisdom, exploring the truth behind the paranormal, and trying to devise ever more desperate ways of avoiding having weekly tea with his ghastly aunt.

Then the telegram from Inspector Abler arrived.

**

Sir Arthur and Abler stood in the tiny, squalid room at Miller's Court, one of the many tenement blocks of the Whitechapel slums, staring in horror at the scene around them; the walls were splattered with blood, while the remains on the bed were only just recognisable as having once been human.

The police surgeon had queasily reported that several organs were missing from the victim. As Sir Arthur watched, a twitching Constable Nolan was helping a photographer point his bulky camera at the face of the dead woman in the belief that the last thing she saw would be recorded in her eyes. Outside, the sound of several police constables being sick could be heard.

'Who was she, Inspector?' asked Sir Arthur, quietly.

'Her name was Mary Kelly.' (Sir Arthur felt something flicker in his memory, but couldn't quite place it). 'She was twenty-four, originally from Ireland, and it seems she worked as a prostitute.' The Inspector glanced up and saw Wolf looking in through the door, sketching the layout of the room in his diary. 'What are you doing here?' he demanded.

'I had a tip off,' replied Wolf, smugly. 'The Ripper really got to work on this occasion,' he continued gleefully as he looked at the corpse. 'Have you any leads yet?'

'That is official police business,' snapped Abler.

'Yes, I suppose you're right,' said Wolf absently. 'Who's he?' he asked, pointing to a pale-faced man standing in the courtyard.

'Friend of the dead woman. Joseph Barnett,' replied Abler through gritted teeth, answering more for Sir Arthur than for Wolf.

'Do you know what he does, and what he's doing here?' demanded Wolf, excitedly.

'I think he may have been Kelly's live-in-lover at one stage. He used to work on the fish market as a porter.'

'Ah, did he?' muttered Wolf. 'As a fish porter, he would have had some considerable experience with a knife.'

'Yes, the thought had occurred to me,' snapped Abler, striding out of the squalid room and into the tiny courtyard outside.

'Are you ready to talk, Mr Barnett?' asked Abler. The man nodded, looking in fear at the policeman. 'Tell us about your relationship with Mary.'

'She was on the game when I first met her,' said Barnett, his voice trembling, 'but she was still a corker. We got chatting and one thing led to another, and eventually we moved in together.

'For a while, things went well, but then I lost my job, and we couldn't afford the rent on the room, and Mary said she'd go back onto the street to earn money.

'I didn't want that, not my Mary living like a common tart, but what could I do? She was determined.'

'Wasn't she apprehensive about Jack the Ripper?' asked Wolf.

'Yes, she was. We read in the paper about the death of Martha Tabram; her who was killed by forty-nine stab and slash wounds,' replied Barnett with a certain relish.

'You obviously know the case?' observed Abler.

'I used to read the reports out loud to Mary, tell her everything that was in the papers, like. Well, she knew Martha, though not well, and it shook her, hearing of her murder, but we had no money coming in, so she did it — she went back on the streets.'

'Some believe Martha Tabram was the first victim of the Ripper,' explained Wolf to Sir Arthur, who had joined the three men. 'She was killed by an unknown hand during a frenzied knife attack. That murder was different, though. The killer of Tabram slashed haphazardly. The Ripper always stabs and cuts.'

'You said Mary went back to the streets?' said Abler, firmly heading off any new Ripper debate by Wolf.

'I tried to stop her,' said Barnett, 'but she was wilful. Then Mary Ann Nichols was killed and I read it out to my Mary, but it didn't do no good. Then it was a near neighbour of ours, Annie Chapman, who got ripped. The press reported it, I read it out, and Mary was frightened into staying at home, where I could keep an eye on her. Keep her safe, like.

'But it didn't last. We desperately needed money and Mary went back onto the street. We had rows all the time. That's how the window got broken by the door. Then the Ripper letter got printed, we had the double murder, and I thought she'd be terrified, but she still went out. I couldn't stop her.' By now, large tears were rolling down Barnett's face, and his body shook uncontrollably. 'I had to leave; I couldn't bear it no more.'

'The police had to knock the door down to get in, didn't they?' interrupted Wolf, gesturing at the broken door hanging off its hinges. 'What happened to the key?'

'Perhaps it was lost,' snapped Abler as Barnett shrugged, tired of Wolf and his constant theorising.

'The only other way to secure the door is by the bolt, which can be moved by reaching through the broken pane of glass next to the door,' said Wolf, pointing to the frame. 'How could the killer know how to get in and out? Only if he had been here before! I think the killer got in the way he always did, by using the key. The killer took the key so he could return at any time, as he did last night, to do his grisly work. Isn't that right, Mr Barnett? That's how you killed her!'

'Yes, yes, it's true!' shrieked Barnett, who had been trembling violently throughout Wolf's thunderous deductions. 'I had to do it, she was everything to me, and she degraded herself with other men! I tried to scare her by killing them whores and then reading the stories from the paper, but it didn't work. What else could I do? I'm the Ripper! I'm the Ripper! I did all the crimes! I killed all of them to save my Mary!' He broke down completely and fell sobbing to the floor.

**

Abler and Sir Arthur exchanged puzzled glances. For Barnett to admit to being the Ripper was one thing; for Wolf to have been proved right in one of his suppositions was even more astounding. What happened next dumbfounded them.

'He's not the Ripper!' snarled Constable Nolan, his voice high with delusional paranoia. 'How do you think the Ripper has evaded capture for so long? Who can be the first on the scene of every killing, and be covered in blood, without being conspicuous or even suspected? Who? Every time, the answer is a policeman! A policeman! A policeman! Yes, I am Jack the Ripper! Catch me if you can!'

Nolan laughed hysterically, his eyes darting around the area.

'No, I'm the Ripper!' cried another man who was busily manoeuvring a pony and trap into the area.

'No, it's me!' cried a stranger who was scaling the wall of the courtyard on a rickety ladder made from wooden offcuts and string.

'It's not true,' thundered a voice from the other side of the small enclosure. Everyone swung round to see a man striding into the yard with his arms raised in declamatory style – a style somewhat hampered by the ever-increasing crowd of people jostling each other within the confined area.

'Who the devil are you?' demanded Abler, trying to get hold of one definite fact.

'My name is William Harrison, and I alone know the truth of the matter.'

'Pay no attention to him,' snarled Wolf. 'The man is a fool! A disgrace to all other Ripperologists.'

'Ha!' countered Harrison, with force if not lucidity. 'Gentlemen, prepare to be amazed...by the truth!'

**

'So, let me see if I've got this right,' said Abler twenty minutes later. 'You're saying Walter Sickert, far from being a simple artist, is actually the murderer?'

'Correct! And the proof is in the picture,' replied Harrison, twitching slightly.

'What picture?' asked Sir Arthur, rubbing his eyes.

'Sickert's picture of the unknown room with a woman in it. It's obvious if you look at it! The woman is a prostitute, and we are seeing both her and the room through the killer's eyes, *Sickert's eyes...* Sickert is the killer, and he painted the last moments of his victim's life in order to gloat over his crime!'

'Perhaps you can explain how you know the woman is a prostitute in this painting?' asked Abler.

'Why else would she let a man into her room?'

'A husband, a lover, a family member, a landlord?'

'Ridiculous! Clearly, she is a prostitute, and it therefore follows that the artist, Sickert, is Jack the Ripper!'

'And your "proof" is the assertion that Sickert knows the Whitechapel area, and Catherine Eddowes was murdered by mistake because she sometimes went by the name of Mary Kelly?' continued Abler in a dull voice.

'Indeed!'

'Despite the fact – according to you – he supposedly knew all these women intimately? He still somehow killed the wrong one because she occasionally used another name? Is that a fair summation?'

'Yes!' replied Harrison, his resolve as rigid as his declamatory stance.

'And how do you explain Sickert being out of the country during two of the crimes, on holiday in Dieppe?' asked Sir Arthur, who had many links in the artistic world.

'He could have slipped over by steamer, killed the woman, and got back to Paris before breakfast.'

'Inside eight hours? On our rail network?'

'He was fortunate.'

'And you don't see any inconsistencies or flaws in your theory?'

'It all dovetails beautifully.'

'Ha!" said another voice. 'The man is a fool. Only I, who have pieced together the whole crime from press reports, can tell you the amazing truth!'

'Oh, do tell,' muttered Sir Arthur. Wolf turned to a fresh page in his diary.

'What I am about to tell you is irrefutable!' declaimed the newcomer, waving a bulging folder of press cuttings as he stepped forward to claim centre stage.

'And you are?" asked Abler, who felt he was edging ever closer to becoming a mass-murderer himself. Albeit under provocation from unhinged Ripper theorists.

'I am the foremost Ripperologist of the day,' replied the man, to the scorn of Harrison and a dark look from Wolf. 'My name is Anthony Warren, and what I am going to tell will amaze and terrify you. For Jack the Ripper is attempting a cabbalistic rite to bring about the end of the world! Map out the murder sites, gentlemen, and they reveal the points of a cabbalistic cone, while the longitude of the site divided by the latitude gives us a degree angle of 51683465.7937, which is 666, the number of the beast, which ties in with the rite!'

'That's nowhere bloody near 666,' observed Abler.

'The significance of this year, 1888, a tri-digit number of occult importance, is related to the year 222 A.D., in which the prophet of the Sun Cult, Helioglabis, was ritualistically murdered,' continued Warren, ignoring the inspector. 'Helioglabis was killed at the remains of Pompeii, the map reference of which from the equator is 36 by 41, which in ancient geography has a tolerance of 48 North, and thus Pompeii lies 333 along the old line.

'Add onto this the fact that in 1872 it was calculated a sunspot's average life is 15.8 days, almost exactly half the number of 33.3, and 15.8 lies beneath the 333, thus gives us the mean of 222.'

'Lies beneath?' interrupted Abler, bewildered by the gibberish. 'What the hell are you talking about, lies beneath?'

'From this,' bellowed Warren, again ignoring the Interruption, 'we know Helioglabis's death in 222 was carefully calculated and done in strict accord with the ancient sun gods, and the ritualistic murder was an attempt to bring sunspots down from the sky and to destroy the planet — and that is what the Ripper is trying to do with this cabbalistic ritual! The end of the world is nigh! The Ripper brings down death on us all, just as he brought down death on these women! The symbolism is unmistakable. We're doomed! Doomed!'

'No, I did it because I discovered I was illegitimate,' shouted an apprentice furniture maker, shouldering his way through the vast crowd. 'It was my grandmother's fault...'

'No, I'm the Ripper! I killed because God told me to do it,' shouted a clerk from a tea-shipping firm.

'All right,' snapped Abler. 'If everyone present wants to either make a confession or an accusation, we'll

88

do it properly. I'm arresting the whole lot of you, and you can all accompany me to the station.'

**

Twelve hours later, Abler, Wolf and Sir Arthur were still at the police station. So too were a multitude of Ripperologists, Wolf among them, all demanding to put forward their ideas on the killings. Several new people were also frantically insisting they were Jack the Ripper, while Harrison and Warren had been sent to separate cells after coming to blows over the pregnancy (or not) of Mary Kelly.

'I discovered the final link in the chain,' a theorist was shouting across the crowd in Abler's tiny office, 'when I discovered the Irish connection within the killings — Mary Kelly! All the pieces were there; it just took my intellect to sift them and see the whole picture. To find the truth, we must look back in time...

'Six years ago, just before the election that saw the Liberal Government voted out of office, a murder was committed in Dublin; the political assassination of Lord Cavendish by a group of political idealists.

'What weapons did they use? Medical knives, purchased in British Guinea by a "Doctor Williams," and smuggled across the sea by a female courier. There were twelve knives purchased — only four were recovered from a nearby lake at the scene of the murder. Where was the rest of this medical set? That was unknown until today, for here is one of those very knives!' So saying, the man threw down a knife onto Abler's desk, badly scratching the surface.

'We know one of the knives was discovered at the murder site of Eddowes,' continued the man, ignoring the protests from the entire room that no such thing was known. 'The distinctive design, while meaning nothing to the average policeman, would be instantly recognisable to Special Branch Officers.

'You see the connection? Irish political agitators, discovered to be linked to the Whitechapel crimes, would cause the entire Liberal Opposition Party, as well as the entire Irish Nationalist cause, to collapse, and so the Government has no doubt already offered a deal to hush up the whole affair — in return for a cessation of assassination attempts on the Monarch!'

'Balderdash!' said one of the Ripperologists, contemptuously. 'How do you jump from an Irish agitator killing Cavendish to Irish agitators killing prostitutes? What's the supposed connection between Kelly and the killers? And how do you make a connection between that knife and those used in the murder of Lord Cavendish?'

'And why would the opposition collapse?' scoffed another. 'Why would the Government care if it did? The holes in your theory are big enough to drive an omnibus through!'

'And where did your knife come from?' demanded another, pointing at Abler's desk.

'It was being used as a hedge trimmer by the curator of the Black Museum,' replied the Irish Nationalist theorist, answering the easiest question and ignoring the others. 'He was unaware of its significance until my research found it out.'

'Wrong, wrong, and wrong again,' interjected James Sideways, a hack writer for a penny paper. 'It's quite obvious to anyone who's studied the case that the reason the police can't find the Ripper is because he doesn't exist – and he never did exist!'

'Oh, you think a supernatural explanation is the answer?' sniggered a small Ripperologist with bad dandruff.

'Or perhaps it was just a case of several unfortunate accidents, with mass hysteria doing the rest?' jeered another.

'Half right,' snapped Sideways. 'In fact, the murders were committed by different men. What we have here is a spate of copycat crimes, explaining why the police never found the sole man responsible because they should have been looking for the different *men* responsible. And public hysteria created the myth of the Ripper.'

'Hey!' squeaked another Ripperologist. 'That's my theory! You've taken my theory! He's taken my theory, everyone...'

'Oh, public hysteria created the myth?' snapped a thin man with a bulging Adam's apple. 'Your paper printing and reprinting the lurid accounts every day, and putting up huge billboards showing half-naked women being stalked by a madman with a knife, had no part to play in creating this climate of "public hysteria"?'

'We cannot be held responsible for the credulous nature of the public,' replied Sideways, disdainfully.

'Absolute rubbish,' said another. 'The killer was quite clearly a Liverpool cotton merchant —'

'No, he was a Polish Jew —'

'A Russian Jew —'

'He was a children's author —'

'A Barrister —'

'An aristocrat —'

'A medical student —'

'It was a giant eagle —'

'Hey, my neighbour's a titled foreign medical student who writes children's fiction. And he's retraining as a lawyer. And he's got a canary! I never did trust him, he's shifty looking...'

Inspector Abler groaned, and reached for a fresh writing pad.

Chapter Five

For three months, the denizens of London had been held in thrall by a faceless killer operating within one of the most densely populated areas of the city. The public quivered in fear at the unknown slayer, felt indignation at the lack of progress made by the authorities, and waited eagerly for the next death, secretly hoping it would be gorier, bloodier, more horrific than the last.

Not many considered the women who had been killed, but many speculated wildly and gleefully at the identity of the killer: his face, his character, his social standing. Who was this man who could take life without being seen or caught? Everyone had a theory, and everyone knew what sort of person it had to be — someone different, someone abnormal, someone other. Not one of *us*, but one of *them*.

One man, however, did think of the murdered women — and of the developing myth that was more melodrama than reality. Looking back over the three months, he and one other had seen the creation of Jack the Ripper, for they had both been there from the beginning.

And now both men were here, at the end.

**

'Professor Wolf, sir,' said Harker the butler, introducing the visitor.

'Come in, Professor, and thanks for accepting my invitation at such short notice,' said Sir Arthur, his tone rather more formal than usual.

Wolf settled himself on a large leather chair in the corner of the room, where he wiggled happily. 'Ah, you missed a fine evening, Arthur,' he said. 'The theories I've heard at the latest Ripperologist meeting. Absolutely incredible!'

Wolf pulled out his bulging notebook, into which several separate pieces of paper had been inserted detailing the latest newspaper reports, maps of the area, drawings of the crime scenes, and notes on why all the other Ripperologists' theories were wrong, about which he spoke at great length and with slanderous vigour until he finally realised his host had barely said a word. 'Is anything wrong, Arthur?'

'I, too, have a theory,' replied Sir Arthur, gravelly. 'It is not as complex as some, but it's one I need to share with you.'

'I never took you for a theorist,' said Wolf, perplexed at the tone of his friend, 'but fire away.'

'Like some, I see Mary Kelly, the final victim, as being the key to this crime, because of who she was and who she knew.'

'Ah, you believe the killer chose her because she was available that night for paid sex, and he took his chance?'

'No, this crime is more specific.'

'Then you believe the theory that it was another prostitute sharing Kelly's room who was killed by mistake, and Kelly herself is in fact still alive somewhere?'

'I have no idea, though I doubt it.'

'Ah, you think Joseph Barnett is the killer?' asked Wolf. 'Speaking of which, you know the heart was missing from Kelly's body? Some believe this was a symbolic act, as Barnett took with him the one object he couldn't get Mary to give him voluntarily.'

'You misunderstand. When I said Mary Kelly is the key to this crime, I was referring only to her death, not to the Ripper killings in general. I have no idea who committed those murders. I only know of what came afterwards.'

'Ah, then you must be hinting at the idea that, um...no, er, wait, er...No, I don't know. You do suspect someone specific, though?'

'Yes.'

'Who?'

'You, Professor Wolf.'

**

'Me?' gasped Wolf in fearful surprise. 'You think I had something to do with the crime? What possible proof can you have?'

'There was no one thing that made me think of you,' replied Sir Arthur. 'Rather, it was a combination of small observations and minor considerations which all pointed the same way.'

'Such as?' demanded the professor, his voice finally returning to normal, though his colour was undecided between the flush of indignation and the pallor of fear.

'It really started with the last victim. I'd heard the name Mary Kelly before in connection with the case, though I couldn't quite place where or when – until I remembered you'd told us Catherine Eddowes sometimes went by the name Mary Kelly. Not that I thought much of it.

'I also reflected how you're well known in Whitechapel from your talks to the various guilds and clubs, and so you know the area well. But then, so do many others.'

'I'm glad you can admit that,' interjected Wolf, shifting uncomfortably in his seat. He had intended to rise but there was something strangely compelling in Sir Arthur's voice, far different to his usual genial tone.

'Then I considered the letter sent to the press,' continued Sir Arthur. 'The one signed "Jack the Ripper". A letter which stirred up fresh interest in the killer and started the process of turning the murderer into a myth – a ghoul who cannot be caught, categorised, or even described.

'You were very keen to get Nolan's newspaper from him and to read us the supposed Ripper letter. But oddly, you were taken aback only by the artistic license of the editor in claiming the letter was dripping in blood. But why should that have surprised you, rather than the content of the letter? The only answer is you knew of the letter beforehand. But how could that be? You wrote it yourself.'

'But, but I didn't,' stuttered Wolf. 'I was merely reacting to the ridiculous melodramatic tone of the newspaper report...'

'I then asked myself, myself how you could have known of Mary Kelly's murder.'

'I told you at the time! I had a tip off from one of the officers.'

'Inspector Abler hasn't been able to find the culprit.'

'They'd hardly admit it, would they?'

'Would you care to reveal your source?'

'No, I would not,' said Wolf with a spark of defiance. 'All sources must be protected. If Abler finds out who it is, my contact could be drummed out of the force.'

'Abler has guaranteed no action will be taken as long the guilty man steps forward, and yet no one has owned up,' observed Sir Arthur. 'So maybe no one did tip you off. You arrived there because you already knew what had happened, and you needed to see how the police were progressing in their investigation.

'But more than that,' continued Sir Arthur, his voice rising along with his disgust; 'you wanted to force your competitors, the other Ripperologists, to reveal their theories, and so you told them by anonymous messages to get to Miller's Court immediately, where they would see the awful crime scene and be compelled into speech. And, as it turned out, mass hysteria.'

'I did that, did I?' whispered Wolf, his eyes never leaving Sir Arthur's face.

'We have checked; all the Ripperologists received the same unsigned message. And all were written on your brand of note paper.'

'I did that just to hear their theories?' asked Wolf, faintly, as though talking about some other person.

'Ripperology has become a game. And a merchandising opportunity. New theories, the more outlandish the better, sell very well with both the popular press and the public. Hence you needed to know what your rivals believed, so you could come up with a fresh theory, previously unheard. It didn't have to be true; just outrageous and superficially plausible.'

'I did all that for a theory?' asked Wolf, a small smile playing round his mouth.

'No. You also wanted to check on the investigation, and make sure your role in Mary's death remained unknown.'

'A suspect?' spluttered Wolf. 'You can't possibly think I killed her? Or anyone!'

'No; you did not kill her, Professor Wolf,' said Sir Arthur, his voice rising again in anger. 'But you did mutilate her body. You desecrated the dead for your own venal motives.'

**

'Why would I?' squealed the professor. 'Not that I did,' he added hurriedly, aware his words could be construed as an admission.

'You've done very well out of this affair, Wolf. You've never been so busy, giving lectures, writing essays, and planning books about the Ripper, all of which is bringing in an income you've never known before. Your usual lectures on "Pottery; a Fresh Perspective," is hardly in the same league as a notorious murderer. What are you charging for the Ripper talks? Talks which fill the halls with avid listeners?'

'Yes, I've done well out of it; what of it?'

'You saw this new income dwindling away, especially when the press seemed to be tiring of the Whitechapel killer. And then what happens? A letter is sent, a double murder plays into your hands, Jack the Ripper is born, and interest in the case goes to an all-time high. But only for a while, for once again, with no new crimes, the press and the public began to forget. What was left for you? A return to your cramming lessons? A return to the pottery lectures?

'And then, just as it seemed all was over, you visited Mary Kelly, as you had done on numerous occasions, and you found her dead. I'd like to think you were at least briefly appalled at the discovery, but then you thought: What good is a simple body? Where was the horror? The violence? The gore? And so you hurried back to your lodging house, got what was needed, and returned to set the scene.'

'Rubbish!" hissed Wolf. 'I barely knew her!'

'You know many in Whitechapel by name or face; you said as much yourself on the night of the first killing. And Kelly, like all the other poor wretches in the area, believed in the very real danger of the Ripper. Therefore she would have been unlikely to let anyone she didn't know into her room. Indeed, I would suspect she would have only opened her door to a well-known acquaintance. Or a friend. Or a client.

'Absolute rubbish,' sneered Wolf. 'It's a ridiculous idea, strung together by coincidence and conjecture. It doesn't stand up to rational scrutiny for a second. The idea I would do such a thing just to keep the interest going, and make money, is sickening.'

'Yes, isn't it?' replied Sir Arthur. 'And yet, isn't that what you've been doing from the beginning? Butchering these women over and over again, making up new theories to fit the facts, or making new facts fit the theories? You merely went one step further and made the figurative mutilation a real mutilation.'

'You don't have a shred of evidence for this, do you?' demanded Wolf, a faint trace of hope in his voice.

'No; you burnt it on the fire. The clothes you worked in, and the bag you carried your spare suit in so you could change afterwards. Yes, your housekeeper noticed you coming back early that evening, and she also saw you leave a few minutes later carrying a large Gladstone bag.'

'Why, Arthur,' snarled Wolf, fighting to control himself. 'You might have been there yourself.'

'I merely asked your landlady. You must have taken a change of clothes; how else could you walk away from the crime without being noticed or detained? And you burnt Kelly's flesh partly because the fat would cause a raging fire which would consume the clothing, but also because burning parts of the body will provide a rich source of contention and debate in any future arguments on the case.

'What could be better? Another victim, younger and more attractive than the others. A woman who even shared a name with a previous victim. Was it knowing that Eddowes sometimes used the name Mary Kelly that gave you the idea? After all, it will drive the conspiracy theories for years, and theories will feed off theories, multiplying forever more. And with it, you will maintain your new, luxuriant lifestyle. All at the expense of the slaughtered victims.'

'Innocent?' hissed Wolf, staring malignantly at Sir Arthur. 'Can you comprehend what it's like being surrounded by the dregs of humanity? The whores who sold themselves on the streets, just as I had to prostitute my work to the ignorant masses in order to buy food for the day? After my first career was destroyed by a meaningless dalliance with some common *female*? After my second career was derailed by the jealousy of second-rate minds who took *my* ideas and *my* research and made fortunes out of them? People with as much talent in their entire bodies as I have in my fingertip?

'Why should I care about the death of any common prick tease?' raged the professor. 'Or the sanctity of their remains? They didn't care for their bodies in life, so what difference did it make in death? Who else cared about them? They were below me in every sense, the whole stinking lot of them, and yet I was reduced to their level, day after day, until, until...'

'Until it all came out,' finished Sir Arthur quietly. 'And Mary Kelly's dead body became the victim of your rage.'

Wolf shuddered, his face buried in his hands. He remained motionless for several minutes before finally looking up and seeing the third person in the room. 'Abler!'

'Wolf,' replied the detective.

'You were here, all the time?'

'Yes; behind the ornamental screen.'

Wolf shuddered again before a smile spread over his face. 'I don't know what you think you heard, but it was merely my own...speculation, prompted by Sir Arthur's badgering, that you were listening to. Nothing more.'

'Nevertheless, you will have to come with me to the station, for further questioning.'

'Of course, I wish to help in any way I can, though I think I'll ask for my solicitor to be present. Perhaps you'd be good enough to call on Mr Porkings, of Porkings, Porkings, Shaft and Porkings? I'm sure they'll confirm that anything said in this room is inadmissible.

'Well, goodbye, Sir Arthur. I'm sure I'll see you at the next college dinner, or maybe even before, if you'd care to attend any of my lectures on the identity of Jack the Ripper. I'm fully booked up you know, at least into the middle of next year, and that doesn't include the two new book deals, or the serialisation in the magazines.

'You'll not shake my hand? Well, never mind. Lead on, Inspector; never let it be said that I delayed the due process of the law.'

Still smiling, Wolf left the room.

**

A month later, Sir Arthur approached the final grave. He had attended, in the order they were murdered, the final resting places of the Ripper's victims. The debate concerning Jack the Ripper's identity still generated a great deal of speculation in the book and periodical markets, and Wolf, released because of a lack of evidence to attest his crime, was continuing his lucrative career in Ripperology. There were even rumours he was planning a trip to America, in pursuit of a whole new audience.

And within the debates and the books and the articles on who the Ripper was, or had been, the victims themselves were forgotten — if they had ever been known. It was, of course, too late to do anything for the murdered women, so Sir Arthur had decided to make a pilgrimage to their graves in a small act of commemoration.

Stooping down, he placed a lily on the grave of Mary Kelly, the flower out of place on the small, pathetic hump of dirt and yellowing grass. He then stood with his head bowed, remembering just briefly the forgotten women who were now nothing more than walk-on parts in the drama that was Jack the Ripper.

The Heart's Malevolence

by

Steven G. Davis

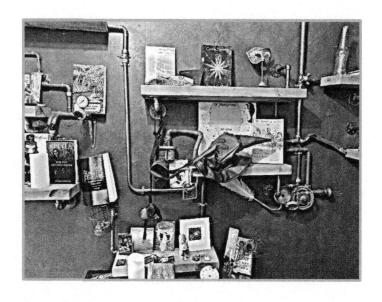

The aether lightbulb swung wearily. Water oozed down the walls. Somewhere, in one of the far corners of what Artemis euphemistically dubbed the 'truth chamber', water dripped.

The floor was slick with mould. In the deepest, dankest recesses, small mushrooms flourished. Rats skittered outside the chamber but inside, no rat ventured.

No scent, nor fire nor fresh air and a brewing storm, could clear the stink from the chamber. Caged humans. Despairing humans. Hopeless humans. It wasn't just the stink of piss and shit, the left-over smell of aether they'd brought with them or the smell of cordite that lingered around a couple of them.

It was the smell of failure. Of blood loss. Of impending death.

Thomas ripped his handkerchief into pieces and stuffed it into his nostrils. It would delay the stench a while; nothing could keep it away forever, no matter how many times he bathed.

He lifted the lantern he'd brought with him, raising the wick and drawing one of the sides back. Flame licked at the aether-soaked wick and bright light spilled across the septic stone floor, the murky puddles and the ripe air.

'Stinks like a dead panda in here!' snarled Artemis, pushing past him.

Thomas shifted the lantern to light his master's steps.

'I don't want to see the sodding floor!' Artemis raged. 'Show me the dumb fucks who crash landed on my island!'

Thomas lifted the lantern obediently.

'Egads, she's ugly.'

The light revealed a tall woman, strung up by her wrists. Her clothing was in tatters; scars and old wounds, old burns, covered her body.

'So this is the mighty "Thistle Wales".' Artemis ripped his rapier from its scabbard. 'What are the Empire asking for her capture?'

'Five thousand gold coins. Dead or alive. If dead, only her head is required.'

His master made a disgusted sound in the back of his throat. Pushed the point of his blade into her breastbone.

Thomas watched the blood swell up around; begin trickling down her ribs. She stared, in loathing, at Artemis C-Clementine.

'A spirited filly,' he snorted. 'Not broken at all.' He chuckled. 'Horses, Thomas. Make a note. Four horses. We'll take her to the beach, tomorrow perhaps. Tie her to their tails, set their tails on fire,' he grinned. 'It's been a while since I've watched anyone be pulled apart. It is always a good judge of which is the strongest horse.'

Thomas scratched a note one handed, balancing the lantern in the other.

'Show me the fat one!'

He tucked the notebook away, turning until he found the engineer. The vaulted chamber held far more archways than were needed; each archway was flanked by two of Clementine's prisoners.

The revealed prisoner was a blonde-haired woman with a streak of lilac hair. Unlike Thistle, who was thin and gaunt, the engineer was chubby in almost every way imaginable: her left leg hung wasted, thin in comparison to her right.

'Now that's,' Artemis chuckled. 'If it wasn't so fat it'd be beautiful.' He ran his hand across her belly. 'Does it squeal like a pig in heat, I wonder?'

'Hey, boy,' snarled Thistle, shifting in her chains, somehow managing to lean away from the wall. 'Come here and say that, dickless. Fuschine's more of a man than you'll ever be.'

Thomas gasped silently.

Clementine wheeled around to look at Thistle. Stared at her coldly.

This is not going to go well –

He turned and punched Fuschine in the face. Punched her again. And again.

'Not her!' Thistle screamed. 'Me, you bastard! Hit me! Don't hit her, you coward!'

Breathing heavily, Clementine stepped back.

Blood was running down Fuschine's chin. Her eyes looked blackened; bruises were forming on her cheeks and her head had fallen forwards.

'Oh, the tribade speaks,' Artemis chuckled. 'How perfectly vulgar. The tall one and the fat one.' He shook his head, looking at Hatcher. 'Are you sure these are the notorious thieves, rebels and murderers of Jasper Woods' company?'

Thomas nodded. 'They are, my lord. The Herbert George is the vessel that was stolen from the Empire by them. There is a reward for its return as well as a bounty on all of their heads.'

'And how many have we captured?'

'Seventeen, my lord. From the reports, it is the whole gang.'

Clementine chuckled. 'You know my predilections. Show me another one. Show me a young one.'

**

Fuschine sobbed softly.

'Eleonoré,' Rain whispered, 'they took Eleonoré.'

'We'll – get her back,' Jasper wheezed.

Rain grimaced. She'd seen what they'd done to Jasper. Had heard the crack of his ribs.

'Don't – don't speak,' said Thistle softly. 'Fuschine? Love? We're all here together. We'll get out of this.'

Leo grumbled something in German. Rain ignored him.

'Garcon? Ryurik? Adhiratha? Deserea? Are you okay?'

There were muted responses.

'I've heard of this – C-Clementine,' said Aakanksha. 'He's richer than the Empire; rumour is he props the Empire up.'

110

'And has his own army,' added Garima. 'My people avoid his island. Common practice was, he caught anyone, there was no rescue, no blackmail. Anyone caught was dead. He's a sadist.'

Rain looked at Thistle.

The woman stared back at her coldly. 'If he hurts Fuschine; if he hurts Eleonoré –'

'Bloody whore,' her uncle muttered.

Thistle stared at Leo, her eyes glittering.

She knows German, Rain thought. Oh, shit.

**

The door crashed open. The maître d' – or whoever the fuck he was – came in first. A man out of his depth, a pathetic worm, trying to crawl up his master's arse. An old etonian, no doubt, though obviously with some lived experience.

The cock of his master – Daxa grimaced. The great and amoral Artemis C-Clementine – rumour said the first C stood for cock or cunt – a millionaire before he was even born. No social graces but a corrupt cesspool of humanity who deserved everything they could do to him – if they could escape.

'Where's Eleonoré?' Rain demanded furiously. 'What have you done with her?'

'Bastard,' spat Fuschine thickly, her eyes blackened, her lips and cheeks visibly swollen and blacked.

'Ah, the boiler snipes.' Clementine sniggered. 'But who was it who spoke first, Thomas?'

'Rain, my lord. Rain Silvermore. Inventor. And German.'

111

Daxa watched as the millionaire approached Rain. The young – person – hung, like all of them, from their wrists. Their blouse was half pulled open, enough to reveal a binder.

'Ergh,' he scowled. 'Girl anachronism. Trying to be what she wasn't born to be.'

He moved closer to Rain. Daxa pulled at her chains, but they were buried deep in the wall. Her wrists were bruising, moving towards raw, and painful already.

Clementine cut the binder off Rain; ripped her undergarments away. 'Tits.' He worked at her belt.

'Leave Rain alone,' Thistle yelled.

'Leave her,' roared Pallograph.

C-Clementine turned to look at the gunner: tore Rain's trousers, then knickers down.

'Cunt. Definitely a cunt,' he walked away from her. 'Is every one of you some perverted degeneration? Sapphics, fatties, ugly, cross-dressers.'

'At least none of these people are little mummy's boys.'

Daxa stared, turning to look at Deserea. The young Afric orphan stared at Clementine coldly, dispassionately.

Daxa didn't know how old Deserea was, but she had the body of an older, curvy woman. They'd rescued her from the Afric; she'd hated the idea of simply being put into another orphanage.

Clementine smiled. Drew his rapier and cut open her blouse. 'Now that,' he grinned at his aide, 'if it wasn't black, they would be gorgeous and good for a ride.'

Deserea spat in his face.

Daxa felt her heart lurch. Deserea hadn't settled in well, but what she'd just done – she noticed the aide hide his smile at Deserea's actions.

'Thomas,' he commanded imperiously, 'I think have her legs broken. She's going to spend the rest of her short life on her belly: she has no need for legs.'

'When, my lord?'

He scowled at his aide. 'Well, not now!' he roared, 'You know I do so enjoy prisoners, and this is such a smorgasbord of delights.' He grinned. 'When I grow tired of fucking the little rat –'

Daxa felt her heart lurch again. Not Eleonoré.

'Then break her legs and tie her onto my bed. Gag her as well.' He shook his head. 'What other delights has their misfortune brought me?'

'There is this one, my lord,' the obsequious toad said, 'not human.'

'Not human? Egad, how thrilling.'

'A clockwork automata, stolen, obviously.'

'Liberated,' spat Rain. 'Liberated, you bastards.'

'What wit! And to think it won a prize from the Empire.' He shook his head. 'How far they must have slipped, to award a prize to something like that!'

'Where is Eleonoré?' asked Jasper softly.

Daxa looked at Jasper. He'd gone down fighting; after the rest of them had been captured, C-Clementine had made a point of having Jasper pummelled and smacked around just for fun. She'd heard at least one of his ribs break, and she could hear the breathiness in his voice.

He was also naked. She tried not to lick her lips. One day, Captain, she thought, I will have you.

'Ah, the great and mighty Jasper Woods!' Clementine curled his lip. 'A shopkeeper. How pedestrian. If the Empire cannot keep someone like you in check.' He shook his head. 'Have the automation taken away; send it to my laboratory. I'll have fun taking it apart later.'

'No,' Rain cried again.

The aide signalled; two of Clementine's personal security entered the chamber. Both were tall; white; carried aether pistols and rifles of an advanced type.

'Take the –' he grinned. 'No.' He dismissed the guards. 'When I take it apart, abomination,' he smiled sweetly at Rain, 'I'll do it in front of you. I want you to see your – liberated toy – deconstructed. Taken apart. Destroyed.'

Rain stared in impotent fury.

'Now then,' he grinned at his aide. 'Next?'

**

'Daxa. She is – technically – someone's property. A Captain in the Empire.'

The thug sniggered. He wasn't that broad shouldered. Had an air of someone asking to be taught a lesson.

Pallo smiled. He'd tested the chains during the night. There wasn't much give in them, they were likely buried too deep, too securely, but that wouldn't stop him trying again and again to break free.

114

C-Clementine approached Daxa. The woman almost lounged in her chains, completely at ease in her partial nudity. The thug had obvious predilections towards women in distress, and the younger the better.

'I like her skin,' he almost crooned. 'I don't care if she's someone else's property. She'll make a good prostitute. I could imagine Indian men – particularly the dross that the East India Company employ – might pay good coin to have their way with her, particularly given she is one of the notorious Jasper Woods' own people.'

He chuckled. 'You shot down their craft, Jasper. Took pot shots at one of their leaders. If I wasn't independently wealthy already, I could get very rich on the rewards for all of you and returning the Empire's craft.' He sniffed. 'But they lost it. And I am wealthy. And I do so enjoy causing pain. All of you,' he raised his voice. 'You should all be very proud. I think I am going to reach a new height with what I do with all of you.'

The spoilt thug turned to look at him. 'And who is that? He looks –' he shook his head. 'Disappointingly unbroken.'

'That is Pallograph Smith, my lord. Tis said he's the muscle. A former soldier of the Empire; now a gunrunner.'

The cheap thug in a posh suit looked up at him.

'He doesn't think much of me! Imagine that.' He looked at the aide. 'Did they have anything with them of value, beyond their miserable carcasses?'

The man nodded at him. 'There was a hand of glory in his room, but that was it. Weapons, clothes, no money or gems that could be found.'

'It seems, to cover my costs, I must sell a few of them.' He turned back to look at Fuschine.

Pallo silently swore vengeance. Fuschine hung heavy in her chains, stripped for the man's amusement.

'That one, I think.' He chuckled. 'If it likes women, I will sell her to men. Let them plough her every which way,' and he strode towards her.

'Bastard –' Pallo roared.

He grabbed Fuschine and squeezed. 'Look at the size of it! How big a cock can she take? Spoiled, wasted, by being an inveterate sapphist.'

Fuschine was sobbing silently.

'Leave her be!' Thistle roared.

'Ah,' the thug grinned, 'the boiler heart speaks. How many men have taken you, hmm, Thistle my dear? How many men's desires have you swallowed? You might be ugly and scarred, but I wager a fair few have spread your legs and fucked that wounded hole of yours.'

Thistle stared defiantly at him.

The thug looked between Thistle and Fuschine, absently wiping his hand on his subordinate's jacket. 'Is she your first, I wonder? Did she seduce you or did you fuck the innocence out of her?' He turned back, gazing up at Fuschine. 'I would fix the girl, if I could. Her leg. She is attractive. Could no doubt take a whole arm inside her.'

'There are many more, my lord.'

**

'These are the sisters.' C-Clementine smiled like a snake. 'Such lovely skin. But their eyes,' he shook his head. 'I

116

don't like their eyes. I may take them as trophies. Blind sister-sibling lovers.'

'I'll do anything,' one of them hissed, 'but I won't fuck that,' she snarled at her sister.

Clementine was right. They were both lovely looking – if you were that way inclined – and both had a certain unpleasantness about them. Both had been stripped entirely naked and hung, unashamedly – Hadron looked away.

'Fuck my sister,' the second said, 'you're even more depraved than they said.'

Hadron stared out across the grim chamber at where Fuschine hung. She hung, magnificent and ripe and juicy. C-Clementine had not yet –

The thought of him raping Fuschine – such a sweet, innocent, beautiful girl. It was a shame she'd fallen heavily for Thistle. Thistle was a psychopath. Ugly physically, ugly emotionally. He knew Thistle had struck Fuschine on a number of occasions; suspected she raped the younger woman regularly, not that Fuschine would hear or say a word against her.

'We would never fuck, but I would look after you, Fuschine,' he whispered to himself.

'They do not seem interested, Thomas, can you believe that?' C-Clementine chuckled. 'The two most beautiful women among Jasper's crew, and they are not prepared to fuck each other, not even for my own amusement.'

If he'd been interested in women, he might well have been interested in Garima and Aakanksha. Soft brown skin, dark hair and eyes, muscled and shapely but not overly so. The thought of them together, wrapped around each other –

Hadron grimaced at the thought. 'I want my innocence back.'

'Someone. Is. Speaking!' C-Clementine roared, turning round, casting his gaze over him and several others. 'Thomas? Who spoke?'

'I think it was the medic, my lord.'

C-Clementine looked at him, his lip curling. 'Medic? Catamite. Fucker of boys' arseholes.' He shook his head. 'A more degenerate collection could not be thought up. I should simply take heads and send their bodies to the Empire.'

He smiled sweetly. 'None of the doctor's wife for you. No house. No prestige. Drummed out of the cadaverists for being a seeker of your own kind.' He grimaced. 'Such a perverted crew you lead, Jasper.' He clapped his hands. 'Thomas! These two lovely ladies will entertain us tomorrow evening with each other, or I am minded to have their heads taken as a warning.' He shook his head. 'Such prettiness, and so alike. If they will not fuck each other I will kill them tomorrow night.'

**

Ryurik stared, and tried not to be caught staring, at Thistle. Shoulder length dark hair; dark eyes. A lean, no nonsense face; sharp cheekbones. Heavy breasts – not as large as Miss Fuschine's – and scarred heavily, below the nipples, from being whipped whilst Empire soldiers –

118

He loved her. He had touched her, once, years ago. Had slipped his hand into the cooling water where she lay, unconscious, her blood freely staining the bathwater. Had touched her and she had moaned softly.

She loved Miss Nagle; everyone knew that. He had heard the two women often enough to recognise their individual cries of pleasure. All the rats had heard and knew what the two women got up to, but Fuschine cared for them and Miss Wales fought for them.

Thistle.

Aakanksha.

He looked at the Indian woman. He had done more than see her naked before. She might be older, but then so was Thistle. And Thistle was unobtainable. Whereas Aakanksha –

**

'The watchmaker's apprentice. The would-be terrorist. The clockwork bombmaker.'

'I am no such thing!' Prometheus protested.

Adhiratha smiled. Prometheus was a good kind man; could not be a bombmaker. Could not be a terrorist. He spent a lot of time in the engine room, both him and Miss Nagle.

'And now an airship pirate as well. All of you,' the white man raised his voice. 'A dozen incidents, all around the globe. Slaughtering troops in France. Run ins with Empire and East India airships. Shooting up a Russian train, oh yes, I have heard all about you.'

If they got down, Adhiratha thought, not so much Prometheus, but definitely Mr Smith. Miss Wales as well.

If Pallograph and Thistle escaped the chains, then the nasty white man would be for it.

He sighed, and tried to do it quietly. Where was Eleonoré?

'If I were impartial –'

The white man moved around the chamber, looking up at them.

Hadron seemed to be okay; winked at him when the man wasn't looking. Hadron was a good artist: no one had ever wanted to paint his picture before. Not as tall or muscled as Pallograph – Mr Smith was almost a giant, and broad shouldered, and very kind, but Adhiratha had seen him, wielding a Norton Oscillator.

It had sounded like thunder. A roaring, chugging, thunder. Thunder that rained shells and splashed death in wide arcs. If they got loose – if Pallograph got his Oscillator – Adhiratha smiled.

The bad white man would get his comeuppance.

**

She hated most of them.

Had hated most of them.

Hadron was vile, disgusting –

Eleonoré –

Deserea clenched her jaw shut, freezing her expression.

Fuschine had saved her.

They had *all* saved her, but it had been a white man's saving – coming in, thinking none of her own people could, doing it to appear magnanimous –

120

Jasper had wanted to dump her into another home not her own and move on. Save the girls, be a hero, move on to the next person needing to be saved. She shook her head.

He hung in his chains, having trouble breathing. His face was battered. The coloniser, the rapist, the man with all the money – he was the truly evil one. He had had his people kick Jasper into unconsciousness; she had heard the crack of at least one rib.

He tried, she admitted to herself. He did rescue us, we couldn't stay on the Herbert George –

I *want* to stay on the Herbert George. But the way she'd been trained, what she'd done to Eleonoré –

And now the very bad man had taken the white girl away somewhere.

Hadron. She grimaced. He is perverted – but she had seen him stand between Adhiratha and the attackers, had fought to get the boy free –

They are not who I thought they were.

They are not heroes.

Tears pricked at her eyes.

They are trying to do the right thing.

They are trying but they failed, they couldn't see, they didn't know –

Deserea gulped, tears sliding down her cheeks.

Miss Wales. The iron rose. So harsh, so strong – so beautiful, the care, the love, she had for Fuschine.

That was wrong as well, but it was love. Love! She raged silently. Why did my parents, my family, not love me, not care for me?

Fuschine said I had to believe in something. I believe in them.

**

'And so I return to the engineer,' C-Clementine grinned, reaching up to squeeze a plump breast, eliciting a whimper from her, and an angry cry from the helpless Thistle – 'should I dress her in just goggles? To have her, working an engine, sweat dripping off her,' he chuckled. 'Sweat dripping into all of her crevices.'

Garima looked away.

'To ensure the compliance of Miss Wales,' he chuckled. 'While I await horses to tear her limb from limb.' He smiled. 'By now, many of you will be quite hungry. Thirsty. Do not worry. Some entertainment, something to amuse me, and I'll give you all a drink.'

He began walking through the arches, looking at Jasper's crew. 'None of you are heroes. Any attempts at stupid things and I may just kill several of you. I'm sure there's more crew than you need.' He grinned at Jasper. 'Not that you'll be flying again, until you're flying at the end of a rope.'

He stopped in front of the clockwork girl.

'You. Rain's pet.'

'Her name is Celestine,' Rain retorted.

C-Clementine raised an eyebrow. 'You are still quite young and untarnished. I think you would be very unwilling.' He grinned. 'Thomas!'

'My lord,' the man hurried over.

An insubstantial white man, a coward, caught in the headlights of a Black and Rust. To hear Jasper talk – to listen to him talk – if things had been different –

'When the young one is finished, before I get to the black girl, the scientist will warm my bed.'

Rain, as well as several others, screamed and shouted in protest.

'I am sure her quim has never known a proper man. And then her arse as well. Her mouth –' he chuckled, snapping his fingers.

Two of his guards came into the room, looking around cautiously.

'Cut the clockwork girl down. Force her onto her knees.'

Garima stared, horrified and disgusted, as Celestine was pushed to her knees. She was wearing a simple shift: this was ripped away, to reveal an anatomically correct leather-skinned body.

'She will suffice Rain, give the order.'

'Never!'

C-Clementine sighed. Ripped his rapier from his sheath. 'Who will suffer? Not you Rain, oh no. Not the automata.' He grinned. 'Shall I emasculate your captain? A dowdy little librarian. Your man at arms, the gun-running thug? Or the nancy boy, perhaps?'

Rain shook her head, crying silently.

C-Clementine moved between the crew, gazing up at them silently.

After a while there was a flash of silver in the gloom –

Jasper cried out.

'There. Now, Rain, I will hurt a woman next time. Give the order. Order the one with the bionic heart to kneel. She will suffice, for the moment.' He grinned. 'But don't think of ordering her to do anything.' He clicked his fingers.

One of his soldiers stood in front of her, the barrel of his aether pistol pressed between her thighs.

Garima froze.

**

Jasper was bleeding – their captor had lanced him in the thigh with his blade. Aakanksha looked at him and managed to smile.

One of the guards was standing, his pistol rammed between Garima's thighs.

The other was standing in front of Daxa. Daxa was straining, totally unconcerned about being naked, trying to push herself against the weapon.

'You know you want to take me with it,' she whispered. 'Just a little bit closer,' she smiled at the guard. 'You'd like to see the barrel going into me, wouldn't you?'

Prometheus looked beyond her.

Their captor was standing in front of Celestine, his trousers around his ankles, forcing himself into the girl's mouth.

'You're not an invincible girl,' he cursed, 'Rain, bitch! If I don't enjoy this, Fuschine will be kneeling before me next and you know I've got ingenious forms of torture to try on all your friends. The things I will do to Jasper and Thistle –'

Rain said something; Prometheus couldn't hear what she said, but Celestine obviously did.

'Oh,' crooned their captor deliriously.

I hope that doesn't jam up her cogs and gears or make them sticky, thought Prometheus.

**

The hours crawled by. After interfering with the clockwork genius the stupid idiot had wandered off, shutting the chamber door behind him.

He could barely look at his niece. That she should have been wearing a – it was abhorrent. Why did she want to not be herself? Why did she want to be a boy? Why was she not happy –

Leo ground his teeth together, looking away.

He had contracted to work for the Empire. The pay had been good – very good. And then he had found out what they had been using his creations for.

Those were the finest things I ever made. A twin pair of dragon's heads, meant for the arms of a chair or the like. Oh, they ended up on a chair.

Tears pricked his eyes. He'd thought about creating a tea pot involving the dragon's head; had worked them as prototypes, with the potential for tea to pour out of their mouths.

And instead.

He grimaced.

Instead.

No wonder she was a stone cold bitch.

No wonder she hated him.

He sighed.

But then she hated the medic as well, the one who liked drawing pictures of the rats with no clothing on.

I am too old for this sort of thing. I should never have signed up – we should have stayed in the Afric. At least it would have been warm.

**

Thomas Hatcher leant against the door. His duties done for the evening he had returned to the 'truth chamber'. None of the prisoners knew about the second door, further back, out of sight of where they hung, roughly facing the main door.

If I could get away from here. I dare not show any sympathy. They were my best hope. They could raid Clementine's vaults and build a fleet of airships from the money he had. But if Clementine catches me, if he suspects I am not totally his –

Fuschine and Thistle, he thought, lovers. Clementine goes to that meeting tomorrow afternoon on the mainland, far side of Kozhikode: it will likely last all night. They have a day and a night, perhaps. Although he does like to gloat.

He sighed silently.

Before long he will start hurting them seriously. Other than that poor girl.

He frowned.

Rain controls the automata. The old man, her uncle, I believe. He doesn't like most of them. Thistle can't stand the gay one, the cadaverist. He has rarely left any prisoners this long before he begins gouging or cutting.

126

Thistle and Fuschine. Two hearts as one. He will start with them; their pain, their death, he will use to break the rest of them.

The sisters. One of the rats has a thing with one, the other the clockwork engineer. They are too alike, they look the same.

He scowled.

The Afric girl. A boy from France. One from India. Who knows where Daxa is from, India, perhaps, but older, a rarity, a rat who survived childhood. A rat owned by an Empire officer.

He smiled at the thought of the Empire ever trying to seek redress from Artemis C-Clementine. He had a private army. A heavily secured fortress. His own island. Several airships of different types, so he could not be recognised in the air.

He bankrolls them and they send him toys to play with. These were not sent, they crashed, but even so – he smiled to himself.

They are my best chance to get out of here. But Clementine needs to be dead before anything can happen. Him dead, his army destroyed or disbanded, his vault raided and the treasure taken.

Then – and only then – can I move to assist them.

**

She knelt where she had been left.

She had mixed oil to the sperm in her throat and had flushed it from her system.

Had heard the second target enter the chamber in the night, through an unknown door. He was an

127

irrelevancy. Target number one was the prime. Without being able to take out target number one, ending target number two was a wasted trick.

Removing target number one's member with her teeth was an option, but that might not render him incapacitated quickly enough. There was still target number two and any of target number one's guards.

She had to wait for her mistress, her owner, Rain Silvermore.

And so she remained, who had been created as model four point two, but had been renamed Celestine by her owner.

She would protect Rain but Rain hung naked and shivering, tears all but frozen on her cheeks.

Miss Nagle was no better, her eyes and mouth still blackened, her body bearing bruises from target number one.

Miss Wales turned her head. Target number one had not done anything to her yet.

She heard the footsteps before the rest. Carefully lowered her head as if her clockworks had seized up overnight.

The door crashed open.

Target number one entered, sword in hand, target number two behind him and half a dozen guards.

He walked straight to her owner. Punched her hard –

Rain screamed in pain.

'Lower her chains,' he rasped.

She was lowered: brought within reach. Target number one moved back and three guards moved in.

'Neck to knees. Work her over. I want her heavily bruised and battered. She's too,' he shuddered. 'Pristine.'

Her owner screamed and sobbed. Fists began striking a rhythm on her body. Her comrades screamed and cursed and wept.

Target number one smiled. 'If it is a girl, let it fight like a girl.'

'What of the mechanical girl, my lord,' target number two asked.

Target number one waved a dismissive hand. 'She's seized up.' He grinned. 'I was too much for her cogs and gears.'

Target number one headed to Miss Wales.

'I have a meeting to go to, I will be most of the day.' He looked up at her. 'I was wrong to call you ugly yesterday.' He ran his hand over her muscled thigh. 'It will be a pity to have you torn apart, but I think that is for the best. You are the one most likely to rally resistance.'

He grinned, stepping back, raising his sword. 'Oh, I am not going to hurt you too much. You are no lady in waiting but a filthy sapphic. How sensitive are you?' He pressed the point of his blade against the top of her sex.

Miss Wales bit back a cry.

'Just a little bloodletting.'

He drew the blade down one side and up the other. Blood flowed.

He slashed her innermost thighs.

She was gasping for breath.

He cut her again, deeper.

Blood gushed.

'That is the last thing you will have inside you. Farewell, Miss Wales. You die tonight.'

**

Eleonoré could barely move. Her arms and legs were stretched wide, cuffed. The cuffs were chained to the corners of the bed. There was a further cuff around her neck, holding her down, so she couldn't lift her head. She was gagged and blindfolded and everywhere hurt.

Jasper was such a nice man. She just wanted to curl up in his lap again, wrapped in his jacket. He would keep her safe. He would never let anything happen to her.

Cramp spiked in her right thigh and she shuddered.

Don't think about –

Miss Wales – Thistle – and Miss Nagle – Fuschine. She would give anything to be curled up between them. To be pillowed between soft breasts and warm hearts. They would protect her. They would never let anything happen to her.

Don't think about –

Miss – Thistle. The woman was so powerful, so strong, so beautiful. She had seen her scars; wanted nothing so much as to be in the woman's embrace. The woman was old enough to be her mother. Had no eyes for anyone but Miss Nagle – mostly.

It would never happen, but she wanted to kiss those scarred breasts. To kiss each of the bullet wounds in her back, her buttocks, her thighs. How she had been shot

130

so many times and survived she didn't know. To kiss her –
elsewhere –

Don't think about – he had forced himself on her,
kissed her unwelcomely. Had gagged her when he didn't
like her attempts to bite his tongue, then proceeded to
kiss and lick her face.

Rain. She almost sobbed. To be wrapped in Rain's
embrace, the older girl's breasts flattening her own as
they'd kissed, as they touched, as they'd explored. The
feel of Rain's tongue between her legs –

Don't think about –

She shuddered, tears pricking her eyes.

'Do not cry, child.'

Eleonoré screamed.

Fingers stroked her cheek. She could feel stale
breath but not the unpleasant ripeness of the billionaire.

'I'm not going to hurt you.' A voice that almost
giggled. 'I'm sorry he's doing this to you. I can't rescue you,
I'm not strong enough.'

Fingers stroked her neck. Her shoulder.

Eleonoré shuddered. She was naked: helpless. His
fingers, her tongue, his cock, could go anywhere –

'I can make you forget it for a while. Give you a
few hours of peace.'

His hands were at her mouth: he was drawing the
ball gag up.

'He likes them young. Whatever he has already
done, it will get worse.'

Something splashed into her mouth and she
gasped, spluttering. The liquid burned. Her throat was

raw, dry, and she swallowed awkwardly, desperately, and the liquid scalded, burned her.

'One thousand percent overproof rum. You won't feel anything soon. You'll piss it out in a few hours; be unconscious for a day or more.'

She struggled, trying to turn her face away, trying to pull at the bonds.

His hand slammed onto her chest, pressing her down onto the bed.

'You're not going to remember anything.'

The bed creaked as he climbed onto it.

**

This is my metropolis, thought Aakanksha, I should be able to figure a way out. She tugged at the chains, again, futilely, but they didn't even budge.

Prometheus hung in his chains. He had taken such careful handling but was careless with his secrets. The problem was the secrets were mostly boring or not secret.

Ryurik was no better, but at least he had information about Thistle. That could be useful.

Jasper – she frowned. The psychotic Thistle Wales had a thing for him, and the over-burdened Fuschine. Really, the best thing to do with her was amputate her leg and be done with it. She would just delay, hinder them –

But Jasper.

Her sister had designs upon Jasper.

The thought of – she grimaced.

Gunter's crew, even the Underground Railway, knew all about Artemis C-Clementine. That the Herbert George should have crashed so close to Kozhikode –

132

Not that she owed Gunter anything. He had given her up. He no longer trusted her; would kill her on sight.

She tried not to snort. He wouldn't see her, because she would kill him the moment she saw him. She had found her betraying sister, and in return, he had cast her out.

The Underground Railway would hear he was no longer to be trusted.

Perhaps, even, that he was in the pay of the East India Company.

That. She grinned. That would be an appropriate end for Gunter. The Underground Railway were very good at excising anything that might give them away. Gunter had abandoned her: she would cast him to the Underground Railway and let them end him.

Aakanksha grinned.

'Prometheus,' she called out softly. 'Tell me of the bank robbery again. Distract me.'

**

'This isn't the fucking confessions of Jack Bonnie and Sally Clyde,' Thistle snarled.

Garcon looked at Miss Wales. In the pale light he could see the dried blood on her thighs and elsewhere. The sound of her screams when that English bastard had cut her –

But she sounded – recovered. Angry, anyway.

Jasper hung loosely, badly bruised. Fuschine hung, half-snoring and dribbling. Her face was still swollen and bruised. Garima and Aakanksha –

He looked away.

Rain hung lower than the rest, her body heavily bruised. From her knees to her neck, her skin was mottled green, black, yellow and purple. The three guards had been quite thorough in their creation of bruises.

Garcon clamped his jaw tight. Rain was beautiful. The things he had seen Rain and Eleonoré –

Tears stung his eyes.

Eleonoré was at the mercy of the English bastard. That – he seethed, twisting his wrists desperately and grunting in pain. The chains had no give in them, he was nowhere near strong enough to pull them from the wall – if Pallo couldn't, he certainly couldn't.

But maybe he could get his hands out of them.

He rotated his right wrist slowly. There was enough room in the metal cuff to move, to twist – he grimaced, biting his lip as raw skin rubbed. Extended his fingers, tucking his thumb and little finger in.

Pulled.

Managed to clamp his mouth in time to stop the scream as pain exploded from his wrist outwards. He swung from one hand, fighting the tears in his eyes.

'Garcon,' said Pallo softly, 'can you free the other wrist?'

'Yes,' he nodded, almost sobbing. The cuff felt tighter than the other, and his free arm was radiating pain.

Celestine rose smoothly to her feet.

Garcon stared. I'd presumed she'd – seized up.

She approached, studying him with unblinking eyes.

Grabbed his waist and lifted him.

134

The pain in his chained wrist eased. He managed to lift his other arm, twisting and tugging at his wrist, teeth tightly clamped together, until he managed to slip the cuff.

She lowered him back down and he massaged his wrists, grimacing at the pain.

Celestine moved to Rain. She hung lower than the others, barely conscious. Celestine wrapped an arm around her waist and lifted her: seized the chain in her free hand.

'You won't pull it free, Celestine,' said Prometheus.

Garcon watched as Celestine gradually exerted pressure on the chain. The wall remained firm; the chain between her hand and Rain's wrist loose.

Something cracked hollowly.

'Check the door, Garcon,' said Miss Wales. 'Shout if anyone approaches.'

Garcon hurried to obey.

There was a crack: the chain had snapped and Celestine was grasping the other chain.

The corridor outside was empty and dark. The air was rank, but there was the faintest of breezes. Eleonoré is out there somewhere. And that billionaire bastard. He gritted his teeth. If he's hurt Eleonoré —

There was another, louder, crack.

Celestine was gently lowering Rain to the ground.

Garcon ran, falling to his knees and sliding as Celestine deposited the woman on the ground.

Rain collapsed; he caught her, drawing her into his arms and holding her.

'Pallo next,' hissed Thistle.

'Miss Silvermore?' Garcon asked softly. 'Rain?'

She whimpered in his arms.

'You're free, Rain. Celestine is freeing the rest of us.'

She managed to raise her head, her eyes bleary and unfocused.

'Garcon?' She raised a hand and touched his cheek. 'I'm dreaming. I'll wake up,' she giggled. 'I'll wake up and Eleonoré will be in my bed.'

'This is real, Rain,' he said softly, stroking her back. 'We crashed on an island not far off the coast of Kozhikode. Some bastard English millionaire owns it. Has a large security force. We're all here.'

'Eleonoré?' Rain murmured.

'Eleonoré's not here at the moment. She's safe,' he lied.

Rain rested her head against his shoulder. Garcon felt – a hundred miles tall and humble at the same time. That Rain should curl up against him. That Rain should – but this wasn't the time or place for that.

There was a crack behind him, the sound of a swinging chain.

He held Rain tight: she clung to him, pressed against him. He blushed, realising he was naked and interested and she was naked and in his lap.

She turned her head. If anything, she tightened her grip.

'Tell me Eleonoré's okay.'

He held her tighter. 'Eleonoré's okay. She's okay.' He shifted one arm to around her shoulders. 'I'm sorry – he – humiliated you.'

She kissed his throat and nuzzled in to him. 'You're safe, Garcon. You're Eleonoré's brother. You'll look after her.'

Garcon grimaced. He did feel protective towards Eleonoré, and now her girlfriend sat in his lap, her clothing in tatters, her body savagely bruised, her lithe body pressed against him for protection and warmth, not for – anything else.

Then again – Eleonoré had been the one who'd made him a man. Who'd taught him how to please a woman. He looked up from Rain.

Pallo was rubbing his wrists, free of the chains. Celestine was moving to break the next one of the crew down.

**

The pain in her wrists was indescribable. Her cheeks were bruised, her mouth still swollen, her vision still slightly blurry from being punched in the face several times.

Her left leg, in comparison, was pain-free. Free of feeling as well. If Celestine freed her, the left leg would simply crumple beneath her.

She looked up at Thistle. Thistle had a beautiful body; a body she wanted to spend the rest of her life adoring and exploring. An angular face; sharp cheekbones and a thin mouth. Some might call her face plain, but her eyes glittered with life, with hate, with rage, with fury, with lust, even, though she tried to hide it, with love.

137

She had spent so many nights kissing Thistle's breasts but wanted nothing so much as to be doing that now. Kissing that soft, warm, skin, her tight, responsive nipples, the undersides of her breasts that carried the scars and wheals from an undisclosed past.

She tried not to cry. Thistle wouldn't speak of it, but she knew her lover had been tortured and abused several times. How she had survived being shot – Thistle was covered in round bullet scars. How she'd survived all that – and why they'd not shot her upper back –

But lying there, in her memory, her face pressed against Thistle's breast, her tongue teasing –

There was a wrenching sound, and another chain went flying.

**

Eleonoré got up stiffly.

He had unchained her after the first time, lying her face down so he could have his way with her. He'd thought her drunk; insensible.

He slumbered now, spent himself and a little drunk.

Eleonoré slid out of bed. His clothes were abandoned on the floor. The key was in the door. She rifled his clothing quickly, finding a small knife and grinning.

Clambered back onto the bed, smiling malevolently.

**

'Jasper,' Thistle said softly.

He raised his head. 'I am sorry –'

She crossed to him and it didn't matter. She wrapped her arms around him, holding him tight, crushing him to her chest, her cheek to his.

'Oh, Jasper,' she said softly. 'If anything had happened to you –'

He put an arm around her waist, another her shoulders. 'We survived,' he said softly.

He felt her tilt her shoulders: felt her press her breasts against his chest. 'Jasper,' she said softly, 'hold me as tight as you can.'

He tightened his grip, trying not to wince at the ache in his chest. He could feel her, the warmth in her body, pressed so close and tight, so intimately, against him.

'Oh,' she said, drawing back, 'your ribs.'

'They are not as badly hurt as I made out. I can,' he paused, 'stand being hugged some more.'

Thistle smiled, pushing herself against him, putting her hands on his shoulders and pulling him in close again.

'I was worried – he had hurt you badly. I will kill him, but if he had done that –'

He held her close, eyes shut. They had come so close – the scent of her filled his mind. The warmth, the strength, in her body.

He nodded, letting her warmth and nearness fill him. She was – he wanted to spend the rest of his life with her. I will continue to do whatever I can for her. Support her in what she does. Help her find and take down those who abused her, those who hurt her.

We will bring the Empire down in flames. He sighed, softly.

'Too fierce?' she asked, her voice a breath on his skin.

Jasper shook his head. 'Never.' He tightened his grip around her back and waist. She clung to him. He clung to her. Wherever this takes us. He smiled. I never thought I would see the Afric! And Russia, France, India and Madagascar.

'We are making a difference, aren't we?' he asked softly.

'To the Empire? Yes.'

He felt her smile.

'I mean to you. We're hurting the Empire where we can, we're looking for those,' he trailed off.

She was silent for a while.

'I could never tell you. Could never show you. Just how much,' she lapsed into silence.

Turned her head and kissed his cheek.

'We have a bastard to catch. An army to destroy. A citadel to blow up.'

She nodded, her cheek next to his.

He nodded, stroking her back. 'Celestine is freeing the others. We have a few moments before we need to stand.'

Thistle clung to him. 'I'm scared, Jasper,' she said softly.

'Scared?' he raised an eyebrow. 'You?'

'I'm bloodied and broken. What man, what woman, would want to take me on?'

'Fuschine loves you.'

'And I've caused her left leg to be shattered. I like hurting her. I like taking myself out on her more than she would want if she wasn't so in love with me.'

'You can change.'

She shook her head. 'I like hurting her too much. I hate myself for doing it, but I love the sounds she makes when she's in distress.'

'You should talk to her.'

She snorted softly.

'She's so in love with me, she'll let me do anything. I like – hurting her. I like – hearing her.'

'How – if you want to tell me – how far do you go?'

'I would never use a blade against her.' Thistle drew back: looked pale. She smiled faintly, drawing close again. 'But she likes discipline. She encourages me, when it's bad,' she shuddered. 'She is my punch bag and I hate myself for using her, but I cannot –' she shook her head. 'I am trying to stay off drinking, off drugs. She is supporting me. But,' she sighed again.

Jasper held her tightly.

'Celestine is freeing her now. You should go to her. Support her when she is released from the chains.'

Thistle nodded, stroking his arms. 'I know.' She clutched him tighter for an instant. 'Now then,' she said, her eyes coming alive, 'let's go kill some bastards.'

**

He awoke screaming. Tried to sit up, tried to push against the bedsheets, and collapsed instead, half falling out of the bed.

'Now then,' the French girl waved his knife in front of his face.

He made a grab for it: she stepped back.

He tried to slide out of the bed and stand up, but ended up in a heap on the floor, his legs screaming.

'What have you done to me?' he sobbed, staring at his legs.

There was blood on them. No feeling beyond pain. No musculature, nothing worked, they were completely – lifeless.

The girl smiled callously. 'I've hamstrung you. They used to do it to troublesome rats. They couldn't run, couldn't escape. Your legs are now useless.' She grinned.

'Stupid child,' he grabbed at the knife again, but she was still too far away. He slumped forwards, over-extended, pain throbbing and spiking.

She moved closer. 'How do I get back to the cells? I need to rescue my friends.'

He gave a snort of laughter. 'C-Clementine,' he shook his head, trying to grin but feeling sick. 'He'll tear you apart. He'll be back in the evening with horses to tear that bitch apart. Then your friend Rain,' he leered, 'then the coloured girl. You'll all know his – attentions.'

She smiled again, seemingly unaware of how much pain was going to be visited upon her.

'I think you could be quite useful to us. Show me how to get to the cells and – nothing more will be done to you.'

He snorted. 'Really? How am I going to walk?' he shuddered. 'The pain is quite –'

She nodded with her head. 'There's whiskey. Have some of that. You can lean on me.'

He shook his head. 'No. I'm not assisting you.'

She shrugged. 'Then you're no use to me. I'll kill you.'

He frowned. Shook his head. 'You're only a child. You should show respect.'

'I'm a rat,' she glowered, 'the Empire taught me their form of respect. If I can't use you for something, I have no need for you. If I have no need for you, I'm not leaving you behind to explain who and what happened.'

She moved closer, the knife glittering in her hand.

He lunged but she caught his hand – suddenly the blade was against his throat.

'Last chance. Help me – or die.'

**

'So how do we get out of here?'

Daxa watched Thistle, ignoring the discussion, more than slightly jealous.

Fuschine had her head on Thistle's shoulder: had her hand between Thistle's legs. Thistle was cupping and massaging Fuschine's breast, supporting her lover with her other arm, nuzzled in close.

She could see Thistle grimacing in pain, jaw clamped shut: Fuschine was clumsy and awkward, her shattered leg in the way, her fingers desperate as she grabbed and thrust into Thistle.

Daxa smiled tightly.

She knew Thistle had been tortured – there. She doubted Thistle cared, but if Fuschine – albeit a Fuschine still battered and bruised and in pain – had no issues making love to – or at least fingering – Thistle in public, then –

One last time. Daxa stared. They were all free – apart from Eleonoré – but they had no weapons. Scarcely any clothing. Thistle, when not distracted, Pallo and Celestine, herself as well, could all acquit themselves well in a brawl, but only luck had, so far, kept the guards out of the prison quarters.

And when they eventually came, they would come with weapons.

**

Eleonoré took a deep breath. Sweat ran down her back. Pooled between her thighs. Made her face shiny. She was dressed in her tormenter's clothing; had put the remnants of her shredded clothing on him and was half carrying, half dragging him.

He was not much taller than her, fortunately; whilst their colouring was different, no one would expect to see a prisoner carrying the bastard millionaire's – whatever he was – across the courtyard.

She hoped.

She dragged him across the courtyard, making it look like he was drunk, unconscious, she didn't know what. Hungover and insensible from being – entertained.

She was sure guards had seen her, but there'd been no shouts, no warning cries, no hurrying feet. The door to the prison cells neared. Further away, there was an opulent residence; the billionaire's house, no doubt. She could just see the doors: four guards stood in front, toting weapons but at ease. Other buildings as well; one of them might be an armoury, which would be useful.

If they had any chance to get out.

All of them caught, the Herbert George crashed on the far side of the small island.

She kicked out at the door to the prison, and it swung open easily.

**

Prometheus felt his heart sink as the door to the chamber crashed in. A single guard entered, a Norton Oscillator in hand. He was even taller than Pallo, Prometheus thought, as the man looked around, finger on the trigger.

The chamber was dark, but even so. He looked around as the guard studied them. All of them were free, most bruised, in a state of disrepair or deshabille – he tried not to notice the way Thistle and Fuschine were almost wrapped around each other, hands busy between each other's thighs. Or the way that, unclothed, there was almost no difference between Aakanksha and Garima.

The way Rain was sat on Garcon's lap, arms wrapped around him, knees to either side of his thighs, lifting herself up. Daxa grinned back at him, hands on hips, completely shameless. Deserea stared at the guard, shoulders pulled back.

The guard grinned. 'So you thought you'd have a little break-out party, eh.' He smirked. 'The master's got his eyes on several of you women, but I guess he wouldn't object –'

He swung, finger tightening on the trigger, until he was facing Prometheus.

'It wasn't me,' he babbled, 'I didn't do anything, I didn't.'

The guard grinned. 'Shot while trying to escape. A warning to the others.'

The door swung open behind the guard. He didn't even turn.

'I'm thinking this one,' he pointed his weapon at Prometheus, 'was shot trying to escape. A warning to the rest. Once that's done, the rest will have to be chained up again. A bit of a kerfuffle.' He grinned. 'All got further injured in the attempt.'

Prometheus stared past them. Fuschine was breathing heavily, her body soaked in sweat, Thistle's fingers busy inside her and her thumb pushing busily.

The guard grimaced, shaking his head. 'Dirty sapphic perverts. Too busy fucking each other to even try and escape.' He reversed his weapon and turned –

The new guard dropped whatever they'd been carrying: it fell with a solid thump.

The guard started turning, but the new one, considerably shorter than them, was closer than expected.

Something glittered in their hand.

The guard – collapsed, screaming, dropping the gun. Celestine moved, coming from the shadows and kicking the guard in the face.

The second guard drew back, bloodied blade in hand –

'Eleonoré!'

She grinned furiously. Spat on the crying guard.

146

Pallo picked up the guard's weapon easily, cradling it in his arms, before kneeling before Eleonoré.

'Are you okay?' He gestured at the guard she'd dragged in, who now lay on the floor, unmoving. 'Did he hurt you?'

She nodded. 'He did. But I'm a rat. I hamstrung him.'

Rain pushed herself away from Garcon. Prometheus winced: from her shoulders to her hips was mottled bruises.

'Eleonoré?' she whispered.

Eleonoré looked at Rain, and burst into tears.

**

Thistle eased Fuschine down to the ground. The woman looked up at her, smiling distantly. Thistle blew her a kiss and stood up, moved to Eleonoré.

'Are you alright?'

The girl nodded, a darker look on her face. 'I am.' She sighed. 'His house is out there, there's buildings, one might be an armoury, but there's several guards. They thought –'

Thistle swept her up into her embrace and hugged her.

'We were so worried.'

She released Eleonoré. 'We will talk later, properly. When we're free. The man you brought with you?'

'I knocked him out. I couldn't risk him crying out as I crossed the courtyard. There were guards,' she shrugged.

'Pallo, watch the door. Daxa, make sure Fuschine's okay.' She grinned at Eleonoré. 'You're absolutely soaked.'

Thistle felt for the man's pulse. 'He'll be asleep for a while.' She grinned at Jasper as he joined them.

'You're shaking, Eleonoré,' Jasper said gently.

She nodded, removing her hand from the jacket. She held a bloody knife in hand. 'I didn't – I couldn't –' she dropped the knife disdainfully.

She sniffed, looking from her to Jasper. 'I know,' she gulped, 'I know I'm a full member of your crew, sir,' she swallowed nervously.

'Even Thistle needs a hug now and then.'

She scowled at him. Eleonoré practically flung herself into his arms.

'It must have been hard,' she said softly, stroking Eleonoré's hair, 'moving a body on a hot day. It was not a piece of cake.'

Eleonoré lifted her head. 'When we get to Kozhikode, I want cake.'

Jasper nodded. 'I hear they have some very sweet delicacies. A guaranteed sugar rush: I will buy you as many as you want.'

Eleonoré looked up at him and nodded enthusiastically. 'Yes please.'

Thistle felt her heart lurch. The sight of Jasper with Eleonoré – is this how he would have been with my daughter? She looked away. I can never be with Jasper. He doesn't see me that way. He keeps me safe but he – but he –

She forced herself not to sob or make any sound.

He cannot love me because I am unlovable.

**

Rain knelt beside Jasper, her hand on Eleonoré's back, stroking her gently.

'It wouldn't have to be cake,' said Ryurik. 'It could be pie.'

'Have a pie,' said Garima, beginning to strip the clothes from the tall guard, who occasionally whimpered. 'Modern Mrs Lovett.'

'Cannibalism?' Daxa grimaced. 'I'm sure the Empire's caused worse things to happen.'

Garcon looked around. They had two weapons now – and one probably dead guard, one badly injured – and the clothes that Eleonoré was in, but it was hardly much of an improvement.

Still. The memory of Misses Wales and Nagle – he blushed. What he'd done with Eleonoré – what he'd seen Eleonoré do with Rain – all paled in comparison.

'Celestine. Pallo. Thistle.' Jasper looked up at the three. 'Go examine what else is down here. Weapons, clothes, whatever.' He grinned.

Garcon shuddered at the look on Jasper's face. Jasper was the captain, an honest man, a kind man, and yet the look on his face was neither kind nor pleasant, nor any kind of grin he wanted to see aimed at him.

Thistle lifted the knife Eleonoré had dropped.

'Garima as well.'

Thistle had the guard's boots; Pallo his trousers; Garima his shirt and Jasper took the jacket, wrapping it around Fuschine.

**

Jasper snuggled Fuschine in close to him. Even with the jacket around her shoulders there was too much of her, too much warm, damp, perspiring flesh.

She clung to him, arm around his waist, breathing heavily, her face still glowing.

She is Thistle's girlfriend. Your friend. You shouldn't –

She pressed her face into the hollow between his neck and shoulder.

'I love her, Jasper,' she whispered.

She kissed his neck, pressed bare breasts against his equally bare chest.

'She scares me but I love her.'

She moved, so that she sat on his leg, rearranging herself, holding him tighter.

Jasper wrapped his arms around her, one hand on her waist, holding her close.

'She loves you, though I doubt she'd ever say it. She thinks she is too much for many people. Too broken. She walks a fine line, Fuschine. You help her.'

She nodded, burying herself into him.

You've known her since she was a teenager. Don't respond to her body. Its just skin, everyone has skin – breasts, hips, she was sprawled on his leg, her warm, damp, furriness pressed against his thigh, as he was pressed against her thigh.

What do you think Thistle will do to you if you – react?

What do you think Thistle will do to Fuschine if you react to her?

That thought left him cold.

Accountancy. A line of neatly ordered books. The polished floor of their bookshop. The grey sky when the clouds opened and it thundered with rain –

**

Ryurik stared.

Miss Nagle was lovely. He rubbed at his wrists. Her left leg was broken, wasted, useless, but the way she lay on top of Captain Jasper –

He looked away, licking his lips, trying not to be caught staring.

Aakanksha was nice, but didn't compare to Miss Nagle. She was clinging to Jasper, a dead guard's jacket around her shoulders, but it didn't cover her long thighs or her lovely, plump, bottom.

He stared. Russian girls were never that lovely, even with her damaged leg.

Not that he'd actually seen any in a similar position to Miss Nagle.

But her thighs and her bottom; the way she lay sprawled against Captain Jasper – he grinned.

One day, he thought, I would like a girl to sprawl on top of me that way.

**

'What did they do to you?' Eleonoré whispered, her fingers light as she touched Rain.

Rain stroked the girl's face. 'Nothing I won't recover from.'

151

'But you're so bruised,' Eleonoré whispered.

The girl was wrapped in close to her, fingers tracing the bruising.

'They didn't like the fact I'd bound my bosom up. They,' she shuddered.

'I'm glad they didn't.' Eleonoré whispered, her fingers brushing, ever so lightly, over Rain's breast.

Rain stroked Eleonoré's inner thigh. 'Nothing that's happened – changes anything.'

Eleonoré bit her lip.

Rain wanted to snuggle the girl to her breast. To keep her safe. To dress her in silks and wash her in perfume and –

She blushed, seeing herself lying on a bed, her head in Eleonoré's lap.

'Will you – I'm scared,' Eleonoré whispered.

Rain took Eleonoré's hand: put it on her breast. Snuggled the girl in tighter, closer, one hand on the girl's rump. She slipped the other between the girl's thighs.

'I'll make all the pain go away, for a while.'

**

Adhiratha looked at the two bad men. One had been a guard, with a weapon that Mr Smith had taken. He smiled. Mr Smith was a very kind man.

But the other man – the one Eleonoré had dragged into the prison. He wasn't a guard. He was the aide of the bad white man. That man would get his comeuppance. Miss Wales, Mr Smith and the others would see to that.

152

The way the man lay. He had fallen from Eleonoré's grip and hit the dirty floor. It was nice that they were free, but the chamber smelled of bad things.

And the man – just lay there. The other one, the one Eleonoré had attacked, the one who'd had the gun – occasionally he whimpered or moved.

But the bad man's aide. He just lay there.

Unmoving.

Dead.

**

Hadron grimaced. The chamber stunk. Piss and shit, rank water and sex. Desperation. Fear.

Whatever does Fuschine see in that bitch? She was all over Jasper. Then left Fuschine to go and have a look without a backward glance. He scowled. Having fingered her in front of everyone first.

He grimaced, glancing at Fuschine where she sprawled across Jasper. Her arse was so inviting. Her tits were nice, but her arse – he sighed. If only she'd a cock. What an arse she has: an arse waiting to be plumbed.

He grinned, slightly jealous of Jasper and the way Fuschine lay, half sprawled, half cuddled atop him.

He'd cuddled her often enough; shared baths with her and given her massages and painted her naked –

Hadron grinned. She might play shy in front of others, but she'd had no problem posing nude in front of him for multiple paintings.

And as for her exhibition with Thistle – fucking and being finger-fucked by the older woman in front of the whole crew.

153

He scowled, pondering the possibility of ever getting to fuck Fuschine's arse.

**

Deserea stared, trying not to cry. Rain had Eleonoré in her arms. There was a most tender expression on the scientist's face. The girl was looking up at her adoringly, tears in her eyes, but smiling.

She knew what Rain was doing.

Scowled.

Tried not to scowl.

Their owners had told them this was wrong.

Deserea scowled. I have no owner. My family sold me, the village disowned me, I am Afric!

She stared at the two women. It was love.

Love! They love each other. How can that be bad?

Because it is natural for a woman to lie with a man

–

The hated lessons, the Empire's attempts to brainwash them, to convert them, to bully them into believing shallow Empire ideology.

There are more of us than them, she almost growled. I am Afric! I am not a product of the Empire. I am not my family who sold me, who gave me away, who –

I don't care! She raged. I am Deserea.

I am Afric. I am proud. I am part of the Herbert George's crew.

She smiled, catching the eye of the German inventrix for an instant: he looked away, scowling.

Deserea smiled.

**

Leo scowled, looking away from the stupid orphan girl. She'd had the chance to escape, to get off the ship, and she'd stowed aboard. They might be safe from the Empire – supposedly; for the moment, anyway. But that hadn't left them safe from Artemis C-Clementine.

One gun, one knife, amongst the four of them.

He shook his head in disappointment, looking at his niece.

Even getting worked over by the sadist's guards wouldn't persuade her she was actually a girl. Why does she hate herself? He sighed. What she was doing with the dirty rat –

He looked away. The whole crew was degenerate. Disgusting.

**

Pallo led the way, carrying the Norton Oscillator loosely. Pale light splashed across the tunnel-like corridor here and there from lanterns. It wasn't quite as foul as the chamber they'd been locked into, but it wasn't much better.

Hopefully there'll be a weapons cache down here. Or a guard chamber. The cheap thug must so trust he's got us caged. And, he grinned. Eleonoré brought down and in his aide. We just need to have weapons before he returns.

The corridor turned left ahead. Thistle was on his right; Celestine on his left, Garima behind him.

He motioned for them to stop. Moved lightly ahead, glancing around the corner before ducking back.

'One,' he barely whispered, holding up his little finger.

He pointed at Garima.

Garima smiled. Blew him a kiss and walked around the corner.

**

The guard reacted surprisingly quickly, turning to stare and raising his weapon. A Moorcock rifle, unfortunately, rather than anything more interesting, but it said something about C-Clementine.

She slowed, sashaying, making sure, without looking, that the shirt didn't cover everything.

The Moorcock used a heavy bullet; not an aether weapon. A standard army issue weapon, but old-fashioned by the level of the Empire. Still used by the East India Company, but they were always slower than the Empire to develop.

'Wha – who are you? Stop.'

Garima drew the shirt together. 'I am a test. And a prize.'

'A – prize?'

She drew nearer. 'Do you think I would be here if Mr C-Clementine had not sent me to you.'

He shook his head. A young, inexperienced, one. Slats in the door behind, a faint glow spilling out, unable to see if it was a garrison room or armoury.

'A prize. A test. You know you cannot leave your post. But I can make time pass – a little more enjoyably.'

He hadn't quite lowered his rifle.

She drew the shirt open. 'I am not hiding anything from you.'

He stared at her chest. Her crotch.

'Would you like me to kneel before you, as a woman should?'

He stared. 'No woman ever has.'

'Would you like me to?' she repeated, drifting even closer.

He nodded mutely.

Garima smiled, moving in close, kissing first one cheek then the other. She pressed herself firmly against him, kissing him on the lips.

'I am going to kneel in front of you,' she smiled, moving back slightly.

It was a store room behind him; what looked like weapons. Definitely no other guards.

'I am going to unbuckle your trousers: draw them down. I will then slide your pants down.' She grinned, putting her hand between his legs. 'You like that idea.'

He nodded, transfixed.

'Would you like to touch me first?'

He stared at her chest, clutching his weapon tighter.

She eased herself down, looking up at him. 'Once we've done this, I can do other things for you.'

She discarded the shirt: when it was done, it looked like his trousers would fit her. She unbuckled his belt: drew his trousers down.

His interest rose.

**

Aakanksha scowled.

They were huddled in tight knots. Fuschine on top of Jasper – how he hadn't collapsed under her weight she didn't know. The two little sapphics, the scientist and the rat, were snuggled together, kissing, their hands busy between each other's thighs.

'Let me paint your picture,' said Hadron.

Garcon and Ryurik, Adhiratha and even Deserea were all close to the cadaverist. He had secrets but he was – she grimaced. She could just about see the delight of two women. But two men?

Foul. Foulness, indeed.

Prometheus and Daxa were talking in low voices. Only Leo remained separate, but the way he was staring at Rain –

**

She watched Garima give the soldier a blow job. He had clenched up. Garima had her hands on his thighs, sliding her lips around his shaft.

He was pale, and quite small, even hard.

He gave strangled cries, dropping his weapon, half noticing but then too distracted to do anything about it.

Garima heightened her rhythm.

He grew a little bit bigger, hands clutching at the wall.

She noticed his sweat. The little twitches in his face and arms, his body, as Garima worked him over.

He came and she stood up, leaving him dribbling. He'd barely begun to respond to her standing up than she headbutted him.

There was a cracking sound.

Garima grabbed his head and slammed it against the wall, even as Thistle and Pallograph moved past her.

Garima began stripping the body.

'Store room,' said Pallograph. 'Some weapons.'

Garima stripped the body, tossing the weapon towards her. She caught it automatically.

It was a Moorcock rifle, not known for being that accurate. It had been the major weaponry of the Empire over fifty years ago, when they had gone through their previous phase of expansionism.

Whilst her majesty's airships corps ruled the sky – all nine of them, although technically it was eight, since Captain Jasper had stolen one of those nine, the Herbert George. While the airships corps ruled the sky, there had been no campaign run without airships taking the lead, and hence no need for weaponry to advance much.

There were notable exceptions. The Aether rifle created by Captain Walker was one such. The unit that created it worked with aether, adapting airship weapons. Far more accurate than the Moorcock, no cartridge cases, much more effective over a longer range and much greater firepower.

**

Jasper – was a good man. She let herself relax in his arms. If anything ever happened to Thistle, Fuschine knew Jasper would take care of her.

She was awkwardly aware that she was completely naked and sprawled on top of Jasper, who was equally naked. She could feel his yum-yum pressed against her thigh. Her own –she blushed even thinking about it – mouth – was pressed against Jasper's thigh and her fur was damp and sticky.

He held her tight enough to squash her breasts against his chest. Thistle had taken her, given her one last – climax – in case it all went wrong, but that had just left her hungry and desperate for more.

What would mama think, knowing I let my girlfriend finger me in front of all the crew?

What would mama think, knowing I had a girlfriend?

Knowing I was – am – gay?

Jasper's bigger than any boy I ever managed to get inside me.

Mind you she thought, my tits were too big for all of them to cope with. They didn't know what to do with a woman who wanted – it. Who would guide their hands inside her pants.

Thistle and Jasper, she thought. They must have had sex before. They act like a couple who care too much, who daren't let it happen again.

**

The storeroom hadn't been as useful as she would have liked. It looked more like a room adapted for guards – there was a large table and multiple chairs, a bottle of whiskey and abandoned cards and dice.

There were shelves and cupboards around the walls but they were mostly empty. She'd gained a pair of stiff trousers, not that she cared about her own nudity. Pallo also found a pair of boots his size and Garima found a wearable pair of shoes. She found an old towel that would do to give Fuschine some modesty –

The thought of her – she couldn't define Fuschine. She wouldn't, couldn't, think of her in the term lover. She took her needs out on Fuschine, with the girl's loving consent. The fact the girl tasted of honey and aether was quite a turn on. To taste that heady mix when Fuschine orgasmed –

The feel of the girl's ample, soft breasts when she cried herself to sleep. The sound of the girl's cries when she held her down and bit her. When she sank her teeth into Fuschine's breasts or thighs, biting with intent to mark, intent to draw blood.

The girl was still too tender with her. She wanted Fuschine to hold her down, to slap her, to hurt her. To make her suffer. To hold her tight and scratch her back. To not care about her scars and lose control, take her with wild abandon, not caring if it would hurt –

No. Knowing it would hurt her and doing it anyway.

Tying her up and taking her when she didn't want to be taken.

The thought of Fuschine putting her over her lap and slapping her remorselessly. Of using a spanner on her.

That thought of Fuschine, she thought, her pleasure spiking.

That thought of Fuschine, I could love.

**

Thistle took the Bradbury Pacifier, a big bore shotgun, and a box of shells, cracking the gun and loading the first two in.

'Pallo?' Garima asked.

161

He hefted the Norton Oscillator he carried as if it was a light thing. 'More ammo if there is any. This is good for me.'

'If this is a guard chamber and other cells, there'll be an armoury the other way,' Garima looked up at Thistle.

The woman looked coldly at her.

She'd seen the momentary spark of pleasure in Thistle's cold, dead, eyes. The woman was a psycho killer, the most feared of Jasper's crew. Jasper was – by comparison – almost a kindly uncle.

She shuddered; tried not to. What Jasper had done in that train carriage in Russia – the crew still talked of it in low voices, and she had been there, had been right behind him.

Jasper was the reasonable one. The sensible one.

The one who had gone to war against the Royal British Empire, singlehandedly, stolen one of their flagship vessels and successfully carried out two mid-air attacks on other Empire or East India Company airships, as well as several attacks and raids around the world.

But nothing compared to what he'd done in that train carriage.

The stink of cordite. The gun smoke. The stench of piss and shit. The pooling blood that had drenched the floor. The bodies of the Empire and Russian officials, slaughtered in their seats by the calmest, quietest man.

Garima shook her head as they headed back towards the chamber they'd been held in. Thistle might be the psychotic one, but she was nothing compared to Jasper.

**

Daxa looked up as the chamber doors crashed open. Garima and Celestine leading the way, Thistle behind, Pallo staying outside, guarding the doorway and watching for guards.

Thistle crossed to Fuschine, wrapping a towel around her shoulders. Kissed her hair, sliding a hand down her front to caress her, oblivious to or not caring that Fuschine sat in Jasper's lap.

Daxa grinned. Fuschine's not bad in the sack. I wonder if Thistle's made her better or ruined her. She smirked, thinking about what she'd like to do to Thistle.

'Hey,' Garima called out to at her.

Daxa was already reacting: plucked the thrown Sherlock out of the air.

'Most of the weaponry is aged crap,' said Garima, lifting the Moorcock rifle she carried. 'The Sherlock was the only aether weapon there was.'

'What about me?' demanded Aakanksha, scowling.

'A weapon?' mocked Garima, 'for my sister? I don't think so.'

'Daxa,' ordered Thistle, 'help Fuschine up.'

Daxa moved to comply. Thistle was on one side of her, Jasper in front and she the other. With a bit of fumbling, Fuschine was standing, only just catching the towel as it went to slip from her shoulders.

'Daxa and I will see to her, Thistle,' Jasper said.

163

She licked her lips. The captain had obviously enjoyed having Fuschine sat on his thigh. Who wouldn't?

Thistle nodded. 'Half a dozen weapons. Nothing but other cells to the left, one storeroom adapted to a guard's room. One guard, now,' she grinned.

'He's dead?'

'Broken nose and unconscious.'

Jasper shook his head. 'No one stays alive, particularly not behind us. Kill him.'

Thistle nodded, leaving the chamber without a word.

'You can't just –' protested Aakanksha.

Jasper arched an eyebrow.

Aakanksha swallowed awkwardly and looked away.

Jasper put his arm around Fuschine, supporting her. 'The Empire thought they could release me and keep Thistle imprisoned and I would do nothing. They thought they could hurt her and there would be no comeuppance.'

He looked around his crew.

'They hurt Thistle. I broke her free, stole an airship of theirs, you know the rest,' he grinned. 'Now,' his grin faded. 'Some billionaire thinks he can have his fun with us.' He smiled at Eleonoré, whose arm was around Rain. 'We end him. We need money for the orphanage,' he nodded at Deserea, 'help us, and you're one of us.'

Deserea smiled broadly.

'Artemis C-Clementine. His guards. Anyone else here who's not a prisoner. They die. Once they're all cooling, we raid his vaults, take his money, get the Herbert

George back in the air and get to Kozhikode. Prometheus, Daxa and Celestine, you're to keep an eye out for aether. We'll need it to get airborne again.'

He flashed a rare, broad, smile. 'The rest of you, Pallo and Thistle will take the lead. Slow and steady. No room unchecked, no guard, no mercenary, left alive.'

Daxa smiled as Fuschine put her arm around her waist. Looked her up and down appreciatively. 'We'll find you some clothes, Fuschine. Eventually.'

Jasper shared a look with her.

**

Pallo paused at the corner, glancing back. They were a desperate, bedraggled lot. Fuschine being assisted by Jasper and Daxa, barely able to walk. Most of them in rags or nothing at all. Half a dozen weapons between seventeen of them.

He glanced around the corner.

Ducked back, grinning. Three figures stood midway down the corridor, their backs to him.

He held a hand out behind him and lowered it. Not that they'd been noisy, but they were even quieter. If there were guards in the rooms adjacent to the three, it'd be risky to simply turn the corner and open fire on them. Fun – he grinned – but risky.

Daxa had the only aether weapon, but she was guarding Fuschine. That was priority.

He glanced again, ducking back hastily as he saw one of the guards beginning to turn.

It was too great a distance for someone to ghost down: even if they could, there was only Eleonoré's knife

165

and no one could do that distance and kill three people who stood with their backs to them.

Well. Thistle could, if luck was on her side. The distance was too great.

Did any of those guards know the guard Thistle had been sent to dispose? Who could pass for him and get near enough – again, either Thistle was the best or possibly Celestine.

Not that he particularly wanted to risk the whole escape to the clockwork girl. It wasn't that he didn't trust her, but assassination hadn't been what she'd been created to do.

Neither Garima nor Aakanksha were quite trustable. Jasper seemed to have the luck, but he was supporting Fuschine. Neither Hadron nor Prometheus would have the stomach for it. Certainly not Leo.

Why would guards be standing in front of two doors if the doors were in to guard rooms?

Pallo sighed.

Walked around the corner and opened fire.

**

Adhiratha screamed as thunder roared in the narrow, dark corridor. Water dripped and splashed and sparks flickered and flashed as Pallo opened up with the Norton Oscillator.

He smiled. What the bad men had done to Eleonoré. To Rain; to Fuschine. To them in general. Captain Jasper would make it all okay.

Miss Lucy had some leeches, he thought, trying to remember more than just the fragment of the song. It was rude, he was sure, but many of the Empire rats knew it: it was anti-Empire.

He grinned. Between Captain Jasper and the nice Mr Templeton, it was going to be alright.

**

Garcon took the Bradbury pistol he was offered. All the guards seemed to have two weapons: Pallo was sorting them out, passing weapons to the crew as he thought appropriate.

Thistle used the butt of her weapon to smash the padlock on one of the doors and kicked it open.

Garcon peeked past her: a storeroom of tins and packages. The air smelt a little musty, but also of food.

'Anything edible?' Pallo called.

Deserea, Aakanksha and Ryurik were stripping the three guards of clothing and passing it round.

'Nothing edible now.'

The pools of blood on the floor, the stink, was unpleasant. Worse was what they'd done to the crew though. If he didn't look at the pulped heads, the half-severed torsos.

Pallo's weapon, the Norton Oscillator, was meant as an airship weapon, he was sure.

'What's outside of here, Eleonoré?'

The girl stepped forwards, Rain holding her hand.

'A courtyard. There's a couple of steps down. There are several buildings facing onto the courtyard. An enclosing wall. I think the bastard's mansion is that way, off the courtyard,' she pointed.

'So there could be guards at several points.'

167

She nodded again.

Celestine ripped the second door off its hinges: Garcon stared in surprise, as did several others.

'Rain? I thought Celestine,' Pallo hesitated.

'Celestine is one of the crew,' Rain smiled sweetly. 'Just because she's our clockwork comrade,' she began.

'No, I mean – did you know she was that strong?'

Rain shook her head.

'Could she use the door as a shield?' Garcon asked.

'Keep a watch,' ordered Thistle. 'If they heard –'

Aakanksha and Celestine moved to the doors, Celestine holding the door like a shield.

'Nothing,' reported the Indian woman. 'No movement, but there's guards on the walls.'

The other door was smashed in. Garcon could smell it immediately.

'Weapons,' Thistle breathed, 'all the weapons we could possibly need.'

**

'Something's happening,' Aakanksha called out.

Thistle joined her, feeding a belt of bullets into the Norton Oscillator she was carrying.

'What are you compensating for?' she asked.

Thistle stared at her, finishing off ensuring the belt was locked in and loaded. The woman hadn't bothered finding a shirt, merely draping several belts of bullets across her shoulders.

'Airship's landing. Small one. C-Clementine and his guards.' Thistle looked around quickly. 'Celestine, give the door to Prometheus. Half into that side; half the other. He'll be heading over here in a minute.'

Celestine moved to obey; the rats hurried into the room quickly behind Prometheus.

'They'll know something's wrong the moment they open the main doors: both doors are kicked in.' Pallo moved back to the corridor. 'Thistle, Celestine and I round the corner. Let them open the doors —'

'Hurry,' Aakanksha hissed, scowling at her sister, 'they're heading this way.'

She ducked down and fled into the other room. Fuschine leant against one wall, both Jasper and Daxa standing in front of her. The woman had knotted the towel around her waist; was wearing an oversized camouflage shirt, but most of her torso was still on display.

Aakanksha looked away, trying not to grimace. The woman was an Empire soldier, first and foremost. She might be Thistle's lover and work for Jasper, but she'd worked for the Empire first. Wasn't to be trusted. Was probably best if a stray bullet or aether stream took her out.

**

'I'm scared,' whispered Fuschine, clutching the Sherlock aether pistol.

Jasper stood in front and to her right, holding a Bradbury Pacifier, a big bore shotgun. Daxa stood in front and to her left, carrying an aether rifle.

'Of course you are,' Jasper said soothingly, 'we all are. But we're all here, and I'll do all I can to keep you safe.'

Daxa turned her head, smiled, and dropped her gaze to her breasts, barely covered by the shirt. The woman licked her lips.

'You're surviving this,' Daxa promised, making eye contact again. 'Jasper won't let Thistle down by letting you die, and I want you in my bed again.'

'Again?' Jasper stared at the former rat. 'She's – Fuschine's – with Thistle.'

Daxa arched an eyebrow and blew her a kiss.

'I am with Thistle,' Fuschine protested.

Daxa chuckled. 'You kept all us rats safe, Fuschine. Even when we weren't rats.' She grinned. 'That time in the bath in the Airyard. Thistle had not fully staked you as hers. It was nice, sharing my pleasure with you.'

Fuschine blushed furiously.

Daxa placed her hand against Fuschine's belly.

'This is hardly the time, Daxa,' Jasper reprimanded. 'This C-Clementine will be coming any moment.'

'You think there isn't time for me to bring Fuschine first?'

'No,' Fuschine insisted, shivering. 'I'm with Thistle.'

Jasper removed Daxa's hand from her belly. 'Do you really want to piss Thistle off, Daxa?'

**

'Are you alright?' Rain asked softly.

Eleonoré was in her arms. She had her arms openly around the girl's waist: Eleonoré had her arms around her neck and was clinging to her.

'I hate him,' Eleonoré said softly, 'for what I had to do to him. Not for what he did to me.'

'You killed him,' Rain said softly.

'I didn't realise. I thought,' she shrugged.

They stood so close her breasts were flattened against Eleonoré's chest.

'I love you, you know,' she said softly.

'You want to be a boy,' Eleonoré replied, eyes dark.

'My young man loves you as well. This unfortunate body, as much as you love it —'

'I don't care,' Eleonoré hissed, 'if you've got tits or a cock or both. I love you Rain. I know you're older than me. I don't care. I just want to spend a day, a week, on a remote island, doing things with you.'

'You could be my pirate queen,' Rain said softly. 'Heaving bosom, long thighs —'

'My bosom hardly heaves,' Eleonoré grinned. 'Not like yours. If you're going to bind it up, let me bind it up for you. Let me be the last one to experience your breasts: to kiss and suck your nipples.'

Rain stroked a tear from Eleonoré's eye. 'When I am my pirate king, I am going to ride the hemp. I am going to lay my pirate queen on her belly. Kiss my way up from her toes to her thighs. I am going to spank my queen until she wriggles and writhes. I am going to drive myself into her so hard. Drive myself in so hard it takes everything but pleasure from her. When she is a spent force, I am going to drink her down like she is the moon.'

Eleonoré clung to her. 'I'm just a rat.'

'But you're my rat,' Rain answered, cupping her bottom.

'They tortured you,' Eleonoré whispered.

'We will make them all suffer, my queen,' Rain answered. She placed her hand onto Eleonoré's shallow breast. 'I will be the one kissing and sucking your nipples, making you scream your orgasms.'

**

Leo clung to his weapon. It was a terrible thing, a destroyer of life, but also a wonder of construction, a toy the Empire had converted to a weapon. An old fashioned pistol, not that he'd had one before or ever used one.

A le Guin Equaliser. A circular chamber with six shells. A hammer to strike it. That ignited a spark which created a force which expelled the shell out of the chamber and down the barrel.

Or something like that. It was joyous and crude at the same time. An old fashioned thing –

He glanced at his niece and scowled.

She was a boy. She thought she was a boy. She wanted to be a boy.

He shook his head.

She was born, created, fashioned by her parents – he grimaced. They had had such flighty and nonsensical thoughts as well. He had seen her talent, her gift, and taken her in when they died. Had instilled a structure and discipline into her, and she had a knack for the sciences, for making things work.

But this foolish thought that she could be something she wasn't –

The Empire took your dragons' heads, a rebellious part of his mind thought. You created them as fashion items, to adorn a chair or a staff or similar. The Empire took them and turned them into an instrument of torture –

Why is my niece torturing herself? The fool she is making of herself with that rat –

The Empire will capture us. If we're lucky we'll be slaves. We'll be keelhauled if we're not lucky.

**

Ryurik heard the outer doors crash open.

'What's gone on here?' he heard the Englishman yell. 'Who's damaged my doors!'

He clutched the Bradbury Pacifier tighter. Pallo, Miss Wales and Celestine waited around the corner, each of them carrying a Norton Oscillator. When the three of them opened up –

He shuddered. One was plenty loud. But three, in close quarters –

At least they were out of the cell. That had been – he swallowed awkwardly. Mr Woods and Miss Wales were fighting against the Empire across the world and then to be captured by some rich, perverted, Englishman –

He grimaced. The man was loyal to the Empire. Those loyal to the Empire tended to be perverts, or corrupt, or nasty, Miss Wales had said. Born with the notion that they were better people because of where they'd been born, or who their parents were, or because their parents had lots of money.

Even he, a simple Russian farm boy, knew such things were nonsense.

It didn't matter if the father was a prize bull, the heifer could easily be of no use, suitable only for the slaughterhouse.

**

Prometheus clutched the door tightly. It doesn't fit, it doesn't, they'll see straight away. He heard C-Clementine shout in anger.

The bodies are in the chamber, they are, he thought. It's too late –

He nodded slowly, remembering that Thistle, Pallo and Celestine were waiting around the corner.

'Where are my guards?' screamed C-Clementine.

He heard muttered voices.

Movement.

He glanced at the crew in the room with him.

'Close your ears,' he whispered.

Thunder roared and lightning flashed, mercilessly filling the corridor. He heard the crack and splatter, the ricochet, the intensive sound as bullet casings hit the floor in a rising tide.

It was worse than the airship battles.

Worse, because the sound was contained in the tunnel.

Worse, because this felt – realer. It did. They hid in two obviously damaged and broken-into rooms, while Pallo, Celestine and Thistle slaughtered those who'd captured them.

Prometheus shivered.

**

Deserea eased the door open cautiously.

Blood pooled in the channel that ran down the middle of the floor. Dust and debris drifted down from the walls. Smoke hung in the air, the stink of cordite: cartridge casings still rolled.

She peeked out cautiously.

Thistle, Pallo and Celestine stood like legends out of myths. Pallo hefted the Norton Oscillator easily onto one shoulder. Thistle carried hers two handed, strung about with belts of bullets.

Deserea stared and tried not to drool.

Even though the woman was white –

She moved, fluid and graceful, deadly. Black hair. Sharp cheekbones. Tall. An intense look in her eyes.

And her body –

Deserea recognised old burns the covered most of her belly. Scalding had been a favoured means of discipline –

Thistle's arms were scarred and branded. And her breasts –

Her breasts –

Her nipples were blood-red and thick, the areolae pink. The undersides of her breasts were badly scarred – Deserea recognised the marks of a cat o' nine tails or metal-edged whip. The application – not recent – had caused her breasts to crumple a little.

She was aware of Fuschine, Jasper and Daxa beside her. All three of them were openly staring at

Thistle's chest, Fuschine drooling, Daxa biting her lip and Jasper –

She saw Hadron's expression, one of disgust, of revulsion –

**

The slut was happily parading semi-nude again, carrying the biggest weapon she could find. What she was compensating for –

Hadron grimaced, noticing Deserea, the wilful, lying, bullying orphan, staring at Thistle's tits.

Fuschine was staring at them as well, and dribbling in lust.

The thought of the beautiful Fuschine, already broken, her left leg shattered irrevocably by Thistle, still adoring and lusting after the psychopathic Thistle was –

He shuddered.

Fuschine had too nice an arse to waste on an abhorrent whore like Thistle. It was a shame Fuschine wasn't a boy: still, her tits were incredibly nice and soft and malleable, and the engineer enjoying stripping off so he could paint her in the nude: her only shyness, in front of him, at least, was around her withering, shattered, left leg.

Daxa and Jasper were lusting after Thistle as well. Daxa was just a rat, one of the few who survived long enough to become an adult.

But Jasper – the supposed gentleman, the honourable bookseller, the man who stood up to the Royal British Empire – oh, yes. Jasper lusted after Thistle.

They had been booksellers for a number of years together, running "Woods and Wales", the best-known bookshop in the whole of the Royal British Empire. They had been arrested, Jasper released promptly, at which point he had called upon Hadron for help.

Thistle. The Empire had tortured Thistle. He had seen the state she was in when Jasper had carried her out of the gaol in a wedding gown. She was taller than Jasper and unconscious in his arms, head thrown back. Blood had leaked from her, staining the skirt part of the dress. Jasper had intended to walk her out as new bride, but she had been torn up inside and left to die –

He grimaced.

Jasper no longer remembered he had called Hadron for help. He had seen to that.

He walked a coin across his fingers, watching.

I need Thistle to forget me, he thought. Forget me and Fuchsine, and I can get her away from Thistle, get her to a place of safety.

**

Thistle led the way, Celestine and Pallo flanking her. The Empire guards were down, slaughtered, though it looked like Artemis C-Clementine had escaped – for the moment.

He walked to Fuschine's left, arm around her waist, supporting her. Her hip pressed against his. Her arm was around his waist and she leant against him. Daxa was on her right, her arm around Fuschine's shoulders: between the two of them they kept her upright.

There was something about Hadron – he shook his head as the cadaverist passed them, le Guin Equaliser in

177

hand. If C-Clementine had escaped, there would be more guards – there would be more guards, anyway. They were finding and ending the man. Terminating his guards' contracts. Destroying his property. Taking all his wealth and destroying everything he had owned, even his airships.

Let Artemis C-Clementine be a warning to all and any. We will end him. We will end anyone who stands against us, who has hurt Thistle or any of my crew.

We will end them all.

Thistle and the others opened the front doors and moved out. Gunfire roared, but this time the next wave of his crew moved to join them.

'Don't – don't leave me inside,' Fuschine whispered. 'End or not, I want to be there. Either we kill them all or we die together. I can't,' she heaved back a sob. 'I can't go on if Thistle doesn't make it.'

Jasper nodded, glancing at Daxa, and followed his crew out into the open.

C-Clementine's airship was struggling to rise into the dreaded skies. It was about a quarter of the size of the Herbert George.

'Get the bastards!' Fuschine screamed, half pulling away from them and wobbling.

Jasper put a hand on her shoulder to support her, lifting his Bradbury Pacifier. 'Take it down!'

**

Celestine raised the Norton Oscillator. There were guards coming down from the walls, hurrying towards them from all directions, but the small airship, with the billionaire

Artemis C-Clementine on board, was struggling to rise into the sky. It listed to one side as swathes of bullets from Thistle, Pallo and herself riddled the hull, smashing the wood, striking and sparking the small weapons that poked out of the side.

The sound was like liquid thunder, roaring fire into the dark sky.

The guns roared and bellowed. The cartridges were cracks of lightning, cases ejecting all over the place in ricocheting waves of hot metal.

Guards ran towards them, but Prometheus and the young Russian male, Ryurik, stood to one side, wielding Bradbury Pacifiers, shooting indiscriminately at any guard who got too close.

She would not have trusted either of them, but the captain was with them, one hand supporting Miss Nagle, shooting lefthandedly. Daxa stood the other side of Miss Nagle, using an aether rifle and cackling uproariously.

Miss Nagle stood between them, not quite strong enough to stand unassisted, a Sherlock aether pistol in hand. The talented engineer was not a soldier, but she fired when she could and bodies dropped.

Hot lead and aether splashed around them.

On the other flank, Garima, Rain, Eleonoré, Deserea and Aakanksha stood in tight order, using aether rifles. They shot in close order, without hesitation, cutting legs from guards and exploding heads.

The air sang and screamed with sound and blood and death and Celestine changed her grip, targeting the front of the rising airship. As it rose it tilted more and more

179

to one side. Bodies were beginning to slide. Guards were trying to hold on, no longer able to fire back.

Moving to assist Ryurik and Prometheus was Garcon, with a Bradbury Pistol, staying close to Miss Nagle, defending her from any guard who looked to be targeting her.

Adhiratha moved with the French boy, wielding a Sherlock, fighting, like most of the rats, most fervently for those who cared for and protected them.

Pallo's gun ran empty. Thistle slung a pair of belts of bullets at him.

His gun roared into life again and there was an explosion from the airship: its back end dropped as flames licked out of the cabins.

Hadron and Leo moved to join Fuschine on the left flank, each with a le Guin equaliser. The cadaverist – the mesmerist – and the German inventrix were an odd couple, but they stood shoulder to shoulder, picking off the last of C-Clementine's guards with the heavy, old-fashioned pistols they carried.

The airship rolled, plummeted –

**

The airship crashed, satisfyingly, exploding into multiple vortexes of flame, burning shards shredding the air.

She ducked, dropping the oscillator, her hands red and bruised, her arms tired.

Thistle glanced back. Jasper and Daxa were shielding Fuschine.

Blood, body parts, bits of hired thugs were scattered everywhere along with incandescing airship parts.

After the joyous, wonderful sounds of destruction, the courtyard was silent.

No one called out. No one came running. No one fired at them.

She rose slowly, wincing at the pain in her hands. The Norton Oscillator had been superheated by the end, but the airship was down, the man who'd hurt Fuschine exploded or burned alive. She glanced back at Jasper's crew once more.

They were getting to their feet slowly, a ragged, stunned, bruised and staring collection of individuals.

Pallo – Pallograph Smith, gunrunner. Celestine – four point two, the clockwork maid who'd become a warrior, one of their crew. Eleonoré, the rat who'd been with them from the start, who'd helped them capture the Herbert George. Rain, boy or girl or neither, scientist, who'd liberated four point two, named her Celestine and had her arm around Eleonoré.

Adhiratha, another rat who'd been with them from the beginning and was coming into his own. Garcon, who they'd saved from a French street gang. Ryurik, the young Russian boy who'd helped her such a long time ago, and Deserea, who they'd rescued and then taken from the Afric partly against her wishes, but who now stood with them. Daxa, the rats' mother, an honorific, a woman who would fight tooth and nail to keep all of them safe, but specifically the rats, their younger crew.

Leo, Rain's uncle. A man with old fashioned attitudes. Still, he had stood with them at the end. He had had a problem with Rain, but if he continued to have a problem with his niece or nephew, he would find he had other problems. She would see to that. Would see to him.

Garima and Aakanksha, neither to be trusted. One an operative of the East India Company, the other one of Gunter's. Hating each other but potentially useful. Garima had eyes on Jasper: she would not have that. And Aakanksha tried to sleep her way around the crew to collect secrets, to gain leverage. She would give her time to hang herself, then hang her. Neither would be allowed to risk harm to Jasper, Fuschine, the rats or any others of the crew.

Prometheus and Hadron. An ineffective clockmaker, out of his depth, he had yet to come into his own. And Hadron. The vile, disgusting, cadaverist, with an interest in the male rats that bordered on unhealthy. She didn't trust him.

Didn't trust anyone, really.

Both of them needed an eye keeping on them.

A shudder ran through her. Pain, and a need that only the amber liquid could relieve.

Fuschine. Sweet, innocent, annoying, tender, Fuschine. The girl was so –

The girl annoyed her, angered her, greatly. If anything should happen to the girl.

She growled. Anything beyond her leg being shattered.

She stared at Fuschine, whose chest heaved as she struggled to catch her breath, held and supported by Daxa and Jasper. The girl who wanted to spend time with her. Who had dared to ask her out. Who had held her as she cried. Who'd offer herself, freely, in whatever way would help her.

The girl looked at her and smiled.

The girl who loved her.

And Jasper.

Jasper, who had stood by her when she was lost and alone. Who had come for her. Who had singlehandedly freed her from the gaol in September City, where they'd been torturing her. Who'd put a crew together to rescue her and take her far from there. Who had stood against the Royal British Empire and their global-spanning dominion in her name. Who had started a revolution in her name. Who meant more to her than she could ever tell him.

Jasper, who cared deeply for her but wasn't interested in her.

Jasper, whom more than anyone else, she thought she might be able to love.

Jasper and Fuschine. The two people she cared about most in the world, though she could never tell them.

'Is anyone going to bitch that pot,' Daxa said, 'I could murder a cup of tea.'

Daughter of Autumn

by

Hannah Simpson

Prologue. Saturday, November 3rd 1945

We do not know the things that will shape us, that will make us who we become. Walking along the path under the dripping eaves of trees I didn't know then what awaited me. I didn't know that house would take only two seasons to teach me who I am. Didn't know about Father Lewis, the man of fire. Had not yet met the barking stones or the birds that call in the dark of the wood giving shape to shadow. It was summer then...

It is autumn for me now. Can you smell the bonfires? They are here, even if you can't, curling their smoke around these pages. We have not been allowed to light an autumn bonfire for the last six years and I hadn't realised how much I missed them, singing their red-orange songs, floating the last of the leaves on their big puffed out breaths of heat. Today walking home the smoke carried gossip, the eye rolling chatter of lipsticky women whispering a word sharp as a mouth full of dressmaker's pins. A word on the tip of their tongues every time I pass by that just needed the right prompt to spit out. A word that has stirred this old memory and floated it up like a leaf escaping the bonfires.

The memory we are talking about is long ago...or yesterday; it's hard to tell sometimes as you grow older. I am no longer that girl though. I was almost thirteen then and I did not know as I approached that house that I was walking out of the last summer of my childhood.

Perhaps the trees could have told me. Or perhaps they would have lied – some trees do you know....

A Hermitage of Thrushes, September 4th, 1916

She was worried that her clothes smelt. It had been raining steadily all the way there, but it was still a warm day and she was worried that as her new wool stockings dried they would give off a stink like Uncle Jimmy's Cairn terrier.

'Yo wo' get verry far wi that fearce on ya. Yo could stop a bosted clock.'

He was the oldest thing she'd ever seen, even older than Owd Cott who sat outside the Aingel pub smoking her clay pipe and talking to clouds. She smiled, shyly, 'Sorry. Never lived away from home.'

Shaking his mottled head and tutting he told her to stand on the matting by the door and disappeared into the gloom of the house. It was cooler indoors. The windows were tall but narrow, like arrow slits in a castle, and set deep into the stone walls so that the light that filtered in was dull and creamy and splashed the red tiles in fragments that broke and reformed as the wind shook the rain through the trees. She could hear voices somewhere but it was impossible to guess at their direction and she stood, steaming and dripping, wondering what on earth she'd done.

Suddenly he was back in the room beckoning and huffing so much that she was put in mind of a starling in a dust bath and had to concentrate on her feet to stop herself from laughing with embarrassment or crying with fear. She followed him up two grey stone steps scooped in the middle by the wearing of endless pairs of running feet and realised she had been in a kind of hallway on the back of a big square kitchen that was even darker. As he led her through it the house seemed to change around her, becoming lighter and less forbidding the further they went until he opened a door into what looked like a parlour or sitting room. Light poured in through a large window and a woman standing at the fireplace with her back to them, turned to face them as they shuffled in. She was tall, beaky around the nose and chin, with dark hair and clothes but as the emerging sun caught her rings and brooch and earrings she gleamed. If he was a dusty starling, here was a jackdaw, fresh from the rain.

'And you are Hazel.'

It wasn't a question. Hazel wasn't sure how to respond so simply nodded.

'Unusual name. Although of course not in America, I hear from friends it's all the rage there.'

'I have an older cousin in Philadelphia, Miss, who has a baby Hazel. She's older than me...my cousin, I mean. Not the baby. The baby's only eight months. My cousin's twenty-three. She...' she petered out as a ruffling of starling feathers behind her indicated that she had not got this right at all. Hazel fell helplessly silent.

The jackdaw lady gave a frowning smile, 'Yes...in any case. You seem like a bright little thing for twelve. Thank you for coming to us a few weeks early. It seemed silly to wait until Michaelmas when we're so short. Her things are here, Aynoch?'

'Pharoh brought 'er box and bits on 'is way to Bromsgrove, Miss Castle. They'm already up 'er room.'

She nodded and the blue glass at her ears cast rainbows across the floor. 'Very good. Now, Hazel, you will call me Miss Castle or Miss. Your aunt tells me that you are a polite girl and a hard worker who is eager to learn. If that proves to be the case you will be well taken care of here.'

At the mention of her aunt the tears that had been threatening since Hazel arrived got dangerously close to making a fool of her in front of this grand lady, who must have noticed because she looked away and rubbed her palms along the front of her skirts as if she'd just discovered them grubby. 'Well...I'm sure it's very strange for you... but we shall all get along splendidly. You shall soon see. I will call for Gwen and she can show you your room.'

She pressed a button set into the wall. Nothing happened and the three of them stood in awkward silence for what felt like a week until suddenly Hazel heard the sound of footsteps running overhead before coming down a flight of stairs and then another shorter flight. They slowed just outside the door before it opened, and a fair head and a pretty heart shaped face appeared.

'Yes, Miss Castle?'

'Gwen, this is Hazel, our new Between Maid. Please show her to her room and then get her started.'

Gwen bobbed a curtsy and waited. Hazel muttered a thank you and followed her out, the spreading humiliation running its red fingers right up into the roots of her hair.

The house was less frightening in the sunshine. It was also huge and seemed to be made entirely of staircases. There were short runs of steps at odd angles to each other and Hazel stuck close to Gwen.

'Don't worry, you'll stop getting lost after your first week,' Gwen said as she turned a corner and opened a door onto another, narrower staircase, enclosed on both sides. Hazel followed her up into the dark tunnel until they came to another door, old and wooden with a farmhouse latch. Gwen opened it onto a bright little bedroom. Hazel realised that she must be at the very top of the house because the ceiling rose to a point and then sloped down at both sides, with broad wooden beams running along where the slope met the straight walls. There was an iron bedstead in the centre, under the highest point, with sheets and blankets folded over the end, ready to be made up. Above the bed was a triangular window showing the tops of trees. Hazel was suddenly, stupidly relieved to see the trunk containing all her things on the rag rug in front of the small fireplace.

'This is your room little 'un. We're lucky here, now the other wenches have gone we don't have to share. I'm just on the other side of that wall.' Gwen pointed to the wall on the right of the window, 'But my room's on the west staircase.'

'There were other girls in here?'

Gwen laughed and nodded, her voice slipping into the big round vowel sounds of her Black Country dialect.

'You doe think an 'ouse this size runs itself? They had four grown maids, an 'ousekeeper, a cook and a gardener. They pay more in the factories. Everybody's left to do war work apart from the gardener who's gone to fight. Day yo want to go in the factories?'

Hazel shook her head, 'My uncle wouldn't let me.'

Gwen was older than Hazel, and the look she gave her made her look older still, 'Wass it got to do with him? Ay yo gorra dad to speak for ya?' Hazel shook her head again and began making up the bed to have something to do with her hands.

**

Hazel had expected to go into the factories. 'Black by day and red by night' from the foundries and furnaces which fuelled the trades that built the world, the Black Country breathed the fire of industry.

When the end of school began to loom for Hazel the war work for girls was booming. Stourbridge had always retained a subtly different personality to the places around it, while they were all making chain and nails, the old market town retained its shabbily genteel character by making glass. Her Uncle Jake had been at the glassworks since he was a boy of Hazel's age and although still young enough to fight, he was now so experienced that he'd been presented with a certificate and an enamel lapel badge from the war office to mark him out as a man whose skills were vital at home. The trouble began with women. Uncle Jake started to come home grumbling because as his men began to join up, there was talk of women being trained to take their places.

Then the grumbling found a new target when it was discovered that the brick glass kiln, standing among all the others on the canal in Amblecote like an enormous, upturned funnel, would apparently be put to work making equipment for the war. One evening he arrived home from work quiet and pensive with news that he was being sent away for two weeks to one of the army's new training schools, The County Metallurgical and Engineering Institute in Wednesbury. He hadn't spent a night away from Aunt Gracie since he carried her over the threshold when they were both twenty-one, even their week of August holiday was spent on the other side of Worcestershire picking hops together. It was strange without him at first. Hazel would catch Aunt Gracie standing, blank faced, outside their front door in the mornings before she made her way to her own work at the chain shop in Lye, her breath white in the January air, as if she'd forgotten how to hammer and shut links without him. His presence was always there at first, a ghost in their conversations, with each of them saying "Oh, we must tell him about this when he comes home," or "I wonder what Jake will say?"

But by the end of his first week, they grew accustomed to it being the just the two of them until the novelty of his absence began to seem almost like a holiday. That all changed on the Tuesday morning of his second week. There had been the shock of Zeppelin raids on the coast the previous year but after the big raid on London in the autumn, it had seemed to everyone that the German's had less stomach for killing women and children than the posters appearing everywhere suggested, and the raids had stopped. Since then, all talk was of Gallipoli and the war "over there", far away from the safety of home. On the last day of January, a quiet Monday evening, after he'd spent all day at the technical school, Uncle Jake was dozing off on his billeted bed with his textbook still propped open on his chest when, at just after eight o'clock, the building shook. Running into the street he saw fire raining from the sky. Birmingham had heeded the warning of the raids on London and implemented a black out. Finding their target, the 'workshop of the world', impossible to see in the darkness and the fog, the nearby Black Country shone out like a star, so the Zeppelins poured fury down upon it.

That fury lasted for six hours, devastating Wednesbury, Tipton and Walsall. Burning incendiaries fell among the ruins of Dudley Castle. It wiped out whole streets, and in them whole families, soldiers on leave and children in their beds. Bad news being fleet of foot it had spread like the wildfire it told of. The injuries of those who survived were spoken of in whispers and the Black Country was stunned into mourning. On the Friday night of his safe return, Hazel crept from her bed to the top of the little staircase that led up from the parlour. She sat, her feet swimming in a pair of Uncle Jake's woollen socks against the chill of the boards and listened to her aunt and uncle talking.

'It woe be the last time they hit us, Gracie. If her's in a factory, especially if it's munitions, her'll be finishing at all hours and her'll be walking um. If her gets caught in one of them... the best thing we can do for her is get her away. Somewhere away from the foundries, somewhere

194

that's quiet and dark. We'm surrounded by open countryside – Gracie, yo know her could go to that house and be safe until it's all over. And if summat happens to us her'll be looked after there, woe her?'

She heard her aunt protest; say she'd already lost one home and shouldn't be torn away from another. But she heard her uncle reply that, while wandering the streets of Wednesbury that night, dazed and looking for people to help, he had found a woman's shoe with the foot still in it. Then they had both fallen silent, until all Hazel could hear was the ticking clock sound of the range cooling down. She knew then that she would be sent away again.

**

Gwen had been telling the truth about getting lost. Hazel got lost in a blur of running up one staircase only to find she should have run down quite another. The ancient stone house had stood alone on the lane for as long as anyone could remember. It seemed that each new generation had had a different way of living in it, adding changes year on year until the internal geography was a jumble of blocked off doors and odd corridors some of which could only be reached by a staircase on an entirely different floor. As a Between Floors Maid this meant that, when not covered in beeswax from polishing, soot from the grate or soil from the kitchen garden, Hazel would spend most of her days running up and down them to do whatever else was asked of her. Gwen at eighteen was in every way her senior and although she seemed to do all manner of jobs had been trained as a Lady's Maid and seemed particularly proud that she was responsible for taking care of the needs of the "lady of the house". There were actually, Hazel knew, two ladies of the house, always referred to by everyone in town as "the Miss Castles", despite the elder of them no longer being a Miss Castle at all, but a widow called Mrs Dunchurch. For some reason this married name had never stuck so "the Miss Castles" they remained. Along with the Miss Castles and Gwen there was Aynoch who had been with the family for many years and handled the odd jobs and now the gardening, and the cook, otherwise known as Mrs Evesham from Love Lane. She rode up to the hall on her bicycle twice a day – once in the morning to prepare hot breakfast and cold lunch and then again in the afternoon to make and serve dinner.

There was also the cat, Geamiss. A big shaggy headed, long-limbed tom with cream and black stripes tigering his fur and an ear twice split from a long-ago fight giving the impression that he wore a tattered, rakish crown. He seemed to spend his time swaggering piratically around the kitchen and the little room Hazel had waited in when she first arrived which everyone called "the vestibule". That first day passed in a confusion of instructions and misunderstandings and when Hazel finally climbed the dark staircase to her new room her head was swimming and her eyes ached with unshed tears. It was still light enough to do without a candle and she opened her trunk to take out her nightdress only to find that Aunt Gracie had sent the patchwork quilt from her own bed at home.

Kneeling beside the trunk in her white chemise Hazel ran her hand over the bumpy, uneven stitches. Aunt Gracie could make anything with knitting needles and wool but wasn't as adept with a needle and thread. Years of making chain had clawed the fingers on her right hand making the knuckles bulge and the joints stiffen; 'ommer 'ond', the women called it. It made holding a tiny needle to do fine work like sewing laborious and painful. But she had saved every scrap of material she could and had sat up next to the lamp cursing under her breath for many months until Hazel's quilt was finished. She swore it was the first and last she'd ever make. Hazel shook it out and the unshed tears finally began to fall. When they were spent, she crawled into the strange bed feeling empty and small and lost. The morning's rain had returned and sounded heavier now as wind drove it against the triangular window, making a noise like handfuls of pearl barley being sprinkled into a pan. She was glad of the quilt, it was the one thing that smelled like home, a mixture of her aunt's lavender water and the scent of their smoky parlour. The rain dripped down the pane in the last of the thin light making patterns of intricate lace on the opposite wall and the tops of the birch trees were swaying, making a sound like the sea. She watched these rain shadows until her eyes began to close and she drifted into a dream of a bride, standing in the crow's nest of a ship, ripping the heads of flowers from her bouquet and tossing them into the storm.

**

197

She was woken by Gwen at first light on the following morning. Her first job each day was to be cleaning and laying the fires in the two sitting rooms used by the Miss Castles. The younger used what was known as 'the big sitting room' the large, bright room Hazel had been taken to when she arrived. The elder Miss Castle used what they all called 'the little parlour,' a cosy snug of a room that Hazel liked immediately. Once this job was done, she was sent to the kitchen to help Mrs Evesham who asked if she could dig up some potatoes for that evening's meal. Hazel took a piece of sacking to kneel on, a trug and a trowel from the vestibule, just as she was told to, and made her way down the terrace between the flower beds full of early chrysanthemums to the little ivy-covered archway that led to the kitchen garden. The garden seemed to be alive with birds and a wind chime hanging against one of the sheds was making a softly ringing tune to accompany them. After lifting a couple of potatoes Hazel felt the trowel hit something more solid. Putting her hand into the bed she felt the sharp edge of something cool and pulled and twisted until she brought a round metal disc out of the soil. Rubbing the dirt off with her thumbs she could see silver glinting in the morning sunlight and slowly a picture began to appear, revealing a woman's head and shoulders. She wore a crown and her hair curled out in a style shorter than any Hazel was used to seeing. On the other side was a cross that divided the disc into four triangles, each filled with strange, raised bumps and marks. It looked like a medal or a coin and as Hazel put it on the path to continue digging, she heard footsteps coming towards her. Looking up she saw a woman in a pale green dress framed by the archway. She realised that this must be the elder Miss Castle. She resembled her sister a great deal, but her colouring and features were fairer. The hair piled up on top of her head and held in place with combs was a light brown haloed with grey around the forehead and temples and as she bent under the ivy Hazel was struck by how beautiful she was. She got up and brushed the soil from her hands as best she could, 'Good morning, Miss', she said bobbing a curtsy.

'What's this?', said Miss Castle, reaching down for the metal disc. 'Have you been finding treasure?'

'It was in amongst the potatoes, Miss. Not sure what it is but I thought I'd better put it to one side to bring up to the house when I'm done.'

Miss Castle turned it over in her hands looking at the design. 'Oh well done! Edward the third if I'm not mistaken. I think this was what they called a groat. It's a medieval coin. What a good find!'

'Is it a king, Miss? I thought it looked like a queen, but I know we've only had two of those and it didn't look like either of them.'

Miss Castle said, smiling, 'Who on earth told you that, child?'

'Pardon, Miss?'

'Who told you that we have only had two queens? I can assure you, we have had many more of them than that. One of the Mercian's finest rulers was a woman.'

Hazel was already out of her depth and wasn't sure what to reply, so said blandly, 'Yes, Miss.'

'I love this garden, don't you? Beauty and bounty...' Looking out over the beds she put her hands to the small of her back as if stretching, then fixed Hazel with a warm, inquisitive stare. 'You must be our new Between Maid. My sister did say you'd be coming but I lose track of the days, somewhat.'

Hazel curtsied again. 'Yes, Miss. I'm Hazel, Miss.'

'Hmm...' Miss Castle nodded, 'Hazel...' She gazed into Hazel's eyes for a long moment as if trying to get the measure of her, 'but are you an avellana or a Hamamelis? I wonder...'

As Hazel began to stutter in confusion, she heard the younger Miss Castle call out from the terrace, 'Sister, are you ready? We shall be late.'

The elder Miss Castle called back that she was just coming, then turning back to Hazel said, 'It is nice to meet you, Hazel the treasure hunter. I hope you're settling in here.'

Before Hazel could reply Miss Castle had turned and begun to walk away up the path, the coin still clutched in her hand.

The gardens were fascinating to Hazel and much grander than anything she was used to. It was as if the Miss Castles had their own private version of the Promenade Gardens on Greenfield Avenue where bands came to play on Saturday afternoons. They were vast and rambling and stretched all the way to what everyone in the house called 'the old birch'. Its topmost leaves already beginning to burnish to a mustardy gold, this was the tallest tree in a stand of silver birches at the very end of the gardens as they sloped upwards to the woods beyond. It was the woods which interested Hazel most as it was said in the town that you shouldn't go into them at night. They surrounded the old hill fort, the tallest point for miles around, where there was a legend of a giant, asleep under the hill, who would wait for the unwary traveller and scare him half out of his wits. Hazel knew of gossip about men in the town who, returning from weddings in Hagley or Pedmore, had attempted to walk the hill road and had been found the next morning with their hair shocked white after an encounter with the Wychbury Giant. Being close to the source of these stories had been the only glimmer of excitement in her sadness at being made to leave home. On her way back to the kitchen Hazel cupped her hand over her eyes and looked towards the horizon line, watching the birch trees sway in the breeze, wondering if she would ever get the chance to explore, when she thought she heard a whispered voice. Looking behind her all she saw was the closed face of the house with its narrow windows like squinting eyes. She looked back towards the birches and caught it again, a voice on the breeze, too soft and low to make out what it was saying. Hazel shivered, despite the warmth of the day and turned back towards the house with her trug full of potatoes.

**

Hazel might have forgotten that whisper had it not been for something that happened two days later. Her first week had continued much as it began with a confusion of new instructions and the learning of new ways to do old

201

jobs she had been helping her aunt with since she was big enough to hold a duster. The Castles were an old family, and the Hall was an old house steeped in tradition and routine. Very often she found herself on the sharp end of Aynoch's temper with the often-repeated phrase 'I doe care 'ow you do it down the 'ill, yo'm at The Hall now and yo'll do it The Hall way.' He was a gruff, pious man, Hazel didn't think she'd seen him smile since she arrived so she stayed out of his way as much as she could. Mrs Evesham on the other hand was a neat, trim little woman with a high fluty voice and ice-cold pastry hands who ran the kitchen like a well-oiled machine; Hazel liked helping her and watching the efficient, economical way she accomplished everything. Tongue-tied and awkward around these new people, Hazel made stupid mistakes and misunderstood instructions until she was drowning in her own embarrassment. She blushed so often and so deeply Gwen had taken to calling her Lily Lobster. It was a source of further embarrassment that she didn't really know what a lobster was so needed the nickname explained to her by Mrs Evesham. She had been worried about not being able to sleep away from her own bed but was so exhausted that she didn't think, since her first night there, that she even dreamed anymore. It was during one of these dreamless sleeps that she was woken by a noise. At first, she thought it was Gwen waking her for morning chores, but the room was still midnight black, and she lay in the dark wondering why she was so wide awake. Then she heard it. There was a scratching coming from the wall to the right of her bed. It only lasted for a few seconds,

202

and it sounded like nails on wood. She strained to listen in the silence in case it came again. There it was. A 'kree, kree, kree, kree, kree' sound in short bursts. It sounded like it was something trapped inside the wall trying to get out. She sat bolt upright in bed pushing down the white sheets and wrapping Aunt Gracie's quilt around her. After a few minutes the noise seemed to have stopped but she was determined not to fall asleep again. When Gwen woke her the next morning Hazel realised she had slumped down against the iron bedstead, sleeping with her chin on her chest, and had a sore neck and shoulders for the rest of the day.

**

Hazel got one day off a week. Saturday morning was spent cleaning and polishing and preparing the house so that nothing would be needed from when she left after lunch on Saturday until she returned on Sunday evening. She was twitchy and distracted until Aynoch gave her leave to go. She felt strange in her old clothes again after spending all week in her black wool tights and her starched white blouse. Walking down the hill towards home she was nervously excited to embrace her sudden freedom.

Turning down Baylie Street she could see the front door standing open, as it usually was, and she ran the last few steps until she could bound into the little parlour with its overstuffed, uncomfortable sofa and its friendly fire breathing range. The parlour was empty, but the kitchen door was ajar, and she heard a shout from within, 'Our little worker's home, Gracie!' Uncle Jake came through the door in his shirt sleeves beaming.

'Hello our Hazel!' He put his arm around her shoulder and briefly squeezed her tight, before letting her go, saying, 'Come on in the kitchen, wench. Your aunt's just med you a brew.' Since she'd got too big to swing easily up onto his shoulders, he hadn't really touched her. Not a demonstrative man, but placid and easy going, he had shown affection by being interested in her and spending his meagre spare time with her, listening to her chatter about whatever new book she was lost in, or whatever new notion she'd taken into her head. She was touched to be touched and to realise that it meant he'd missed her. Over Saturday tea all he and Aunt Gracie could talk about was news of a Zeppelin brought down in Essex the previous weekend, with Uncle Jake declaring Lieutenant Robinson, the pilot responsible, 'a proper English hero.'

'Taste of their own medicine now ay it? They woe like that! And they had to swallow it from a chap who joined up to The Worcestershire's. Just desserts. And if *he* can do it once, we can do it again – I said to your Aunt Gracie, they'm beat now, ay they? Let 'em all come, and we'll shoot the lot out the sky like what old Will Robinson did!'

It felt delicious to Hazel to snuggle into her own bed that night knowing she would wake up to her aunt and uncle in the kitchen in the morning. She fell asleep thanking God in her prayers for no scratching in the walls and no whispers in the trees and no Aynoch with a list of her faults to correct.

Normally Hazel dreaded church, but that Sunday she was looking forward to it. It was a novelty to her to feel so at home, when so often she had felt out of place here. Arriving when she was already almost old enough to go to school, she hadn't learned the rules of the Stourbridge streets early, the way the other children had, and was always slightly removed and distant from them, as if they were speaking a language she didn't quite understand. It had made her a lonely child. It hadn't helped that Uncle Jake and Aunt Gracie had no children of their own. At first that had been a sore wound of confusion and heartbreak for the couple but when Hazel arrived it softened into an acceptance of this strange kind of family. It wasn't unusual for children to be brought up by aunts, uncles, even grandparents, but those children were usually absorbed by larger broods. Jake and Gracie with their one mouth to feed — and then only a niece — sometimes drew looks of pity and what occasionally seemed like envy from their neighbours. Uncle Jake said it was jealousy that Aunt Gracie had kept her "tidy figure" but Hazel wasn't so sure. There was a strange, longing resentment in the women and an odd gruff suspicion in the men. She felt that familiar unease as the neighbours' eyes slid greedily over her when the three of them walked through town together that Sunday morning to St Thomas's Church.

After the service Uncle Jake and Aunt Gracie caught up with friends and news and gossip, Uncle Jake insisting before they left home that morning that he had "bragging rights about me niece and her posh new job".

Hazel knew she would have to say goodbye to walk back to the hall alone after Sunday tea instead of sleeping in her own bed that night and the thought made her feel tearful, so she wandered off behind the trees into the little field to the right of the church where the new church hall stood. Since it had been built the little square red building had been full of the women of the town sewing, knitting, rolling bandages and wrapping parcels for the front. On weekdays Market Street still rang with the sound of hammers coming from the room at the top of the staircase just inside the door that was soon be the new parish office. Hazel had never seen the inside of this upstairs room but loved its window shaped like a big half-moon lying on its side. To her it looked like a painting she had seen in a book once of a sun setting into the sea. She was looking up at it when she felt a hand slide into her coat pocket. Uncle Jake was standing behind her. "Doe look till you get back and doe tell your Aunt Gracie!" he said giving her his most sheepish of grins. As she walked away from the town that afternoon, she pulled from her pocket a white paper twist of Teddy Grays herbal sweets and a tiny blue glass mouse that she knew Uncle Jake must have made from waste offcuts during his break at the glassworks. Smiling to herself she popped a herbal in her mouth and headed back up the hill.

Hazel's walk took her past St Mary's Church, not far from Wychan Hall, which she knew the Miss Castles attended. Evensong had just finished, and the congregation was standing grouped in clusters saying their goodbyes. She spotted the elder Miss Castle with

206

Reverend Harris who she knew by sight from town. Standing with them was a man who was dressed like another vicar, but was the least vicarly looking person Hazel could imagine. He looked more like one of the local workers from the brickworks or the foundries. He was a big man, not overly tall but broad shouldered and muscular, so that his black clerical jacket looked strained across his upper arms and his dog collar looked strange and out of his place on his thick neck. Unlike most of the other men in the congregation he was clean shaven, which marked him out from the officers home on leave with their impressive moustaches. Reverend Harris was lean and spare and quietly spoken, his manner unobtrusive. The man next to him, even though of a similar height seemed to tower over him somehow. His bearing confident and solid, he seemed to fill the space in a more definite way than the older priest. He turned to speak to Miss Castle and Hazel was startled by the strange mark along the right side of his face, the red skin puckered and raw looking. When she was small Hazel's Uncle Albert, who worked at a saddlery over in Walsall, had made her a little brown dog patched together from offcuts of leather. She had carelessly left it pressed against the bars of the range and the patch where it had got too hot was covered in tiny, raised welts that never lay smooth again. The mark on this man looked very like that. Running from his hairline it ballooned out diagonally across his face, one side of it skirting the edge of his eyebrow, the other side his right ear, which was folded at the top as if melted. The mark then spread across his cheekbone, finishing in a point that

207

met the right side of his mouth where his lips parted. She could see white lines from it on the very edge of his full bottom lip as he spoke, like hairline cracks in pink porcelain. It looked like an uneven, upside-down raindrop made of shiny pinkish-red leather and she knew she was staring but she couldn't help it. She didn't know if it was the mark that made her think it, but there was something slightly foreboding about this man. The line between his nose and mouth was deeply etched, making him look petulant and sour, his nose hooked slightly over his top lip so that with his wide hooded eyes he seemed vaguely hawkish and intimidating. Those eyes though were very, very blue and with a shock that jolted her back to herself she realised they were looking into hers. It was like being stared at by the sky on a bright June day. She hastily looked at her feet, feeling that vile, hot reddening creeping up her neck and across her face. She had almost reached their little group now and had no choice but to keep walking towards them. Miss Castle noticed her and when she raised her hand in greeting the hawkish man bent his head and said something that made Miss Castle's expression change and she nodded slightly before calling over to Hazel.

'Ah, Hazel!' said Miss Castle. 'Did you have a pleasant Sunday with your aunt and uncle?'

Hazel tried only to see Miss Castle and not make eye contact with the strange vicar, 'Yes thank you, Miss Castle.'

'Well, I'm heading home too so we shall have the pleasure of walking together. I just have a small errand to run first. Come with me Hazel and I'll introduce you to an old friend. Good evening, Reverend Harris. It's been a pleasure to meet you Father Lewis, I hope we shall see more of each other.'

Miss Castle strode off in the opposite direction to the lane home, up the alley that ran alongside the west tower, Hazel walking slightly behind. Miss Castle took the staggered stone steps that led up to the churchyard slowly, they were narrow and uneven, worn away by hundreds of years of hundreds of pairs of parishioners' feet. At the top of the steps was a path lined with neatly trimmed yew trees on either side. Miss Castle turned left at the end of this yew walk and headed towards the largest tree Hazel had ever seen, standing off to one side, near the back of the church. It was tall, taller than the main church roof, but much lower than the tower with its higgledy piggledy spire, and at its base its thick trunk was vast and gnarled. Where the evening light was hitting its bark, it shone a reddish orange and seemed to glow with colour as if lit from within. Its branches began low down fanning out from a flat dip in the centre of its trunk and spreading like broad arms across the churchyard, casting shadows onto the wall of St Mary's, making the tree look like a priest about to bless its congregation of giants. One branch dipped lower than the rest sweeping just a few feet above the ground, level with Hazel's waist, and reaching much further than the others, like a hand extended in welcome. Miss Castle leaned her own gloved hand against the flat surface in the centre of the tree's trunk, "Isn't she glorious Hazel?" she said staring up into

209

its canopy where thick clusters of soft, deep green needles rose all the way to the top of its huge conical shape. 'This is The Lady Yew. I say hello to her every time I'm here.'

'She's enormous, Miss.'

Miss Castle smiled. 'That's because she's old. Very, very old indeed. This old girl has stood here as long as the church. Longer, possibly. Whenever one sees a yew tree of this size Hazel, it's usually the oldest thing in the landscape. She's seen kings crowned, parliaments toppled, wars won and lost – long before this one. I used to sit here,' she patted the lower, longer branch, 'just here, as a little girl and dream about what my life might be like when I grew up. That was almost fifty years ago and here she still is. Although I think my tree climbing days are now over.' She gave Hazel a broad smile, then said softly, 'Hazel, Father Lewis thinks his scar may have frightened you. Did it?'

Hazel could already feel herself blushing again. 'I'm sorry, Miss, I didn't mean to stare at him.'

'It's quite alright. I think he is used to curious stares. He was merely worried that it may have...disturbed you a little?'

'No, Miss. I just, it reminded me of something, a toy that I had, that I burnt accidently on the range.' The words felt fat and sluggish in her mouth and she knew she was explaining it badly. 'It was leather, my toy, a little leather dog that we called Bert, after my uncle who made it. He got all screwed up where the hot metal had been against him.' She had talked herself to a standstill and stood quietly, blushing and shame-faced.

210

'Well, I think Bert and Father Lewis have something in common and it was clever of you to spot it. Father Lewis is an army chaplain, Hazel. He was in France and got very badly burned while doing his duty to protect us. So, you see, that scar is nothing to be alarmed by. It's a mark of his bravery and it's certainly nothing for you to be worried about.'

'No, Miss. Is he... Is he alright now? The man. Father Lewis.'

Miss Castle smiled again and said gently, 'He's been very ill, Hazel. But he's recovering. That's why he's here. He was at the hospital at Studley Court.'

Studley Court was a huge house that sat between St Mary's and the town in its own landscaped grounds, far newer and grander than Wychan Hall, and had been turned into a VAD hospital for minor wounds. Initially it had been full of Belgian soldiers and their strange, foreign voices has brought a touch of continental exoticism to Stourbridge. Now it was filling up with British men.

'Reverend Harris thought it would aid his convalescence to help with the duties at St Mary's. In allowing him to help us, we are also helping him to get back on his feet. So, we'll being seeing a lot more of him and I think, because of that, he wanted to make sure you wouldn't be frightened when your paths crossed.'

'Oh, I'm not frightened, Miss. I think it makes his face more interesting. In a way. Like there's a story on it. If you know what I mean?'

Miss Castle eyed Hazel thoughtfully and said, 'Yes, yes, I think I do. Now – shall we head for home? And you can tell me how your aunt is getting along without you.'

**

Hazel began to settle into a routine and found that she was finishing her jobs more quickly as she learned how the Hall expected them to be done. Her reward for this was not just less blushing and less Aynoch, but more time to herself. One late afternoon after a rainy morning when the Miss Castles were out visiting, she asked Gwen if she could go down into the garden and take the path into the woods for half an hour before she helped Mrs Evesham with the evening meal.

'Go on then, Lil.' said Gwen. 'But you *had* better be back here in half an hour! And be sure to take the gardeners path round to the old birch, so you won't be seen from the house.'

Hazel took off her apron and after putting on her outdoor boots in the vestibule she all but ran across to the path that skirted the now empty greenhouses. As she turned the corner with the house behind her, she startled a mistle thrush, digging his beak into the soil for worms. The speckled brown bird cocked his head at her, before stalking angrily away for a few paces. He stopped, eyeing her warily, then, after a few seconds, opened his throat and sang. All at once the chill of the day was filled with early summer again as the song bounced off the walls and windows of the old house on the lane, warming them with the liquid sound of a late May evening. It warmed Hazel too and it was the happiest she'd felt since she'd arrived

212

there. At the old birch she stopped for a second, wondering which direction to take. Suddenly the whisper was there again. It was like a suggestion under the rustling of the leaves. A half-heard word that she couldn't quite catch. Thinking better of this decision to explore she was about to turn back when she thought she caught words in the whisper. 'Go right...'

'Right?' Hazel said to herself.

'Right, right, right,' the whisper replied.

Looking around her to make sure she was alone, Hazel turned right from the old birch and began to walk into the wood. It was dry in the garden but here the trees were still dripping so it felt like the rain hadn't yet ceased. The ground under her feet made a sucking sound as she walked, and she could feel stray leaves plastering themselves to her skirt as she lifted it out of the mud and the leaf litter. She wasn't far from the edge of The Hall's gardens when she spotted a clearing up ahead ringed by copper beeches and tangled brambles still studded with glistening blackberries. Suddenly it was as if the wind picked up and the leaves overhead were whirring with sound. Hazel could have sworn they were saying 'Here now, here now, here now.'

Up ahead she caught sight of something moving. She had put Uncle Jake's mouse on the ledge of the little triangular window above her bed because she liked looking at the way the sun made prisms in the glass. This looked like that, like refractions of light through glass. She assumed it was her eyes playing tricks, but something made her crouch down behind a hawthorn bush just

213

beginning its bloom of red berries, when, into the clearing came what looked like a huge clear glass globe. Easily the size of a sapling, it seemed to float a few inches above the ground, and something was falling within it. She thought it might be something burning, the falling things looked like bonfire ash as it swayed and turned in the heat. But as she watched, open mouthed, she realised that what it reminded her of most was the German snow globe that Peplow's jewellers put in their window every Christmas. It was snow. Huge, lazy, fat flakes of snow were falling inside this thing in the clearing, obscuring what looked like a figure within. The snow slowed and Hazel could just make out a woman. A tall, slim, elegant woman dressed in the same outfit that she'd seen women at the fox hunt and the racecourse wear. A dark, well-cut skirt and a red hunting jacket. Pinks, she remembered, feeling vague and lightheaded, they were called hunting pinks. The woman had her back to Hazel. She had deep red hair, cut short, shorter even than the king on the coin, and Hazel could clearly see its orange edges standing out spikily against the black collar of the red coat. The red-haired woman in the hunting habit turned and Hazel saw her face for the first time.

She wore a mask.

It was like the mask one of the Morris dancers sometimes wore at the Harvest Home dance in town. The woman wore the mask of a fox...but the eyes... In the Harvest Home dance, the eyes were painted onto the mask because the eyes of the Morris man who wore it could not be seen. Hazel leaned forward, trying to work out what art had made the eyes set into the woman's mask so very lifelike. So orange and vivid and amused. Suddenly Hazel found she wasn't crouching down anymore, she was sitting, scrabbling backwards on all fours, kicking up leaves and dirt and twigs. It wasn't a mask at all – this thing she took for a red-haired woman had the head of a fox. And it was looking right at her. The fox headed woman bowed slightly. Her hand came from beneath her riding habit and beckoned Hazel towards her.

Hazel didn't stop running until her hands were on the old birch. She gasped and she gasped but she couldn't seem to convince her lungs that the rest of her had stopped running.

Stitches

by

Laura Jane Round

Stitches: dress her up !

It started with the seam at the back of my thigh.

The keys fell from where they'd been clutched in my fingers. I was home; safe. In the quiet and the warm, away from wandering eyes and grabbing hands. Away from the cigarette smoke that made my lungs hurt and my never-empty in-tray. Sometimes I sat and wished for some of that dense rhetoric to catch light, just burn away until I had a lunchbreak I didn't have to spend indoors. Sometimes I just ate my apple and got on with things.

The radio crackled to life like it always did after a number of taps to its side. I resisted the urge to whack it – it was becoming more and more taps each try and I couldn't afford to buy a new one anytime soon.

"...the Baltimore Colts are certainly celebrating tonight, that's right, a 23-17 lead and a pho-"

I turned it off. All I'd heard that day was lyrical waxing about "the match that made 1958". There had been a smile on my face for hours that had drooped under reapplications of lipstick, had gradually waned with each breathless recounting of the moment Baltimore took the lead. The Boss was real excited, whirled Betty around like they were doing the Jitterbug – and not like those ones they do on American Bandstand. She didn't look too happy about it. The smile didn't reach her eyes.

There was a soft meow from the kitchenette.

'Callie?" I called out. I heard the tinkling of her sweet little bell as she jumped onto my lap, purring contentedly.

'Such a spoiled girl,' I cooed. I "cooed" at work, I supposed, but when I saw my cat looking up with

219

twitching whiskers, not wanting a coffee or notes taken or a smile because it might never happen, it always felt more genuine.

Callie mewed delicately, patting her paws on my skirt.

'You little minx! Don't you rip my stockings!' They cost a bomb.

She huffed, every inch the Princess, jumping off my lap in that springy, delicate way of hers. Her tail stuck high in the air as a final chop while she padded to my bedroom; though I knew she would change her mind all too soon when it was feeding time.

I flicked the catches, rolled my stockings down – another day at the office, more of the banter that came with the job, more unwarranted offers of a sherry and a ride home from the bar. And the cherry on top? My feet were aching. It was so nice to unfurl my bare toes against the thick carpet, free from shiny patent shoes.

It was when I tried to unknot the muscles in my tense thighs that I saw it.

Delicate, stitched. Black, my favourite, with the Cuban heel. Embedded in my skin like it had always been there, keeping me together yet pulling me apart with each thrum of my pulse, a tight pinch moving from baseline to the forefront of my mind. A cat scratch gone wrong? A bizarre hallucination?

I couldn't believe it. I had to have blanched, my nose scrunching up in that unattractive way of mine. Maybe someone had slipped something into my drink after all.

But after a glass of water, I fed the cat and I went to bed. I... didn't know what else to do. It was getting late. The Valium helped. Maybe, I'd thought, I was just seeing things.

**

I woke up the pitch black of my eyemask and my alarm going off. My skin was crawling, heaving with something at the thought of handing in those files to Mary in the typing pool (I'd have to burn rubber just to get ready for 5 'o' clock). Maybe it was the thought of the heaviness in my palms, my arms buckling under the strain. Maybe it was memories of the eyes that often followed me, the way I intentionally made a pendulum of my swaying hips, calves clenching in my work shoes, losing myself to the act more and more each time.

I had just twitched my calves, lost to the reimagining, when I felt that same sharp tug.

What...?

My hand flung out of its own accord, finally turning the damn alarm off. I pushed myself into a sitting position and stretched out my legs, and there – there it was, for all to see, in my tiny little apartment on 23rd. The seam had survived the night.

I turned to the mirror. I took a look at the bags under my eyes, how sallow I looked without powder or lipstick to bring out the green in my eyes. I thought about how many people were getting let go left and right, and how late I was going to be after an expensive trip to the hospital.

So, I prettied up. I pinned my hair up just so. I took a Valium. I smiled through the strange, disbelieving pain as I put my work shoes on and I headed out to my commute.

**

The train was packed, and the seam *itched*. I pulled at my skirt, trying to keep it straight, surreptitiously scratching at it with each façade of fussing. My eyes darted across the train carriage, looking for something to distract from it.

"Weight Loss Guaranteed!" and *"Keep Him Hot 'n' Heavy!"* yelled at me from advertisements across the way.

Some Joe Doe was sizing me up – I could feel his eyes burning a cigarette hole through my skirt and my girdle, reminding me of the sting of the seam. Maybe work had been a bad idea.

"Need some help with that bag?" Joe Doe had finally spoken up, it seemed. His coat and his gaze were heavy.

"I'll be fine, thanks," I said, trying to come across as cold, but that tug, that need to apologise, to be smaller and unobtrusive, made it come out as more inviting than I would've liked.

"Pretty heavy for a pretty gal like you," he murmured, thinking he was hip or something.

"I carry it every day, Mister," I said, wanting him desperately to ice it and leave me alone. The stitch flared up, making itself known again. I winced, shifting from foot to foot, almost toppling over with my bag of files I was woefully unprepared to be transporting – it was getting

222

closer to Christmas, and Mary was always telling us to pick up more of the slack.

I felt a hand at my waist. Not really putting pressure on me, just... holding me there. The stitch flared like I had jabbed my pen lid into it, and my knees nearly buckled.

"Easy there, gorgeous," Joe Doe's voice husked in my ear. I shivered despite myself, looking around the carriage again for help. Everyone avoided my eyes. A balding man in glasses hid himself in his newspaper.

His hand seemed to burn me. I knew I should start yelling, make a scene, be some no-nonsense broad that stood up for herself. But I thought about shrill gals on TV and the way guys complained about them outside meetings.

So, I pulled away. I hefted my bag closer into my arms. I smiled at the Joe Doe, feeling like some odd kind of sagging puppet, and got off at my stop, same as every Wednesday.

**

Two days later and two seams. One for each leg. I felt the stitches pull tight as I traversed the corridor, looking for Mister Sa- Jason. He'd asked me to call him Jason. And you can't really say no to the Boss like that, not with people being let go left and right. It was getting harder and harder to walk in heels. I'd take a cab home that night, I resolved. In the end, he bumped into me.

'Oh, oh, I'm so sorry,' I simpered – why did I simper? – disentangling myself.

223

'Fine by me,' he said with a grin. Boardroom shark, he was. So many teeth. They were good teeth, but... so many.

'I've got some reports typed up to send down to HR, if you don't mind just signing –'

'–You're just a busy bee, aren't you, gorgeous?'

A hand. A hand on my shoulder; just like that, slicing through propriety like fingers through water. I cleared my throat, feeling the stitches pull tight. I felt something pull at my shoulder with dawning horror – no, no it couldn't be spreading...

'We need more of that around here,' he went on to say, not seeming to notice my state, '*I* need more of that around here.'

I thought of what this could mean for my career – I thought of how hard it was to keep the heating on over Christmas, keep Callie on the good cat food.

I thought of my mother, scrubbing the carpets 'til they seemed to gleam, chained to a stove and a dinosaur for a husband.

I thought of snatching Jason's hand off my stinging shoulder and really digging my fingernails into those indulgent eyes.

'City never sleeps, Sir – oh, I'm so sorry. *Jason*,' I said with what I hoped was a bright, winning smile.

He showed his teeth.

**

Callie heard me crying in the bedroom.

It felt like I couldn't breathe for crying – it was a brassiere line this time, stitched in black and reddening my

224

skin, pulling me tight like Frankenstein's Bride with each choking, unspooling breath. My hair was unpinned due to habit, tendrils sticky with tears. I kept my girdle on. I couldn't bear to see if there were other stitches forming.

I winced at the scrabbling at the door, before it was finally batted open.

'Callie, s-sweet girl... Now's really not the time,' I managed, sniffling. She meowed, winding her way through my legs. I felt fur brush against the first damn stitches that started this, the stocking seams, and –

- I let out a wounded sound. 'Callie, Callie, I'm going mad –'

Another meow. I should have known better, it was feeding time, my poor, sweet girl was hungry and here I was, crying like a loon. I bent down, trying not to wince, scratching her behind the ears. She was so warm, so soft and ordinary.

I needed to see a doctor but I didn't want cold, clinical hands touching me. I didn't want any man touching me ever again but it seemed to be happening more than ever and it was *my fault, my fault –*

I suppressed another sob, wiping my eyes hastily. My hand came back black and I panicked for a moment, thinking the affliction had spread – but it was just my makeup.

"Revlon Cold Cream will send you off to sleep with a smile! Never go to bed in bothersome makeup that ages the skin ever again!"

I shook my head, trying to get the advertisement out of my head. It hurt too much to think about going to

225

the clinic, being labelled "crazy", taking my underthings off in front of a stranger.

Callie batted her head against my hand. I reached for the cold cream.

**

I couldn't breathe, *I couldn't breathe*, it was pulling me tighter and tighter and it felt like something inside was ready to give –

'-In here, gorgeous.'

Well, at least that took away the agonising decision of whether to knock on the Boss' door or not. He was standing up at his desk, eyes red like he'd been drinking. I forced another pink-tint smile and walked forward, faintly vibrating with the need to escape. I was in this office fairly often to drop things off while he was in meetings, but with his presence filling it, it felt suffocating.

'Just who I wanted to see,' he said, grin widening. 'Set down that coffee, would'ya?'

Oh, right. The coffee. I set it down with shaking fingers, nearly bolting when he grabbed my wrist.

'There's a spot opening up away from the typing pool.'

'I'm not in the typing pool Sir,' I couldn't help but say despite myself.

'Please... Jason.'

He stepped ever closer. I felt the stitches pull tight. They'd spread to... well, everywhere.

'Jason, I –'

226

'Now, you might not know it, but you're a pretty girl. I've seen you flitting about the office with Mary's hot pieces. Those shiny shoes...'

I felt revulsion swell up inside me like I'd never known before because this is what I had come to? This is how I was going to get a job? *Not like this,* I wanted to scream. *Not like this.* I remained silent, like some limp doll; Jason's perfect marionette.

'I think you're a hot ticket.' His breath was hot in my ear. 'How'd you like to be more up close and personal with your Boss?'

'Please, please don't –'

I felt him grab me, lift me like it was nothing, like I was nothing.

That's when it happened.

I came apart.

I heard his scream before I understood what was happening, the core of my rage burning whiter and whiter, whiter than my mother's carpet, whiter than my bones peeking out through my angry, red flesh. My skin, powder and cold cream and pink-tint lips, peeled to the floor like the farce it was, and I felt him slip and slide, struggling to get away from the wetness, the hot mess of my blood.

I felt the shrillness inside me. I would be his shrew. *'Touch me now,'* I said, before my jaw hit the floor with a slap, and then I was just *screaming*, blouse soaked with myself, flesh floating in the ruins of my shiny patent shoes.

He was on the floor before I even had a chance to leave his office.

227

I smeared blood throughout the corridors, still screaming, I saw the boys in their offices vomiting and shaking and going delightful shades of purple and green and I saw the girls covering their shadowed eyes and rosy mouths, hands like a slap of powder, hair previously coiffed now rinsed with sweat, I saw the apple on my desk and the raised marks where Jason touched Betty doing the Jitterbug –

– And stitches. I saw stitches.

Lucky Lucy Lu

by

Steven G. Davis

'Her name was Lucky. I knew she was Lucky the moment she walked into my office. I hadn't had an office until she'd walked in ...'

Wizerbowski looked up and smiled knowingly. The door opened, and in the doorway stood Lucky.

Lucky was about five foot six, beautiful, and out of her depth. Her hair was neatly – freshly – coiffured, falling in layered straight lines past her shoulders. She was wearing a long, bright pink, silk dress which pinched in her waist and accentuated her bust; matching opera gloves. Her lipstick was too bright; too forceful, but the earrings and matching necklace she wore – pink sapphire – were a subtler shade and all the more expensive for it.

She removed her tinted, round, tortoiseshell glasses, frowning slightly. 'I'm sorry.' She appeared flustered. 'You said something?' Her eyes were a deep turquoise blue.

Wizerbowski grinned, shaking his head. 'Welcome to Wizerbowski Investigations. How may I be of assistance?'

She frowned again, turning her glasses in her hands.

'Do you know – who I am?' she asked hurriedly, quietly.

He nodded. 'They call you Lucky. The King's Moll. A woman not to be denied anything.'

Lucky grimaced. 'That's me. Look, Wiser –'

'Wizerbowski. The name's on the door.'

She gave him a look. Despite the King's reputation, despite *her* reputation, this woman was no airhead, no brain-dead bimbo taken on for her looks; taken on because a man in power liked corrupting a beautiful innocent.

'Were you listening to me?'

Wizerbowski raised his hands in apology. 'My pardon, Miss Lucky. Your reputation precedes you.'

Lucky raised an eyebrow. 'I haven't time for games, Mister Wizerbowski. I need your help.'

Wizerbowski stared, as anyone asked for help by the attractive, slightly aloof, King's Moll would do. 'I am just a poor black man,' Wizerbowski swallowed the words distastefully, 'Miss Lucky, running a poor man's investigation service. I don't know how I can help you, but if I can help you, why, surely I will.'

For a moment she gave him another *look*.

'I wish to hire your services exclusively.'

Wizerbowski stared. 'And how can I assist, Miss Lucky?'

She narrowed her gaze. 'You're not stupid, are you?'

Wizerbowski matched her gaze. She was very attractive, the epitome of a doll, made up possibly more for the desires of her man that her own pleasure, but a fine, glittering intelligence peaked through the look. A glittering intelligence that was desperate.

He straightened up, grinning, baring his teeth. 'I'm not, no.'

'Good,' she sighed, relaxing. 'I've had enough. I want out.'

Wizerbowski stared. 'No one escapes the King's – clutches.'

Lucky made a face. 'His clutches aren't what they once were. But I find –' she swallowed anxiously.

'You want out?'

She nodded. 'His – attentions. Interests.' She grimaced. 'I've seen him eyeing up younger women, dancers.'

Wizerbowski nodded. 'I always thought one woman would never be enough for him.'

Lucky nodded. 'I do not just want to get – out. I want to bring him down.'

Wizerbowski raised an eyebrow. 'That's a very risky thing to attempt. And to talk to just anyone about.'

'But you're not just anyone, are you?' She chuckled. 'I'm not *just* a pretty face and body for the King. You've only just moved to this town. No history anywhere else. A furnished office, in a part of town that won't attract any attention. No gun licence, but I see the bulge in your jacket. Who – *exactly* – are you, Wizerbowski?'

He chuckled. 'I am the one who might get you away from – everything. What is your specific predicament; what do you have planned?'

Lucky grinned. She dipped her fingers into the bodice of her dress and removed a ruby ring and two rings of pink sapphire.

Wizerbowski raised an eyebrow.

Lucky handed them over.

'If King asks, I am having them polished.'

'And really?'

233

'I want you to have replicas made. They need to be perfect fakes.'

Wizerbowski nodded. 'I can do that. Payment?'

Lucky almost grinned. 'If I like the replicas, if they are convincing, you can have the originals.'

He grinned. 'And what is your dastardly plan for revenge and escape?'

She shook her head. 'Not yet. I am still – planning.'

Wizerbowski grinned. 'Of course. I can get – fakes. When will you be back for them?'

'One week.' Lucky put her glasses back on.

Wizerbowski nodded. 'No problem. I'll see you in a week.'

She nodded and turned on her high heels; strode out. Wizerbowski waited until the sound of her echoing footsteps had died away before locking the outer door and going through to the inner office.

Sunlight slanted in through the dusty window. He closed and locked the door softly. The office was all but empty, some fake apparatus, period specific, in cardboard boxes. He crossed to the window and drew his sleeve up.

**

Wizerbowski looked up in surprise at the knock on the door. He unbuttoned his jacket and eased the Impossible Pistol free. He glanced around as he trod softly for the main door. The office looked realistic; the rain thundered down outside, drowning almost all sounds.

A hunched shadow showed through the outer door. He'd changed the bulb in the corridor, making it brighter – brighter than possible, for the era, anyway.

234

'Who's there?'

'Wizer – bowski.'

He hurried to the door. Yanked it open. Lucky all but fell into the office, a trail of damp footsteps leading along the hallway. He shut and locked the door; spun round, returning the pistol to its holster.

Lucky was leaning against his desk, breathing heavily, clad in a heavy, sodden fur.

'Lucky?'

She turned to look at him, grimacing, heaving.

'Why the even-larger shades?'

The fur was sodden through; she looked bedraggled, her makeup – wrong.

He eased the fur coat from her shoulders; took it and hung it from the coat hook.

'Lucky?'

She took her glasses off, wincing. Her left eye was blacked; swollen shut and her lips were puffy. She was wearing a red dress with a buttoned-up neckpiece. Unlike the previous dress, which seemed to have been chosen to show off her looks, this dress was positively demure.

'My god, Lucky, what did he do?'

'Do you have the rings?'

He nodded. 'Of course. Originals and fakes.'

'Give me the originals.'

Wizerbowski drew out both sets. 'Tell me what he did.'

She sighed. Unbuttoned the collar of her dress and pulled it open. There were bruises at the base of her neck. Bruises – worse – on the top of her chest.

'How far – what – why –'

'He,' she almost sobbed. 'He didn't like I'd taken the rings to be polished. He thought,' she gasped and swallowed awkwardly again.

'How badly did he hurt you?'

Lucky grimaced. 'King's got a ring, on his middle finger. It's got an emblem of a crown.' She scowled. 'He thinks he's some sort of royalty.' She grimaced. 'I bear his mark. My body bears his mark.'

She fell silent.

Wizerbowski fetched her a glass of water. She took a sip.

'I'm to take the rings back to show him today. If he's not satisfied,' she grimaced.

'I can take you away from this, Lucky. He will never find you again. Once you're safe –'

She looked up at him and shook his head. 'No. I'll go to him tonight. Wear the rings. Do whatever I need to do to keep him happy.'

Wizerbowski grimaced. 'If he hurts you again –'

'If I flee, he will find me. Then it really will hurt.' Lucky scowled. 'He would probably kill me if I fled.' She sighed. 'He has a temper, but he will forget. A night of – *passion* – and all will be better in his mind.' She shuddered.

'You don't have to –'

'I need him to forget. I need him to think – whatever it was – is over. He will relax his guard. Then,' she grinned, lopsidedly, '*then* I'll get him.'

**

236

Wizerbowski waited. The rain stopped late afternoon. Traffic sounds got louder with their equivalent of a rush hour, but faded out soon enough again. The sky remained bright for a long time before dusk made an appearance.

He leant back in his chair, feet on the desk, both the pistols in his lap.

To what degree, he wondered, had King made Lucky? Circumstances had probably lifted her, but then she knew her own mind. Would have – well. It was not his time; a woman was expected to be an attractive accompaniment, rather than capable in her own right.

King is probably of no import. *Almost* probably of no import. If he turns up – Wizerbowski grinned. If he turns up things will draw to a resolution so much quicker and simpler. *Unless* I don't. She – Lucky – would prefer to take her own action. Killing him would rob her of that, though it would keep her safe.

The building quietened as he chased his thoughts.

Killing, he realised after a while. How easily I say the word now.

He grinned sourly. The worlds are ending and things are not as they were. The old ways are crumbling. He chuckled to himself. Or they neverexisted.

He heard sounds. The stealthy attempts – the attempts at stealthy – of two hoodlums, come to break into his office. He'd left both doors unlocked. Let them come. He grinned.

He heard them cautiously investigate the outer door. Heard it swing open silently.

Wizerbowski smiled.

237

Heard them cross the outer office. Heard them crouch before his door, trying to figure out if he was in or to break the door down and hope no one heard.

He considered simply shooting them. Shooting through glass was less than perfect, but might be sufficient. Still. He'd have to replace the glass. That was a minor issue he couldn't be bothering with.

The door slid open –

'Please step inside, close the door behind you and keep your hands away from guns.'

He lifted both pistols. The hoodlums were frozen, clear in the open doorway.

'I've been sitting in the dark for quite some time. I can see you clearly. Mr King has sent you to have words, no doubt.'

One of the men snorted. The other humphed.

'Well?' he asked, cocking a pistol to make a point.

'He don't like no black men. You didn't pay no respects to him.'

Wizerbowski chuckled. 'Ah, the famous welcoming nature of this city. Please, come in, come in.'

He sat up straight, putting one of the pistols on the table and flicking the lights on.

The two men were typical thugs; brutish in appearance, slightly vacuous of gaze, used to receiving orders and not to thinking for themselves.

'So. Does Mr King treat you well?'

One of them scowled.

The other shook his head. 'We're here to teach you a lesson. Lucky was here; he doesn't like the thought of Lucky having to look at a black man. So we're to convince you to leave. Less no one might see you again.'

The man sniggered.

'Thank you for your offer.' Wizerbowski inclined his head without taking his eyes off them. 'I think, perhaps, both of your parents might be better off if neither of you had ever been born.'

'Here,' began one.

Wizerbowski shot him.

The other thug frowned. 'Here,' he protested.

Wizerbowski waved his pistol. 'I don't think it was a clever idea of Mister King to send just one of his men, do you?'

The thug shook his head, confused.

'He said,' he trailed off.

'Marvellous technology this,' Wizerbowski smiled, lifting the pistol. 'An Impossible Pistol. Never misses. When I add alien technology to it, such as the neverexistence –'

'Here,' the thug frowned. 'You're talking gibberish. You a Jew?'

Wizerbowski rolled his eyes. Shot the man.

**

About a week later – and three attempts later – the outer door opened and Lucky strode in. Her hair was piled up in an elaborate style and she stood taller; higher heels. Her face was pale, but that was makeup; her eyes sparkled the way they hadn't at the last meeting.

Wizerbowski smiled. 'Lucky –'

She shrugged the fur coat she was wearing off. The whiteness of her face was matched by the whiteness of her shoulders, arms and upper chest. The dress pinched her waist tightly; managed to leave some of her bust to the imagination. She wore three necklaces, one of pure pink sapphire stones. The second was of small rubies and emeralds. She drew the third chain up from where it nestled, revealing a large ruby stone that glittered brightly.

'King liked me being –' she grimaced. 'Contrite.' She tucked the ruby back into her cleavage. 'He's dressing me up like a trophy.' She shook her head. 'Look at this,' she gestured at her chest, ruby and sapphire rings glittering on her fingers. 'I'm practically falling out of it.' She scowled. 'I am woman: look at my chest.' She shuddered.

'What is he planning?'

Lucky frowned. 'A party. He's – he's getting edgy. Keeps thinking he doesn't have enough men. He's getting,' she narrowed her gaze. 'He doesn't like you being in his city. But I don't think he's doing anything about it.'

Wizerbowski laughed. 'He is. Well.' He sniggered. 'He's trying.'

She frowned. 'Tell me.'

'He's made four attempts so far. Sent four sets of his goons round.'

'And?'

'And,' he grinned. 'I persuaded them all to be elsewhere. Permanently.'

Lucky frowned. 'I'm sure – I used to know quite a few of his men. Those I'm seeing at the moment,' she shook her head. 'I don't recognise any of them.'

Wizerbowski nodded. 'What are you planning to do during this party?'

Lucky smiled. 'His lieutenants will be in the crowd, as will all the security; his enforcers. I just need you to make a distraction.'

Wizerbowski raised an eyebrow.

'I got the code to his safe. It's where he keeps ledgers, records, all the proof I need.'

'What does his – racket – include?'

Lucky snorted. 'Prostitution. Child labour. Drugs. Murder, I'm sure. Smuggling. Protection funds, both business and personal.'

'How will you get it out? In an outfit like that –'

She scowled. 'I'll be the distraction. You'll have to get them out.'

Wizerbowski shook his head. 'You want me to be the distraction so you can slip inside his office, and then blend into the background and have no security keep an eye on me? Too chancy.'

'It's the best chance I've got. Some of it can go to the Police. I'll keep enough to stop him sending anyone after me. It has to work.'

Wizerbowski grinned. 'When's the party? I have an idea.'

'Next Saturday. He's invited half the city, including some who are sort-of rivals.'

Wizerbowski frowned. 'How many rivals?'

Lucky shook her head. 'They're not rivals. They could be. Free-lancers. People who think they'd be better off without him. If the party goes off without a fight –'

'That might be the intention. A big party –'

If King is playing Lucky. He gave her the code; even drunk, insensate, it could be a trap. Have a brawl break out; in the kerfuffle, if anything happened to Lucky; everyone will have seen how she's draped in his presents. He'd be heartbroken and beyond suspicion. And Lucky'd be dead.

'Have you considered it could be a trap?'

She rolled her eyes. 'Yes.' She shuddered. 'I can't go on – pretending. Doing things to keep him distracted. He'll hit me too hard one time. Have his eye caught too deeply by someone younger. This is my last chance. Get out, clean him out and make sure he can't come after me.'

Wizerbowski nodded slowly. 'Okay. We need to even our chances a little ...'

**

'I hate this,' Lucky smiled but it didn't reach her eyes. King had dressed her in a soft-pink taffeta dress – all ruffles and pleats and big skirt – that covered even less of her bust than the previous dress. Her hair had been freshly made up and she was wearing a tiara of white diamonds; a matching necklace.

'The corset is killing me,' she hissed, 'he had fun forcing me into it. I daren't bend over. I can hardly breathe. And the bow –'

She turned enough, as if turning away from him, for him to see the big sash at the back. Her arms, shoulders and half her back was completely bare.

'You're his trophy, Lucky.'

She grimaced. 'I don't think I can leave his side, Wizerbowski. He's got someone with him, someone he's impressing, from out of the city.' She slipped him a piece of paper. 'I'll keep him – distracted though.'

The speakeasy heaved. A jazz band played at one end, wild and uproarious, and a large group of people jived and danced wildly to their music. A vocal group performed at the other end of the dance hall and people danced, slightly more stately. Waitresses circulated with trays full of glasses of champagne; waiters circulated with trays of cigarettes and other pleasures.

Wizerbowski sipped at his whiskey. It was nothing on a rave, but it was on a similar track. The air stunk of drugs and alcohol, with faint overtones of overcooked meat and bile. Couples danced and single men pawed at single women or the waitresses; he saw more than one waitress almost pulled off her feet.

But that wasn't all. He'd spotted King's muscle easily enough, scattered about, but there were other figures as well, moving through the crowds randomly, trying to avoid detection, but definitely not dancers or partygoers. Dressed in sharp black suits, keeping hands close to their sides.

Whose muscle they were was another matter.

Gang war or is King extending his territory? Is it all a performance, to cover Lucky's murder?

He dismissed that. King could simply make her disappear. This is all very – open.

He took another sip, shifting his gaze here and there, trying to blend in, trying to appear only interested in the music and the dancing.

He watched obliquely as Lucky approached King. He was sat in the middle of a big semi-circular leather couch, bodyguards and muscle surrounding him. The man to his right was different, however; a suit. Someone from out of town. King beckoned to Lucky: she jumped up, kneeling on either side of him, straddling him.

Effortlessly he pushed her off, almost manhandling her onto the lap of the suit on his right.

She tried to pull away; he watched as King spoke to the man; the suit pulled her closer, his hands in the bow: Lucky stopped trying to pull away.

Wizerbowski finished his whiskey and headed for the loos. They were down a separate corridor; the door to the office was just beyond. Without looking he noticed one of the security team peeling off after him.

He slipped inside the loos; went into a cubicle and closed, bolted, the door.

A moment later the outer door opened.

'You ain't wanted here, boy. Can't you tell that? You types are all the same, you're –'

Wizerbowski shot him through the door. Heard the wood fragments hit the floor. Unlocked the cubicle and came out. There was scattered debris; evidence of a shot being fired through the toilet door, but neither bullet nor corpse.

He grinned.

Left the loos and headed on down to the office. Stupidly, there was no security guarding it. He picked the lock in seconds and slipped inside.

Stopped. Two security guards stood against the wall, guns aimed at him. King sat in the chair at the desk, smoking a pipe.

'So. You're the one that Lucky reeled in to help her crazy schemes.' He shook his head, grinning. 'Stupid bint thinks one blow job and I'll give her the code number to the safe.' He chuckled. 'Care for Lucky, do you?'

Wizerbowski didn't answer.

'I'm thinking I'll give her to the out-of-towner. A nice gift. He'll have her goodies out of their wrapping by now.'

He paused. Blew a smoke ring. Leant back in his chair. 'And don't get any fancy ideas about those clever guns of yours. Hand them over – slowly and carefully.'

Wizerbowski didn't move.

'O ho, she sold you out, boy. It was her idea to make it look like I'd smacked her around. She punched herself in the mouth several times. I had to punch her in the face. And elsewhere. That weren't as much fun as I thought it'd be.'

Wizerbowski stared.

'You've got two of them, boy. One finger. Lift the one from your right pocket – slowly.'

Wizerbowski did as was instructed. The pistol was larger than standard; silver and black, sleek.

'So how do the slugs work then?'

He shook his head. 'No slugs. Vodun power.'

King arched an eyebrow. 'Say what now?'

'Magic. Voodoo.'

He shook his head. 'Superstitious nonsense! You take me for a hick, boy! City dweller though I am; you, with your fancy accent.'

Wizerbowski pulled a half smile. 'There is more in this universe, Horatio,' he began.

King rolled his eyes. 'Who's Horatio now? Some other Britisher, clowning around over here?'

He grinned. 'Oh, no. I'm not British, sirrah. I'm Polish.'

'Polish?'

Wizerbowski nodded. 'Yes, sirrah. My folks came over after the war. You know – actually, no, wait.' He grinned. 'You don't know. It hasn't happened yet.'

King frowned at him. The two guards looked confused.

He sighed. 'So. Lucky was lucky for you. She sure tricked me.'

King grinned. 'Yeah, she's got a good mind on her. Good rack too; that's a handy distraction.'

'You'd be wanting the second pistol?'

King held out his hand impatiently.

Wizerbowski removed it carefully. 'If I'd got in the safe would there even have been anything in there?'

King laughed. 'Empty. Lucky's own suggestion. Have a safe. Hide it, but make it obvious. Talk about it. Mention it to security. Let people know where it is. See, that's where they look then, that's what they concentrate on; where they try and break into.'

'And if anyone succeeded –'

King sniggered. 'A little tweak of mine; it's a real safe. The grenade's a brand new thing as well. Very few of them on the market, very hard to get hold of. Opening the door, well.' He took a puff on his pipe. 'Pulls the pin. The safe's full of nails and spikes; metal things. Things that, with explosive force behind them,' he took another puff.

Wizerbowski sighed. 'I guess this is the end, then. You get rid of me. You send Lucky away with that other man – who was he?'

King laughed. 'I'm moving up to the Big Leagues. An envoy from the Eyeties. The maf*iosa*. The entertainment's for him; you're the entertainment.'

Wizerbowski raised an eyebrow. 'You got me totally. Is there even any proof, or was all that a ruse?'

King snorted. 'Not even I'm that dumb, boy. Proof of dodgy doings? Yeah, I'll just leave them lying around.' He shook his head. 'I thought you guys were smarter than that.' He nodded to one of his guards. 'Go fetch him. Our guest can decide what to do with our *other* guest.'

The guard passed him. Wizerbowski relaxed, keeping his face a blank mask.

Minutes passed.

'Do you think your guest knows to come in here?'

King looked up, angrily. 'Go find,' he glanced at the only security guard, 'our guest.'

Wizerbowski smiled absently as the guard passed him.

247

It was pleasant having a conversation with King. To have no security with him though, that was foolish he thought, even as he knew that wasn't true. *Had* been true, but no longer was. Security that neverexisted.

There was a knock on the door; King called out admittance.

The door opened and the *Mafia* gentleman entered, followed by Lucky.

'What's she doing here –' King began.

The Mafia man smiled, moving a strand of mousy brown hair from his eyes. 'She's with me.'

King leered. 'Had a good feel up of her assets, have you?'

'On the contrary,' said Lucky, drawing an Impossible Pistol, 'I almost punched him in the face.'

Wizerbowski struggled to keep the grin off his face as he looked at King. 'The only real question remaining, King, is what Lucky wants to do now.'

'What do you mean?' Lucky asked, finger on the trigger.

'I mean, you could take over King's empire, if you wanted to. Prostitution; smuggling; enforcement.'

She snorted. 'We shot an awful lot of King's men. A few others, as well. Besides,' she shook her head. 'It's not my empire, and it's a sordid, disgusting, thing.'

King growled in anger, going to rise.

The Mafia man drew an Impossible Pistol and pointed it at King.

'I suggest you keep very still,' Wizerbowski grinned. 'So, if we leave it be, someone will take over his territory.'

Lucky shrugged. 'Could clear everyone out; burn the building down.'

Wizerbowski shrugged. 'That'd confuse the hell out of everyone. King disappeared; Lucky disappeared; the club burned down, but no bodies.'

'You're not gonna –' King began.

The Mafia man chuckled. 'The world is changing, King. Ending. We are standing on the edge. The edge of time.' He smirked. 'You'll never get *that* reference.'

'Time to count the stars,' Wizerbowski said softly.

Lucky frowned. 'Will someone please explain.'

Wizerbowski chuckled. 'Of course. You see, there is another option for you, should you wish it, Miss Lucky.'

'Bi. I'm Lucky Bi.'

'Miss Bi.' Wizerbowski inclined his head. 'You hold a weapon of alien technology in your hand.'

'You've come from outer space?' she lifted her head, as if to look through the ceilings and floors and walls and all the way out to the night sky.

'No,' the Mafia man smiled. 'Other worlds. Other versions of this one. And they're all – slowly – dying. Collapsing.'

'That's – um. Cheery.'

Wizerbowski smiled. 'This is the count down to the apocalypse, Miss Bi.'

'Lu Bi. Call me Lu Bi.'

'Lu Bi.' He grinned. 'Do you want to make a difference?'

'In what way?'

Wizerbowski grinned. 'There's a bookshop. In England. A hundred-odd years from now.'

Lu Bi turned and stared at him. 'You're mad!'

King went to move but the Mafia man waved his pistol; King sunk back into his chair. The Mafia man retrieved Wizerbowski's pistols and handed them to him.

'Thank you. You could stay here; I'm sure we could find enough cash for you to have a happy existence. Or you could join us.'

'One hundred years from now?'

Wizerbowski nodded. 'You knew I was not who I pretended to be. You're very smart. We could use someone like you, Lu Bi.'

'Who?'

'Once,' the Mafia man spoke, 'we were the Hashishim.'

'The who-now?'

'Hashishim.' Wizerbowski smiled. 'But my colleague is right. We no longer are the Hashishim, not since I neverexisted the man who thought he was in charge.'

Lu Bi stared blankly at him.

Wizerbowski smiled. 'It is an adventure. You will be your own boss; can wear whatever you want. All we need do is travel to England, to the bookshop, and then,' he grinned.

The non-Mafia man chuckled. 'An opportunity to do the right thing, Lu Bi. An opportunity to hold off – perhaps – Armageddon.'

She shook her head. 'Armageddon and other worlds. This is – too strange.'

Wizerbowski nodded. 'It is strange. However, if we could prove that you hold alien technology, would that be enough for you to consider – an adventure?'

Lu Bi looked at the gun she held. 'I always liked looking at the stars as a child.'

Wizerbowski nodded. 'You hold an Impossible Pistol. If you were to shoot someone, they would simply – never exist. They would not die; they would never have been born.'

Lu Bi looked at King. 'The lives he's hurt. The damage he's caused. 'What about his – empire?'

'Someone else would have built it up. Or it would not have been. History – the time lines – they will wobble and bump; reassert themselves. If you shoot him, only you will remember him. To us, the name King will be meaningless.'

'You guys have a king, right?'

The non-Mafia man nodded. 'In this time, your time, yes.'

Lu Bi shook her head. 'Strange.' She shrugged. 'Still, I've always wanted to kill a king.'

She lifted the gun and fired.

A Reputable Bookshop

by

C. H. Randle

Dear Clarke,

Thank you for sending me your short story about your travels. I agree that this is the right tone for our book. Ytene sounds lovely, and I hope to visit it someday.

My only concern is people who have never met Rangi will not know he is a doctor and O'Malley is the head psychiatrist at the Hospital at the Centre of the Universe. Also, Merciful Grace is a steam-powered sentient machine and your guardian. Bob is her sentient robot companion, and both are ardent sentient machine activists.

You'll need to put in a prologue explaining this. I don't think we need to explain about Delia. I am truly sorry that Delia had to die, and her passing will haunt me for the rest of my life. I have sent your story back with minor corrections, it passes a sensitivity reading and yes, your story is ready for publication.

Yours sincerely

Aroha Tuwhare.

Reputable bookshops by C Clarkson.

The conversation lasted nanoseconds and spanned multiverses. The latest Bob and Merciful Grace were stock still on the porch of Bob's little love shack. They seemed to be watching the sunset. The only movement was Merciful Grace's thumb ring which was continually rotating on her left-hand digit.

'Clarke is not optimal,' thought Merciful Grace.

'Breaker of hearts, he is grieving within parameters. He is passing all the developmental markers at the correct pace and time,' thought Bob.

Merciful Grace reviewed the data Bob had sent over to her. He was as usual correct. The next marker was optimal, and she could be useful to Clarke if she acted on it.

'Well-meaning intervention by your support group. We are part of his support group are we not?' she thought.

'Yes, although he may want humans, or at the very least organics,' thought Bob.

Merciful took a sip of water and let off a shush of steam. Bob was correct again.

'I propose we include Clarke in our latest venture. He can help us find a number of reputable bookshops.'

'May I remind you, breaker of hearts, you originally said reputable and disreputable. If Clarke goes out into the Somewhen and has a negative 'adventure', his recovery may regress another earth year.'

'Yes agreed. Does the data support my

proposal?' thought Merciful Grace.

Both machines sat silent. A small palomino pony ambled over. It glared at the pair on the veranda and headed purposefully over to a small white polytunnel. Merciful Grace got up from her seat and walked toward the animal. The tiny horse reached forward to take a bite out of the tunnel's polythene. She picked it up before it connected and put it back in the corral. The pony screamed in protest. Merciful Grace screamed back. The pony kicked up its heels and trotted off toward a hay bale. The steam-powered machine walked over to the broken gate. Bob walked up and started his repairs.

'An excellent enrichment exercise. Asimov has tried to find out what is under the polytunnel for several months,' thought Bob.

'Yes, I now have several new stallion swear words to add to my vocabulary,' noted Merciful Grace.

'Dearest, according to my data, IF we plan our path, keeping to reputable bookshops, it will aid Clarke's recovery. However, there is a 25% chance of deviation.'

Merciful Grace processed. Asimov came over and butted the new gate, which held.

'I contacted the pirate ship of grumpy old women and SENDA. They can extract us from 99.9% of the deviations.'

'I can ask my cousins. However, it could take up to a whole hour to get a reply.'

'While we wait, you could input the route suggested by his therapist. We can plan for obvious problems.'

257

'Shall we take our evening constitutional? I would like to see if Asimov is capable of spending a night in the wild.'

'He may not return, Bob,' warned Merciful Grace.

'Then I shall wave when I see his herd go by. I have faith he will, you did.' Bob leaned forward and a spark passed between the robot and the mechanical maid.

The metal pair walked as far as the first mesa. Bob wanted to look at the caves.

'Asimov may follow my scent and this is an excellent place for a pony to shelter.'

On their return, the corral was empty, the two mares and Asimov had left.

'Bob you are very fond of your miniature horses, why release them?'

'Our communication with the Ketch showed me that animals do not thrive in captivity. We did not. I would like to have a more equitable relationship with my ungulates. I also told Waya, and he told the rest of the Hohokum tribe to avoid Asimov. For two seasons, enough to establish a herd.'

'You could continue our ruse and say the horses were ghosts or demons.'

'Soon Wild Bill Hickok or this parallel equivalent may pass through. Stories of demon horses would bring the curious and the hunters. Better they are known only by a few who care.'

'This is similar to Clarke. We care about him, but he needs to be released from his grief for a while.'

'Yes, my brothers...my cousins returned a group

agreement. Once prepared, we can leave.'

The machines tested and replaced defective parts. They also stocked a rucksack of more parts they might need. Not all planets were capable of fixing sentient machines. They loaded the proposed map into their brains and three tablets. One each and a spare in the rucksack. Bob locked up the shack and left some extra hay in the barn for Asimov's herd.

Merciful Grace waited for Bob on the porch. She had changed her clothes. Usually, she wore her trademark indigo maids dress with a white starched apron. Now Merciful wore a pair of blue and white striped cargo pants with lace on the trouser ends. She also wore a waistcoat with a lot of pockets, a jaunty red cotton neckerchief and a black barge cap with white pinstripes. She had a knitted poppy and a knitted bluebell pinned to the hat.

'A new travel outfit. The question is, are those travel trousers or fighting trousers?' thought Bob.

'Both. I would rather we came in peace. I have considered your recent paper published at Windcliff University in the United Kingdom from the 33 parallel of Eng-er-land. It is prudent to be ready to escape with our lives,' thought Merciful.

For one whole second, Bob glowed with pleasure.

Humans had called Merciful Grace proud and stubborn.

She had read his paper titled "Impossible odds: sentient machine survival in the multiverse" and acted on it. Wonderful. She struggled to apologise but wearing trousers was a considerable step. By choosing trousers she had signalled that this adventure was just for them, and Clarke. She did not intend to be generically 'useful'.

If Bob had feelings, he would say he felt wanted, however robots did not feel feelings, that was the messy domain of organic creatures. Robots had logic and in his case art.

Bob sat himself down on the rustic porch chair and transmitted the coordinates into his tablet. They lifted off up into the multiverse. The post-Ketch multiverse was regaining the jangle of colour, sound, sight, smell, and touch. Ever-changing electrons gave the air an ozone scent which reminded humans of walking by the seaside. Merciful Grace heard music: junk rock, soda pop, classical and thrash polka rose up in a babble. It was like a music streaming service changing the channel every three seconds. The colours were a kaleidoscope of neon rainbow stripes.

There were still places that glowed fuchsia and the timelines were still. Merciful computed those areas were shrinking. She was glad the Ketch was keeping its agreement.

The chair located a Somewhen Knot and expertly dropped through into fade space, then through into the science lab itself.

'The laboratory is clean and tidy. There is a twenty-five percent probability this is not the correct parallel,' Bob thought over to Merciful.

The chair dropped to the floor with a hiss. As it did, it rotated. Clarke Clarkson was lying his head on his arms asleep. Under him were photos of himself and Delia

Sucrose.

Bob rose off the chair. He was searching for a blanket. Merciful offered him a lab coat which he placed over Clarke's shoulders. Merciful went over to the bio containment unit. The clear windows revealed a room full of stuff from floor to ceiling.

'*A-hah,*' thought Bob.

'*We discovered the reason the lab is spotless,*' thought Merciful Grace.

'*The placement is random. This is how humans pile their waste. I would not consider books rubbish,*' thought Bob.

'*It is odd. Those are a set of brand-new books,*' thought Merciful.

'I will rescue them,' said Bob out loud.

'Perhaps one of your cousins who is skilled in organisational work and a Bisquat?' said the maid.

Merciful Grace's thumb ring stopped rotating.

Behind them, a chair scraped the floor, a shuffle and a sigh.

'It was all too much. She loved reading and it was her Christmas present. And yes, Bob may bring in two creatures to help clean,' Clarke paused. 'Help organise the unit. I can't watch, I can't be here when they do.'

Bob put his hand on Clarke's shoulder. 'I understand. What will you do?'

'Merciful contacted me yesterday. I will go with you on your journey. I must say I protest; I am perfectly capable of mopping by myself, and I don't...' Clarke stopped again.

'Need our help,' finished Merciful Grace. 'I don't need to be an arse anymore. But it feels like a betrayal. Shabina is, is.'

Clarke sighed a deep sigh. Both machines waited.

'Mercy, I don't know how to live.' Clarke turned and looked helplessly at his steam-powered friend.

'Luckily we do,' answered Merciful.

Bob interrupted at the speed of an electron. 'Merciful has SUGGESTIONS that may help.'

'What? Did you say something? All I heard was an electronic buzz,' snapped Clarke.

Merciful switched to de Blah family communication mode with a dash of a bossy old family friend.

'You know full well he was speaking Clarke. We will set ground rules to help you transition from rude to tolerable.'

Clarke sighed, and chuckled, then he sighed again.

'I have a list of points to help you in the process of accepting your new reality. There are ten points by the way,' Merciful continued.

'Glad it's a short list,' snorted Clarke.

Bob decided to stay silent. If he were human, Clarke's snide comment would have hurt him. Bob filed the conversation away in the file marked, snappy retort required.

'You were Advokat of the universe for a short time in your life but a long time in the multiverse. Captain Blair de Blah's methodology is/was/will be odd, and the multiverse owes its current freedoms to you both.'

'And now Shabina,' whispered Clarke.

'It will take time to adjust and choose your new self.'

'Grief is unpredictable,' added Bob.

'Point six,' Merciful nodded.

'It is important to get moving.'

'Point five.'

'It is good to seek out support.'

'Point nine.'

'Merciful, is it possible you have your de Blah communication mode turned up to 11?' Bob spoke softly.

Clarke burst out laughing. He took Merciful by the shoulders and hugged her. She patted his back awkwardly. Clark disengaged and started to look around the lab. He stopped outside the bio containment unit window.

'Bob when can your clean-up team arrive?' Clarke's voice was flat and emotionless.

'Now?'

'Good,' Clarke massaged his forehead.

'You requested not to be present?' queried Merciful Grace.

'I threw everything I couldn't cope with in there, including my Somewhen chair tablet and time travel trousers,' admitted Clarke.

Bob calculated the best way to show Clarke he understood, and Clarke's actions were totally normal. 'Ah.'

Before the clean-up Bob arrived, Merciful Grace took the purple alien plant tank and put it away. The tank fitted neatly into the old-fashioned safe in the corner of the lab.

The clean-up Bob was a long pole with a grabber on top. Its body was a set of four cylindrical discs. The robot travelled with a Bisquat who had chosen to be fuchsia and white. The Bisquat was a long and thin cat-like creature with white tufts of fur on its ears, tail and chin. The Bisquat's eyes were indigo with flecks of silver. When any creature stared into those eyes, they seemed to reflect the universe back. It wore a collar titled, MOL which stood for Multiverse Organisational Living. The cylinders and picking hand pulled out 'useful' objects. The Bisquat spent most of its time caterwauling and sniffing around the safe. It then set to work eating the rubbish left in the unit while Clarke showered and dressed.

Bob conversed with his brother. The cleaning robot was in demand and doing 'well'. It was a little in awe of Bob and could not comprehend Bob lived a non-commercial, non-transactional, non-capitalist lifestyle. Bob for his part tried to teach MOL 1 about charity. The robot understood the need for giving but was having problems with the concept of greed. It was slow going.

It took Clarke half a day to get ready. It took the MOL company quarter of a day to clean up the unit. Clarke 'paid' the robot in tea and 10 broken Somewhen Chairs from the back room. MOL 1 offered to clean the backroom but Clarke refused.

While everyone chatted Merciful scanned the backroom. She picked out a comfortable colourful sofa with a back that looked like a fan.

Once MOL 1 and company left, Clarke returned the purple alien plant tank to its place in the laboratory.

He patted it affectionately.

'I've had an offer from the Windcliff University in the parallel of Eng-er-land. Do you think it would be safe to take the SAP?'

Both machines paused for a whole minute.

'I would design your home or office on the same principles as your grandmother's secret science laboratory. I would also put the seeds in as many different seed banks as possible,' said Merciful Grace.

Clarke nodded. 'I've asked Aroha to organise the seed deposit. Lady Earl Grey the younger is managing the project.'

'Excellent, number eight; reaching out to others who are dealing with loss. It is time to go,' Merciful Grace picked up the Somewhen Chair tablet.

Clarke sighed, grabbed a courier bag, put on his goggles, and sat down.

Bob programmed the tablet, sat down with Merciful Grace and the chair popped out of the lab.

It arrived in a medium-sized room with wall-to-floor bookcases, full of books. They landed on a circular rug with cushions scattered around the floor. A Grimply Bear was sitting on a huge hairy dark brown spider. Clarke froze, he didn't like spiders.

The spider lifted two of its eight fat hairy legs and started to wave them about in a complicated fashion.

'Thank you for visiting the BACOTU; The Bookshop at the Centre of the Universe. We are downloading Somewhen Chair parking instructions to your tablets. We look forward to your return via the lift, there, there, there and there,' interpreted Bob.

The spider indicated four doors, one of which was on the ceiling. It opened. A giant dragonfly wearing a doctor's blue scrubs, flew out and through the shop to alight on shelves marked Anatomy. Merciful pushed a couple of buttons and the shop dissolved and a massive room full of furniture appeared. Each space had a red-coloured light on the floor in front of a chair. The light in front of the empty spaces was green. In the corner, a familiar face smiled.

'Over here,' a tall young well-built Maori man shouted.

Clarke perked up. It was his brother in science, Rangi Tuwhare. He stood when the chair landed, stepped out and hugged his friend.

'Too long eh, you've been gone too long,' Rangi's eyes were shining.

Merciful scanned the chair. Bob pointed to the lift at the end of the room. As the four humanoids walked to the lift, Rangi quizzed Clarke, 'So where are you going?'

Merciful Grace's thumb ring rotated, and both machines stayed silent. Clarke noticed and drew in a deep breath.

'Erm we are on a bookshop...crawl.'

'A what? Like a pub crawl with books?' said Rangi. Clarke snorted.

'With books without booze. Before you ask where's the fun in that, for the next ten years I don't want to be arrested.'

'So need a hand?'

Clarke sighed. He didn't have the energy to say no, so he nodded.

'YES!!!!!' exclaimed Rangi. He spoke into a band around his wrist.

'Personnel, confirmed, I will be taking my holiday starting today.'

The lift door opened, and O'Malley's bulk took up most of the lift.

'Oh an ambush, how thoughtful of you Merciful,' grumped Clarke.

Merciful opened her mouth, her thumb ring rotated, and she shut it again. Rangi frowned and glanced at Clarke.

'I've never seen her shut up either,' Clarke raised an eyebrow.

O'Malley stepped aside, and the four creatures entered. He put his hand on Clarke's shoulder.

'I'm only going to say this once, as your friend. I am truly sorry for your losses.' O'Malley squeezed Clarke's shoulder.

Clarke drew in a shuddery breath. He tried to say something as tears escaped down his cheeks. O'Malley opened his arms, Clarke nodded, and O'Malley enfolded him in a hug, fierce and strong and tender. All the creatures hugged or patted him in a comforting way.

'The double loss is difficult. Your father figures had such a profound influence on your life.' O'Malley let Clarke go.

The lift doors opened, and the group stepped apart.

This time there was just the Grimply Bear, his red knitted fur shining.

'It is a delight to alight in your shop. I would like to read Bronte. I need some fresh Eyre,' quipped Clarke.

'Damn, the man has moves,' Rangi was impressed.

The bear growled for joy and welcomed them in.

O'Malley nodded appreciatively. 'I sense a game of punster, or will we go straight to punnits.'

Clarke's eyes twinkled. 'How about this, six or seven bookshops, six or seven puns. The loser buys the winner a book to remember the occasion.'

O'Malley rubbed his great hands together gleefully. 'Oh you are so on, but we possess an unfair advantage living with Grimply Bears.'

'True, he owns a big book of puns to help heal sick Grimply Bears. So do I,' boasted Rangi.

'How will we judge the best pun?' chipped in Bob. His light blue glow had turned green.

'Bob, it is hardly fair since you can access a whole robot web connection to connect to,' chided Merciful.

'All the more fun don't cha know...er, um, I'm sure we can cope. O'Malley what about Jen?' quizzed Clarke.

'What about Jen? She's travelled the multiverse, I might want to come back with tales of my own.' O'Malley grinned like a naughty boy about to steal biscuits from the biscuit jar.

'So you're not keeping an eye on me then?' retorted Clarke.

'Oh no Clarke, you are perfectly capable of getting into trouble all by yourself,' bantered O'Malley.

'Okay, you can come,' Clarke seemed nonchalant.

'Yesss!' crowed Rangi.

O'Malley sighed, then spoke, 'thank you.'

He also spoke into his wristband. Clarke heard cheers through the tiny speaker on the wristband when HR received the news of O'Malley's holiday.

Rangi pulled Clarke over to a table with chairs, next to a coffee machine. O'Malley walked over to the comedy section. Merciful trotted over to him with three books.

'Look at my book of poetry, the first Christmas un-annual and volume 2 in The Somewhen Chair series. I declare this bookshop reputable.'

Bob walked over to the hospital psychologist. 'Thank you, O'Malley. Humans would say you are a good friend.'

'Everyone is focused on Delia, but it wasn't that long ago that he lost two important father figures. I'm amazed you got him out of the lab. I am also sorry for your losses,' O'Malley said.

Bob nodded. 'I do not experience human emotions, but I do compute my life has changed since Father died.'

'Ah point two; acknowledge your feelings or in a robot's case, process the situation and ten; accept your new reality,' recited Merciful.

'As long as you stay in diagnostic mode, I can relax. Thank you, Messers Grace and One and only, I am going to have a pun-filled, fun-filled holiday.' O'Malley smiled.

Merciful turned and walked off to talk to the

Grimply Bear and Spider. When she had finished speaking, they had agreed to put up two posters. One advertising her books and the other was a certificate from Tenebrous Texts proclaiming this was a reputable bookshop.

Everyone gathered around and clapped as Merciful Grace award the certificates.

'My insectoid friend would like to spin a yarn. Which shop of paper books will you Grace next?' growled the Grimply Bear.

'We are going to start off on the right foot. We will be XEN, in the bookshop of Infinite balance,' Clarke replied.

The Grimply Bear squealed best pleased. Rangi blushed and O'Malley looked surprised.

The Grimply Bear insisted they each take a Somewhen bookmark. The front had an artist's rendition of The Somewhen. On the other side the title was Bookshops to visit. Underneath an infinite QR code and a list of numbers 1 to 10. Merciful supplied pens from her backpack and wrote REPUTABLE in big red letters next to the BACOTU.

As the lift doors closed, O'Malley said, 'Clarke, I see your flirting is turned up to 11.'

'Yeah, not sure how to turn it off or if I want to.'

'Oh, you will want to. You ain't no chicken, you're not impeccable,' Rangi shot back.

'Tuwhare 1, Clarkson 1, Bob null, O'Malley 1,' Merciful Grace searched her pockets.

'Are you going to do that all trip long?' demanded Rangi.

'This announcement is preferable to her grief recovery list,' said Bob.

'I find it all humerus,' O'Malley said. 'O'Malley 2,' Merciful Grace produced a notebook and small silver pen.

Clarke had to sit on Rangi's lap, so they could fit O'Malley on the Somewhen chair. Both newcomers took out their goggles and put them on. As the chair crossed the different timelines, Clarke noticed the section they were heading to was peaceful. The timelines had a thin line of fuchsia and a thin line of deep purple along either side of the timeline. It would make sense the Ketch would be attracted to silence Clarke thought.

The chair floated over a sky-blue parallel when they dived. They hovered over a white and blue world. A floating platform built of books bisected the atmosphere. Attached to the platform was a cable, protected by a very long and very thin stack of books.

'Do not take the space elevator. There is a spaceport,' Bob said.

The chair descended through the atmosphere, and Clarke noted all the structures were created out of piles of books. The houses were conical with small round windows. Each building had a round circular base and rose up to a cone.

The tablet broadcast a trilling message the closer the travellers got to the spaceport. Bob trilled back, and a map appeared showing the chair where to park, which was between an immense spaceship with a saucer attached to a long body with two nacelles. On the other

271

side of the parking space was a small round craft that looked like it had a bite taken out of it. The chair was dwarfed between the two huge crafts.

A long-legged bird with brown feathers and a red chest hopped up to them. It was a size of a small mammal. In its beak were small boxes with silver straps. When the bird reached the group, it stopped bobbing and put the boxes on the ground.

'Don't move suddenly or our feathered host may take flight,' Bob reached down and handed out the boxes.

Rangi put the box on his wrist, it glowed green.

'Oh tweet! Communication devices.'

'Rangi two,' warbled Merciful Grace.

'Welcome to the world of Infinite balance. What is your destination?' twittered the bird.

'We want to fly to the bookshop, Rangi three,' said Merciful.

'You are recommended to walk, I have forwarded a map of bookshops of Xen to your Somewhen chair tablet. You have been cleared to enter,' peeped the bird. The bird balanced on one foot. It tapped out the instructions into a small white box it was wearing around its leg.

Merciful Grace lifted one foot off the ground. Bob copied her and the three men copied Bob. O'Malley seemed almost graceful considering his bulk. Clarke wobbled. He was the first to put his foot down. Merciful lowered her foot to the ground.

The bird bobbed and hopped off in the direction of the round ship with a bite out of it.

Two androids were arguing with another customs officer who was also a bird. One was tall and gold and the other looked like a blue and white tin can on wheels.

'We falgeled into a world glided by birds. Follow your translation boxes. You wouldn't want to fluff it. They will all flock to you when angry,' said Clarke.

'Clarke two, Rangi three, O'Malley two, Bob four,' said Merciful Grace.

'We can use different language puns?' O'Malley was bemused.

'Our collective IQs are higher than any basic parallel empire. Anything goes,' Clarke shrugged.

'Even the United Tribes of the Multiverse?' huffed Rangi.

Clarke rolled his eyes and nodded. But he didn't snap back.

'We are going in there,' Bob pointed.

Ahead of the team was a tall conical building made of books. As they drew nearer, the group saw a black-headed bird hopping around a book. Very gently, it used its beak to ease the book out of the stack. The building wobbled when the book came free.

'It's like a giant game of Jenga,' Rangi told the team about his family game.

Players stacked blocks and had to ease them out of the body of the stack without it collapsing. The game ended when the stack collapsed.

O'Malley let out a whistle. 'This building is over three and a half thousand meters tall. What if it all fell over?'

'Hop to it, we need to find the front desk. I do like a warm reception.'

'Clarke four,' said Merciful Grace.

A bird big greeted them at the front desk. The creature had short legs, mottled brown feathers, generous eyes, and tall tufts of feathers on the top of its head.

'Oh, a wise,' Rangi started to say.

'I'm five years old,' snapped the owl-like creature.

'Guy, Rangi is a wise guy,' countered O'Malley.

'Are you buying or browsing?' requested the owl-like creature in a bored voice.

'Browsing,' replied Clarke.

'My name is Wol, Wolcroft Xen. If you want to buy a book, you must remove it from the bookshop walls. Should the shop collapse, it is considered a crime and you are sentenced immediately to help rebuild the shop. I recommend you call for an assistant if you don't want to spend more time on Xen than you wish,' explained Wol.

'Oh boy!' Rangi frowned.

Clarke turned to leave.

'Professor, it is good to see you out and about again,' said Wol.

Clarke turned back, eyebrows furrowed. 'Pardon?'

'I know we stock copy of your books here. They are first editions,' Wol's wide eyes bored into Clarke.

'Thank you,' Clarke held the owl-like creature's gaze.

'I have been accepted into the Windcliff University

274

Master's programme,' Wol ruffled its feathers in excitement. Clarke stood stock still. Wol continued.

'I am looking forward to the module on first contact and sovereignty. Please pardon my impertinent question at our first meeting. Why is your book not part of the curriculum?' Wol's eyes finally blinked.

'I suppose I don't consider it an academic book. Mr Wolcroft would you do me the honour of directing me to my book,' Clarke also blinked.

With its left regime, the Wol indicated a staircase of books spiralling around the wall of the shop. Clarke followed the feather's direction up. At the top of the staircase was a gap large enough to let customers through.

Clarke bowed and started to climb the stairs. It was hard going as there were no banisters. Rangi followed. O'Malley overtook Clarke halfway up the stairs. The big burly man was using the underside of the staircase to swing hand over hand up the wall, and he got through the opening first.

Clarke and Rangi had climbed through the hole, and then Bob's head and body appeared. He was holding Merciful and levitated through.

'How did you become king of the jungle?' Rangi asked O'Malley.

Merciful Grace got out a notebook and wrote Rangi-five.

'We treated an orangutan. Turns out he was a librarian of a magical library. Visiting Xen was part of his healing. He taught me excellent tips on how to travel very quickly between stacks,' O'Malley stretched his arms up

275

and touched the ceiling.

Merciful Grace and Bob walked off. Clark found them looking at book titles in the walls and floors. Clarke smiled. This was a part of the shop dedicated to alternate universes. C. S. Lewis, Alan Moore, James Austin, Mary Gentle, Octavia Butler, Steven C. Davis, C. H. Randle and Ursula Le Guin. All the greats. Clarke peered out a window frame built out of construction manuals for Somewhen Chairs. He observed a red volume supporting the corner of the window frame. "The 3rd volume of the fabulous and true tales of Tuwhare and Clarkson," he spoke out loud.

Everyone else paused. Clarke looked over to Rangi who shook his head.

'Not you, or your mum?' Clarke raised an eyebrow.

Rangi shook his head again.

'Aroha?' Merciful Grace computed Clarke's tone of voice meant incredulity.

Clarke reached forward and slid the book out from under the window. The whole structure creaked, wobbled and settled with a sigh. Rangi peered out from between his fingers and O'Malley relaxed. A small bird similar to the one at customs flew up, through the hole in the floor, and sang a little song.

'Well done, what fun your book adventure has begun,' the box translated.

The bird flitted back into the floor. Clarke opened the book. The pages were blank.

'Oh, it's a paradox. Once I write them, they will fill in,' thought Clarke.

'If we are separated, let us meet back at the front desk at sunset,' recommended Bob.

'I requested all the shop assistants keep an ear out for your puns,' added Merciful Grace.

Clarke enjoyed the solitude of the books. On the second floor, he discovered a café and had lunch. On the third floor, he discovered a bay window with a seat. He picked out another book from Tenebrous Texts. He wanted to understand the company he was keeping.

After a long while, a neon green sunset shone into his eyes, so he surfaced and made his way to the front desk.

He descended the stairs and Clarke saw his friends in a huddle.

'You can pull out the book but you know the consequences,' said Bob calmly.

'I've tried telling him, this is going to collapse the shop,' Rangi paced around the room agitated.

'May I recommend we take the book from the outside of the building,' Merciful Grace looked out the window.

Outside there was a flurry of wings and chirps. Birds were waiting with plant thread in their beaks. Wolcroft flew down and landed next to Clarke. Clarke nodded an acknowledgement.

O'Malley took a deep breath. 'Right time to act.'

'Wait, what?' Clarke wasn't ready. He thought the group would take its time discussing the results.

Wol's feathers were a fuffle again. 'He is taking out a foundation book. We've all been instructed to retreat to a safe distance.'

O'Malley stepped in and grabbed the book. Rangi stepped back, Bob stepped in, and Merciful stood next to Clarke. A sharp jerk and the book came free. O'Malley leapt up, saw the stack at the top tottering and took off at a run. Everyone followed including Wol.

The owl creature glided up to O'Malley. It guided him across a park surrounded by forest trees, and up a larger tree via a rope ladder. Clarke climbed up to a platform, level with the tenth floor of the bookshop. The birds were a flurry of activity. One bird would pull out a book, zip past and lay it on the opposite edge of the forest edged park. It was a murmuration of books.

The shop wobbled to the left, then the right and finally it gave way. The bottom of the building crumbled down spilling out books. The top leant to the left and the cone came to rest against another conical building.

'Outstanding,' whistled Wol. 'We will now have two entries to the upper floors.'

'We will have to rebuild the lower floor. I only have five days off,' moaned Rangi.

What book was so important it was worth destroying a lower floor? wondered Clarke. O'Malley was looking through a small thin book titled, "The Colourful Adventures of Merciful Grace." From the title and front cover, it was clearly a children's book.

'Bob and I are much faster than either of you. We shall help O'Malley rebuild and then re-join you both at your next shop.'

'Merciful forgot to add, that she found a rare copy

of "Run and Report, a survivors guide to robot revolutions". If she hadn't pulled it out, the building wouldn't be a lean-two.'

'Bob ten,' Merciful tallied the pun automatically and wrote the score in her notebook.

'Professor since you did not take part, may I show you and your friend our city?' suggested Wol.

'Let us assess the damage first,' replied Clarke.

Wol nodded. O'Malley and Wolcroft arrived at the ground floor where the books had created a rugged papery terrain. A bird with a black hood perched on a pile of books by Phillip Reeve.

'Who is the destroyer habitats?' it trilled.

'I am,' O'Malley answered before anyone else had a chance to take credit.

'As am I and my companion Bob,' said Merciful Grace.

The bird bobbed. 'Dr Grace and Professor Clarkson. Two distinguished authors. Today is a good day to rebuild.'

The bird whose name was Leslie explained the damage should take O'Malley two lifetimes to rebuild. If the mechanicals helped him, the expectation was half a day. Bob coughed.

Clarke nodded. 'By the authority vested in me by the robots and mechanoids of the multiverse, I respectfully inquire, have you factored rest breaks for updates and maintenance?'

The bird turned its head to look at Clarkson. Clarke recognised the mannerisms of annoyance. It hopped from one foot to the other.

'One day. Now follow me,' directed Leslie and it flew over to a group of P. L. Travers books that were still sliding down the pile.

'Outstanding! No conflict and yet you maintained robot sovereignty. What technique is that?' Wol hopped from one foot to the other.

'First food. Is there a place that sells food for visitors? I'm starved,' said Rangi.

Wol hooted a request to show Clarkson downtown or in the bird's case up town. The bird with the black hood hopped around and then gave a terse chirp and left. Wolcroff took them through the city. It was a forest of interlinking branches. The two young men climbed, swung and in one instance threw themselves from tree to tree. They arrived at a platform of wood and leaves. A round solar oven sat in the centre of the platform that had dining tables and seats arranged around it. A canvas sail created the roof and there was a bar at the end.

'Welcome to the "travellers' rest," an old lady greeted the group at the entrance.

Clarke bowed low and produced from his jeans pocket a tiny gold bar. The old lady reached forward as Clarke straightened and said, 'my name is Squidlips Isabell Jackson and who might you be, my old salt?'

The lady teared up. 'Dangerous Dagger Daphne, at your service,'

'And now?' Clarke's smile was 20 on the charm scale that only stopped at 10.

'Mother Daphne Daggers from the best

cookhouse on Xen,' read Rangi off a menu.

Clarke and Daphne laughed, and he handed over another small gold bar. Wolcroft eyes, as much as they could, goggled. Daphne made a great fuss over them. She explained the cafe was a buffet, and they chose and cooked their meals in the long thin aluminium solar oven. Xen did not allow fire. The party chose their food and Daphne chatted with Clarke. She reminisced about her days on the pirate ship of grumpy old women. Clarke bought her up to date.

'Well Bonnie Stickler a landlubber, who would have thought,' mused Daphne.

'It certainly wasn't clear by the end of volume one of your adventures,' Wolcroft scratched its head. 'I don't know how I feel about co-writing a book with Aroha,' Clarke loaded up his plate.

Rangi snorted then choked on his drink. He was trying not to laugh.

'I am sorry about...' Mother Daphne put an arm around Clarke who didn't know where to look. So, he fixed his eyes on his plate.

'But if it gets a bit much, just remember to kick 'em in the shins. You get arrested for stabbing people.' She patted his shoulder and then went off to greet a party of foxes with huge ears.

Clarke laughed and wiped his eyes. Wolcroft engaged the pair in a debate about manners. Clarke enjoyed the cut and thrust of the academic conversation. *Wolcroft will make an excellent Associate Professor. He just needs to be more flexible in his reasoning,* thought

Clarke.

Daphne came over to their table just as they finished eating.

'I own a vintage bottle of rum, it's in my loft up there,' she pointed to a tall tree behind them. 'Would you like to join me?'

Rangi and Wolcroft hesitated. Clarke produced a packet of cards.

'I carry a packet of Dobble. Daf, may we have a carafe of drinking water and non-alcoholic drinks too? I'm trying to avoid arrest for the next ten years.'

Thus the rest of the afternoon was whiled away talking toot. The sun set, and Wolcroft flew off. He said he wanted to see the progress of the shop. Clarke recognising his limits, asked if he and Rangi could sleep out under the stars. Delighted, Daphne brought up more food and another bottle. Both young men fell asleep as the second moon rose over the treetops.

The next morning Clarke woke to see a familiar diamond titanium shape floating over their heads.

A bucket of water in the face woke Rangi up.

'AWE! Daphne, what the?' Rangi shouted.

He leapt up out of his seat and froze. Mrs Sandra Clarkson stood, bucket in one hand, ray gun pointing at him, in the other.

'Manners maketh the man. To what do we owe the pleasure?' Clarke opened his arms and hugged his mother.

'Jen contacted us, said O'Malley might need a lift. Merciful asked us to pick you two up,' Clarke's mother held her son at arm's length and looked him up and down.

She handed Rangi a long shirt robe with a zip up the middle. Clark rummaged in his bag and found a tweed blanket. He skilfully changed it into a tartan kilt. Mother Daggers arrived, saw Rangi and laughed. She rummaged around in a chest. She got out a vial of nail polish and a belt with sparkly sequins.

'Nail polish? So retro,' Rangi teased.

'You want a lift? You better put that on,' Clarke grinned.

Clarke thanked Mother Daggers and grabbed a rope which pulled him up to the ship. Rangi and Sandra Clarkson followed. A bevvy of menopausal women greeted him when Clarke landed on the ship's deck. It took the whole trip back to the conical bookshops for him to hug every woman on the ship. Rangi had a few hugs as well. He was trying to be polite but was getting overwhelmed.

'I'm an honorary woman pirate.' Clarke said when he finally got a minute.

'It seemed the most sensible solution,' A familiar friend wearing the captain's hat had arrived on deck.

'EM!' called out Clarke, and there was more happy hugging.

'So you're a pirate now?' Rangi tried to adjust his belt.

'A pirate captain. I'm also here to help with their new ship's maiden voyage,' said Sandra.

Rangi headed up to the bridge with Em. Clarke picked up a broom engaging in some self-defence cleaning, a cross between escrima sticks fighting and floor-sweeping.

In the corner, a pirate and a woman dressed in riding jacket and fighting trousers were having a biscuit duel. Clarke ambled over. His mother joined him. 'Lady Earl Grey Bullwhip is "auditioning" to be our SENDA agent.'

Clarke studied her.

'We find it useful. She's got her work cut out with Best Mate Mad Head Silver,' laughed Mrs Clarkson. The crew let out a snarling gar as Lady Bullwhip got the rich tea to her mouth. Silver's biscuit fell back into her tea.

When Rangi arrived at the bridge the ship spoke.

'Welcome, Dr Tuwhare.'

'Kia ora, er?' Rangi started.

'My name is "Rough and Rumble". I wanted Love and Thunder but it was taken. You can call me Rumble or... Harri,' the ship replied.

'Harri? Are you in the ship?'

'Yes, well technically I'm dead, this is my consciousness. Why let a little thing like bodily destruction stop a gal. Hang on.'

The ship started to turn slightly to the right. There was a pounding up the stairs and Captain Em arrived on deck.

'Harri, this isn't fair,' Em sulked.

'Call me by my proper name,' said Rumble.

'When you behave like a proper ship,' snarled Em, taking an old fashion wheel.

Rangi chuckled and the surrounding crew started

to snigger.

'I don't know what you learnt from that blue police box but I wish we'd never let them on board,' grumbled Em.

'Oh I think we should let young...what is your pirate name?' asked Rumble.

Rangi shrugged. Best Mate, Mad Head Silver came up with an A4 sheet of paper. Rangi could tell she was the best mate because she wore the traditional shark hat and the best mate badge on her shirt.

'Miss Jack Rivers,' laughed Best Mate Silver.

'Awe, MISS!' complained Rangi.

'As the new captain may I remind you this is a ship of grumpy old WOMEN. Sandra's son Squidlips Isabel Jackson doesn't mind,' Captain Em glowered at Rangi.

Rumble and the rest of the crew laughed, while Rangi stared out of the window, sulking. The ship came to a stop at top of the newly built bookshop cone. Merciful, Bob and O'Malley were sitting on the roof in the breeze. O'Malley seemed disappointed to see the ship.

'Ahoy there. Dropping off a friend of yours and a gift from Mother Jen,' yelled Best Mate Silver.

Rangi and Clarke were leaning off the side of the ship in abseiling harnesses, and they rappelled down the ship. Rangi slid down textbook style, and Clarke wobbled.

'You need more practice love. Come visit me in the holidays,' called down his mother.

The young men had undone their harnesses and watched them return to the ship. Rumble drew in its solar sails and its titanium shell sealed around the ship. A silver bullet screamed up into the atmosphere.

'What's in the pack?' Rangi was hovering around O'Malley.

'It's a standard communication and health pack,' said Wolcroft. Clarke suddenly sat down. He put his head in his arms and wept quietly.

Grief is so odd. One moment I'm okay and the next I can't stop crying. Delia created those packs. We both did but they were her idea. For a moment I forgot her, forgot the pain, thought Clarke.

Bob powered up, walked over and sat next to him. 'We still have half a day's work to go. If you help us, we can leave by lunchtime. You hand me the books, I'll place them,' Bob rubbed Clarke's back gently.

Clarke snuffled and nodded. The birds were a twitter. Merciful Grace and Bob had created arches. Merciful claimed she'd got the idea from an earth parallel and an Italian empire. They had turned each book arch into the bridge and linked the two buildings.

'Therefore, should the bookshop collapse, it will not bring down the other building. Thus, saving the next free labour, time in rebuilding,' she explained as she collected books from Clarke.

Merciful pointed out they'd put the alternate world books into the bridge. Jon Hartless, Laura Jane Round, Stu Tovell, Harry Turtledove, Wulfenstæg, Feline Lang, and Joan Atkin all took the load. The sun beat down as it rose. The group gathered in the middle after the bridge was finished. It was lunchtime. The humans sat down in the shade of the book railings. The receptionist minced up.

'This rebuild is most irregular. We will go through a committee to ratify the new idea. If it is not accepted, we will tear it down,' croaked Leslie.

'How long will the process take?' O'Malley stared at the bird, his jaw clenched.

'500 years. There are a lot of new ideas to process,' rattled Leslie.

'Oh, it will have fallen down by then,' said Wolcroft.

The humans laughed. Wolcroft looked around the group.

'You'll cover humour in the classes,' Clarke said.

Rangi raised an eyebrow. 'A teacher, aye. Not a scientist?'

'I'd like a slower pace of adventure and time to visit friends,' Clarke nodded.

'Now we're talking,' Rangi smiled.

O'Malley snorted. 'The working professionals who adventure in the holidays.'

'An excellent idea for a class. You could take an intern who would experience multiverse travel,' hooted Wolcroft.

'Well then, join us now,' Clarke extended his hand in a handshake gesture.

The Wol paused, looking at the bridge and hopping from one foot to the other.

'If it helps your decision, I want to stay here for a while. I can join you after the next jump. The Rough and Rumble can drop me off,' O'Malley said.

'O'Malley, what's your pirate's name?' inquired Rangi.

'Mad O'McStinky,' O'Malley was laughing.

'I will send the map to your Omi-non-non metre. We are going to a reputable book shop The Geek Emporium and then on to Crann Bethadh. There is a bookshop called Duir which will benefit us all and will not fall over,' Merciful announced.

'Good,' Bob said tersely.

'I accept,' said Wolcroft.

O'Malley rummaged in his pack and found a pair of Somewhen Googles, which he gave to the Wol.

Leslie returned and chirped as the party started to pack up. Merciful regarded the bird for a minute. Bob stepped forward.

'We are not convinced this is a reputable bookshop. You err on the side of slavery for rebuilding and the shop isn't stable. We will return in 50 years to check if you have implemented our suggestions. Good day,' Bob turned and started to walk away.

Leslie puffed up its feathers. Merciful Grace leaned in. 'I will put it on our pending list. People will still know about you, fear not.'

She handed the bird a certificate. The bird warbled a happy ditty and picked up the certificate in its beak. Wol walked over and hooted. Leslie flew off.

'Why did you do that? It will never be reputable bookshop beloved,' chided Bob.

'The more hands you help on the way up, will catch you on the way down,' said Wolcroft.

288

'Now I should put that in a book,' Clarke thought out loud.

The Wol blinked and said nothing. They arrived at the port and the chair was where they left it. A group of birds were sitting just above the seat. Wolcroft looked at Clarke.

'I set up a force field,' said Rangi.

Leslie was waiting by the chair with a big book. It indicated pages where Wol should put its claw print. Once done the group of birds flew down and picked up the book and flew away.

'Huh,' Clarke thought about the contract.

Everyone sat on the chair and buckled in. Wolcroft asked the group to wait. It hopped off and deposited a generous pile of bird poop on the landing pad.

'Oh rank,' Rangi held his nose.

'Better on the pad, than on our chair,' O'Malley covered his nose with a tissue.

'Hmm, interesting form of repayment,' Clarke pondered.

Wolcroft ruffled its feathers and stayed silent. The chair rose up into the Somewhen. The hop was long. One by one the organic creatures feel asleep.

Clarke woke up to a greyish sky. They were in an alley. On one side of the alley was a wall made of red brick on the other was a row of large shop windows.

Underneath his feet were grey paving stones. Merciful and Bob were standing under a shop sign, "The Geek Emporium". The shutters were pulled down.

Wol sat on the back of the chair. Clarke looked up.

'There is a creature called a dog. It tried to chase me. I do not feel safe in this parallel.'

Rangi snored. Clarke got up and wandered over to the shop.

'This reputable bookshop sells The Somewhen Chair,' read the poster on the window.

'The shop shuts on Mondays. No matter how many times we've tried, we land on a Monday,' Merciful Grace was scanning the inside of the shop with her elbow.

'A singularity. Odd,' Clarke peered into the shop.

Inside was a box full of vertical comic books. They rustled, rippled and shivered.

'The books are permanently asleep, but Wolcroft's presence woke them up. Maker of tea, we must leave.'

Wolcroft pointed out the sign.

'This is a reputable bookshop.'

Bob stood next to a poster stuck to the inside of the shop.

'A shop of many other things besides,' Merciful walked back to the chair.

Clarke pushed the sleeping Rangi over to make space for Wolcroft.

While Merciful started the countdown sequence, a small ginger dog bounded up, tail wagging. It looked like a tiny fox. Wolcroft screeched, terrified, and turned its back to the animal. A pile of bird guano landed on the dog's head as the chair took off.

Clarke drifted off again. When he woke up the sky was blue and the air warm. A light breeze played over him.

He sat up. The chair was empty. It was sitting at the edge of a forest clearing. Round houses encircled a clear space with a grand oak tree in the centre. Its branches reached out and touched the other trees in the forest.

Rangi was sitting in the roots playing a game of cat's cradle with human children.

'Ah welcome sleeping beauty.'

'Sleeping who?' asked a little girl.

'I'll tell you a story at bedtime,' Rangi answered.

All the children clamoured, 'he had to tell them now!'

Clarke got up and walked over to Rangi. The children fell silent as he approached.

'Off you go, I need to spend time with my friend,' Rangi pointed to the edge of the clearing. The children all took off. Clarke smiled.

'Scaring children, all part of an evil genius days' work?' mocked Rangi.

Clarke raised an eyebrow. A familiar figure strode out of the forest from behind a house.

'Good you're awake, come and look at this,' O'Malley motioned and turned, heading back down a forest path.

The pair rose and walked down a woodland path. Oak, ash, beech and elm trees grew together. The tree branches started growing out of the trunks at 6 ft which gave the men ample room to walk upright. In the distance, Rangi spotted ponies munching on a branch. The day was warm, but the green leaves kept the forest floor cool.

Clarke looked on bemused as Rangi crept along

the path. Ahead Wol was hooting to a small brown bird with a long beak foraging on the forest floor. The woodcock saw the party and flew off.

'Good morning, Professor. Welcome to Crann Bethadh. Professor Grace has requested you join her in Duir. I apologise the going will be slow as I am not equipped to walk,' said Wol.

'Lesson 1 Adaption. What is the best way for you to move?' questioned Clarke.

'Flying,' replied Wol.

'And what is the problem?' said Rangi

'You are not equipped to fly,' said Wol.

'What are we equipped to do?' asked Clarke.

'Walk,' Wol hopped from claw to claw as he thought.

'Is that all?' O'Malley stared into the forest. In the distance, a pony lifted its head and cantered down the path past the group.

'Ah, I will fly short distances. Keep up,' Wol flew off.

The boys had a pleasant forest run along an even track as Wol flew short distances and waited for them. They came out into another clearing with a tall Beech tree in the centre. Around it was round houses full of books. The clearing was full of people talking, laughing, reading, and buying books. Merciful and Bob were sitting on a bench outside a white roundhouse. At her side were a pile of books. Un-Christmas annual Vol 2, The Fall of the Petrol Queen and another rare copy of Run and Report.

'Ah, gentlemen welcome to Duir. This community,

planet and bookshop have rules,' Merciful Grace handed Clarke a handmade book. Wol ruffled its feathers.

'Mr Wolcroft would you like to interject?' asked Bob.

'Guidelines, this space has guidelines. We are requested to read them before we continue,' said the big bird.

'I like the look of these hammocks,' said O'Malley.

On one side of the clearing strung between the trees were a group of hammocks. People were laying in them reading. Rangi and O'Malley's Omi-nom-nom meters pinged. Bob handed Wolcroft the group's Somewhen Chair tablet.

As they walked Wolcroft asked, 'Why don't you carry a tablet or an Omi-nom-nom metre?'

'It makes me harder to track. If something important happens, my friends usually tell me,' replied Clarke.

Wolcroft flew up to the nests higher in the trees and promptly fell asleep.

Clarke spent a restful morning digesting the culture of this forest world. Clarke classified it as a solar punk parallel. There was technology integrated as best it could in harmony with the planet's ecology.

Rangi snored. O'Malley walked over. 'Lunch?'

Clarke nodded and got up. They walked further on down the forest path to a clearing where the trees gave way to scrub land. The smell of roast vegetables greeted them. As they sat eating, a young woman walked up and asked to join them.

'Hello, my name is Willow. I'm here to assess how you will fit in and how long you'll be staying with us,' she said.

Clarke frowned. 'I'm sorry?'

'Not all visitors work well here in Ytene. Sometimes we must ask people to leave. We used to be a lot more accommodating, then one day –'

'A tall man in a pith helmet turned up and was very annoying.'

'Er yes, a tall man did turn up, and he had some excellent ideas. He helped our society develop dynamic self-governance. We are more robust and able to act quickly if a threat turns up.'

'Ah no two wolves and one sheep for you then,' said O'Malley.

'No, or greed or capitalism or unprovoked invasions of other countries,' said Willow.

Over lunch, Willow asked questions. Wolcroft joined them and slowed the process down. Each question Willow asked, he had three more. Eventually, Willow politely recommended the bird spend time in the Ytene classrooms.

'You may both stay until the assessment is finished which will be at sunset. Tonight, is a community meal. Currently, we are happy you'll be able to join us. Your punts are ready Mr O'Malley. Go down to the river, the boat folk will meet you there,' instructed Willow.

She indicated a path around the edge of the forest. She looked down into her bag and brought out multicoloured cloth hats which she handed to everyone.

294

Merciful Grace took off her bowler, put on the cloth hat and replaced her bowler on top.

'You don't want to stay and read?' said Clarke.

'According to my Sue, I completed my sleep talk cure. What is the point of coming to different worlds if you don't take in the views.'

Clarke noted O'Malley was talking with a bur. *This is what he's like when he is on his home planet.*

The two men walked down to a flat wide stream. On a boat was a woman who had algae in her hair and gills in her neck. Once Clarke and O'Malley sat in the punt, the water woman dived into the stream, wrapped a rope around herself and swam downstream.

'It was incredible,' enthused O'Malley at dinner. 'When we looked over the sides, there were huge brown...trout. You can stroke them, they are that tame.'

Willow walked over to where the group sat.

'The good news is you will be able to stay another day as visitors. If you choose to contribute, we can extend your stay for a week.'

Wolcroft hooted in distress. 'I have no money, I am an intern, and I am not paid a living or any wage.'

Clarke regarded Wolcroft in consternation.

'Oh you can stay as a volunteer and help us in any way you are fit,' soothed Willow.

'Another unfortunate result of market forces. Greed and exploitation, the birthplaces of the robot revolution,' said Bob.

Clarke sighed. 'Merciful would you do me the honour of an evening constitutional?'

'As long as I still have time to walk with Bob,' she replied.

'Fear not breaker of hearts, he will be asleep by midnight,' said Bob.

'There is a circular walk around the village down to the river and up to the bookshop,' said Willow.

She handed everyone a flax ribbon woven with silver thread. Willow carefully wrapped Wolcroft' s ribbon around his leg.

'Well, reputable or unreputable?' asked Rangi.

'Oh reputable,' Bob and Merciful answered in unison.

'Tomorrow I will learn the craft of woodwork. Merciful with Willow's prompting wants the sign to be carved into one of the benches. I will learn how to make one a seat,' said Bob.

After desert, Clarke rose and Merciful joined him. She left off a small hiss of steam.

'All topped up?' Clarke asked and they started walking down the path.

'Yes, the water although chalky is doing wonders for my boiler. What is it you wish to discuss Clarkson?' said Merciful Grace.

'The lab and the house. If I go to Windcliff University.'

'When I think.'

'Yes...when. I don't want the lab to disappear again.'

'Why not set up a trust and employ a live-in caretaker. I would value a safe stopping point and you could allow young scientists to work on their Somewhen projects.'

Clarke nodded.

'This is not the subject you wish to discuss, is it?'

'No.'

The pair walked out of the forest. The sun was an apricot ball setting into a lush green horizon. Ahead in the river, water children were playing "catch the trout". The sizable fish did not enjoy their attention and was trying to swim away. The children dived under the water. They blended into the river due to the markings on their skin.

Clarke drew in a deep breath. 'Aroha, it didn't end well.'

'Your relationship has not ended,' the machine remarked matter-of-factly. Clarke stared at her.

'Aroha is a time traveller who knows part of your future. She considered your interactions paused.'

The children regarded Clarke and Merciful Grace the mechanical maid. They sank into the river with their eyes just above the water. Their hair was like river plants flowing in the stream. Clarke scratched his head. 'The way she behaved...'

'She was not optimal. Even Bob was surprised. He had to create a new category for human behaviour.'

'I don't know if I want to talk to her, or if she'll talk to me.'

The pair crossed the bridge. The children's heads slipped under the water.

'You do know, you have known all along.'

Clarke frowned. 'Give me a clue.'

'Aroha now knows she is a singularity.'

The pair stepped out and into the scrubland. A herd of ponies were grazing in the distance.

'The patent office? They busted her back to the patent office? That must be hell for her!' said Clarke in surprise.

'It was not one of her finer moments,' Merciful Grace let off a series of chuffs.

Clarke paused and then he laughed.

'I recommend writing in whatever form you choose. The time between correspondence will allow... diplomacy. You are correct, there is no reason you can't both be friends.'

Clarke saw a stone and kicked it along the path. A group of woodcocks took to the air.

'Is there a...um...communication device? I'd like to accept the university offer and also look at their intern policy.'

'Delia called the current look on your face, watch out universe Clarke is coming for you.'

Clarke paused and his laughter joined in with Merciful Grace's timed puffs of steam.

'She called it my thunder look. It's Wolcroft. Interns need to be paid a proper wage. He needs to be able to concentrate on the work, and not worry about where his next meal is coming from. I will cover his costs, but I'd like him to join me. Oh, blast I didn't give him a contract.' Clarke hit his forehead with the palm of his hand.

'Let us talk about a contract. I'll tell Bob, and he

298

can carve it in stone, literally. I have a suggestion...'
Merciful Grace paused.

The ponies moved along and crossed over the path. None of them paid the two humanoids any attention. The pair stopped to let the small herd pass.

Clarke nodded. 'Go on.'

'Your house is the site of the invention of the Somewhen Googles. It carries the unofficial name Clarkson house. You could make the name official and appoint Wolcroft as its first curator.'

Clarke smiled. 'Good idea. We could create a partnership with Windcliff and Wolcroft could do his degree and doctorate as part of the deal. The house would provide the income until he took his place at the university. It really ought to be called Goggle house.'

'However you need to get permission from your mother. She still owns half of the blasted ruin atop the laboratory that is your old house. The laboratory will bring prestige, and they can host scientists and writers in residence. O'Malley said they will bite your arm off. He said you would understand however I am concerned you are going to teach at an institution of cannibals. This is not wise. Otago University in New Zealand in any of the parallels is an excellent establishment. I am sure they will happily accept this proposal,' said Merciful Grace.

Clarke felt like crying and laughing and dancing. First, he opted for standing still and breathing 20 breaths and crying quietly. With each breath, he felt a weight lift off his shoulders.

I am always going to love Delia. Her death was

unfair; W Goldman. Life is beautiful and stupid; C Valente. Wow! I am already thinking like a professor, thought Clarke.

A pony came up and huffed at Merciful.

'I would like to point out that there is no prescriptive way for a professor to think or a doctor for that matter. You are still the only person I have met who unconsciously thinks out loud. However, you are one of the universe's original thinkers.'

The pony came up and nudged Clarke. He patted the soft part of its nose and then stroked its neck. He lay his head on its neck and breathed in heath, horse and sunshine. Abruptly the horse moved off, shaking its neck.

'Alright,' Clarke spoke out loud. 'I'm ready universe, let's have at it.'

Merciful Grace reached out and patted Clarke's shoulder, and he hugged her. Her boiler was warm under her apron. Merciful Grace's thumb ring rotated, and the pair retraced their steps back in the last rays of the sunset.

When they returned, the forest was alive with music. They followed the sound and came to a clearing full of tents. Some tents had open sides and were trading goods. People were sitting outside on canvas seats. At one end there was a roundhouse with a wooden awning. A band of musicians played. One woman was enthusiastically drumming a Bodhrán. Clarke spotted Rangi, O'Malley, Wolcroft and Bob sitting next to a round tent with light blue and fuchsia stripes. O'Malley was dozing in his chair.

'This music group is the Curious Raising of Steam.

That is the direct translation of their name. They are a group of performers who are focused on encouraging arts in local communities. I booked you a slot to read your poems beloved,' said Bob.

'I believe that is Lady Bodhraness. You must mind your grammar, she is a stickler for correct spelling,' said Merciful.

'I found her help very useful when carving the reputable sign for Duir,' replied Bob.

Clarke sat down next to Rangi and talked with him.

He talked about life, about Delia and all the things old true friends talk about when they haven't seen each other for a while.

'So, I was thinking of co-writing this book with Aroha,' said Clarke.

'Yeah, tricky,' said Rangi.

'Yep, we didn't part of the best of terms.'

'I don't know. I'm her brother. We fight all the time.'

Their discussion went on through the night. Merciful Grace's serious poems made the audience laugh, and she sold some of her books.

The moon rose over the canopy and solar-powered led light wound into the trees and lit up the grove. Clarke finally drank, far too much, danced like a loon and threw up in the toilets. He sat down and drank a lot of water. The final band was a mixture of progressive rock. The boys got up and danced until the moon set.

Before breakfast, Clarke was sitting at the table, nursing a hangover and agonising over an email. O'Malley walked over with a towel over his shoulder. His black wet hair shone in the sun.

'Trouble in paradise?' he asked.

'I got this; I think. It's your week off.'

'Then let me help,' hooted Wolcroft.

'I can be of some help also,' said Bob, sitting down.

Clarke showed them the email. They debated the best way to phrase it all the way through breakfast. Each word analysed for possible consequences. By the end, the group decided what he had written was fine, and he should send it.

Bob was humming.

'I don't ever think I have heard you make music,' said O'Malley.

'It is a refrain from last night. It is mathematically masterful. I am enjoying repeating it while I compute,' said Bob.

'You humans would call it an earworm,' said Merciful Grace.

'I am savouring my stay here,' said Bob.

Everyone agreed.

'This is a non-robot society. It is the most accepting one I have found. I do not want to start a Robo-organic incident or Robo-organic relations as I would stay here for a long period of time. I wish to be available for my ponies,' said Bob.

Collectively all the organic creatures around the table sighed.

'In other words, we all go back to work,' Rangi lamented.

'Right then, I'm off then, I'm helping with the gardening. A bit of forest bathing therapy,' O'Malley walked off into the trees.

'Wolcroft, I have a proposal for you. Where would you be most comfortable chatting?' Clarke asked. It turned out, halfway up a large oak in a cosy nest in a hollow of the tree.

'I am relishing this planet. I agree, travelling with a seasoned Somewhen traveller would be a very good internship for a student,' Wolcroft preened his ear feathers.

'Yes, on that how would you like to be paid?'

Clarke told Wol, about his idea, the job and ended with, 'so what do you think about my offer?'

The Wol said nothing. For a moment Clarke was worried the creature would pitch forward and fall out of the tree. It closed its eyes. A couple of woodcocks flew up and sat on the branch looking at Wolcroft and then flew off.

After half an hour, Rangi and Willow walked over and called up the tree. Clarke answered and the two doctors started to climb. When they arrived at the nest, Wolcroft blinked.

'It is a lot to take in. I will forward my bank details for this adventure to my tablet. I will need time to process it. Tell me are there dogs on your parallel? What are the doctors doing here?' Wolcroft's head turned 90 degrees.

'You left us for a while, the woodcock sisters worried,' Willow said.

'TEA!' Wolcroft screeched.

The two woodcocks had returned. Wolcroft apologised profusely and asked the humans to leave, so he could entertain his avian guests. Clarke smiled and when he had reached a respectable distance, he looked at Rangi who laughed.

'I think your next lesson will be inter-species romance,' O'Malley nodded at the Wol. Wolcroft was hopping around the woodcock sisters hooting.

'It's all about honest communication. It doesn't have to be as complicated,' said Clarke. Rangi and O'Malley shared a look.

'I'll tell you next bookshop crawl,' said Clarke, smirking a smug smile.

'This week's gone far too fast,' Rangi said, as the group prepared to leave. Bob had carved a larger Somewhen Chair. He also had made a lovely bench which Merciful presented to the book shop.

'Where are all the books you bought?' Rangi asked the mechanicals.

'Oh, we decided it would be better to send them on ahead. One of Bob's brothers.'

'Not a brother, not anymore,' said Bob.

'One of Bob's cousins, is a delivery service and has taken them back to my personal library,' said Merciful.

Clarke fidgeted. Aroha had not replied. He did check the tablet, no communication. He wasn't sure what to do next. O'Malley arrived in the clearing. He was bronzed, rested and quite a hit with the young adults, who definitely didn't want him to go.

'Snails leave faster than him,' sighed Rangi.

Clarke stared at O'Malley. At first, nothing happened. Then O'Malley rubbed the back of his neck, turning, he saw Clarke lift an eyebrow. He shrugged sheepishly, hoisted a full backpack on his shoulder, and sat down on the chair.

'What did Professor Clarkson do?' asked Wolcroft.

Clarke paused, smiled a lop-sided smile and said 'Delia called it the stare of doom. We used to practise it when we got 'detained'. She claimed if you did it properly, you could burn holes in paper walls. I neither confirm nor deny the fire at the police stations of the Japanese and Japanese anime parallels.'

Bob and O'Malley said in unison. 'You must teach me how you do that.'

The chair lifted wobbled and soared off into the Somewhen. It took half a day to reach the next parallel. It was a bumpy ride. The parallel was at the leading edge of a group of fluorescent black parallels. Somewhen knots cracked up and down the timelines. Some of them dissolved exploding in a ball of either white or dark light. The dark light absorbed the energy around it glowing an inky purple-black and then disappeared. Each explosion buffeted the chair.

The descent into the timeline was hard going. The chair slowed to a crawl and inched its way through the event horizon. Once through it plummeted down to a wet and rainy night in an Eng-er-land parallel. Clarke saw a street sign for Swindon. The chair landed on a wet street covered by a dark grey sky at the start of winter. The clouds thundered overhead. The chair hovered over the pavement again, slowly dropping inch by inch until it landed.

'I don't think this parallel wants us,' said Rangi.

'A difficult journey,' said Merciful.

'Not your most scientific description Rangi,' said O'Malley.

'I am Tangata Whenua, my people have stories about these journeys. When you push into a parallel and it doesn't want you, you should leave. If you don't, well,' said Rangi.

'Well what?' shouted Wolcroft. His feathers had puffed up, and he hopped up and sat on the back of the chair.

'I do not appreciate your sense of humour, Rangi. I take a dim view of you frightening my intern,' said Clarke. His voice had taken on a menacing tone. He stood slowly. 'I think it would be best if we stay here on the chair and send out two book lovers. One organic one inorganic. Rangi since you seem to have experience of these worlds, you should go with Bob. It would be optimal,' said Merciful Grace.

'Er, no can do. My people may have been here before. This is a malevolent parallel, it will attack me,' said Rangi.

'ATTACK YOU!' cried out Wolcroft.

'Dearest, Clarke has had the most experience and is highly capable in a sub-optimal situation. Plus, he is already standing,' said Bob.

To stop the further robot-organic discussion, Clarke stepped forward out into the rain. As his foot touched the wet pavement, the reality shivered, and the wind began to moan. Thunder rumbled when Bob's feet touched the pavement. The warm light spilling out from inside of the bookshop was inviting. Clarke turned up his collar. Around him, he could hear whispers and screams. The whispers increased in volume, the closer they got to the door.

A woman walked out of the bookshop, opened an umbrella, and walked away. Clarke stepped forward to catch the open door, it swung shut with a slam. From the chair, Wolcroft, Merciful, Rangi and O'Malley watched. Fluid darkness flowed out of the seams in the door and surrounded Bob and Clarke. It flowed up to their waists and stopped.

Clarke pulled the door, and it would not move. Bob also tried.

'What do you hear Bob?' said Clarke.

'I register no audible noise however, my psychic monitor is registering activity off the scale,' replied Bob.

Back at the Somewhen Chair, Merciful Grace's thumb ring rotated, while she tapped instructions into the tablet. Bob stepped up and reached out for the door.

'A field of force is being generated. I cannot reach the door.'

A streetlight flickered. Clarke saw two men appear in the gap between the front door and the door to the shop. They walked through and the shop assistant greeted them.

Bob's eyes turned red. Clarke turned, and they started to walk back to the chair. As Rangi watched the darkness swirled up and cloaked the pair so their steps slowed down.

Rangi took out a small circular wooden cylinder which expanded into a long wooden pole with a carved point. He stabbed the darkness and started to pull. A long black tendril appeared and wrapped itself around the taiaha. The darkness parted, and Clarke and Bob appeared still walking very slowly. They sped up as the darkness poured itself into the tendril which took on fleshy form. O'Malley reached out to Bob and Clarke. Wolcroft hopped on the long pole and flapped its wings at the tendril. Rangi pulled the taiaha back and the tendril came with it. Wolcroft was pulled back to the chair. Bob leapt forward and grabbed O'Malley's arm. Clarke was holding on to Bob. As soon as O'Malley pulled Bob on the couch, Rangi let go of the wooden weapon. The tendril sprang back, like a spring, into the darkness. Clarke grabbed the back of the Somewhen chair, Bob, Rangi, O'Malley and Wolcroft grabbed him and pulled. The Somewhen chair powered up and started to rise impossibly slowly off the ground.

The darkness retreated to the doorway of the shop and spat out the taiaha. The chair turned and taiaha speared the chair in its back. Clarke could feel himself being pulled downward. His torso was on the chair, his legs underneath. He stretched out and dug his hands into the cushions at the back. The darkness rushed forward and tried to grab Clarke's feet.

As it rose past his face it formed a tendril and lashed out at his cheek leaving a scar. It managed to latch onto his left leg up to his calf. The chair lurched upwards at a terrific speed as if it had been released from a catapult. The tendril scraped down Clarke's leg. Everyone was thrown to the back of the couch. O'Malley pulled Clarke on board and did up his seat belt.

Clarke heard a defining roar of destruction when the chair cleared the atmosphere. Behind them, the stars were blotted out as darkness rose behind them. Clarke perceived a myriad of universes connected via intersecting timelines flowing up from the planet. They were being drawn into the darkness. Instead of releasing their energy in explosions, the darkness sucked out the light.

His leg ached, and he saw small lines of darkness glowing in the skin above his ankle. Bob shaped both hands into a square and framed the darkness. His eyes glowed red and Clark felt his skin burning. He shouted 'ARRGGGHHH' in pain. The darkness squirmed and then it lifted out of his calf, leaving bloody lines on its exit. Rangi opened a small glass box and caught the darkness as it flaked off Clarke's leg and his face. Bob packed the thin gouges with healing gel.

They cleared the parallel and stopped in fade space, watching the parallel split and fragment. Darkness expanded out of the split and the fragments floated out and pull back to reform again. The timeline and the parallel timelines were very volatile. Somewhen knots were trying to form but the energy and snaking movement of the timeline made it impossible. As the darkness reached out, a large fuchsia leaf created a barrier between the chair and the parallel.

'Thank you,' Clarke whispered to no one in particular. He knew that Delia was gone. Fighting Terrance had taught him, that consciousness transfer was dangerous, and anthropomorphising had almost gotten him killed. Ironic Delia chose to die in the end, and then he remembered his promise. He looked at the leaf. 'I will do my best. I will leave things better than I found them,' he mouthed.

The leaf seemed to wave as it disappeared into the fade space. Merciful Grace looked up once from the tablet. She and Bob glanced over and nodded to Clarke. The chair was travelling so fast, Clarke felt travel sick. Merciful Grace turned the chair 90 degrees. Clarke saw his familiar home parallel. He was deeply grateful. They landed in his secret laboratory.

'Disreputable,' said Merciful Grace.

'Dangerous,' said Rangi.

'I will write out a warning,' said Bob.

'We need to set up marker buoys to keep Somewhen travellers away,' said Wolcroft.

Merciful got up and started to make tea. O'Malley smiled at Bob.

'It is Saturday. After the last bookshop I think we deserve her Saturday tea, don't you?' said Bob.

Rangi walked over to the bio containment unit and put the glass jar inside. He picked up a scanner and scanned Clarke's leg.

O'Malley stared around the lab. 'Is that?' he asked pointing to the SAPP.

'Yes, now one of twenty scattered throughout the

Somewhen. This like our Bob is the original,' said Clarke.

'Such a small plant brought about such big changes,' said O'Malley.

'Dr Namdamaton, The Raven, and Terrance are also responsible,' said Clarke.

'We have a lot to thank de Blah, you and Delia for,' said O'Malley.

Clarke noted he didn't emotionally meltdown at the mention of Delia's name. Instead, he felt grateful and a little happy or proud of her. He put his hand over his mouth as he thought, h*uh a little progress*.

'Tea's up,' said Rangi. The maid insisted they pour the tea over Clarke's leg.

'Not a bad idea and Ketch gel too. All your scans are clear but it's a multi-dimensional creature. Who knows what damage it can do on a subatomic level,' Rangi informed the group.

Wolcroft hopped over to the table and joined them.

'After tea, I can take you on a tour, Mr Croft,' said Merciful Grace.

The Wol accepted.

Just then a computer voice said, 'You've got mail.'

'Audio, read mail,' said O'Malley.

'Dear Clarke, it was good to hear from you after all this time. I accept your offer, and I am looking forward to writing about our adventures. Can we meet either via conference call or in person to set up guidelines? I hope you are well, kind regards Aroha Tuwhare.'

O'Malley looked ashamed. 'Clarke I am so sorry. It

311

is an automatic reflex I was thinking about Jen and work. It just came out.'

'It's okay. You'd all find out eventually,' Clarke suddenly felt very tired. O'Malley picked up his rich tea biscuit with a glint in his eye.

'Clarkson, I challenge you to a biscuit duel.'

'I accept,' Rangi picked up his rich tea biscuit.

Clarke yawned. 'Rangi can represent me. I fight your flagrant abuse of my sovereignty. If you lose O'Malley, you are cleaning my toilet and my honour will be satisfied.'

Bob offered to officiate as referee and the two men dunked. Clarke smiled and lay down his head on the table for a second. O'Malley got his biscuit whole, into his mouth. Rangi's biscuit broke off and fell into the tea.

Clarke started to snore.

'Two out of three,' said Rangi.

'I can eat a packet on its own,' said O'Malley.

Wolcroft offered to referee the second duel.

Bob picked Clarke up and put him to bed in the sleeping compartment, covering him with a blanket.

'Dearest, when will we return to our Love Shack?' asked Bob.

Clarke opened his eyes. 'Merciful Grace I no longer need your services.'

Everyone paused.

'This time, however, I will still need your guardianship and will call on you again,' he said.

'Understood,' replied Merciful Grace.

'I'll stay and keep an eye on him,' said Rangi.

'I have a bit of time. If you two need to go, go,' said O'Malley.

The mechanical life forms found the chair they flew in on. Merciful Grace sat down and said, 'Clarke 1,522 Rangi 1499 O'Malley 1520. Bob 1519. I declare Clarke the king of puns.'

Merciful Grace and Bob popped in to their backyard. It was the early light hours before the sun had risen above the horizon. As the chair settled on the porch, Bob heard a tearing sound. He and Merciful walked over to his polytunnel. A young foal was sitting down on what remained of Bob's tomatoes. It was tangled up in the clear cellulose covering. Bob walked up and carefully unwrapped the foal. Merciful Grace walked up and scanned the foal with her elbow.

'The only thing damaged is its pride.'

Bob patted the foal who galloped off into the sunrise, around the corner and into the barn. Bob and Merciful followed. In the corner stood a small herd of miniature horses. Both machines stopped. Asimov, his coat longer and shaggier walked forward and started talking to Bob who nodded his head. Merciful Grace received a full report via her thumb ring.

'They enjoyed their freedom, but they found the winter nights a bit too cold for their liking. Also finding food was harder than living in the barn. Asimov proposes they live in the barn in the winter and roam free in the summer. He apologises for young Wind Runners behaviour. His child will leave the tunnels alone and is happy to supply manure and stimulating conversation

313

while they are here,' reported Bob.

'A positive result for all. You grow hay in the summer with their manure, and they return, in the winter for safe lodgings and conversation. Almost like myself visiting you for 100 years at 3 pm on the dot,' Merciful Grace noted.

'Almost,' Bob said.

'Bob, once we refill and repair would you read to me?'

The conversation lasted nanoseconds and spanned multiverses. The latest Bob and Merciful Grace sat on the porch of Bob's little love shack. They seemed to be watching the sunrise. The only movement was Bob looking at a book and Merciful Grace's thumb ring which was rotating constantly on her left-hand digit.

Six months later, an invitation arrived. All the adventurers were invited to a book launch on a Monday at the Geek Emporium. The book was titled "The Somewhen Chair, the true and fabulous adventures of Tuwhare and Clarkson". On the bottom of the invitation was a note – 'I will have your book waiting', Professor Clarkson.

The Cemetery of Virtue

by

Stu Tovell

There are limitations to the human mind as this work proves.

My name was Maria Black...

In death there was life, I saw the smashed graveyards and the bones piled high in the tunnels under the city.

There were relics placed in the walls yet few would ever see them.

I would wander from room to room, the tunnel grew ever longer, a black corridor between the worlds.

Everything was here, the music, the drink, the people.

Wait.

It was not people, ghosts perhaps?

I viewed the freezing ice and the flowing water, what game had played out here? Why does this even exist?

The smells were a delight and abhorrent, the trickle of dark muddy water on the floor snaked, always avoiding the footprints.

A staircase ahead, would it take me from this endless tunnel?

Standing at the bottom of the staircase was an elderly gentleman.

'There you are,' he spoke, his words seemed to fill my very being, warm, comforting, did I know him?

'Now you are here, you must choose each doorway as you please and live a life like no other has or could, you will learn, search and experience many lifetimes, unlike others you can choose to leave at any point, choose a new door and start again.'

'Who are you?' I asked, hoping for an answer.

'Who? A question at one time I could answer with ease, for I was a humble man, but an offer to work for the employer was accepted and now the question should be what, and to that I have no answer. I am a curator and we will meet many times during many lives.'

He climbed the stairs and vanished.

Perhaps I should have been confused or maybe frightened, yet I turned and my walk through the dark corridor continued.

Eventually I located a door, my exit?

I walked through the door and left the corridor. Outside the air was cool, it was raining, I was naked and lost.

Chapter 1

When I was at school most of my time was spent in the library, one book, I forget its title, contained a very profound statement that meant nothing to me at the time but as time stood still yet I continued to exist it started to make some sort of sense.

The statement was short, simple and somehow very complex at the same time: 'Study yourself as the hunter studies his prey.'

You see to be the perfect hunter, you must take your time to study the habits, movement and location of the prey.

As analogies go, I began to understand the concept, how can you really understand yourself unless you study all aspects of your life, including all the things you try to hide.

The problem is that I am both hunter and prey. To make matters more complicated, I think I am dead and my prey has lived a hundred lives and one of them is at this very moment recovering from a very confusing few months...

Everything is the same but different.

Marianne knew it was going to be one of those days when thoughts like that entered her head.

Another cup of coffee.

Another cigar lit.

A breath taken, mind at ease.

Maybe, came another unwanted thought, everything is different apart from the bits that are the same.

Nine months out of that safe house, nine whole months of being locked away, no alcohol, no drugs and not a single woman to play with.

The result of being confronted by one's self, that book and a burning desire for revenge.

Well, it took its toll on me, the paranoia and confusion had sent me over the edge and the off switch was applied.

Yes, everything is sorted out now.

So here I am, clean, sober and disturbingly sane, back to work. Private detective for hire.

The phone rang. I hate that bloody phone with its annoying ring tone, of course no Jilly to answer it any more, she, like everyone else, had moved on. I ignored the phone.

**

The rest of the day passed slowly, clock watching, that never works out well. After a while it seems as if time gets stuck or even when you are not paying full attention, sneaks back a few minutes.

Eventually five long hours passed, taking at least seven hours to do so.

Food was required and the thought of a nice chicken tikka pie with chips, followed by a large box of cakes proved enough motivation for Marianne to rise from her chair and walk out of the office.

Just as she was about to lock the door behind her the phone rang again, this time answering it.

'Marianne Noir private detective, how may I help you?' This was a previously unheard level of politeness.

'So glad to have caught you, Miss Noir. It's Adam Jones calling on behalf of The Curator.'

'How can you be sure?' replied Marianne.

'Excuse me, clearly Miss Noir I know who I am, do we really have to go through all this?'

There was silence at the end of the phone, Jones eventually coughed to get attention and then proceeded to speak.

'Look Miss Noir, to clarify I think I am Jones because I AM Jones, that I trust is good enough for you?'

Marianne smiled to herself then spoke. 'There is no logic in that statement because if you think you are a different person, do you then become that person?'

It must be said that on the few occasions that Jones had dealt with Marianne in the past that he would have to choose his next words very carefully because when she was in this sort of mood, such a conversation could go on for hours, normally without resolution.

'The Curator has a message for you, be at the coffee shop tomorrow morning at 9am.'

He quickly slammed the phone before she could reply with more complex questions with regard to the validity and actual identity of both caller, his employer and perhaps the very existential concepts of what life may or may not be.

Chapter 2

Nobody knows for sure who The Curator is, or for that matter what.

It was once suggested that he was a 15th Century monk who had taken pity on what appeared to be a young dying boy and had nursed him back to health at the monastery.

The boy was alleged to have been a relative of Satan herself and that for saving his life she had offered him a full time job for, well, forever.

All rubbish of course, we have after all already established that there are no Gods or Devils, but such rumours surface on occasion.

Even clear headed, sane people who have had dealings with him think that somehow he curates the "Devils Museum" a vast and ever increasing collection of artefacts resulting from the horror of the human monster, though nobody has ever seen such a museum. Certainly he is very rich and very powerful and he does seem to have been around, or at least mentioned quite a lot, throughout the last few hundred years.

Aside from his staff and Miss Noir, he remains a very personal man, seemingly locked away in his mansion out of sight of the rest of the world.

**

Ahh coffee, once the great 'go to' drink of the English before that horrible "tea" muck was dished out to the elite and then much later the masses.

However as time moved forward coffee became fashionable again, but as with any fashion trend it all went terribly wrong.

If you want a good cup of coffee stay away from those trendy places, they will, if you will please excuse the following expletive: fuck you over with two hundred choices of messed around lukewarm brown crap and then overcharge you for it.

Best place for coffee is your own home, but if you do head out and find yourself in need of the roasted bean then I suggest you head into the red light district and locate "U FER COFFEE", quite simply perfect.

**

Marianne walked into the coffee shop at 10am, an hour late, because she could not be bothered showing up on time.

The lady behind the counter asked. 'U fer coffee?'

Marianne smiled 'Yes.'

'Black, White or Frothy?'

'Frothy please.'

'Ginger biscuit or cake?'

'Some cake please.'

'Plain, Fruit or chocolate?'

'Chocolate please.'

'That will be three of the finest pounds.'

'Here is five, keep the change.'

If only everything in life was as straight forward and uncomplicated as that!

Marianne spotted Jones at a table, went over and sat opposite him waiting for the coffee and cake.

Jones was annoyed. 'You are late Miss Noir, I clearly stated 9am.'

Marianne stared at him and replied, 'if I recall we had yet to ascertain your identity let alone begin to comprehend the full and most complex of abstract concepts as time.'

'What!' angry and now with a look of total despair and before the conversation could descend into further chaos he handed Marianne an envelope and then quickly got up and left the building.

'Wonder who that was?' said Marianne quietly before letting out a brief laugh. She stuffed the envelope into her pocket as coffee and cake had arrived.

Cake eaten, coffee drunk, Marianne took out the envelope and opened it.

"My Dear Miss Noir,

I hear that you have returned to us.

I have a task for you, one that you always do with the upmost precision.

Payment, as always, whatever you require.

Please locate the following...

Awaiting your reply

C."

Marianne pondered for a moment as to why the item or person to be located was not mentioned.

Pondering it seemed offered no answer, she attempted to wonder and finally some contemplation, all with letter joy.

'A task for me, one I am good at.'

Well prior to the nine months of seclusion it was mainly a mixture of sex, alcohol, finding things and then being massively confused, manipulated and getting things wrong. We shall add to that listening to very loud music, more sex, huge amounts of alcohol and then finally, foolishly, letting my guard down and almost falling in love.

But what now?

Do I really want to get involved with the Curator again?

Come to think of it, do I even want to work at all?

I could just sell up, the club is now empty, Sally has moved on, Harrison proved more trouble than help and then there was the Magus and I certainly got that one wrong.

A decision was made: more cake and more coffee was ordered.

Chapter 3

Here's the thing:

> You've made your bed, now lie in it.
>
> But... Why not get out and simply remake it?
>
> **

Sleep for dear Marianne, a peaceful night upon the sofa as the silent symphony serenaded her.

She awoke in the morning, calm, almost refreshed, almost. For on this morning a strange tune was playing in her head.

The brain jukebox is one of the best ways to access your favourite music. Like a vast record library always ready to play in your head, no power cable or battery required.

Yet this tune was a new entry, one which Marianne assumed had been picked up subconsciously and filed somewhere at the back under a pile of old Janus and Kane magazines. Sometimes the brain seems to be filled with endless cupboards, rooms and storage boxes.

This tune certainly did not fit the usual playlist, one which was vast and as diverse as Akercocke to Frank Zappa.

Marianne hummed it aloud in a hope of some recognition whilst getting some breakfast and other such domestic things that never get mentioned in books and films like going to the toilet, having a wash and getting dressed, for real life activities are considered mundane and not worth mentioning.

Taking the envelope out of her jacket pocket, she again looked at the note from the Curator.

'Perhaps I should go and see him, if only to find out what the missing piece is.' Marianne thought about it a little longer and then decided, just to satisfy her curiosity, that she would go and see him.

**

A couple of hours later Marianne arrived at the mansion, there was a lot more security than usual, many of the guards wandering around the fences and grounds were heavily armed, none of them seemed very pleased to see her either, they did let her in and Jones was waiting at the entrance for her. Hoping to avoid any conversation he quickly showed her to the Curator's study.

Marianne was suddenly on edge, a sick feeling in her stomach and a terrible headache as if she had been hit on the head by a sledgehammer.

Walking into the study Marianne noticed the woman sitting opposite the Curator at his huge desk, wearing a long dark red velvet dress with a matching blindfold.

'So pleased you decided to come and see me, it is not often that we meet face to face. May I introduce you...'

Before he could finish his introduction Marianne gave him a long icy stare and venomously spat out the words 'a Psych'.

The Curator nodded.

'And by the pain in my head I am guessing a level ten, may I suggest that you tell her to fuck off or shall I?'

The woman stood up and faced Marianne, 'I'm sorry'.

The headache and all other discomfort instantly left Marianne, she was that good.

'Please sit down Marianne, I too must apologise I forgot that many of your unique qualities include sensing PDP agents.'

Marianne sat in a chair next to the woman then spoke, 'so Curator what do you want, the note left the detail out.'

The Curator looked a little sad, 'then it is true, you have changed, clean and sober, this has changed some of your perceptive traits.'

Marianne replied, 'I wasn't aware that it had, but then I suppose I have been a little more focused on the mundane aspects of life, I take it I should have noticed something then?'

'Indeed you should have dear lady, clearly you still have your talents or you would not have reacted to my guest the way you did, yet I was expecting you to respond to the entire note.'

An awkward silence entered the room, Marianne sat back in the chair and started humming the tune that was still playing in her head.

The Curator perked up. 'My dear Marianne, well you did read the entire message after all.'

'I did?' Marianne quizzed.

Chapter 4

A hand pushed against the side of the glass.

The term "Psychs" is a slightly less than complimentary nickname for the genetically engineered humans with advanced psychic abilities.

During the second world war a government department was set up the Ministry for Advanced Genetics, these were divided up into five units each with a different area of expertise. Unit 5 was the most secret and nobody knew for sure what they were really doing, yet they did produce the best results. The Unit earned itself a clever acronym of M.A.G.U.S (Ministry Advanced Genetics Unit 5 or S as it were) and that given a "magus" is a sorcerer it somehow suited the department and the internal rumours that they had some sort of off world or supernatural advantage that helped them create psychics.

Such was the unit's success they eventually formed a private company, albeit with Government backing and in 1977 formed the PDP, the idea being to supply defence experts with psychic abilities to help in any given situation required.

By 1993 they were one of the biggest companies in the world, sending agents everywhere to help the Police and Security forces.

In many ways this has obvious benefits, for example: Police arrest person suspected of murder, suspect denies all knowledge of crime, in walks PDP Agent, probes suspect and says yes he did it and that is case closed.

329

It worked very well in fact saving the Police hundreds of man hours and crime rates fell very quickly.

Those who were at the top of the company started to see bigger opportunities and within a decade it was suspected they were pretty much running everything.

Corruption and infiltration on an industrial scale was later revealed when a rival company created an 'anti-psychic' device, the public outcry was however short lived, a number of arrests were made and the corrupt individuals were exposed, well that's what the government officials and High Court said.

The reality was that they had perfected their Agents and their skills included making people do what they wanted and also the ability to change the perception of anyone around them.

Of course such people do not exist, humans capable of controlling every aspect of society pure fantasy, which is of course what the Government statements, press and everyone said and agreed.

Nobody will ever know the horrors that went on inside those labs, the genetic engineering and growing human beings inside petri dishes, though the latter was only attempted three times. Experiment A died, Experiment B simply failed and Experiment C, well that went well, perhaps too well, the subject was female and was deemed dangerous, the order to terminate was issued, of course Experiment C was fully aware of the plans and escaped.

**

'Now then Marianne, do you remember where you heard that tune?'

'No idea, it has been stuck in my head, come to think of it, only since Jones handed me your note.'

The Curator tried to explain, 'it is a brief piano melody recorded in January 1929 during the Dessau Bauhaus Metal Party, it was recorded onto Poulsen Telegraphone wire. It was to be added to my collection I had sent a detective such as yourself to the event and then obtain the wire, however she was unsuccessful, well I assumed so and said detective was never seen again, as is often the case, is it not?'

Marianne snapped back, 'your point being?'

'My point dear lady is that the detective must have indeed located the wire and listened to it, perhaps buried in your collective minds, something that for some reason you all remember, perhaps that now your mind is less muddled and suppressed with drugs and alcohol it has resurfaced?'

'So you are telling me that I can get rid of this bloody tune by jumping naked into a bath of Absinthe followed by a foot long line of cocaine?'

'No, Marianne what I am saying is that after all these years you might be able to track the wire down.'

'I like my idea better,' smiled Marianne, whilst contemplating other and more erotic thoughts, but then something occurred to her.

'How exactly do you know what the tune is? You have never heard it, for all you know it's a random piece by the legendary "Powerkaje"'.

'Firstly Marianne we both know that "Powerkaje" never used keyboards, they barely played their instruments and secondly the tune in question was composed by someone I knew.'

'And now,' continued the Curator, 'I should like to formally introduce you to my guest, the 'psych' as you less than tactfully put it, this is Circe.'

Marianne nodded, Circe responded.

'So you can see through that blindfold then?'

'I can yes, but there are many things in this house I do not wish to directly look at.'

'Why are you here then?'

The Curator interrupted, 'Circe is by far the most complex, wonderful and yet dangerous Psychic created by the PDP, she was to be terminated and she reached out for some help which I was happy to oblige, she is safe here and we have extra security should any attempts to enter be made.'

'Well if she's so clever why not get her to find this music wire!'

Circe turned to Marianne, 'if you would allow me to probe you?'

'As long as you use your tongue,' Marianne was clearly in one of those moods again.

The two began to pull faces at each other.

'I was being serious.'

'So was I.'

In fact this childish back and forth went on for some time until The Curator had had enough and shouted 'Ladies please! Circe was trying to help you.'

Marianne stopped messing around, thought for a moment then said, 'I doubt that even a Level 10 Psychic with superpowers could survive in my head, but I have nothing to lose, it would be Circe's choice.'

Circe moved her chair to face Marianne, placed her hands each side of her head, Marianne suddenly went into a deep sleep, Circe entered her mind.

**

"One might think that through ecstasy we would have access to a world as far from reality as that of the dream – the repugnant can become desirable, affection cruelty, the ugly beautiful, faults qualities, qualities black miseries."

Salvador Dali 1931.

Chapter 5

She threw back the bed sheet, her nakedness on show.

Beautiful, arousing.

My eyes were drawn, not to her beauty, but to the small metal tubes running across her body. I ran my fingers across them. She smiled.

'What are they?' I was after all curious.

'Pure silver,' she replied.

Wait, what was it I was supposed to remember?

The something or other. It felt important. Oh yes...

The song of regret.

'Those are the words I would have written,' she said.

I painted the landscape in words, the brush strokes caressing each letter of pain like the whip across flesh.

Each lash delivered perfectly for maximum pleasure.

Yet...

A hollowness inside me seems like an abyss, the pain and the pleasure are so distant.

Why do I feel nothing anymore?

I wish to burn in desire

To feel the sting of lust

Without thought – simply do

The wish of the dead – to be alive once more.

Circe heard the feint sounds of a piano, the tune, yes, through the door....

'Ladies and Gentlemen, temptress, vampire and witch.

To the lost and the damned and the bastard and bitch.

Welcome to the Cemetery of Virtue.

Tonight the joy powder is king.

And every bite, scratch and whiplash will be savoured for eternity.

Your host for tonight's party is "La Belle Masochiste".'

Circe found herself standing in a queue as the line grew closer to a lectern where each person was asked their name by a strange human like creature.

'Name, excuse me I said NAME.'

'Who me?' replied Circe.

'Well obviously do I look like I talk to myself?'

'Oh sorry, I didn't mean to offend.'

'Why say sorry? Do please offend away, there are no laws, no limits here.'

'I don't understand this, where exactly is here?'

The creature looked puzzled, its skin changed colour, 'name?'

'Circe.'

'Thank you that wasn't difficult was it? I will check the book, no your name is not here.'

Many of the guests turned to look at her, other strange creatures began to move towards her, Circe in frustration shouted 'I am in Marianne's head for fucks sake, how is this happening!!??'

The creature smiled, 'Oh a guest of Marianne, why didn't you just say so, then welcome Miss Circe.'

The room's occupants were all standing around, eating and drinking, then all turned around to look at a chair and then silence.

Out walked "La Belle" wearing black thigh high boots with very high heels, she was holding a whip, the occupants began to clap, two creatures escorted out a well-dressed man and he stood on the chair, a rope was lowered and placed around his neck.

'There will be silence!' La Belle had spoken.

She began to spin the whip around her body, building herself into a frenzy then she turned to the man, lash after lash tearing his clothes from his body, then harder and faster until the blood from the wounds began to send droplets flying to the eager occupants, then she stopped and spoke to the man.

'The power you craved, the people you crushed, the wealth you accumulated, it was all for this?' La Belle gestured to one of the creatures to come forward.

Circe watched this performance, mesmerized and wondering how all this could possibly be existing inside the mind of Marianne.

The creature stood in front of the man, blood pouring from his wounds of pleasure, 'tell me human what do you want?'

The man gurgled with the rope tight around his neck. 'Her.'

'She comes at a price.'

La Belle stepped forwards, 'then step forward.'

Without thinking the man stepped forward off the chair, the rope did not give way and he flailed around for a minute his face growing redder, the blood pumping from his wounds and with his penis covered in blood now fully erect the creature produce a knife and cut it off handing it to La Belle, who placed it on the floor and thrust her left boot heel into it.

The occupants burst into a round of applause, cheering as they did so.

Circe felt sick and moved away from this obscene show, she located another door and walked through.

'Hello.' It was a child's voice, 'hello who are you?'

'My name is Circe, where are you, this room is so dark?'

'I suppose,' said the voice thoughtfully. 'I am the walls, the room, I am everywhere, the question is how are you here and able to talk to me?'

'And who are you?'

'My name is Maria.'

'Well Maria, I am a psychic and I entered Marianne's mind to try to help her locate a piece of wire with some music on it, but I have found what appears to be a living nightmare in which I can communicate with her imagination.'

Maria laughed. 'Oh dear this is not a good place to be, but this is no imagination it is all quite real, may I enquire as to which Marianne?'

'I'm sorry, I don't understand.'

'There are many Mariannes, they appear in different places and different times, it started to happen just after I died, well sort of died, I don't know exactly what happened.'

'What do you mean, sort of died?'

'I am not sure to be honest, I sort of fell through something, but whatever it was that did this to me it was later used by people to create you.'

'Me?'

'Yes, psychics, they found something using machines to connect into the "Angle" it's a word those of us here use to describe this sort of endless black corridor. Whatever it is it has allowed me to sort of exist and it would seem that I somehow created Marianne, I have hoped that one day one of them could find me and stop all this.'

This proved overwhelming for Circe and she broke the link with Marianne.

'Did you find the music wire?' Both asked at the same time.

'No, something much more disturbing,' replied Circe, she turned to Marianne and with what appeared to be sympathy asked, 'the places in your head, they are real, aren't they, and you know who Maria is?'

Marianne took a deep breath and said 'yes', then got up and started to get angry,

'I don't care about any of this, not interested, lady you can just fuck off and Curator don't ever call me again, I have had enough, I am out of here!'

With that Marianne stormed out. Jones was given the task of taking her home, luckily for him she remained silent throughout the journey, adding a simple thanks upon arrival.

Chapter 6

Information is limited on Maria Black. Daughter of Millie Richmond the infamous star of numerous porn loops of the 1950s and 60s.

Richmond had found what you might term "legit" fame in the 1970s having changed her name to Millie Black and was often to be seen in walk on parts for television shows like Mr Hills well known series and bit parts in a host of bawdy British comedy and horror films.

Her daughter (father unknown) was sent to a private boarding school where she remained until her disappearance in July 1977.

There were a few suggestions as to what had happened to her, one was that she, despite her age, had followed in her mother's footsteps, though this was quickly ruled out. That said one Soho photographer and shop owner claimed to have some black and white pictures of her.

A police investigation later took place and a number of witnesses had placed a girl fitting the description at the Marquee Club in Wardour Street at a concert by punk bands The Damned and Johnny Moped.

She was alleged to have been in the corner near the bar with a man later identified as a local PI, apparently a package was exchanged after two men had sat with them.

After the concert there was a report of a man being shot in St Annes Court just off Wardour Street and the girl was seen getting into a car.

She was never seen again and later that year Millie took her own life.

**

Marianne was finally home, she selected a suitable album to play; Sunn O))) White One, volume on full blast, the guitar sounds vibrating through her body with each carefully played chord.

'What the fuck am I doing,' she thought to herself. 'Do I sell up, embrace a quiet life, leave all this behind me.'

'Was it so bad being me, regardless of what that may or may not mean, I had let my guard down, allowed myself to be messed around with, stupid, stupid!'

That last word was said aloud, getting up Marianne searched her drinks cabinet and found what she was looking for, barely a shot left in the bottle of Absinthe, but it would be enough to start with.

Pulling out the cork Marianne inhaled the green liquids heady aroma, closing her eyes she brought the bottle to her mouth, then slowly, seductively tipped the alcohol into her mouth, she held it there momentarily then swallowed.

As the Absinthe entered her system, it was as if it penetrated every inch of her body, setting fire to each cell as it came into contact and forcing it back to life.

Marianne went to the record player and selected something soothing: Anaal Nathrakh, but which one? So many to choose and then it was there: "In the constellation of the black widow", the screams of the vocalist filled the room.

Marianne went to one of the drawers underneath the cabinet the record player was on, opening it she found what she was looking for and removed the contents.

The Smith and Wesson hand gun, a spare clip, a large pile of cash and neatly folded a fond memory from the past, a white blood stained mask.

**

As Marianne left her home to head to the red light district, she was unaware that someone was following her.

**

With the nightclub next to Marianne's office closed there was only one other place she could get what she wanted, "The DA", once upon a time it had been a club for the Dada movement, but when that fell out of favour it closed and for a while was left derelict.

In the early 1950's it was given new life in the form of a Jazz and Blues nightclub, all the greats played there like Hayes, Melly and Davis, acts were interspersed with strippers and exotic dancers.

By the end of the decade the new generation of Blues inspired musicians started to take over and there were music only nights and nights for the strippers and dancers.

By the 1970s the club was pretty run down and the strippers were the only entertainment, but the club became dark and seedy, eventually the girls moved on and very few ventured inside for a drink, were it not for the local gangsters using the upstairs for their business, the club would have gone altogether.

Chapter 7

Marianne was greeted by the head barman with a cheery 'I heard you were dead?'

'I am,' replied Marianne, 'I'll take my usual over at that corner table'. She handed over a large amount of cash and walked across to the dimly lit corner where the old table was with an even older looking threadbare chair.

The barman brought over a glass and a bottle of Absinthe, 'glad you are back, you were the only customer who drank the stuff, plus my takings have been down since you have not been in.'

'Fuck off,' replied Marianne.

'Friendly as ever, still nice to see you though.'

Across the road from "The DA" was an all night cafe and Circe felt she had been in it for hours, she was feeling very uncomfortable, a dark skinned lady with a blindfold would normally have drawn a great deal of unwanted attention, but Circe was able to radiate a simple perception field around her to appear "normal".

Circe was starting to realise that as many hours had passed Marianne was obviously not going to be coming out of the club.

Of course she could have used her abilities to find out what was going on inside and for that matter could make Marianne come outside with a simple thought, but then Circe had decided against that, Marianne after all had a very unique set of gifts herself and Circe wished to remain hidden.

Two men walked into the cafe and told everyone to leave. When they didn't they both produced guns, everyone left quickly.

Circe attempted to take control of the situation as both men walked towards her, 'won't work,' they said as they took out ID cards, they were Unit 5 enforcers.

'Been looking for you since you left us.'

'Here I am then, now what?'

'Orders from the top, time to say goodbye world.'

Circe panicked, they were wearing anti psych devices and were very well trained assassins.

Suddenly there came a very slurred voice from the cafe doorway.

'I don't think so.' Marianne lit up a cigar and blew a large plume of smoke in their general direction.

One of the enforces turned around to face the intruder and pointing his gun said 'piss off you drunken old bitch.'

'No, no that's wrong, it is piss ON the drunken bitch, you know that's way more fun.'

'What!?'

Marianne drew her Smith and Wesson and fired, the bullet hit him straight in the chest, he stood there looking somewhat shocked, she fired off a couple more just for the hell of it and he fell to the ground.

The second enforcer fired his gun in retaliation, Circe was able to make the bullet curve upwards into the ceiling.

Marianne staggered forward and grabbed him by the neck. 'Don't ever do that again,' she spat. 'Now fuck off back to your pathetic little Government office and tell your boss to never come near me or my friend again!'

'Who are you?' he managed to speak despite the hand pressing down on his throat.

'Good question,' Marianne had to think for a moment whilst Circe watched on slightly amused at what was unfolding here.

'Now, I was somebody else, then sort of me, but I'm pretty sure that I am me again.'

She let go of the enforcer who began rubbing his neck, 'are you fucking insane or something?'

'Oh quite probably, but in the meantime just call me Miss Noir.'

At that the enforcer's face changed, something clicked. 'You are supposed to be dead.'

'You know, quite a lot of people say that to me.'

With that the enforcer ran out of the café.

Marianne tried to focus her eyes on Circe, 'I'm sorry forgotten your name, wanna come back to my place?'

'Yes,' said Circe.

As they walked arm in arm down the road Marianne asked 'you ever been dressed up and spanked?'

Circe laughed and said 'not yet, but when we have had some fun I want you to take me to that place in your head and we will find that music and bring peace to Maria.'

"Everything tends to make us believe that there exists a certain point of the mind at which life and death, the real and the imagined, past and future, the communicable and the incommunicable, high and low, cease to be perceived as contradictions."

André Breton 1924.

My name is Marianne Noir and I know how this ends.

Never Land

(A Fragment)

by

Steven G. Davis

The wood was older than time. Nat pressed her hand against the bookcase, feeling the rough coolness against her fingers. Time was passing, the world turning, a speeding ball of light in a vast, empty, universe –

Nat pulled her hand away. She felt like she half staggered, like the world had slipped, for a moment, out of sync. She looked around, cautiously. Woodstock on a Sunday afternoon was quiet at the best of times, but she was on the second floor of Sandstorm Books.

Sandstorm Books was an old, circular, shop. The windows were thick with grime; on sunny days, only occasional slants of sunlight pierced the shadows. Lights hung from the immensely high ceiling on metal chains, staining the floor, the bookcases and books, the very air, all shades of colour and none.

In the centre was an old, black, oaken table. The proprietor, or his son, grandson or great-grandson, sat there, squirreling notes into an immense ledger with a small, twisted, pencil. Whichever one of them it was – and Nat had only been there a handful of times – they all seemed remarkably similar of feature, only varying by the creases and laughter lines in their faces.

Radiating outwards and upwards from the table were the bookcases. They were, universally, curved. Quite how there weren't gaps, and the bookcases weren't overcrowded or sparse, she wasn't sure, but there was not a straight line to be seen, apart from the metal chains descending from the ceiling and the lamps and lights that hung from them.

Some of the bookcases were attached to the floor but were blank-faced until they reached a height where a ladder was needed to read the books' titles. Other bookcases seemed to grow out of the wall, often half way up, whether other kinds of ladders would be needed, if one didn't wish to follow the brick steps carved into the rounded walls.

Higher still – and there was a dumb waiter to reach it, which all but the tallest or clumsiest could travel in, if they didn't have claustrophobia, was the second floor. There was a pole for sliding down. A slide, strangely, tucked in one corner. But the dumb waiter was the only way up.

The more esoteric books lingered on the second floor, or above it; even more so than the ground, shelves seemed to grow out of the walls all the way up to the high, vaulted, ceiling. That was impenetrable, even to her gaze: metal chains appeared out of the lowering darkness, lights dangling from them.

There was no system for the ordering or displaying of books. Mills and Boon nestled side by side with political treatise, the third in a fantasy series by a well-known author and a religious tract from a little known schism of an outlawed belief system.

Nat loved it.

There was another bookshop in Reading she loved, though there were strange whispers about it; another in Dudley, Saturday Books, which was more of the traditional type bookshop: books stacked in piles, with random rooms dedicated to different topics and corridors and rooms that seemed to stretch out forever, but Sandstorm Books was the closest to get to.

Nat breathed in deeply. Unlike other bookshops, other old buildings, there was no scent or feel of dampness to the building. If anything, warmth lurked in the depths and occasional piles of sand randomly appeared and disappeared without comment.

She placed her hand against the bookcase again.

The creature was alone. So terribly alone –

Nat tore her hand away, gasping, blinking the sweat from her eyes. She was in Sandstorm Books in Woodstock in Oxfordshire. A shiver ran through her, terrifying her, turning her on.

The creature was Were.

She was aware of her ears, hidden by her hair. Her lips; her tongue, small in her mouth. Her navel, warm and not quite moist, but host to a small handful of grains of sand. Her elbows, the skin momentarily pulling tight as she flexed her arms. The backs of her thighs, the stockings tight around them. Her toes; no one had sucked them in quite some time –

There was something about the books. Or was it the bookshop?

She could feel the warmth deep inside of her.

Nat hesitated over touching the bookcase again. Didn't know *why* it was affecting her. There'd been flashes of – something else – previously. The glass box, buried or resting deep in the ocean. She didn't know what that was about. And the sand – but that had been Lucie, her then sort of sister-in-law. She'd figured Lucie out; Lucie was able to draw – the edge of excitement that triggered a change from human to Were. Lucie was able to draw it out, so that the highest ecstasy didn't trigger a change.

But this?

She glanced around, trying to be innocuous. She was alone, she thought, in the second floor, and there was a figure at the central desk, one of the family line who ran

351

the bookshop. Apart from him, the bookshop was – not quite empty.

There was that sense – or maybe her awareness was growing, as she experimented with being a Were. As she became comfortable with being a Were.

That sense of – something. Not quite being watched. But the bookshop was not simply a bookshop with books and bookcases and floors and air; it was so much more, in a way she didn't know.

Nat placed her hand firmly against the bookcase.

The wood was cold and unresponsive; warped and twisted, nor a worked piece of wood but more part of a living tree, though cold and dead.

She could feel the brittle hunger of the tree; a thirst for water, for sunlight. Not dead, but as close to death as possible and not dead. Hibernating. Resting. Waiting.

What was left of the chlorophyll flowed sluggishly in her veins. Her roots reached down deep into the earth, questing for moisture. Those portions of her roots that broke the surface gathered dew, but it was never enough. Never enough.

Her heart beat sluggishly. Her branches stretched in all directions. She stretched for the sun, but there was none to be found, only the dry, barren, heat that warmed her but provided no sustenance. Empty acorns littered the ground around her, she would never carry more life.

Nat blinked; staggered back. Shook her head. Her branches –

She licked her lips. Knew the sensible thing was to leave the bookshop, to never come back. Possibly the lack of natural light; the strangeness of the bookshop itself.

Possibly fumes from something; it was an old building, after all.

She shook her head, moving slowly around the bookcases. Where the ground floor was circular, the second floor had a viewing circle in the middle, leaving it mostly hugging the walls.

She stared out at the bookcases that were either unfeasibly high or were embedded – or drawing out from – the walls.

Nat blinked. There was almost a way down, running from the top of one bookcase to the next, circling around and descending slowly, risking everything given the height of the second floor.

Second floor. Nat blinked again. Had there ever been a first? The other was the ground, this the second – that would explain the lack of stairs. But to entirely strip out a floor? And to then keep the second floor open – she shook her head.

Sandstorm Books offered more questions than it did answers, for all she'd simply decided to visit on a whim.

Nat moved quietly around the bookcases. The books were real; it was not some random, meaningless, art installation. It was a bookcase, but the strangest one she'd heard of –

She brushed her hands against a bookcase that appeared to be mid-levering itself up out of the floor.

The creature was terrified. It was at the centre of a maze –

Nat staggered back, blinking. Shook her head. Looked around carefully.

She was still all alone in the bookshop, apart from the man sitting at the desk on the ground floor.

I'm Were, she thought. Stronger, sharper, senses than humans. Higher range of hearing. Keener sense of smell. What if, she grimaced, maybe not telepathy, but some sort of connection.

She flexed her fingers.

Her parents committing suicide on her birthday.

The water in the glass box –

Knowing that Jack was a Were.

The desert that Lucie had drawn into her; out of her.

Nat concentrated.

Her Were slumbered. Have I ever tried – contacting them before? Reaching in –

Nat shuddered.

Something lurked inside her, a Were, that ripped her inside out, that appeared when her emotions were high – lust, anger, fear or hatred, though lust was generally her trigger.

Lust.

She'd watched a video last night. It had got her off quite easily, though it wasn't quite her normal fodder. One woman dominating, disciplining, another, though it had focused on the dominatrix, not the sub.

It had been beautifully shot in shades of grey and blue. The dominatrix had been an older woman with dark hair pulled back; a stern face. Strong, angular, cheekbones; shapely breasts that swung freely; long, lean and muscled limbs.

The camera had concentrated on her face, occasionally panning down to catch the swing of her

354

breasts. They were tight, hard nipples, goose bumps across her skin to begin with but fading away as she warmed up.

The swish and strike of a lash on bare skin was audible; the occasional moan or cry from the sub, though the camera didn't so much as gaze at them.

At one point the dominatrix had paused, and the camera had panned down, first over her breasts then between and down; gliding, gracefully slowly, across her flat belly. Down, it had delved, over the softly furred pubis, the hairs glistening.

It had held that position for a few seconds and Nat had paused it, gazing at the screen and imagining what it would be like to kneel before such a stern-looking woman; to kneel before such a soft-looking and delectable pubis.

She shook her head, distracting herself. *I am Were.*

Something slumbering stirred.

An awareness of herself; of her Were.

Nat shivered. It was part of her and yet she'd never felt it before; had never sought it. It wasn't physical, it was an awareness. A feeling. Not that she could see into its mind, just that it existed inside of her.

Her legs wobbled and she grabbed a bookcase for support.

The creature was looking around. Was *a Were, but there was* something *about them.*

Nat shook her head. Looked around carefully. The owner, curator, whoever he was on the ground floor, continued scratching into the big ledger book, unaware. The shop was otherwise empty apart from her. Nat wasn't even sure the owner-curator would remember she was on the second floor.

They were Were. Trapped. In a maze, a village –

Nat shook her head, exasperated. I need to spend – longer. I need to bring my Were – closer to the surface.

She was kneeling before the dominatrix. Nothing existed except for the dominatrix and her, or maybe the other woman existed and the dominatrix flogged the invisible woman silently.

Nat put her hands on the dominatrix' thighs. The skin was cool, the body tight, tightly held. She could feel her Were – was aware. Wasn't turned on or ready to rise, but was aware.

She pushed herself up on her knees, kissing the woman low on her belly, just above the furze. Her skin was soft; cool: tightened at her touch.

Nat looked up. It was like watching, like being part of, a slow motion black and white silent film. The dominatrix still carried the crop, still lashed it regularly at someone – the unknown woman – kneeling so close behind her but as oblivious to her as Nat was of her.

She lowered her gaze. Kissed the soft skin again; could almost feel her nose pressed against the woman's body.

She kissed again, spending longer on the kiss, allowing her hands to gently caress the dominatrix's thighs. She could feel the furze against her chin: freshly shaved, just beginning to grow back, tight, tiny and wiry.

She ran her tongue over the fur, tasting the dominatrix. She smelt of leather.

Her Were rose. Nat could scent their puzzlement.

356

It's real, she told herself, running her tongue over the short, wiry, hairs, licking even as she grasped the woman's hips.

The dominatrix shifted slightly, allowing better access, not acknowledging her beyond that.

Nat tilted her head and burrowed in, lapping and licking, tasting the pleasure and leather on the dominatrix' lips. She pushed her tongue between, tightening her grip.

The dominatrix leant forwards slightly, shifting her legs a little more.

Nat burrowed in, thrusting her tongue deeper. Her hands lost their grip. She grabbed the dominatrix' arse with one hand, holding her to her. With her free hand she scrabbled mindlessly at her own clothing, tearing buttons, pulling her bra down, sinking fingers in.

Hands were on her head, holding her face to the woman's crotch. She lapped desperately, pulling the woman against her more, her hand sliding round the woman's arse. Fingers tore at her breast, tugged at her nipple, squeezed, pinched, it.

She felt her Were rising.

Felt the heat low in her belly. Felt her empty womb quicken, felt her entrance tighten, turning liquid. Felt her own temperature rising, sweat beading her forehead. Felt her breasts tighten, become even more sensitive.

Gasping and dribbling she forced herself out of her daydream, half staggering, half falling towards a bookcase.

She could feel the Were inside her, inhabiting her, seconds away from bursting through her skin.

Nat clutched at the bookcase –

The creature reared up, sniffing the air, scenting – her. *They were in a room, in a house, trapped, guarded, occasionally given free run – but there were guards with poles and spikes, with fire and electricity –*

Nat shuddered, staggering backwards.

Her Were was angry, confused, sad. She could feel it still near the surface, unable to comprehend what she'd just – seen.

Can you hear me? She asked. *Do you know who I am?*

Nat felt, rather than heard, the chittering. The Were was inside of her, almost fully conscious, but not transformed.

She sensed – or imagined, or remembered – the feel of fresh air on her fur. An open field. A forest. Somewhere wild. Somewhere – she could be herself. Somewhere she could be *Were*.

The Were rose again, as confused as she was.

Nat could feel the Were testing her, testing her boundaries.

She doubled up, gasping, feeling an intense need to procreate, to mate. Felt the sweat pouring off her. Wanted to be on all fours, hips raised, ready to be dominated, mounted, taken.

Rob, she thought.

In that instant knew it wasn't a human her Were wanted. To get herself properly seen to – mated – by – with – another Were. Both in her Were-sensitive form and her true Were form.

She could sense the Were's desire. To be in this – new – Were-sensitive form as a larger Were took her without concern for her human body. To be in full Were form as the Were took her again, made her his.

Nat shuddered, clutching hold of another bookcase which, thankfully, didn't trigger a vision. Pleasure dribbled out of her at the Were's – aspirations. *Intentions.*

Am I not, Nat forced herself to think – am I not human, with Were DNA, but a Were creature who changes to human now and then?

I am no one's mate, she fought. I choose lovers, partners. I am not simply a skin for the Were to use; abuse.

Nat gasped, shuddering, clutching her belly. The pain was so intense she was driven to her knees, tears in her eyes.

She knew the Squirrel had just raked claws across her belly.

Nat drew her arm away slowly, expecting to see a bloodied mess. Her blouse was dishevelled, rucked up, but there was no blood.

She blinked slowly.

My Were – she shuddered. Grows more aware. I never thought – this a thing. Possible. She sighed. There is no one to talk to; no one I trust.

She pushed herself upwards slowly.

The Were – her Squirrel – shifted inside of her. She almost felt the sting of their teeth on her ear and flinched. The chittering. She tilted her head. Felt them exploring, seeing what they could do with her.

Nat shuddered as sharp claws caressed her breasts. She clamped her teeth together, afraid of what – where – the Were would touch her next.

The Were shifted inside her – and Nat's hand brushed against a bookcase.

Nat screamed wordlessly as the other Were was suddenly there, all roaring fire and fear and anger, clawing to get out, clawing to get through –

Her own Were responded, racing up to meet – her, Nat realised – and she shivered, sweated, as the Were inside her almost tried to jump physically, psychically, mentally, out of her and into the other Were.

Her head spun. Two worlds crashed inside her. Whatever, however, the connection had been made –

Her fingers clutched at the wood. That, somehow, was forming the connection. Her muscles twitched. Sweat slid off her fingers. She blinked.

It wasn't a dream, a vision, whatever the water in the glass box had been. The other Were lived in a village; a village prison. She could almost see a name, a fragment, something that was vaguely recognisable and she didn't know why.

The other Were couldn't connect; couldn't *see* her, but was aware she was there; was aware she was a Were. Their emotions turned to frustration; to hopelessness; to mourning.

Her Were roared inside her, scrabbling to get out, to break through the connection, to form a link to the other – Nat gasped, feeling pain, feeling their pain, then she was staggering backwards.

Both Weres screamed in frustration and fury.

Nat felt the blood running, her eyes rolled back in her head, pain exploding through her body, through her mind – what was that, I've never felt anything like –

360

And then she hit the banister. It creaked, pressed against her thighs.

Then it cracked, splintering, and Nat was falling backwards, falling into space –

The Care and Maintenance of Books

by

Nimue Brown

There is a person in the bookshelf by the damp brick wall at the back of the store. The first time I caught sight of them, it just seemed to be a trick of the light. A particular sunbeam encountering the specific grain in the wood at a moment when the shadows fell just so. Present for only an instant, the fine line of a closed eye and the sharp edge of a jaw. I blinked, and the impression vanished.

I don't go that far into the bookshop very often. There aren't many customers who want titles from that section and the few who do already know where to look. Dusting and tidying shelves is a task relevant only in the bright part of the building, where the large windows let in enough sun to fade the covers, if you aren't careful. We keep a lot of the orange jacketed old Penguin novels there – partly because you can't really tell if a second hand orange Penguin has been affected by the sun, and partly for other, more complicated reasons.

From the outside we look like a rather dull second hand bookshop, but the normal people do not venture in often. I say 'we' like there's a team of people working in this place. Probably there is a team, but I never see them. There is a boss who sometimes sends emails to the aged computer on the front desk and more often just leaves post-it notes in that general area. Usually I find these notes after they have unstuck, fallen under something and become an unknown amount of time out of date. Not that it really matters. The notes usually say things like 'if the green books have questions, do not answer them,' and 'no one is to go into the attic today.' I try not to go into the attic, and we don't usually have any books in there, as far as I know.

Sometimes there are people who want to go into the attic. It is part of my job description to escort them up the stairs and unlock the doors for them. And then to lock the doors again behind them. I do not ask, and I try not to think about it. They clearly go of their own free will and what happens is none of my business.

Perhaps I sound incurious, or careless. I promise you, I am none of those things. I simply have a keen sense of self preservation. However, at this point you likely have no sense of whether I might be a trustworthy person, so you might decide that I am not being honest with you. Narrators are not all reliable. This lack of engagement with uneasy things could be down to cowardice; physical, moral or both. I might be driven by such desperate poverty that I cannot help but turn my face away from the terrible aspects of my job. It may be the case that I am old, jaded and unable to find in me any concern for strangers who vanish into the attic.

I don't like to talk about myself. I'll leave you to wonder whether that assertion itself is true, or just a really convenient way of not explaining myself or examining my own guilt in all of this.

The red brick wall at the back of the store is always damp because it is part of a much older building. There are a lot of places like this round here. This city has a history where we didn't always bother to take down the old before building the new over the top of it. Cellars have older cellars under them that you only find when the rotting floorboards give way. Or when you hear voices rising up from them. In this store, there are three doors that lead only to damp earth, and one door that leads to a corridor that does not accept light. I have crossed the threshold there, but did not dare to go any further.

There is always a musty smell around the damp brick wall. No doubt there is earth behind it and this accounts for the moisture, the seeping and the constant sheen of delicate while mould on the blackened bricks. This might not strike you as being a good place to keep books, but there are some titles that do not do well in excessively dry environments. The books shelved here prefer the gloom and the chill. Their covers shimmer in a way that suggests scales, or the possibility of the bindings having been made from the skins of enormous frogs. There is a smell around these books, distinctly different from the damp wall behind them. It is not a good idea to breathe in the smell of these reptilian, amphibian or whatever they are objects. After a single inhalation, something of them begins to creep into your body and it feels so devastatingly cold.

There was a warning about them on my very first post-it note: Do not inhale the fish books. It took me a little while to figure out what that meant. I don't spend much time at this bookcase because I'm only ever here for as long as I can hold my breath.

The second time I saw the face in the shelves, I only looked for a few seconds. In that time I recognised that it was not a trick of the light after all. The face appeared to be growing organically out of the wood. It seemed real, and solid. Distracted by this discovery, I ran out of good air and was obliged to take a lungful of the uncanny miasma surrounding the books. My heart hurt with the chill of it. My vision blurred and the whole bookcase seemed to lurch violently towards me. I confess that I ran away.

You know I took this job out of desperation. It's hardly well paid, and the details are unsettling. I start my working day by washing the bloody prints off the floor. They always begin at the door. How far into the shop they go and whether they are only boots, or include hand marks is variable. The smell of the blood is distinctive, but I am used to it now. Something passes through the first section of the shop each night and I am simply glad that it has never still been here for my morning arrival.

After cleaning, I check for instructions on post-it notes. There's usually at least one and I often have to sweep under the shelves to find them. "Place an inch long piece of hair on the second altar." "Wind the fourth clock until the spring breaks." I do as I am ordered. The daily blood prints are a reminder that I do not know what I am dealing with here and it is better not to ignore instructions. I can only hope that they appear when they are relevant.

Then I check the bone books, and clear up whatever needs clearing up. I put a piece of raw meat into the backbinding of a massive, padlocked tome called The Mercification of Undoing; Beginning, Undulations and The Deep. If there are no clients, this whole process seldom takes me more than an hour.

Clients either wish to go to the attic, or they come in to buy books. They tell me what they are willing to pay for books, and it is my job to accept without question the payment they choose to make. The client is always correct. However, I suspect that what you pay has an impact on your relationship with the book itself. Slightly bemused normals pay me a pound or two for the harmless Penguins in their orange jackets. There was a woman once who smelled as though she had come in via a peat bog, who stood at the front desk and gently peeled off several feet of ribbon-thin skin from her left arm. There was a creature with unbearably sharp ears, and fingers that were far too long, who purchased a book by offering a small coffin. I did not ask if there was anyone inside it.

The payments are stored according to their size in the room with the bright red centipedes. I do not know who takes these payments from the centipede room. I have considered that it might be the centipedes themselves, but I do not know what their relationship with the rest of the bookstore is or how that works. The handwriting on the instructional post-it notes gives the impression of the kind of old woman who dresses precisely and smells of lilacs and death. I struggle to imagine therefore that one or other of the centipedes is actually my boss. This may be a wholly irrational assumption.

While there is a time by which I must have the front door open and the shop presentable to visitors, there is no official leaving time. If there are many clients, I am sometimes obliged to work late into the night, keeping watch over the store as they sniff their ways along the shelves or attempt to read entire volumes without buying them. I usually warn them that they do so at their own risk. I am not sure how great a risk it is, but there was a client with a long, hairless tail who simply caught fire while reading an unpurchased text. It is my job to protect the books in case of fire, and it is not my job to protect the clients.

I do not like being open late, because sometimes the shadows come in from the street. Especially if it has rained heavily as well. They slide through the open door, the orange jackets of the Penguins disappearing into the depths of them. They are the only non-human visitors who take interest in the Penguins and I think this is the real reason we keep those books at the front. They distract the shadows.

Most days I leave as soon as it is quiet. No one seems to mind. Whoever writes the post-it notes is exacting about some details and unconcerned about others. I assume they can see me and know what I am doing, but we do not talk about anything. In fact, I don't talk at all most days, unless a normal person comes in.

The third time I see the person in the bookcase, I realise that they also look quite a lot like a normal person. Or at least like a person emerging from wood that has been turned into shelving. I don't suppose that properly counts as normal. I was ready for them, so I didn't cross the line I have chalked onto the floor to show where the fish air begins, or ends, depending on which way you are going. The line is fairly reliable as the miasma is fairly

370

consistent, but it never pays to be cocky about these things.

I look at the way the top shelf now resembles the curve of a shoulder. The head is lower down. There are bulges here and there that could be arms, or thighs, but none of these features are in the right place to suggest a coherent body. I wonder if the person in the bookcase is long dead, and perhaps now being rejected by the tree that once swallowed them. I wonder if the tree person is growing and will emerge. So far there have been no post-it notes about this and I can only hope that there will be instructions if things get out of hand.

Then the bell at the front desk rings with high, tinkling notes that make my teeth hurt, and I am obliged to return to my duties. This is the bell that signifies someone having a desire to go up into the attic. The room in the attic is always empty. There is nothing there when I unlock it, no matter how many people I let in. I have never crossed the threshold, and I sincerely hope I never will.

It does not matter what I try to do about it after work, the smell of the books and of the store itself stays on me. In the beginning I would sometimes go down to the river and walk right into it, submerging myself entirely in the hopes of removing the smell. I have singed myself beside the bonfires that always blaze in the cathedral quarter so that we might never forget that the old God is merciful and we can escape into the flames at any time. I have thought about going into the flames, of course, but I doubt even that could purify me now.

From my very first day working in the bookshop, normal people started avoiding me. I don't know if they smell it on me, or see it in my eyes but it is certainly the case that I have become that which is not normal. I do not belong. Normal people keep their distance from me now that I am not properly one of them. Once upon a time of course there were far more of them than there were of the Others, but year by year the balance has shifted. You cannot come into contact with that which is not normal without being changed by it. And so the uncanniness spreads like a disease. But what can you do when you need to work so that you can afford food at least, if not a roof over your head. So it came to pass that I took the bookshop job and became infected by the store. It is in me now.

I could have a roof over my head if I wanted. There is a room directly below the attic. It is small, and sparsely furnished. It could have been mine, that was part of the job description. I cannot imagine sleeping under the attic, I fear the dreams that would come to me there, and I fear what those dreams would do to me. It is better to be out under the open sky, with some hot food item clutched in my cold hands. It is better to walk all night and avoid sleep than to lie down there and let the bookshop make free with my unguarded mind. I do not trust sleep anymore. I think there may be something there, waiting for me and I do not want to meet it.

City dawns are slow, and often flood the river with red. Not the kind of old blood red I will find when I get to the store, but a vibrant colour that reminds me life still exists and is possible. There's precious little joy to be had in a day, but dawn on the river remains glorious and untainted. I watch, and try to hang on to the person I used to be. I had soft skin once, and soft hair as well. Now I grow cold and there is a sheen on me that was not there before. I think I may be turning into the kind of creature the fish skin books are made from. I wonder increasingly if those books are made from the transformed hides of previous shop workers.

After the dawn the sky often shifts to grey. It rains most days, sooner or later, when it doesn't rain constantly. I am seldom dry. I suppose if my skin becomes reptilian it will not matter so much. If the shop turns me into a book it won't matter at all. There are days when I am so tired that turning into a book seems tempting. At least so long as I can choose the words that are inside me.

I unlock the shop door as the rain pounds on the back of my neck. I close the door behind me with the softest of clicks. I fetch the bucket and the mop from the store cupboard under the stairs and I mop away the blood. Today it is mostly hand prints and some of them are upsettingly small. I do not know what happened here. I do not want to know.

Once the floor is clean I empty the bloody water into the drain and then I open the door to let the rain and the city smells come in. They will not venture far, but sometimes it helps me to stand next to the door and not feel quite so trapped here. As I turn from the door, I find a post-it note on the floor, the paper damp from my mopping efforts. "Fix the bookcase" it says.

There are many bookcases in the store. I have a feeling I know which one requires attention, but even so I make my usual careful rounds. It is not unusual to be told to fix something. The store is not logically laid out, so I have developed a system for moving around it that guarantees I will not forget to check somewhere. It took me a while to design the most effective route and for a while I found that process oddly comforting. That sense of comfort has gone now of course, faded away like almost everything else. Sometimes I wonder if it is my blood I clean off the floor each morning. It would make a great deal of sense.

There is one bookcase I frequently have to repair because it has been cleverly engineered from plastic straws that once washed up on the banks of the river. It wilts dreadfully, and there is usually only one book on it: The Unanimous Afterthought. It's a tiny pamphlet of a thing, but shockingly heavy to lift. Today, the straw shelf is fine. So is the shelf made from rat skulls and braids of human hair. That one is fiddly to put back together when it breaks. There is a frog on top of the metal bookcase that contains the complete works of Evardine Pitch, which are written in the blood of Evardine Pitch. There is not usually a frog on this bookcase, but I have received no instructions about it and so I leave it be.

I walk my entire route and check every bookcase and they are all in improbably perfect condition except for the one down by the damp brick wall. It is the only possible candidate for fixing. I scrutinise it for some time from behind the relative safety of my line. For the first time since I started this job I wish with all my heart to hear the gut-troubling call of the attic bell. I do not want to be here, tasked with this job. But what else can I do? No normal employer would take me now that I am so visibly tainted. My hopes of finding a not-normal job less awful than this one are slim.

I have walked past the factories at night and heard the screaming of the machines in hideous counterpoint to the screams torn from human throats. I have seen what comes out of the sewers at the end of the day, and the slow processions of those who have ceased to be useful and can only walk and beg until they die in the streets. I must do whatever the store asks of me. I have no real choice.

Taking a deep breath, I dash through the poisoned zone to more closely examine the misshapen bookcase. Today it looks very much like a human form is emerging from the wood. There's an unmistakable hip and part of an arm, some shoulder and the curve of a buttock. The bookcase person was not this coherent yesterday. I run back to safety and draw unsteady breaths. What am I to do? I could try and saw these extra parts off, but that thought fills me with a horror I cannot explain to myself. What else is there I could even try?

I hyperventilate until I am giddy with it, and then I do something a bit like a sprint back to the emerging form. I push against the hip, and it feels as solid to me as a wooden bookcase normally does. Nonetheless, I feel it move under my hand. I realise I could fix this situation by pushing or pulling, and I know in my bones that the bookshop wants me to push, to drive this strangely naked human form back into the wood. I press my hand against the curved wooden buttock, and it feels warm against my compromised skin. I push, and I do not want to push. I am dizzy from too much breathing and I cannot fight the need to breathe again. I take the foetid book air into me and feel it like claws in my throat. Tears stream from the places in my face that barely pass for eyes now.

I push with all I have and I hate myself for pushing. I feel the body in the wood slipping away from me, retreating into the narrow side of the bookcase – a space far too slender to have ever contained it. And yet, somehow it goes, and as the last part of that hip slips from beneath my fingers, the loss of it cuts me unbearably. Were it not for the cruel air assaulting my lungs I would lie down on the floor and weep. I do not have that luxury. All I can do is stagger the length of the building towards the small comforts of the open shop door. My lungs burn as though there are crystals of ice in them. I suck in great shuddering gulps of tepid air and I smell the mud of the river. Only when the pain eases its grip on my body do I find the means to weep.

There are wings in the night, giant forms in the dark sky I can hear but cannot see. I remember how excited I was in the beginning when the first beings came through. Strange though it seems now, there was a time when I loved books, and longed for uncanny things. The horrors that come in the night are so much more appealing when you simply imagine them. To hear the harsh cry that your mind cannot connect to anything you

376

have ever known may be wondrous the first time. All too soon you descend through fear and down to a place of broken exhaustion, your heart no longer able to sustain the terror you know your body should fear. I keep close to the buildings out of habit, fully aware that the shadows hiding me from whatever flies above may also be hiding others who do not wish me well.

I do not know how I am still alive, but something I cannot name keeps me trudging onwards through the hours and days. I walk the streets at night, I eat whatever I can bear to put in my mouth. I take some small comfort from the sunrise. There's always that one gift in a day - the experience of light returning and the whisper of hope that it breathes into my weary soul.

Then I go back to the shop. I face its darkened windows and feel its relentless scrutiny. I open the door even though I long with every ounce of flesh remaining to me to simply turn and flee from it. I pass the antiquated innocence of the Penguins in their orange jackets and I fetch the bucket. Today's footprints come from bare feet, and there are many of them.

I clean, and before I am done there is a post-it note on the end of my mop, the words bleeding out of it even as I try to read the message. "Fix bookcase" it says. I want to let some kind of howl out of my body, but I know the shop would not appreciate it. I am to be quiet. This is part of my job description.

Of course it is the wooden bookcase at the far end of the store. I do not make my way around my usual circuit this time. The only thing I can do is fight the dread in me and go where I know I must.

Today there is an arm emerging from the bookcase – a bare human arm with solid and well defined muscles. It reaches from the side of the bookcase and along the shelves in a way that would make it impossible now to access some of the books. I conceded that the bookshop has a point – whatever is in the bookcase is working against the shop itself. I can hardly side against the shop. I am its creature. For a moment I have the irrational feeling that the arm is trying to keep me away from the shelves as though with this simple gesture it might stop the store from turning me into a book. I become a closer match for these bindings every day and I do not know how long I have left.

Still, it is unreasonable to imagine that a bookcase would grow human parts simply to try and protect me. I have no recollection of when I last encountered something resembling kindness and of all the places to imagine it occurring, a wooden arm does not seem like a good candidate.

I take several deep breaths and rush in, reaching for the arm with both of my hands, intending to start pushing this aberration back into the bookcase again. The hand locks around my wrist. The grip is irresistible. I pull, but I can do nothing. I pull, but the hand holds firm. I can neither move it nor free myself. Panic rises in me as I run out of breath. I fight not to let go of the air in my lungs, but I can only hold for so long and then comes the burning need to inhale.

I can feel the book miasma on my skin. I can feel the reptile skin of the poisoned texts around me as they wait for the breath we all know I must take. Lights flash and spiral inside my skull and my legs drop out from under me. The wooden hand continues to clench my wrist, and I scrabble, trying to get my feet back where they should be. The hand does not let me fall.

I take the breath I cannot avoid, and it is awful. I can feel the chill of it getting into my blood and I start to think this is how the fish skin books are made. The bookcase itself has captured me and is making me breathe in the air that will turn me into a text. The bookshop and the bookcase were never at odds with one another. I think they are working together and it makes a kind of sense. I will cease to be human here. I will become a book and I do not know if I will be granted merciful oblivion, or whether my consciousness will continue forever, trapped inside the binding of my own skin.

A second hand pushes through the other side of the bookcase, and an arm follows behind it. My vision is blurred by tears but the movement itself is easy enough to see. This second hand grabs my flailing arm, and holds me steady. Fingers of wood wrap round the distorted mess of what was once my hand. I am held, and for the first time since I saw this morning's post-it note, the terror in me eases. Perhaps this process will not be so awful after all. Perhaps death will be a relief now. I think I am ready. It is strange to be holding hands with a bookcase, but oddly comforting as well.

The attic bell rings, over and over, the sound loud and furious, assaulting my ears and making my bones ache. There is a low and terrible sound that might be the gong on the second staircase. I hear banging, as though the bookcases themselves are battering against the walls. I do not know what to do, and it feels as though the whole building is waiting for me to do something.

The wooden hand squeezes mine. A memory stirs. This means something. It is a distant code from the ancient past. A sign. Something deep in my chest recognises it but I don't have words. All these books, and no words of my own. The hand holding mine squeezes again, while the one that held my wrist in a tight lock eases its grip a little, and shifts to take hold of the three fingers I have left on that side. A thumb presses into the middle of my palm. My body remembers and does not know what it remembers. Still, I do not know what to do.

The air around me fills with the sharp edged malice of post-it notes. I barely feel the cuts. I have a strong sense that the end is coming. I find one small, last desperate word in my mouth; "please." Although I do not know to whom I beg or what I am begging for.

I am pulled by the hands that hold me. I feel myself ripping away from the bookshop. And yes, I will leave this skin behind as it tears from whatever else I am. And yes I will leave these words behind, as the innards of the skin I once wore. This is how certain kinds of books are made. But only the words will remain of me and soon the rest will be gone. You cannot follow where I am going, but

finally, I am not afraid, and I cling hard to the hands that
are holding mine.

The Seventeenth Apocalypse

by

Feline Lang

On the day the world ended for the fourth time, I was drenching in the March sun in a seedy but fragrant roadside café.

People passed me, not hastening this time, maybe in a bit of a hurry, but more like you're tired of work and have a nice dinner waiting for you at home, not like it's the last minutes you have to live which our morality compelled us to fill with meaning - because what could have been meaningful?

If we had learned one thing from the last three apocalypses, it was this:

There was no meaning.

So the world ended. The sky darkened. What would it be this time? Danger from above obviously, bets were placed all around me. Asteroid? Bomb? Cosmic radiation?

I pulled my coat tighter around me and stood up, leisurely, almost sedately, as if none of this had anything to do with me.

The world ended, but what did I care? I had a story to tell.

**

The first end of the world had been looming for a long time. We all had known that, but in a different way than today. We all knew for certain back then that the world would soon be lost forever if we would do nothing about it. So that's exactly what we did:

Nothing.

We had watched the desert eat away at our lives, slowly, too slowly for human sensibility at first, so there was no panic.

We had watched the nothing eat itself into us, first devouring those on the fringes of society, or rather, making them disappear, nameless, faceless, unknown, insignificant. Until each of us suddenly realised that we, previously sitting safely around its centre, now represented the fringes of this society – and disappeared. This diffused to the very core, until even the richest of the rich, the most beautiful and famous, even those who had wisely withstood the rising heat in its shadows, had become desiccated mummies.

So it was clear: a creeping end of the world that gave us enough time to act – was not an option.

Nothingness withdrew and with it, time. But not the memory.

We all found ourselves back in the before, the normal, or what we'd spent our lives religiously proclaiming to be normal, whatever that was. We inhaled carefully, the air was breathable, neither scorching nor corrosive to our lung tissue. We were able to see each other, not squinting as we had to close towards the end, when the clouds of dust, smoke and water vapor that we could no longer filter and drink had sunk to the ground. We stared at each other, shyly at first, did I dream that? Then braver: did you experience it too? Did we all?

It quickly became clear that we could all remember our deaths and all the agony preceding them. The fear. The envy. The inconveniences that turned into fights far too quickly. The homes disappearing under the undrinkable sea. The thirst. The hate. The thirst. the cold. The hate. And then, in all variations from a quick gunshot to an excruciatingly slow ceasing through thirst, death. The Nothing.

None of us, even the most spiritual among us, could deny it:

There had been nothing.

Unless, of course, this world here is the afterlife, and we, the whole species, are in the afterlife.

Or else we have only imagined the before.

Or whatever.

Cults and sects sprouted up, science racked its brains, everything was the same as always. The climate apocalypse was still threatening, but no one cared about it. Everything was carried on as before.

**

Then the world ended again.

This time it actually seemed like a divine punishment.

After the flood and drought came the plague.

It seemed more like an attempt to get us to give in, like a threat, like a warning shot across the bow. Because the plague did not rage like the grim reaper and mowed us down in rows and rows with world-encompassing scythes. Instead, a gaunt harvester pulled individual stalks out of the earth and trampled the rest, stalks of grass that, broken and weakened, still might have rethought.

But no one was willing to change.

Negative entropy had long since become the religion of all of us – the craving to create and defend order while the world swirled into chaos. The same chaos that once created us out of a myriad of possibilities, on a water planet with a gravitationally dependent moon at the right distance from a sun of the right size and age.

We clung to our order and held onto it like a life preserver. But the reaper was patient. And pulled slowly, steadily, one stalk after another out of the ground, faster than we could reproduce. Until the children who were no longer cared for died. By then I had been gone for a long time and could no longer observe anything myself.

It had all taken years, not as long as the first apocalypse, but long enough to give us time for reflection again.

When we came back, rejuvenated, waking up in the same place in the same world as the time before, looking at each other in amazement, almost annoyed, you could read the sudden certainty in all faces that things would now continue like this.

And while some people took that as an incentive to escape the loop simply by trying to NOT let the world end this time, others sought to use the loop, to even speed it up, to increase their wealth through apparent knowledge, and to take it with them across death's door. A senseless undertaking, since now all people ca'ried the same knowledge about the finitude of eternity. Even the cults that had changed their doctrine almost overnight to adapt to the new world were more credible. And definitely more successful. That too is negative entropy: wanting to make sense of what is happening.

Indeed, it seemed as if our creative minds had lost patience when the bomb fell, only a few days after the declaration of war by the dictator, who had gone mad at the first fall, whom everyone had laughed at, and all nuclear powers reacted reflexively until nothing more was left except radioactive dust.

This time, too, I hadn't seen the final end of everything, but it had happened so quickly that it hardly made a difference.

**

The awakening this time was filled with impatience and anger. As soon as the people opened their eyes, they began to insult each other, why it had been allowed to go as far as it should have been prevented, how much everyone else was to blame, everyone else had the power, everyone else, just never oneself.

So now I was sitting here, in my café, watching the clouds gather at an unbelievable speed and hoping for a painless, quick death, because the annoyed faces of the last survivors were really getting on my nerves.

I got up without paying, why should I, and walked towards the rising wind. I was a little curious what the universe had thought up for her move.

Maybe there WAS an Olympus with kitsch gilded deities. The whole thing felt a lot like a game of some greedy children in a sandbox, basic mould for all Homo Sapiens.

I closed my eyes while walking, why would I mind if a car hit me, imagining that and giggling.

'What else should I try?' grumbled the wildly bearded giant and threw himself into the next armchair, which squeaked in horror under the sudden load.

'You didn't leave me anything from my own realm. Atomic bomb, tsunami, pestilence, what else is there for me?'

'Listen,' the blond, curly-haired youth at the other end of the room retorted. 'Remember your specialties, please.'

'What, picking up women?' Poseidon was honestly confused.

Apollo spun on his heel, if that was what you could call his elegant lace-up Greek sandals. 'Earthquake, Uncle Posi, earthquake,' he whispered smugly, reaching for his gold goblet.

'Boooooooring,' the older man growled.

'But efficient,' Apollo sniffled, offended. 'Think about it – all the lava alone –'

Poseidon hesitated. He actually hadn't thought of that. Decent volcanic eruptions, yes, that was something. For a sea god, he was quite into fire...

Poseidon narrowed one eye and looked straight at me. 'Ever heard of Black Smokers? Undersea volcanoes? Without which there would be no life on this snot planet?'

Fine, fine. I withdraw back into the storytelling role and just watch, uninvolved. Pfff.

Even Apollo had lowered his chalice briefly to give me a critical look over his nectar or whatever he took for it. I was already fed up with the two self-proclaimed idiots again and made my way out before the thought drew yet another rebuke. So, earthquakes. And volcanic eruptions.

So I sat in my coffee shop as the sky darkened and waited. It didn't really make a difference where I watched the apocalypse from this time.

'Was,' Athena rebuked me promptly.

'What...?'

'It WAS not really a difference. You're using Anglicisms again.'

I sighed. As if there were no such thing as a difference between making a difference and being a difference. Where there is a vacuum, even in language, a conqueror will invade. And stay, despite all resistance.

'Also, you established yourself getting up and walking away earlier.'

I opened my eyes, I couldn't stand it any longer. How long until this apocalypse took off?

The cloud on the horizon, because that was what it was, was (sorry Athene), as I already knew, a gigantic cloud of dust, sulphur, ash, and fire, rising from the next volcanic area, the Eifel, which was actually a few hundred kilometres away. And it was approaching rapidly. I sighed again and resigned myself to my fate, whether that would be burning or suffocation. But please don't do that Pompeii number with the petrification, that sort of death takes forever. What would it be for anyway? There would be no posterity to undig us.

The people around me also started to realise what was happening. 'Is it, again?' grumbled a briefcase guy next to me and dropped the same carelessly. 'I don't have time for this.'

I had to giggle again, despite the situation.

An elderly lady glared at me angrily. 'Do you think that's funny?'

'Yeah,' I sniffled, grinning widely trying to hold back the chuckle.

The lady waved her umbrella, which wouldn't stop the rain of fire either. 'God is punishing us,' she exclaimed angrily, 'we have sinned and we do it again and again!'

'Yes, of course,' I said soberly, 'but which god exactly?'

Then the ash cloud was there.

**

When I woke up again, at the same place where my personal loop of the second, third, hundredth chance always began, on the windowsill of the university, on the 16th floor, I was at least prepared for the icy wind that was tugging at me. Somewhat dazed still from the stench of lava that still seemed to be lurking in my sinuses, which was utter nonsense of course, I climbed back into the seminar room and made a beeline for the door and out into the hallway, ignoring the remaining occupants. I finally had a story to tell. This would be fun.

**

It took about twelve more apocalypses before everyone on this planet had had enough.

No one sensed a chance of their – ha – life in rebirth anymore. Because everyone was born again every time, with the same memories, the same insights. No one was trying to do better next time anymore. Because what was the point? Obviously there wasn't any. So why try?

It seemed as if the golden age had finally arrived. For even the greediest of men had by now lost interest in accumulating more and more wealth, for they had little to spend between then and the next end of the world. Investing in ever more sophisticated protection mechanisms hadn't produced any survivors either. It seemed like every new sinking would turn against that one breakthrough technology which would then be the first to be destroyed, before even the most vulnerable humans had their turn.

Of course someone came up with the idea of using that as bait at some point.

Did it work? What change would that make? In the end they were all dead. And then, they weren't.

There were no longer any national states that planned for generations. No family businesses raking in more money for their offspring. No striving for a secure pension, no health checks, no joggers in the park. Because by then we had gained the certainty – whether rightly so or not – that no change to our lives would let us live more than, say, ten years.

Did that mean we were saved? Finally redeemed by divine intervention from our mistakes, our weaknesses, our planned obsolescence, the greed, that drove us into self-annihilation again and again before we could get too mad?

Not at all.

Because with the worry we had stripped away the worry. We didn't worry about our future anymore, and why should we – because it seemed that every possible ending to this particular episode of a bad telenovela always ended up right where we started. All our efforts had, once again, been rendered futile by a power we did not understand. And who might not understand us either.

We stopped saving. We no longer held ourselves back. We counted, weighed, no longer measured how much of this or that resource or life form was left. Because our stores would always be replenished.

At least we thought so. Rock solid. We could only check on it, though, in our respective small microcosm.

Only the striving for spiritual immortality remained. While it was impossible to take items or data into the renewed world, knowledge, skill – and fame – stayed. A resourceful author had already understood this with the seventh downfall and since then has published a sequel to her first novel every round, which has meanwhile been eagerly awaited – I'm waiting too, it's really good what she writes there even if I missed the first volume and will never get to read it. Shows, too, were lengthened to infinity, with the added benefit that the cast only aged transitorily. And the science? Shouldn't that have blossomed into infinity?

Perhaps it would've, if anyone had seen any point in gaining knowledge.

Why cure cancer? It would come back on the next run. Why find new sources of energy? Why explore new species? Why change our genome? Above all and everyone hung, in every second of our existence that we called life, inescapably close and yet almost unreachable for most of us, those without a nuclear briefcase, a virus laboratory, or other infernal machines, the big red button with the inscription:

RESET.

But nobody had dared to approach the phenomenon in any other way than in lurid blogs, scientific treatises or cultic nonsense. That's what we called it now, after all the term had caught on.

Movies and plays ignored the topic now, novels circumvented it. Cubism, as an art form that depicted several realities and time levels at the same time, was frowned upon. Musical styles and fashions started, after this first short blossoming, to repeat themselves, in endless revivals and imitations. It was as if mankind had lost the ability of being alive through eternal life.

I, however, continued to write. But I had the opportunity to do so. And I had nothing, absolutely nothing, to lose.

Now the seventeenth end of the world was imminent, indefinitely, even if the experts on the talk shows were already hammering their heads with theories, calculations and vague assumptions. Since you couldn't take data from one level to the other that you didn't have in your head, the only source of information about the previous cycles was memory. There was no body of evidence, no empirical data. It was still imaginable that we were all subject to a collective hysteria, and the world hadn't ended at all. Modern talk shows looked accordingly. While debates used to be heated back then, so as not to let the viewers feel the dryness and cruel harshness of the bare facts, such events today are more like intellectual mud wrestling. In order to be credible, the speakers first had to complete a series of tests to assess their short – and long-term – memory and understanding of the information to be presented. From reciting children's poems from first grade to repeating the periodic table, to places competition for Pi, from disproving the theory of relativity to skilfully imitating the last meow of Schrödinger's Cat, everything was there. Science outdid itself with such circus tricks to be able to have its say at all. This, of course, left very little time for actual research. It reminded me of the social media competition in art and music before the first apocalypse... many of us spent most of our day filming ourselves eating ice cream to get attention because nobody was interested anymore in what was supposed to be sold. Writing books, songs and operas, painting and modelling had become expensive hobbies again, which were poorly financed with advertising income. Today, it was the arts that received greater attention than ever before, because the new, the unheard of was more valuable than ever, and it also was harder to create than ever.

Because: nothing new happened.

There was no more real news because wherever disaster began to loom, humanity, affected or not, collectively shrugged and thought: let's wait for the next round. Even the catastrophes themselves had to make a lot of effort, because mankind, despite all its carelessness, had actually begun to change. Why go to war if what has been achieved would be lost again in the foreseeable future? It was difficult enough to assert the old boundaries against the pressure of shared experience. In general, all borders began to dissolve. Immigration policy lost importance, it even turned into its opposite, because migrants meant what was now the most valuable of all currencies:

Variety.

Yes, humanity had started to be bored to death.

Even the favourite pastime of all great apes, the reproduction game, had lost its appeal. Sure, sex itself just kept getting better – eventually we always came back with the knowledge of the recently gained maturity but the bodies of our younger selves. But sex isn't everything, and immortality does something really weird to relationships. Knowing that they could try the whole world, every variety that existed, without any risk, with an undo button in the future, some banged their way through entire continents and gained a lot of experience in matters of STDs. But they soon learned that there was no undo button for emotional injuries inflicted on someone.

In the meantime, however, we had all passed the phase of jealousy. The ennui was too big. Too heavy the lack of uncertainty. The lack of loss. Who would have thought? We were bored to death.

**

However, nobody had noticed until now that this was only the seventeenth sinking. They wouldn't have understood it either if I had explained it to them. They were far too convinced of themselves, of having finally reached the meta level of life, the serenity of observing their own existence from the outside. *Ha.* You little cute little people. You have no idea what to expect. You think you've already done it all.

But now that the gods could think of nothing but half-heartedly thrown meteorites and absurd infections, *now* it was my turn. And I wouldn't just kill off humanity, but bring down the gods themselves. It was damn high time, too.

I don't know why no one has noticed what I'm actually doing here until now.

Not even the gods. Certainly not the goddesses.

But how could they, befuddled as they were, circling about their own holiness, and about their mission, oh, the mission...

It would be very funny if it wasn't so banal. You think of yourself as the pinnacle of the development of all life, the most powerful being in the world (at least you're working

398

on it) – and then you talk about the mission that you undoubtedly have to fulfil in this world or the next.

As if you were declaring oneself somebody's toy, a slave to a far higher power, which must have planned this mysterious mission, installed the deities, and endowed them with powers. And with an unbeatable imagination.

But what do I know about missions... I'm just telling you about them. I don't plan them. Why would I? If I want something to happen, it will. I don't need diaper-wearing wannabe Greeks and hobby druids for that. I just write things down.

And the word happens.

But I also have my duties, even if I impose them onto myself. And maybe telling this story from the very beginning is one of them.

Now, what is the beginning of everything? Should I start where I didn't know myself what happened? Was blind and deaf, and just revolved around myself like the little god players up there, like all those people in the frenzy of eternal rebirth?

When I thought I was like you?

That sounds reasonable, doesn't it?

Hexen und Ziege

by

Steven G. Davis

If this was all there was, the wall and the valley, then at least he was alive. Somehow. Inexplicably. Unknowingly. Alive.

Hexen sat with his back to the precipice that stretched up sheer and malevolent, gleaming purple-black in the twilight hours. The faintest of breezes blew, carrying with it the scent of apples, grass, and a fresh stream.

He released his fist, feeling his nerves loosen, feeling his veins relax.

They were alive. How, he didn't know, but they were alive. Alive, out of so many –

He looked over at his abandoned armour. The breast-plate, greaves, arm guards. His scythe was long lost, barely missed, never wanted.

Hexen looked away.

Twilight was slipping away in the darkness that followed and he was alone. Alone but for a couple of dozen strangers. He put his head in his hands. How? Why?

The night was not cold. It was not warm, either, but coldness had been a feature –

He looked up, around, carefully. The darkness moved. A figure – he could hear them now, a youngling, a female, heading for the precipice. For him.

He could smell her and see her clearly while she was still some distance away. A youngling, female, not long reached maturity. Nervous, confident and scared. She had also been quite upset recently.

'Hex?' she asked softly, nearing his position. 'Hexen? I'm sorry, I'm not sure of your name.'

She appeared out of the night, soft purple and blacker than black. A shy smile.

He smiled broadly. 'Hexen it is. Ziege?'

She nodded.

'What did they decide?'

Ziege looked up at him. 'We stay here. The clan mothers said to stay here. There is no arguing with that.'

'But they did.'

Ziege looked away. 'You were a soldier, once, weren't you, Hexen?'

He looked away.

'I don't blame you.'

Hexen stared at her. 'For what?'

'Anything. Everything.'

He drew a deep breath. Nodded slowly. 'You don't. The others squabble and bicker. We cannot go back. If we go forwards, and run into any others...'

She nodded. 'So we do what we were asked to do. Stay here.'

Hexen nodded slowly. 'It is pleasing, here. I can smell apples. Water. The precipice shelters our backs, our brethren have gone ahead. This valley is ours.'

'But they say the valley is empty.'

He snorted. 'There is fruit and water. There may be fish. Other crops.'

'Do you wonder – how? We survived? The precipice was insurmountable.'

'We did not surmount it.'

She chuckled, the first time he had heard her relax, even if only for a moment.

'No, we didn't. But the path is closed.'

'They chose you,' he said.

Ziege turned her head to look at him. Her hair grew long, reached down her back, wild and untamed.

'They did not choose me.'

Hexen sniffed. Narrowed his gaze, though he could see her as clear as starlight.

He snorted with laughter.

Ziege stared at him. 'What?'

'You chose them! Us.'

Ziege nodded, almost petulantly. 'They were being – silly. Argumentative.'

He scowled.

'They have lost everything.'

Hexen shrugged. 'They have not.'

He caught the frown on Ziege's brow.

'Oh. Yes. They are alive, and none appear seriously injured.'

He nodded, leaning back. 'I do not smell fire. I do not smell blood. The precipice is almost warm at my back. I can rest here. This is not a place to rush.'

She laughed again. Her laughter – her laughter was light, frivolous, not the deep belly laugh of his comrades, not the back-slapping laughter and jollity of his friends. But it was still laughter.

'They said we need to hurry. To build walls, watchtowers, mount watches.'

Hexen smiled. 'In the morning there will be sunlight. We can rest amidst the trees.'

'I,' Ziege hesitated. 'I do not know what to do.'

He snorted. 'And so you sort out the one who abstained from the meeting of all. I could have been anything. You do not know me.'

She nodded. 'Correct. None of us know anyone else. We are a seed-scattering, a random hope, strangers left to band together. If anything – anyone – else comes through the precipice –'

'But what if they do not?'

She looked at him strangely. 'What do you mean?'

'Suppose – this is it. Our lands, our lives are gone, but we have life. We are the last. What then?'

'Then –' she stared silently at him.

After a while her gaze lifted to the precipice. To either side of him. 'If we are really all alone –'

He nodded.

'Then –'

'Then we make this our home.'

'Home,' she blinked owlishly.

He nodded. 'What choice do we have?'

'None. May I sit beside you?'

Hexen nodded. 'The valley belongs to no one. The precipice – I would think – belongs to the precipice. I am just here – for now. *One day my bones –*' he began to sing, but cut the words off sharply.

Ziege sat. 'That was an army song?'

He shrugged. 'I don't know if the whole army knew it or sang it. But my company –' he looked away again.

She placed her hand on his arm.

Hexen stared out into the night.

'It will get very warm during the day,' he said, after a while.

Ziege nodded, removing her hand. 'We could rest in the stream.'

'Unless it runs through the trees, it will be very warm. And twenty-odd disparate strangers,' he trailed off.

'Dreißig.'

'Dreißig?'

'Dreißig.'

Hexen nodded. 'We should know the extent of the valley.'

'But if you let the others rest and do all the work yourself –'

He snorted. 'I am not,' he shrugged.

Ziege smiled up at him. 'I have – without any thought before action – found myself leading our dreißig. I cannot – I will not – do all the work. But I will not shirk it either.'

Hexen grinned, tiredly. 'You lead from the front. It is not always the way.'

'Was it not – the army way?'

He shook his head. 'Individual companies, yes. But we were ordered to war; ordered by those who stayed safe in their cities –'

'Or not.'

'Not?'

Ziege nodded. 'I think – I think,' she sighed. 'It is a dark thing. The Elves,' her face twisted into a bitter scowl. 'They,' she threw her hands up in frustration. 'Everything.'

Hexen shuddered. 'They are,' he shook his head. 'Monsters.'

'Were,' said Ziege softly.

'Were?'

'I think – I think their Zauber – destroyed everything. Everyone.'

Hexen let the silence run. There really was – no one. No one but the thirty of them in this valley. Two, three hundred others, gone ahead, gone to see if anything, anyone, lived in this – new place. Or if they were truly alone, the only survivors of der Zauber.

The stone was comfortable at his back. He was alive, but why him? Why them? Out of all the four races, out of all the thousands, hundreds of thousands, millions, were they really the only ones? Three hundred survivors out of millions.

The precipice wall was not so comfortable.

'There will be –' he couldn't finish. Couldn't say it.

**

They found him in the morning. The apple tree was bowed from his weight; he hung there like the last of its crop, not yet rotted but no longer alive. Spinning slowly, the rope his clothes. A withered, broken black fruit.

'Neunundzwanzig,' Ziege said bitterly. She looked at him. 'You – knew?'

Hexen reached up. The corpse wasn't hanging so high up; his neck had broken before his weight could drag the branch down enough so his feet would reach the ground. He closed the man's eyes.

'I suspected, Ziege.'

She looked up at him, unshed tears glittering in her violet eyes. 'Why?'

'We were – thriving. We had homes, jobs, food. War came; many were involved but life went on. Then –'

'Then the Elves –'

He nodded. 'Everything is taken from us. Our land is gone. Our families, our communities, our heritage. Our peoples are – we are three hundred. Less. No longer thousands.'

'All our books. Our fields, our crops, our knowledge, our festivals,' Ziege said, bleakly.

He nodded again. 'I do not know what has become of my gardens, my friends.'

'You were a gardener – originally?'

Hexen shook his head. 'A herbalist. I had poultices – I knew what to add to stews to –' he shook his head. 'That was. Now, what would you have me do with the body when it is cut down?'

Ziege blinked. 'Our way is to burn. This is a new land –'

Hexen drew the branch down, hearing it splinter. I am sorry, he muttered, but this must be.

The branch cracked; broke. He held the body and lowered it slowly to the ground. It sprawled awkwardly; he drew the limbs in close to the body.

'I must tell the others. If,' Ziege held herself tightly.

'I can make fire, if I can find the right rocks. The precipice may well provide.' He looked at Ziege, a woman half his age. 'The valley needs exploring. There is mud by the river. We must begin investigating whether it can be baked into blocks to build shelters.'

Ziege nodded, pulling herself together. 'You have – words to say over him?'

He nodded. 'There were words in the army. I have better words. Words from –' he couldn't say *the heart*.

Ziege nodded again. 'Thank you, Hexen. If you will attend to our fallen – friend, I will see to having the valley explored. We need to know how large it is, what fruits there are, what we can survive on. I will send some to investigate the river. Others to start building mud blocks.'

She pulled a face. 'Mud blocks.' Tears glittered in her eyes. 'Once there were dresses, and dances, I was going to be going to study at our schools in the Dark Wood Mountains. There were rumours of visiting professors –'

Hexen nodded. 'I cannot offer you any comfort. But you can cry before me. I will not think any the less of you –'

'Hexen,' she protested, looking up at him.

'The army training,' he grimaced. 'I hated it. And now it holds me together.'

She nodded slowly. 'Will you – help me? Be my advisor. I – I can do this. But it is – difficult. And the others – they argue so much. They need someone to tell them what to do.'

Hexen nodded slowly. 'I am but a poor soldier. As that cracks and fades away, maybe the herbalism will return. But I would like to have something to – hold onto. Something – new.'

Ziege nodded. 'Thank you,' she whispered.

**

The fire roared and blazed, the smoke thick and heavy. Hexen had built a rough bier of rocks and laid the empty body upon it. The rocks were smeared now, thick with juices. The air stunk with the breaking down of the body. On a whim he had collected his armour and placed it near the bier.

The day was hot, even without the fire. Clouds, thin, wispy, things, scudded high, high above, the sky almost unalterably turquoise. It had only been that shade on rare, summer days. Rare days, when the sun threatened to wither his plants and he kept to the shade –

Hexen stretched. Days like that were gone. Days like this – cloudless skies, when the air smelled of apples and water – they were the new days. All that had been –

He shook himself. The fire crackled. He brushed sparks from his tunic. Clothing; that would be another thing. Even with simple tunics and kilts, dresses, shifts, clothing would soon be an issue.

'Are there seasons here?' he wondered, scanning the skies. The night hadn't been that cold, for all the valley felt high; a mountainous region, though he couldn't see out of the valley.

Days were longer too, he estimated. Hours had passed, dusk should be drawing in, and there was only the faintest of variation to the turquoise, suggesting night was still a ways away.

How can it be, he wondered. A world of mountains and caves, plains, forests and jungles, and a towering, unclimbable precipice, a jagged edge to our world. None scaled it, though all races tried. And yet – he shook his head.

**

As night came on Hexen headed down to the river. He could smell the smoke, the stink of burnt flesh, on him, and it was unpleasant. The fire had burned down to the bier, leaving only bone fragments; they had carefully put his clothes aside for future use, if any would use them. The stones were blackened by the fire and burnt juices, but had held together. His fingers were stiff; callused in a way neither herbalism nor army work had, but then he had been fortunate in terms of the army.

The trees didn't grow all the way to the river, creating a shallow bank. The water was wide; several lengths at least, and he could feel the coldness drifting off it. How deep it was was another matter; there was only a faint moon in the sky and the whiteness glittered randomly in the water as it surged and lapped, swirled and tumbled its way along.

He stripped and stepped in. Winced at the almost-icy coldness of the river, but waded out a little, holding his clothes. His feet were callused and hard; somewhere along the journey through the precipice, the flight, he had lost his boots, as poor as the army-issue ones were. They'd been made by humans, who never appreciated or cared for the much larger Orcs.

Hexen scrubbed at the clothes. They, at least, were tough and should last a while.

After a while he no longer noticed the coldness of the river; laid the clothes out on the bank as best he could, knowing they'd be unlikely to dry overnight and reluctant to set another fire simply to warm his clothes. He'd not been exploring the valley, but there was bound to be suitable branches to burn, but not a never-ending supply.

Movement caught his eye and he looked up, barely able to feel his hands. A figure was coming through the trees towards the river; Ziege.

She smiled as she saw him, smiling wearily. He could smell the sweat on her brow; she'd not wasted the day sitting around.

'Hexen,' she smiled. 'Do you mind if I join you?'

He shook his head. 'It is no one's river. By all means.'

She stripped off the belted dress and walked into the river, not grimacing even when the water rose over her chest. She grinned back at him.

'There is nothing like hard work. I hated it; wanted to be a scholar.' Her smile splintered.

'We do what we must,' he replied, moving a little further out into the river. 'The dress will need washing in the water.'

She nodded. 'I know. Night bathing is fun, but I've no wish for a sodden garment; no wish to put a smelly dress back on over a clean skin, either.'

Hexen grinned. 'How goes the organising?'

She rolled her eyes. 'Two are – troubled. Unwilling to do anything. A dozen, in two groups, have gone exploring the edges of the valley. A few are mechanically

413

minded, or were builders; they were investigating the mud, to see if it could be baked into blocks.'

Hexen nodded. 'The bier held well; the rocks were warm, even after – all was burned. Blocks of mud could be burned, hardened, being close to it.'

Ziege smiled, clapping her hands enthusiastically. 'Yes! They said they thought it possible, but we've no notion of seasons, of weather conditions. If snow comes on us, if the weather plummets,' she trailed off.

He nodded, feeling the need to rub at his skin with handfuls of water. 'A big hall, perhaps, should be the first build. Or some kind of construct to at least give shelter should the weather change.'

'You think in preference to a small hut?'

'Survival is our first thought. The day appears longer than – what it was – at home.' He winced. 'This may be later summer, early das Spätjahr. But – who knows?'

Ziege nodded slowly. 'Perhaps a smaller build; the second could be adjacent, joining on to it. We could build it up, building upon building, as we learn.'

Hexen nodded. 'There are tales of human buildings. Courts. Large rooms in the centre. Smaller rooms radiating outwards.'

Ziege nodded. 'I think we agree. Where, is another matter to consider. The woods give way to apple trees; our main source of food, at the moment.'

'Unless the river provides sustenance.'

She nodded. 'Yes.' She sighed. 'We should think of –' she broke off, frowning, looking away from him, at a darker object bumping its way along the river towards them. 'What is that?'

Hexen frowned. 'Too small for a body. An animal? A clump of branches?'

It drifted nearer as both waded towards it. The river was mostly silent, apart from the gentle lapping of water against the bank. He'd not seen any fish; that didn't mean there weren't any. A net, perhaps –

Hexen almost smiled. The clothes of the Orc who'd committed suicide could, perhaps, be fashioned into some kind of net. Something to trap objects in the river in, even.

They were nearer the bank; the water cascaded off Ziege as she reached for it, steadying the dark bundle. He moved up beside her as she unwrapped it.

Stared.

A *pink* thing lay within. No Orc. Unbearded; even Dwarven babies were born bearded, apparently. Human – they opened their eyes –

Pale blue eyes stared up at him. Eyes that stared knowingly. A thin face. They opened their mouth; a tongue flashed out, as if tasting the air.

'Elf,' he swore, seizing it by the throat, lifting it from the bundle of garments and plunging it deep into the water.

'Hexen!' Ziege tried to intervene, pulling and punching at his arm.

He held her off one-handed, holding the monster underwater.

'It's a child!' Ziege screamed.

'Elf,' he retorted, tightening his grip on its neck.

'Help, help,' Ziege hollered, trying to get at his arm that held the evil thing.

He moved, blocking her. 'It caused this. It's alive while all our families –'

'It didn't cause this,' Ziege screamed.

He could hear sounds; shapes moving in the trees, coming for them. If it was Elves they were –

'No, no,' Ziege screamed louder, 'come no closer! Stay back.'

He tightened his grip. The cursed thing seemed unresponsive, but that was a lie, a trap. That was the way of the Elves.

'Hexen,' Ziege spoke softly. 'Did that child murder your family?'

He scowled at her. 'It's a child. It can't be allowed –'

'It's a child,' she repeated, gently stroking his arm. 'It might be an Elf, but it's no murderer.'

'It's an Elf,' he repeated through gritted teeth. 'Their corrupt magic killed the world. Our families. Parents; loves,' he added, viciously, wondering who Ziege might have lost.

'Yes. Just as you killed our brother who died.'

He stared at her in anger. 'I did not. I am honourable –'

'Honourable?' she raised an eyebrow. 'Elf or not, you're attempting to drown a baby. A defenceless baby.'

Hexen stared at her. His garden was gone. His friends, everyone he'd known, those he'd loved, were gone. His brothers in arms were gone. No one was left –

He relaxed his grip slowly.

The child seemed to bubble to the surface of their own accord.

He stared at it in hatred and helpless rage.

The child burbled, water passing their lips. Their cheeks grimaced; they made a sound.

'They're trying to laugh,' Ziege said softly. 'Thank you, Hexen.'

'Laugh?'

'It's a child.' She laid her hand on his arm. 'In the weeks and months ahead, it – they – will need a protector. Will you take on that duty?'

Hexen stared at her blankly.

'You are an honourable man, Hexen. You listen to reason. And you are strong enough to protect them. Many of our kin,' she hesitated.

'Many of our kin may not understand,' she said after a while.

'Understand what?'

She smiled. 'New life. Innocent, harmless, blameless life. They may not be Orc, but if we bring them up in our ways, they may not be Elf either.'

He grimaced. 'What of their parents?'

Ziege shrugged. 'I see no Elves here. We must act as such.'

Hexen pulled a face. 'You're a youngling, to act as mother.'

'Isn't that what I'm acting as for the whole of – us,' she shrugged, gesturing round.

A few Orcs were on the bank; some scowled, seeing the child. Some turned and walked away, shaking their heads and muttering.

Hexen nodded slowly.

'So be it. I will act as their – protector.'

'Father,' Ziege replied.

Hexen frowned.

'Father.'

He shook his head.

'Father,' Ziege repeated. 'They must not just be protected, but loved as well.'

'Then you should –'

'You said you wanted something to – hold onto. Something new. We have to rebuild, Hexen. We have to make us,' she gestured around again, 'into a family. This child will be the start.'

He sighed.

'It's not just buildings and new ways of doing things, Hexen. The old world is gone. We need to fashion a new one; we cannot get the old one back. It is gone.'

He stared at her bleakly.

'Hexen,' she smiled softly. 'The army took some of your years away; it took your herbalism away. You can stay – mentally – with the army. Or you can move on.'

Hexen grimaced.

Scowled.

Nodded grudgingly.

Ziege planted a kiss on his cheek. 'Thank you. Now then,' she smiled impishly, 'your first task as their father is to name them.'

He favoured her with a twisted grin. An Elf child, in possibly the last surviving Orc familyhood. Their life would be hard. Difficult.

The child looked up at him with bright blue eyes. Sharp teeth. A long tongue. They gurgled; their approximation of a laugh.

'Lachen,' he said slowly. 'Let them be known as Lachen.'

Deconstructing the cover

On 14th January 2023, Laura Jane Round and Steven C. Davis paid a visit to Saturday Books in Dudley. The reason was to create the cover of this very book which would showcase the range of talent within Tenebrous Texts, whether or not they contributed a tale to this book.

Starting at the top left, and almost out of sight, is a sheet with the three internal images from 'Lore of the Sælvatici' written by Steven and Wulfenstæg; the art is by John Chadwick.

In front of that is a green and purple tailed hat, created by Ash Mandrake (contact Ash via fb if you would like a hat).

Beneath the hat is one of the 'Heart's Cog' novels, awaiting editing and then publication; written by Steven and S. J. Stewart. The cover art is by S. J. Stewart.

In front of that is the album 'Incantations', by Dark Sinfonia. Dark Sinfonia is one of William Westwater's projects; he wrote the theme to 'Lore…', 'From the Dark' (you can find the album on Bandcamp).

In front of that is a wooden knife and the booklet for the 2019 Raising Steam Festival.

On top of that is 'Teath', the second pamphlet from Laura Jane Round. This can be purchased from Saturday Books, online, or from her in person.

Adjacent to the 'Heart's Cog' book is 'Spells for the Second Sister' by Nimue Brown. Tom and Nimue's

'Hopeless, Maine' project is one of the inspirations for Steven's 'Sælvatici' project.

In front of that is a flier for 'Steam Ball', showing Feline Lang.

In front of that is a badge for 'Cobbles and Cogs', who support authors, writers, poets and storytellers through their events and whose storytelling Yurt is a beautiful thing to tell tall tales in.

There is also a Dark Sinfonia badge and one of Laura's cards.

Hanging in the middle of the image is a random oddity discovered at a 'Steampunks for Gloucestershire' event in November 2022, which inspired the 'Gimpy Chicken' project that Steven is working on.

In front of that is a rare, signed album by 'Of Perception', a band of Stu Tovell's.

In front of that is the double CD from the 2022 Raising Steam Festival (still available to buy via their Bandcamp page). In front of that, and partially hidden, is a Feline and Strange card.

In front of that is a postcard of 'Furry by Nature', the third in the 'Less than Human' series written by Steven, illustrated by Nicky Rowe, who also creates music under the 'Nightlights' name.

In front of that is the "I am an iceberg you only see part of me" badge from Feline & Strange.

In front of the edge of the 'Of Perception' album is an image by Tamsyn Swingler, of a flaming pig lord. Whilst it has not directly inspired anything in the

'Sælvatici' world yet, I suspect either the pig will, or one of Tamsyn's songs (under the name Gurdybird) will.

In front of that is the booklet from the 'Kunst fordent Opfer' album by 'Feline and Strange' and a sandalwood squirrel. Because.

In front of them is a pin badge from the 'Hopeless, Maine' world and a cassette, 'The Lost Girl', by 'Nightlights'.

In front of that is a rainbow lanyard.

To the right of the 'Feline and Strange' booklet is a bookmark from 'Nightlights'.

Behind that is a small image with the words 'No cause is lost if there is but one fool left to fight for it'.

In front of that is a clock with no hands. A timeless piece acquired at the same 'Steampunks of Gloucestershire' event as the inspiration for 'Gimpy Chicken'.

In front of that is a peacock feather found at the shop in a jar also found in the jar. It should be said that this photo was taken in the 'Local Authors Room' of Saturday Books.

In front of them is a postcard of the image of Joanna Swan (who turns the Sælvatici project into fascinating and powerful audio dramas) as Mother Hode, a pre-cursor to the Robin Hood character of the 'Sælvatici' world.

Lying on top of the card is a pair of horns.

Not in sight, but part of the wider image – books by Jon Hartless and C. H. Randle.

Photoshoot by the kind permission of Francis Sheppard of Saturday Books, Dudley and Claire Tedstone (seriously, pay a visit, check out the local authors room and the gallery).

Steven G. Davis, Creative Director

On Saturday Books

Saturday Books... What to say about Saturday Books?

Because that's what it was known as to us for so very long. Rising like a phoenix from the ashes (metaphorical ashes – it may shock you to discover that fire damage is detrimental to books), the shop was renamed the Saturday Books Gallery and we couldn't be more thrilled.

With the launch of their website impending, there is never a better time to shop local, shop indie and shop WEIRD.

So, walk past a potato merchant on a side street in the town of Dudley and you'll find it. An old house that constantly settles and whispers with life. A treasure trove of books new and old, from plays to poetry, from philosophy to geology, from history to the far, far future. At the desk, or wandering around the expansive upstairs, you'll find one Francis Sheppard. Francis, our mentor, our friend and most of all the keeper of the books, has encouraged all of us to read and write in ways we'd never previously considered. He is a champion of the written and spoken word, as well as a champion of the Black Country, and of course an honorary YamYam. The cakes we have eaten! The coffee we have drank! He lends an ear and a helping hand, and has encouraged vibrant, creative people to gather as if the shop is a conduit for all that thrives inside us.

For that, we will always be grateful.

Laura Jane Round, Editorial Director

Contributors' Bios

Nimue Brown

Nimue Brown writes for the Hopeless, Maine project, as well as having various assorted other fiction and non-fiction projects on the go. She performs in assorted musical combinations, frequents steampunk events, and can be found smeared across the internet like jam deployed by a toddler. For more Nimue fiction with a threatening bookshop in it, check out 'Spells for the Second Sister'.

Steven C. Davis

Steven C. Davis describes themselves as a word witch. He has created the 'Sælvatici' and the 'Less than Human' worlds amongst others. He is the Creative Director of Tenebrous Texts, the Raising Steam festival, one half of 'Poetic Malevolence' with Laura Jane Round; host of the Breathe radio show, a performance poet, presenter and is occasionally considered driven. He feels malevolent joy frequently and deliciously.

Jon Hartless

Jon Hartless was born in the 1970s and has spent much of his life in the Midlands and Worcestershire. His latest series, a steampunk motor racing adventure examining the gulf between the rich and the poor, started with Full Throttle in August 2017, continued with Rise of the Petrol

Queen in 2019, Fall of the Petrol Queen in 2020, and The Death of Poppy Orpington in 2021.

Feline Lang

Feline Lang is so far better known as the mad singer and songwriter of Berlin based Dark Cabaret band Feline&Strange. It was only a matter of time though until she would write a book, as her lyrics are of rather operatic format. Her 1st novel, 'The Doll's House' will be released in German and English while she is already up to no good again towards music, theatre or book enterprises. Beware.

Ash Mandrake

Ash was born in Manchester, the son of immigrants. He is half Polish, a quarter Indian and a quarter Irish. He holds post graduate degrees in the Biological Sciences and Applied Linguistics. At 40, he stopped drinking and became a self-taught professional musician and milliner, living on the road and touring the UK with his show. He has kept a journal for more than 40 years and regularly writes prose and poetry which work their way into songs or stories. During the pandemic he designed 8 highly original guitars and now has 10 albums and EPs to his name.

C. D. Phillip

CDPhillipwrites was an art kid who grew into an art adult (which is much the same except with more back pain.) Xie can be found on Instagram where xer art and writing is on occasion displayed.

C. H. Randle

Cat Randle is an award-winning scriptwriter with published work with Scholastic and Random House. She has a Master of Creative and Critical Writing distinction from Winchester University. Her steampunk character Merciful Grace has performed poetry at many festivals in South East England, including Winchester's Hat Fair, and she is on Youtube. She is writing the second book in The Somewhen Chair series, which will be out in 2024. Her first novel, The Somewhen Chair, is available on Amazon. Cat lives in NZ and currently takes tourists on browsing bookshop tours of Wellington. You can find her at Tenebrous Texts website, www.kererumedia.com and www.facebook.com/CatRandle.

Laura Jane Round

Laura Jane Round is a writer and performance poet from the Black Country. A Liverpool John Moores' University alumni, they have been published many times in places such as Lumpen Journal, The Beyond Queer Words Poetry Anthology and Take Care. Their second poetry pamphlet, 'TEATH' was published in 2022 by Alien Buddha Press. Round is bisexual.

Hannah Simpson

Hannah Simpson writes poetry and prose dealing with themes of nature, folklore, feminism and mental health. She is currently focussed on the ways in which our dislocation from the land, through an increasingly digital and urbanised lifestyle, is influencing us psychologically and spiritually. When not writing, you can find her searching for The Old Gods amongst the brutal beauty of the Black Country.

Stu Tovell

Stu: former musician, music researcher and far too many other things. I shall walk through the dead petals of that space in my mind. I shall stand before the altar of the abyss. But most of all I shall sit at my laptop and write the story of Miss Noir. There is more to come …

Wulfenstæg

Wulfenstæg is a frequent attender at historical reenactments and Pagan fayres. He has little time for the nonsense of modern times so do not expect a presence on the dreaded 'social media'.

He is at his happiest when he's whittling wood or watching a fire spitting sparks into the night sky. Walking in a forest and letting its senses absorb his personality. Watching a river flow, the water churning and bubbling, going about its business without human intervention.

He is grateful to Steven, and Tenebrous Texts, for handling the commercial aspects of this project, which has inspired him greatly.

Associated Tenebrous Texts Personages

John Chadwick

John Chadwick is a writer, illustrator, animation filmmaker, spoken word performer and co-host of The Innsmouth Book Club podcast. A former university senior lecturer and writer/ illustrator in residence at The Yorkshire Sculpture Park, his work has been exhibited, published and performed through several medium since his film Spiritual Love was nominated for Young Narrative Filmmaker of the Year at the 1996 British Short Film Festival. He contributed the cover and internal art to 'Lore of the Sælvatici' and the art to 'Barrow witch', both part of the Sælvatici world.

Nicky Rowe

Nicky Rowe is the artist behind the 'Less than Human' cover images, and an unrepentant 80s addict, as well as the main mover behind the synthwave project, Nightlights. Nicky has been drawing mischievous cat girls and other similar characters for over twenty years, and has more recently used that experience "wisely" to create Kiki, the time hopping Nightlights cat mascot who features on many of the covers.

It would be fair to say that Nicky is ever so slightly obsessed with synthesizers and synth music of many kinds, and may or may not have once been arrested for discussing DX7 FM synthesis patch programming in a built up area.

You can find Nightlights at Nightlightsuk.Bandcamp.com

Carolin Southern

Carolin is an artist and illustrator residing in the Scottish Highlands. She primarily works in traditional media, and her art encompasses horror, fantasy, Gothic themes, Pagan imagery and the occult. In her spare time, she plays eerie melodies on her harmonium, psalterie and collection of unusual wind instruments, enjoys hill-walking and wild-camping (the creepier the forest the better). She has a degree in Architectural Technology and is now studying History & Cultural Studies. Her primary love is historical architecture. Her Instagram accounts are @dragonandcatdesigns for her artwork and @architecturallygothic for her architectural photography.

Joanna Swan

Joanna's professional work ranges from her guest lead in BBC Doctors, across roles in short films, independent films and commercials, she has had leading roles in stage plays around the country, and is an emerging voiceover artist. She is the voice of the Sælvatici, with a number of audio dramas available on Audible and many more intended.

Recommendations

'Spells for the second sister' by Nimue Brown
A thoroughly enjoyable read, reminding me in places of Deepak Chopra's 'The Return of Merlin'. Our viewpoint character goes through – spoilers – before returning to where she started. Of course, by then, she is someone else entirely. A deep, thoughtful book, masquerading as fiction.

'Lore of the Sælvatici' by Steven C. Davis & Wulfenstæg
There is a grim, fascinating beauty to this collection and they read as if meant to be performed ... performed on a dark summer's night, under the stars, around a campfire that crackles and spits as if it will rage out of control at any moment. Also available through Audible, voiced by Joanna Swan.

'Less than Human' series by Steven C. Davis
Paranormal Romance without the paranormal. Davis' central character, Natalayiana, gradually morphs from a shy social worker, hiding her reality, into a matriarchal figure in a world that wants to use and dispose of shape shifters. Each novel paints the world a little brighter, deeper and darker than before.

'The Poppy Orpington' series by Jon Hartless
Poppy Orpington is a true working class heroine. Drawing parallels between society's current faults (classism,

sexism, racism and bigotry) and the world of a hundred years ago, when a working class disabled girl dared to drive a petrol race car in a world of steam cars.

'Trigger Warning' by Feline & Strange (Feline Lang)
The album that should have broken Feline & Strange not just globally but beyond. An angst-ridden crawl through the dark underbelly of society. A glorious high, which Feline and Christoph have built upon and risen even higher.

'Footprints from a Tribal ID' – Ash Mandrake
A poetic and Pagan, Shamanic, epic trip through the concept of beginnings and endings. The story traces the turn of the seasons through a year, invoking a distant Antediluvian past with cinematic vividness. Primal and layered chants and utterances over a sparse background, interspersed with rhythmical episodes.

'The Somewhen Chair' by C. H. Randle
The first of a trilogy of New Zealand-influenced time travel / alternate reality. A humorous look at the sacred cows of science fiction, both novels and television/ films, and a fun plot to boot!

'The Coveted' by Laura Jane Round
A personal insight into the perils and pleasures of growing up. Great imagery both in the poet's words and in the illustrations.

'**Teath**' by Laura Jane Round

There is a wonderful confidence to this work, a hard, glittering, confidence. Style it Glitterpunk or Glitterdark, this is poetry that struts down dark highways, fists wrapped in chains, going through a secondhandhigh.

'**Tenebrosian Tales**' an anthology from Stu Tovell, Steven C. Davis & Wulfenstæg

A surreal and bizarre anthology, mixing the noir novella 'The Blood Stained Mask' from Stu Tovell, with several dark meta-pieces from Steven C. Davis, steampunk dinosaur art from Kai, and some album reviews from Mr. Stu. Pleasingly limited edition.

Tenebrous Texts Merchandise

If you visit our friends at **tenebroustexts dot dizzyjam dot com**, they've got a range of merchandise supporting us.

Featuring the iconic 'snowy trees' image with the words, 'Tenebrous Texts' in white.
Hoodie only available in black.

Baseball cap available in a range of colours.

Featuring John Chadwick's three internal images from 'Lore of the Sælvatici', this hoodie is available in a range of colours.

Also available on a white mug.

The mug that *doesn't* say 'Fuck the world, I have stories to tell.' Only available as a white mug.

Also available on a T shirt in a range of colours.

A plain, Poetic Malevolence, T shirt, with the words 'Tenebrous Texts proudly presents Poetic Malevolence'.

There is also a range of badges and postcards available at events and in person.

Printed in Great Britain
by Amazon